LETHAL ACTION

A MASON SHARPE THRILLER

LOGAN RYLES

INKUBATOR
BOOKS

Published by Inkubator Books
www.inkubatorbooks.com

Copyright © 2024 by Logan Ryles

Logan Ryles has asserted his right to be identified as the author of this work.

ISBN (eBook): 978-1-83756-505-4
ISBN (Paperback): 978-1-83756-506-1
ISBN (Hardback): 978-1-83756-507-8

For Alice, Lizzie, and Claire –

Thank you for everything.

1

SIX YEARS EARLIER

L ong before the US Army CH-47 departed Camp Lemonnier in Djibouti City, Sharpe knew in his gut that something was wrong with this mission. Maybe it was the unusual speed with which he and three fellow US Army Rangers were deployed, without any time to scope out the terrain or properly plan the operation. Maybe it was the case full of nuclear, biological, and chemical protection suits that he and his fire team were instructed to wear—or the matching suits that the three members of the Chinook's aircrew wore.

Most of all, it was likely the unexpected passenger rushed last-minute up the loading ramp of the twin-rotored cargo helicopter, the fastest bird in the Army's rotary wing fleet. She wasn't military—she wore tan pants and a light blue long-sleeved shirt overlaid by a dark blue vest. On the back of the vest, printed in bold white letters, was the logo of the World Health Organization—the medical wing of the United Nations.

The doctor was ushered into a seat along the port side of

the Chinook and strapped in by the crew chief. Sharpe spun his index finger in the air, indicating for the flight crew to get the craft airborne. Jet engines screamed as he took his own seat, double-checking the M4A1 rifle held across his chest by a two-point sling. He'd tugged on the awkward NBC suit only fifteen minutes prior, but already its interior was slick with sweat.

And he had hours to go inside this thing. Maybe most of a day. At least the altitude would help.

The Chinook roared above Camp Lemonnier and turned west out of Djibouti, nose down as it beat a path at one hundred sixty knots toward Ethiopia. The noise was deafening, the crew chief who loaded the M134 Minigun mounted to the Chinook's starboard side anything but reassuring.

They were going in fast. They were going in hot. It was just like any number of missions Sharpe had executed during his eventful tenure with the US Army's 75th Ranger Regiment...

And yet totally different.

Rising back to his feet, Sharpe steadied himself on overhead handholds running the length of the chopper's ceiling. He looked out the open tailgate at the blur of African safari rushing by, then glanced to Corporal Gunter, the second most senior man in the fire team. The two men locked eyes, and Sharpe saw in Gunter's tired face a reflection of his own unease.

Something wasn't right.

Pulling his headset cable from the chest rig-mounted radio, Sharpe plugged it into one of the Chinook's interior intercom ports and hummed to activate the mic.

"Hammer Actual to Eagle-Eye. What's our ETA?"

"We're forty-three minutes out, Sergeant." The first lieutenant seated behind the left stick of the Chinook spoke with perfect ease—the voice of a man who would remain safely inside his armored cockpit over the next hour.

"Be advised," the lieutenant continued. "Once we reach the LZ we'll be switching to your ground frequency. We'll be right there in your ear from entry to exit."

Gee, thanks.

Sharpe thought it, he didn't say it. He yanked his headset cable from the wall and stepped across the cargo bay to where the doctor sat strapped into her seat. Surrounded by heavy blue duffel bags also printed with the WHO logo, she sweated a lot, but Sharpe couldn't tell whether it was due to the brutal African heat or her own anxiety. As he squatted next to her he noticed for the first time how young she was.

Mid-twenties—about his own age. Brilliant green eyes, strawberry-blonde hair. A small mouth pressed into a hard line. The name tape on her vest read: *Dr. E. Landry, MD.*

She was very pretty. She was also very tense.

"First time in a chopper?" Sharpe shouted.

Landry looked up from the med kit in her lap. She shook her head.

"No...well. Yes. First time in an Army chopper."

Sharpe forced a grin. "They're just like any other kind... only louder."

Landry didn't smile back. She looked out the tailgate. Her tongue ran across her dry lips. She breathed a little too quickly.

"Hey," Sharpe called, patting her arm. Landry looked back. "We've got a Predator drone on overwatch. The guys back at base are tracking the entire region—there's no sign of militant activity. We should be good."

Landry held his gaze, not blinking. Her next words chilled Sharpe to the bone.

"I'm not worried about bullets, Sergeant."

Sharpe said nothing. He simply nodded, retreating back to his seat and settling in. From the front of the cargo bay the crew chief snapped the receiver closed on the minigun. He made eye contact with Mason and held up three fingers, then a circle with his thumb and forefinger.

Thirty minutes.

2

"Gear up!" Sharpe shouted down the length of his men, reaching for his own NBC mask as the Chinook leaned into a hard bank—the final approach. Sliding over his head and sucking tight across his face, the mask fogged instantly as Sharpe exhaled damp air. The chopper leveled off and he adjusted the seal, waiting for the mist to clear.

Visible through the open tailgate, the sparse Sahara terrain had vanished, replaced now by thick tangles of vibrant green jungle. Northwest Ethiopia looked like a rich green carpet, stretching to the horizon in every direction. Sharpe attempted to inhale through the constricting mask filter and muttered a curse.

He could hardly breathe. He could barely see. The rubber suit covering his body, pinned in place by a full chest rig, constricted his movements by a factor of half. He was dumping so much body fluid via sweat that he half expected to pass out when he stood.

But orders were orders, and these orders were crystal

clear—full NBC protection. Not for concerns of the N or the C...but the B.

Biological.

Sharpe looked down the length of his fireteam and found Gunter ready to go. The third man, Private Tate, was also suited up and wielding a squad automatic machine gun like a favorite toy. The last guy, Private Moyers, was still struggling with his mask.

The new kid.

"Hey!" Sharpe shouted. "Stop fooling around!"

"It keeps fogging, Sarge. I can't see a thing!"

"So fight blind! Stop whining."

Sharpe jabbed a thumb, and Gunter moved to assist Moyers. Beneath his boots the vibrations of the giant chopper slowed as the jet engines wound down. Sharpe checked his M4 for the sixth time since departing base. He motioned for Tate to take up the pair of twin, collapsible stretchers laid out next to Dr. Landry's medical bags. Over his headset, the left-stick lieutenant called into Sharpe's ear.

"LZ in sight, Sergeant. All looks clear. We're going in!"

"Good copy. We're ready."

Sharpe braced himself with the overhead handrails as he stepped across the cargo bay. He reached Landry and tapped her shoulder. She looked up through the medical version of the NBC mask he wore.

She appeared just as strained as Moyer.

"Listen carefully, Doctor. Once we're on the ground, you do exactly as I say. Okay? You step where I step, you don't touch anything I don't touch. If I give you a shout, you get down and stay down until I come for you. Understand?"

Landry nodded, her mask lens systematically misting

and clearing with each rapid breath. Sharpe squeezed her shoulder.

"Relax, Doc. We do this all the time. You stick close and we'll be in and out before you know it."

Sharpe winked. He turned toward the open tailgate and caught Gunter's eye. The Corporal's eyebrows rose. Sharpe shot him the middle finger.

"Shut up, Gunt."

The Chinook stopped in midair. It orbited once. It thundered in place. Then the lieutenant called over the radio again.

"LZ clear—we're going in!"

At the tail of the chopper the already open tailgate descended into the landing position. Sharpe advanced along the handrail as Gunter called Tate and Moyer into position. The dense jungle below stretched out in a patchwork of mahogany trees and tangled vines, the jungle floor itself dense with bright green undergrowth. Sharpe observed a pair of monkeys swinging amid the trees. He noted a flock of birds exploding into the air as the Chinook's rotor wash flushed them out of their nests.

Then he saw the village—if you could call it that. It was really just an expanse of muddy orange dirt, occupied by a pair of thatch-roofed shacks with cloth-curtain doors. There was an old Toyota truck, battered by abuse and abandoned near the tree line. A skinny dog braced himself in the mud and barked at the incoming helicopter. Wild pigs ran for cover into the underbrush.

But there were no people—and what was more, no signs of people.

"We go first!" Sharpe shouted to Landry. "Wait for our signal."

Then the Chinook touched down, landing gear sinking into the orange mud. The rotors continued to churn as Sharpe led the way down the tailgate, rifle held into his shoulder, Aimpoint red-dot optic scanning the tree line. The other three Rangers fanned out behind him, Tate and Moyer covering Sharpe's blind spots on either side while Gunter walked backward, sweeping the jungle perimeter.

It was a solid defense mechanism, but Sharpe still felt fully exposed. This part of Ethiopia was *miles* from the developed, relatively stable capital of Addis Ababa. Deep inside the jungles of Ethiopia's poor and undeveloped Benishangul-Gumuz Region, Sharpe stood at the epicenter of ethnic tensions between Oromo, Gumuz, and Amhara communities.

Those tensions had spilled out of control of late. Heavily armed and highly militant militias roamed the countryside, indiscriminately attacking each other and anyone who dared to trespass on their territory. They would have heard the chopper as it thundered in for a landing.

And yet there was still an even bigger threat. A more insidious, invisible enemy.

Get in, get out, Sharpe thought. *Focus on the mission. Protect your people.*

Sharpe cleared the first mud hut. It was empty—just abandoned stick furniture and a dead cat. He proceeded to the second, sweeping the cloth curtain aside and breathing heavily through the NBC mask. Sweat ran into his eyes. The interior of the hut was inky dark, sheltered by the sun with windows covered in blackout curtains. Sharpe thumbed his weapon light.

And then his heart stopped. The second hut was not empty—it was occupied by two figures, both European. Both clad in the same light blue shirts and dark blue vests as Dr. Landry—members of the World Health Organization. The first lay face down on the floor, a pool of dry vomit surrounding her head. Motionless—also dead.

The second, a male, lay on his side on a cot, covered in a blanket. As Sharpe swept his weapon light over the man's form, the head twitched. Eyes blinked. An arm rose, lifting a handgun.

"Stop! Don't!"

Sharpe jerked back as the handgun cracked. A sloppy shot tore through the hut's doorframe. The gun toppled to the floor with a clatter. Sharpe pivoted the door frame again, rifle up, finger on the trigger. He placed the red dot over the man's chest.

The guy didn't move. His arm hung off the side of the bed.

"Net call, Hammer Actual. I've got two persons in Hut Number Two. One appears dead. One alive. Send the doctor!"

"Copy that, Hammer. Sending the doc."

Sharpe withdrew from the hut door and motioned with two quick jerks of his hand to Gunter. The corporal and the two privates fanned out to establish a security perimeter while Landry rushed from the tail of the chopper. She made a bee-line for Sharpe, hefting a medical duffel bag along with her, strawberry-blonde hair torn by the Chinook's perpetual rotor wash.

"In here!" Sharpe pointed to the second hut. Landry ducked right through the curtain without hesitation. Sharpe followed her inside, lowering his rifle and ripping the Streamlight MacroStream from his chest rig. He flicked it on, dumping light over the first person Landry stooped over—the motionless woman clad in the blue WHO vest.

Landry placed a gloved hand over the woman's stiff wrist, checking for a pulse. Shook her head. Proceeded to the man on the cot, brushing the fallen handgun aside. It was a Makarov PM, a popular sidearm among the aforementioned warring militias.

"He's alive," Landry said, voice distorted by her mask, but still sounding calmer than it had aboard the Chinook. The doctor had regained control of her nerves.

Pushing the man onto his back, Landry dug into her medical bag for a portable bottle of oxygen complete with a rubber mask. She snapped it over the guy's face as he moaned. Sharpe stood back with the MacroStream held up, casting nervous glances over his shoulder.

Too long. They'd been on the ground too long. Battlefield instincts honed and perfected in the slaughter valleys of Afghanistan warned him that it was time to move.

"Sarge!" Gunter's voice crackled through Sharpe's headset. The earpiece wiggled, and Sharpe wanted to adjust it. He couldn't reach it beneath the suffocating hood of the NBC suit.

"Go ahead, Gunt."

"Back of Hut Number One. You'll want to see this."

Sharpe cast a look out the curtained door. From across the clearing the Chinook continued to churn, the nose of the minigun twitching as the crew chief swept the jungle—just as nervous as the Rangers.

Tapping Landry on the shoulder, Sharpe passed her the light. "Take this. I'll be right back."

He jogged out of the hut, sweaty rubber legs swishing against his uniform pants. Moyer kneeled just outside Hut

Number One, his M4 held up and ready for action. Sharpe passed him and found Gunter and Tate gathered at the back of the hut, Tate's SAW sweeping the tree line, Gunter overlooking something at the base of the hut. Sharpe turned the corner. He kept his rifle up, finger pressed against the receiver. He surveyed the ground.

Then he saw them. Two men, both black, both dressed in muddy brown fatigues. Both dead—but not like the plague-ravished occupants of Hut Number Two. These men never had the opportunity to die the slow and miserable way—they'd been both shot in the chest, multiple times. Thirty-caliber holes with gaping exit wounds.

Hallmarks of AK-47 fire.

"The bodies are still limp," Gunter said, voice alive with tension. "This just happened."

Sharpe's gaze snapped back up to the tree line as he instinctively took a half-step back, rifle locked into his shoulder. He surveyed the jungle but saw nothing save darkness interwoven by vegetation.

Yet he knew—something was out there.

"Fall back," Sharpe radioed. "Everybody fall back to Hut Two. We're extracting now!"

The Rangers moved on command. Sharpe radioed the chopper, confirming that the pilots were ready for immediate takeoff. The Chinook's engines wound up in response. Sharpe reached the second mud hut and ripped through the door. Landry looked up, the MacroStream held in one hand, her face washing suddenly pale. She stared wide-eyed at Sharpe.

"Positive?" Sharpe asked.

Landry nodded once. "It's Ebola."

Sharpe breathed a curse and looked back over one

shoulder, dragging air through the mask filter. "Tate! Bring a stretcher."

He turned back to Landry. "Pack it up, Doc. We're moving out."

"He's not ready," Landry objected. "There's too much fluid in his lungs. I need to stabilize him first."

"You can stabilize him in the helo," Sharpe said. "Pack it up!"

Again Landry shook her head. She opened her mouth.

She never got the words out. From the jungle beyond the hut, a bark of gunfire burst like the snarl of a hundred rabid dogs. A chatter, followed by the hiss of bullets slicing through the air. The thatched roof of the mud hut exploded into a shower of dust, and Sharpe dove toward Landry, body-slamming her to the ground.

3

Sharpe and Landry hit the deck as Tate, Gunter, and Moyer opened fire outside, the snap of M4s punctuated by the heavier chug of Tate's SAW. In a split second the calm of the jungle descended into an absolute maelstrom of small-arms fire, bullets thudding into trees and walls, Gunter shouting into his radio.

"Tangos inbound from the east! Multiple muzzle flashes, heavy small-arms fire. We need that minigun!"

The crew chief aboard the Chinook answered the call with a curse, his shout barking through Sharpe's earpiece.

"I can't get a shot at them! You boys get back here—we're clearing out!"

Pushing himself back to his knees, Sharpe grasped Landry by the hand and pulled her into a crouch. The gunfire outside had redoubled, but none of the rounds were penetrating the wall.

At least, not yet.

"Gunter!" Sharpe called. "Get us some cover!"

"Copy! Throwing smoke."

Outside the hut a grunt singled the corporal's deployment of multiple smoke grenades. Tate's SAW chugged on, and Sharpe leaned close to Landry to shout into her ear.

"We're leaving! You wait by the door for my signal. When I give the word you sprint for the chopper—don't stop no matter what. We'll cover you!"

"What about—" Landry turned for the man stretched out over the cot.

"I'll get him," Sharpe cut her off. "Do what I say!"

He pushed her toward the door. Landry went, abandoning her medical bag. Sharpe turned back to the motionless man on the cot, scanning a face swollen with inflammation and starting to turn purple. The unconscious doctor's eyes were bloodshot, his lips crusted with vomit.

He might never make it back to base. He might already be dead. Sharpe would haul him out anyway.

"Gunt!" Sharpe called. "Prepare to cover the doctor. She's coming out on my signal."

"Copy that. The smoke is good. Ready when you are!"

Sharpe moved to the door. He swept the tree line, noting multiple muzzle flashes obscured by thick gray smoke. As the Chinook's rotors spun, bullets pinged off the armored metal sides, and the lieutenant screamed into the radio.

"*Sergeant!* Get your men back here!"

"We're coming," Sharpe said. "Stay calm."

He reached for Landry's arm. "You ready?"

Landry didn't respond. Sharpe turned and found her looking back at the woman lying spread across the mud floor amid dry vomit. Motionless.

"We gotta take her too," Landry said. "She has a family."

Sharpe bit back a curse, pulling her toward the door. "We don't have *time!* Now move for—"

He never finished. Gunter's scream of "*RPG!*" burst through the earpiece only a split second before the hiss of the rocket-propelled grenade ripped out of the jungle. Sharpe watched as the weapon streaked straight for the Chinook. It missed the bird by mere inches, passing above the rear ramp and slamming into a mahogany tree at the edge of the clearing. A blast of fire and smoke sent a shockwave ripping through the jungle, shards of wood and vegetation exploding against the side of the helicopter. The lieutenant shouted. The crew chief opened up with the minigun, firing blindly into the trees.

Sharpe grabbed Landry by her arm and dragged her out of the hut, no longer waiting for permission. He sprinted across the clearing, firing one-handed toward the muzzle flash as Gunter, Tate, and Moyer closed into a protective circle around him, lighting up the jungle on all sides. The minigun raced. The Chinook's jet engines howled. Sharpe reached the end of the tailgate and pushed Landry into the waiting arms of the helicopter's flight engineer.

"*Get down!*" he shouted. Releasing her, Sharpe made a circular motion with his right hand, jerking his head toward the chopper. "Everybody on board!"

Then he turned back for Hut Number Two. Gunter saw him go and called after him. Sharpe ignored the call and reached the mud hut even as the Chinook's engines wound up. Diving through the curtain, Sharpe dropped his rifle on its sling and scooped up the limp WHO doctor from atop the cot—the one who might still be alive. He spun back for the door. He sprinted.

The Chinook was lifting off. The lieutenant hadn't yet applied enough collective to send the twin-rotored behemoth shooting into the sky, but he was flirting with the line.

The nerves were getting to him as bullets pinged off the armor. Sharpe reached the tailgate as Gunter and Moyer extended their arms, ready to help him on board.

But he didn't run aboard. He passed off the body, shoving it into Moyer's outstretched arms. He made eye contact with Landry where she sat against the Chinook's wall as the flight engineer strapped her in.

Then Sharpe turned back again.

"What are you doing?" It was the lieutenant who shouted. The radio dissolved into a storm of cursing and confused demands. The pilot declared his intentions to take off.

Sharpe just kept running. Back to the hut. Ripping through the door, kneeling alongside the body of the dead woman—scooping her out of the dirt even as the Chinook screamed to takeoff RPM. He turned to the door and was met by a sandstorm of rotor wash. He couldn't see, choking even through the filter of the NBC mask. He fell back, stumbling. Over the radio Gunter dog-cursed the pilot, commanding him to stay on the ground.

The lieutenant wasn't listening. Another RPG roared out of the jungle, hissing past the Chinook's cockpit. That was more than enough for the young officer. He applied the collective. The bird lifted off. Sharpe hurled himself out of the shack and ran for the tailgate, the body in his arms stiff and leaden as his boots tore through the orange muck.

The world around him descended into slow motion— much as it had during all of his worst moments in Afghanistan. The bullets zipped by. One sliced through the leg of his NBC suit and cut into his calf. Another blew the filter off his mask.

Sharpe kept running even as the Chinook lifted six feet

off the ground and began to turn. The minigun screamed, dumping white-hot fury into the surrounding foliage. From the edge of the ramp Gunter leaned out, held in place by a safety harness as he grasped for Sharpe's hand.

"*Move!*" Gunter screamed.

Sharpe threw himself forward. He hurled the body upward just as he reached the tailgate. Gunter leaned down and caught the dead doctor by her arm. Moyer and Tate pulled on his harness from behind, dragging both Gunter and the body into the belly of the chopper. Sharpe reached for the edge of the tailgate but missed it by two inches as the lieutenant unleashed power to the rotors. The Chinook was climbing—pivoting toward the haven of open skies. Sharpe fell face-first into the orange clay, his busted mask crushing against the ground. He fought his way out of the goop and clawed the mask off, gasping for air. The clearing around him looked like the eye of a hurricane, trees and undergrowth torn by the rotor wash, loose leaves and foliage swirling amid the gunfire. He was caught in the open— nowhere to go. No place to hide. He clawed for his rifle.

Then the safety harness fell to the ground next to him, dangling at the end of a long strap. Without thinking, Sharpe hooked one arm through the harness, pulling it tight against his chest.

A split second later he was yanked off the ground like a child's toy plucked from a sandbox. His body rocketed upward, pain shooting through his left shoulder. Bullets zipped past his boots and brass rained in a column from the ejection port of the minigun. The jungle swirled on every side. He swung like a pendulum, a hundred feet of empty nothingness opening beneath his boots.

"Hold on, Sarge!"

It was Moyer. Sharpe looked up to see the vibrating edge of the tailgate, twenty feet overhead.

Then that twenty feet became nineteen. The strap moved, tugging him upward. Hearty men grunted through the radio, heaving together. The Chinook raced skyward and banked toward the east as Sharpe dangled beneath. He clung madly to the harness, heart hammering.

He reached the tailgate. Muscled arms reached over the edge and pulled him up and over. Sharpe landed with a thud on the ramp and his three battle buddies dragged him into the cargo bay of the chopper.

He came to rest on his back, staring up at a metal ceiling as jet engines howled. Gunter kneeled beside him and stripped away his chest rig, feeling across his body with two gloved hands.

"You hurt?" Gunter called. "There's blood!"

Sharpe gasped for air, body still choked by adrenaline. He shook his head, wiping sweat from his face.

"Leg," he managed. "Flesh wound."

"Where's your mask?"

"Busted," Sharpe wheezed, heart still hammering. "Did we bring a spare?"

Gunter simply shook his head, then deployed a folding knife and cut away Sharpe's right pants leg to inspect the bullet wound. As he worked, Sharpe rocked his head to look up the belly of the helicopter, making eye contact with the left-stick lieutenant as the pilot looked over his shoulder.

The lieutenant blinked behind his mask. Then he faced forward.

Sharpe looked back to the ceiling, rolling his eyes. He inhaled a long breath and forced himself to relax a little of the tension in his body. There would be ass-chewing back at base. If Sharpe had his way, that lieutenant would never fly a combat mission again.

But for now...he was simply glad to be alive.

A soft hand touched his arm. Sharpe looked up into the kind green eyes of Dr. Landry, her full-face mask still misting and clearing with each breath. She reached to brush the dirt from his face, then withdrew her hand. Maybe remembering that her gloves could be contaminated.

She shouted over the jet engines instead. "Thank you."

Sharpe managed a grin. "Any time, Doc."

That brought a slight flush. Landry's gaze dropped bashfully. "Evelyn. My name is Evelyn."

Sharpe pressed himself up onto his elbows, rising into a sitting position. Bunching his gloved hand, he tapped his knuckles against hers.

"Mason," he said. "Pleased to meet you."

4

PRESENT DAY

Bitter winter wind cut through my Carhartt coat as I killed the bandsaw, remaining behind the cutting head until the whirring metal blade reached a full stop. I'd fought all day to keep the machine running, waging a losing battle with the soapy water mixture that dripped onto the blade, providing both lubrication and a cleansing agent against the natural accumulation of pine resin.

Iowa in the heart of early February was a brutally cold place, and despite the shelter of a pole barn and the warmth of the mill's diesel engine, the soapy water mixture froze inside its tank every half hour, forcing me to stop the saw and deploy a heat gun to thaw it out.

I might have complained, but in truth, I didn't mind the break. I'd spent the week cutting shipping dunnage for a nearby steel mill—three-by-three sticks of oak and pine for the truckers to use as spacing strips between heavy I-beams. Paid on production at a rate of twelve cents per board foot, with six board feet per stick of dunnage, I was able to churn out as many as fifty units per hour.

It wasn't bad money. Paul Schroder, the easygoing old-timer who owned the sawmill, provided all the equipment and paid for the diesel. He even kept a refrigerator loaded down with canned iced tea, which I sometimes dumped into a coffee mug and warmed in the office microwave whenever the Iowa cold became too much to bear.

It never truly warmed me up, but at least it kept me going.

"Say, Mason!" Paul called from the open rolling doors of the pole barn.

I cast a glance over my shoulder and noted that it was snowing again—substantially. Giant white flakes landed on Paul's rancher-style felt hat, his breath clouding in front of his face.

"We're about snowed in," Paul said. "You better call it a day."

I shot him a two-finger salute and proceeded to loosen the sawmill's bandsaw-style blade, cutting off the lubricant nozzle even though the lubricant was frozen. In the event that it ever thawed, I didn't want it flooding my workspace.

Outside the barn I tugged off my work gloves and followed Paul across a snowbound yard piled high with mounds of unsawn logs and stacks of lumber ready to be shipped. It was a small operation—Paul, myself, and some college kid who worked only a couple days a week were the only personnel. Most of Paul's business originated from the steel company, but he also sold rough-sawn lumber to cabin builders, hobbyists, or pretty much anybody with a dollar in their pocket.

I'd found the place after bumping into town three months prior with a nasty left-leg limp and my own pockets nearly empty. I inquired about a job at the local diner, where

Paul was kicked back at a booth sipping coffee. He sized me up and said I'd last a week.

I hadn't quit yet.

"Let's get you paid." Paul led me to a table inside the dim block office, shifting aside stacks of paperwork and supply catalogs before locating a pencil and a legal pad. He worked the numbers by hand, adding my total board footage for the week, multiplying by my twelve-cent fee, and circling the number. Only after he was finished did he consult a calculator to ensure his own accuracy. He offered me the pencil, but I waved a hand in dismissal.

I'd checked his math before. It was never wrong.

Paul wrote out a check and I folded it into my pocket. Outside, the snow shower had become a downpour, piling atop the freshly painted hood of my 1967 GMC pickup. The windshield was covered. The camper shell laden with a thick blanket.

Beyond the truck a hundred-acre cornfield lay barren for the winter, with Paul's two-story, yellow farmhouse and adjoining barn rising out of the emptiness like the focal point of a postcard. Snow paved both his yard and the field beyond in pure white, with a pair of brown dots standing off in the distance that I soon recognized as a doe and her fawn. They walked gracefully through the swirling flakes, ears twitching against the cold.

It was picture-perfect, and Paul and I stood watching it in silence for a long while, both enjoying the crisp cold of the unheated office.

At last I shot him a smile. "Now that's beautiful."

Another two-finger salute and I promised to see Paul Monday. I piled into my truck and pumped the gas pedal a couple of times before twisting the key. I didn't pull the choke—I didn't need to. After several weeks of detailed restoration at a shop in St. Louis, the old pickup ran so beautifully that even in the bitter cold it started up on the first try. I gave it a few minutes to warm, then cleared the snow with my wipers, and turned toward town.

Prairie Junction, Iowa, was little more than a dot on the map. Situated in the northeastern quadrant of the state amid endless miles of corn and soybean fields, the town boasted a population of nineteen thousand—but most of those residents claimed Prairie Junction addresses only by virtue of the town's arbitrarily expansive city limits. The nearest metropolis of any size was Waterloo—sixty-six thousand people, but two hours away.

What Prairie Junction *could* claim was charm. A metric, Midwestern ton of it. With sleepy streets, a handful of churches, and a whole bunch of dirty-booted locals who appreciated kindness as much as they appreciated juicy gossip, Prairie Junction was my kind of town.

It was simple. It was quiet. It was the sort of place where you'd often find John Deere tractors parked in front of the courthouse while farm boys enjoyed lunch. It was just the right spot for me to recover from the St. Louis gunshot wound to my left thigh while I refilled my pockets with some hard-earned cash.

The GMC's heater ran well, and I was downright comfortable as I rumbled onto Main Street. Despite the snow, all the usual dives were alive and hopping. It was Friday night, and Iowans don't take a blizzard seriously until they have to dig their way out of their houses—sometimes, not even then.

I pulled my truck into an angled parking spot near my favorite restaurant—Millie's Place—and enjoyed the crunch of my boots in the snow as I walked. More than a few passing locals greeted me by name. An alley cat that everybody called "Schmuck", but nobody claimed, danced out of the shadows behind Millie's Place and seduced me into stopping to give him a scratch behind the ears.

The cat was fat, well fed by scraps from Millie's, with a little bed in the corner of the restaurant's kitchen that the health department knew nothing about. Who was the schmuck, anyway?

I pushed through the glass door to a welcome wash of warmth, walking right past the hostess stand. Everybody sat themselves, and this particular night the place was nearly full. I had almost resigned myself to waiting when a call rang from the back of the room.

"Mason! Over here. Grab a seat."

The booming voice was that of Ransom Jeter. Specifically, *Chief* Ransom Jeter, chief of police for Prairie Junction and the de facto sheriff of the community, given those expansive city limits lost inside an even more expansive county.

Jeter was another old-timer, pushing seventy while he could easily pass for late fifties. He was fit. He was salty. He was an Army veteran like me. He loved American football in every form, and enjoyed swapping war stories over tall glasses of craft beer.

I liked him.

Taking the proffered seat, I ordered hot coffee and the Salisbury steak from the waitress, waving a dismissive hand when she warned me the food might take a while. I wasn't in a hurry. Jeter didn't appear to be either. He was sucking on a bottle of Tank 7 Farmhouse Ale from Boulevard Brewing Company in Kansas City, a specialty beer that Millie ordered just for him. By the flush of his cheeks, I could tell it wasn't his first. Probably not even his third.

I'd never seen the man enter a gym, but beneath his sweatshirt heavy muscles bulged. The sweatshirt was blue, printed with the skull and leather helmet logo of an upstart arena football league that was gaining rapid popularity across the heartland. "American Gridiron", the shirt read. "*Yard by bloody yard.*"

The barbarity of that slogan was more than advertiser's bravado. I'd sat at the local watering hole and viewed a couple of games alongside Jeter, who was an enthusiastic fan of the arena league's brutal, unregulated brand—a brand that featured as many fistfights as touchdowns. The tempo seemed to suit Jeter's rough-and-tumble nature.

"Championship's coming up, isn't it?" I jabbed a thumb at Jeter's sweatshirt. He chugged beer and nodded.

"Later this week. Gonna be a banger! Baltimore made it."

"You gonna go?"

"Couldn't get tickets. The dern thing was sold out!"

"Nothing quite so popular as violence," I said, only half-joking.

Jeter laughed. Then he held up a finger. "That reminds me. Look what I dug up."

He sifted through his cargo pockets and produced a color photograph, faded and worn by age. I accepted it and squinted at the image. It was mostly green—a green mountain backdrop, a green Huey helicopter, men dressed in green squatted in front of it.

"Hey," I said. "That's you!"

Jeter grinned. "Dang right. Second day in Grenada, me and some other boys from the Seventy-fifth. That fellow on the right—" he stuck his finger over the picture and pointed.

"We called him Squirmy. Guy could wriggle through barbed wire like a snake. Turns out, he was a pretty good shot, too. We were taking the airfield and this Cuban punk was raining grenades on us with some Soviet grenade launcher. Not very accurately, mind you, but he was getting closer. Well, he was hiding behind all this undergrowth, and we couldn't get to him with our M-16s. So Squirmy, he snatches up this ninety-millimeter recoilless rifle. You know the kind."

"Tank gun," I said.

"Right, right. Well, Squirmy says, 'I'll teach him to chuck grenades', and fires that ninety millimeter at him. And would you believe it? Blew that sucker in half, right through the guts!"

Jeter guffawed. I laughed too. It was ugly humor—no doubt the Cuban's descendants weren't laughing. But when you've seen enough bloodshed and carnage, you find a way to manage the mental toll.

The waitress brought my steak and I carved in while Jeter continued to reminisce about days gone by in the Rangers. Most of his stories took a very different tone than mine. Grenada, Panama, and vague "assignments" in an unnamed country that we both knew was Nicaragua. It was a time of covert action and small wars. Gunfights alongside the Contras and adventures in the jungle.

Yes, a very different war than the endless mire of grinding bloodshed I'd faced in Afghanistan, but that made Jeter no less a soldier. With very little technology and fewer safety mechanisms than I had enjoyed, in some ways, he was more of one.

I leaned back with a full belly and drained my coffee. I reached for my wallet, but Jeter waved me off.

"I got it. Thanks for the company."

I nodded my thanks. Threw him a casual salute. I was just pushing my chair back when the diner door exploded open with a howl of winter wind, and a wild-eyed man dressed head to toe in Vietnam-era BDUs barreled in, breathing hard and dusted with snow. He scanned the room, ignoring a waitress who offered him a startled greeting. His gaze settled on the back corner—on *me*, I thought.

Then I realized he was looking at Jeter. He barreled through the tables. He was shouting long before he reached us.

"I got 'em, Chief! I got proof. *They're here.*"

5

The guy was tall, maybe six-five and broad-shouldered, but not heavy. If anything, he was underweight. With gray hair and a face creased by lines, I judged him to be in his late sixties—and those sixty-something years had been hard ones. He wore the BDUs like a man who learned to button them in basic training. His eyes, the color of washed concrete, were wide and strained.

He wasn't paying any attention to the diners he shoved aside on his way to our table. He didn't seem to notice anybody at all—anyone except Jeter.

By the time the newcomer reached our table, Jeter was rising out of his chair with a scowl on his face, motioning with an open palm for the guy to slow down.

"Dang it, Taggert, calm down. You're disrupting folks' dinner!"

"*I got 'em,*" Taggert said, smacking something onto the table. It was another photograph, color like Jeter's, but not green. No, this one was predominantly gray, a little white. A lot of snow.

Printed in the bottom right-hand corner of the photo was a date and time. The date matched the readout on my watch —the photograph was brand new. The time was earlier that morning.

And the subject of the photo was a car. Some compact, imported SUV, black in color and covered in snow slurry. The windows weren't tinted. Behind the wheel a dark figure huddled as he or she drove—the car's heater hadn't yet caught up to the cold.

"What's this?" Jeter sounded more annoyed than interested. Taggert pressed the image toward the police chief, and as he did I realized that it wasn't one image but a stack of them.

"Go on, Chief. Have a look."

An exhausted sigh. Jeter tugged on his beer. He blinked through watery eyes and shuffled the photos.

He shook his head and tossed them down.

"Taggert, for the last time. You can't be following people like this. If this fella were to complain I'd have to arrest you for stalkin'."

"Don't you recognize him?" Taggert demanded, eyes wide. Jeter didn't answer, and Taggert dropped a heavy finger on the top photo. "*Do you recognize him?*"

"No, Clay. I don't."

"So there you have it. He's Middle Eastern. Maybe from the Levant, by the look of him. So is his buddy. Jordan, Lebanon, maybe Syria. The car is a rental. I caught them out past one-oh-nine, not far from the nuclear plant. Now what's a bunch of foreigners doing out there?"

"Taggert..."

"It ain't right, Chief. I been telling you for years this place is primed for a terrorist attack. Now you got ragheads running around—"

"*Taggert!*" Jeter's voice snapped. He slammed his beer bottle down and the dining room grew suddenly quiet. Jeter cast an apologetic glance at his neighbors.

Then he leaned in. He lowered his voice.

"For the last time—stop bringing me this stuff. You ain't got nothing here but some creepy-ass photos and some hapless tourists lost in Iowa. You—"

"They're ragheads, Chief!"

Jeter raised a finger. His face radiated the warning wrath of an exhausted teacher, and to my surprise Taggert capitulated. He shrank a little. Jeter measured his words.

"That's an offensive slur, Taggert. And ignorant. For all you know, these are good people."

"They look like good people?"

Jeter laid his worn hand on the photos. He shoved them back at Taggert. "As a matter of fact, they do."

Taggert muttered a curse and retracted the photos. He jammed them into the open cargo pocket of his BDU jacket, muttering about 9/11 and ignored warnings.

Then, as though for the first time, he seemed to notice me. His slate-gray eyes fixated on my face and he frowned.

"Who's he?"

I relaxed in my chair, cocking an eyebrow. Jeter sighed.

"This is Mason Sharpe. He's new in town. Been working down at the mill with Paul."

"You a raghead?" Taggert barked.

I didn't blink. Jeter gritted his teeth. Taggert flushed a little.

"Sorry... I can see you ain't. Where you from, anyway? Whatcha doin' here?"

"Sitting," I said. Taggert's lips twitched. He seemed to be unsure whether I was simple or simply yanking his chain. I decided to let him wonder. He hadn't offended me—it takes a lot more than careless prejudice and paranoia to do that.

Besides, I could see behind the concrete, deep into a troubled, crazed soul. This guy *reeked* of post-traumatic stress disorder. It was something I understood.

Taggert directed his attention back to Jeter. He tapped the table again.

"You can laugh all you want, Chief. Make fun of my tin hat. That nuclear plant ain't got near enough security, and I'm *telling you*...those guys are no good."

With that Taggert pulled a BDU cap from his pocket, shook it to open it, then jammed it atop a crown of dirty hair. He nodded once.

Then he left, as suddenly as he'd come. I watched him go, noting the catch and pull of his jacket against a concealed object within his waistband. Something hard, and bulky.

"He's fun," I muttered.

Jeter grunted. He motioned to the waitress and she produced another bottle of Tank 7. She topped off my coffee. I decided I had another five minutes.

"Clay Taggert," Jeter said. "Served in Vietnam with the Marines. Got captured and spent ten months in a Vietcong prison camp."

"Rescued?"

"Escaped. At least...physically."

Right.

"He's eccentric," I said.

Jeter snorted. "He's insane. Big-time prepper, got himself a whole compound out in the county. Guns, beans, the works—or so he claims. He's always crashing into my office to report the next 9/11. There's a nuke plant 'bout six miles west of town and he's convinced it's a target."

I knew about the nuclear plant. Half the town worked there. I also knew that the facility was about the safest place in America short of NORAD. Armored, fenced, and patrolled by ex-military guys with rifles who weren't afraid to use them.

But for a guy like Taggert with a few screws loose, I could only imagine the rabbit trails of paranoia that kept him awake at night. I'd met the kind before. Not everyone who returns from war ever makes it home.

"I'm sorry," I said simply.

Jeter met my gaze. He tipped his beer. I stood and slapped a ten-dollar bill on the table.

"Thanks for dinner. Next round's on me."

Jeter grinned.

I LEFT my truck parked in front of Millie's Place and walked the two blocks down Main Street to my current residence— the law offices of one Lyle Pritchard. While exploring the American Southeast I had developed an affinity for camping and spent most of my nights stretched out on an air mattress in the back of my truck, my head hanging out over the tail-gate so that I could see the stars. But in Iowa—specifically, in *winter* Iowa—sleeping outside was something worse than ill-advised. It was downright suicidal.

Lyle Pritchard was a practicing attorney in his mid-sixties with a specialty in divorce, civil litigation, criminal defense, real estate, business law, and literally anything else he could turn a buck at. He owned a two-story brick building on Main Street directly across from a hardware store and two doors down from the old movie theater. A few years back, Lyle had been involved in a car accident and was paralyzed from the waist down.

He'd sued the pants off the offending driver, making bank from their insurance. He'd purchased a modified van that allowed him to drive with only his hands. He'd moved all his legal clutter to the front room of the office building and installed his bachelor apartment in the back room.

That left the second floor empty, as it had remained for several years. After rolling into town I struck up a conversation with Lyle over a game of dominos at the local coffee shop. I needed a place to stay warm through the winter. Lyle offered me his second floor at a reasonable rent. I inflated my air mattress on the worn hardwood and had been calling his address home ever since.

Lyle sat behind his sprawling legal desk as I entered, kicking snow off my boots on the door mat. The office was heated by a gas furnace, and Lyle had the temperature cranked up someplace north of volcanic. Within seconds I was stripping out of my Carhartt coat as Lyle hung up his phone, scratching a bearded cheek and staring at the handset.

"What's up?" I said. "Long day?"

Lyle looked up. He blinked, seeming to notice me for the first time. With a grunt he pushed his wheelchair out from behind the desk and rumbled over to the coffee bar.

"Been fighting for a settlement on the Willoughby case all afternoon... Looks like we're going to trial. Freaking insurance companies!"

He fixed himself a cup of tea. Steam clouded in front of his face. There was something in his eyes.

"You good?" I asked.

Lyle nodded, stirring honey into the cup. Then he looked to the office's front windows, squinting at the gathering snowfall swirling between the streetlights.

"Haven't heard from Mama in a couple days...couldn't get her on the phone. Unusual."

He shook his head and returned to the tea. I could tell he was more concerned than he let on.

"You check with Maggie?" I asked.

Maggie, the ostensible maid of Mrs. Pritchard's expansive family farmhouse, was more of a family friend. I'd met her on a couple of occasions. She kept close tabs on Lyle's mother.

"Phoned her an hour ago," Lyle said. "She checked on Mama yesterday...was supposed to clean the house. Mama sent her away. Said she wasn't feeling good."

Lyle paused over his tea. He sucked his teeth and looked toward the office's front windows again.

"You wanna ride out to the farm?" I offered.

"Van can't handle this much snow," Lyle said. "I'll have to wait until the morning."

"What about my truck? Better ground clearance. I've got snow chains."

A snort. "Can't fit my chair in that thing."

I resisted a grin. "I could carry you."

Lyle snorted and tossed the honey bottle at me. By the time I caught it he was laughing. I walked past with my coat over one shoulder, sweat already running down my back as I wished him goodnight. I climbed to the second level. I walked past a bathroom to a wood-framed door with a frosted glass insert. On the glass, faded golden letters read "Gordon Golf, Attorney at Law." Lyle's old partner—another victim of a car accident, this one fatal.

Inside the now barren office I kicked off my boots and cast a glance around the sparse interior. Besides the air mattress inflated in one corner, the only contents were a large duffle bag where I kept my clothes, a backpack where I kept my personal effects, and a violin case where I kept the obvious.

One chair sat next to a low end table, overlooking Main Street through a trio of tall windows. I approached the glass and tugged the blinds open, standing for a long minute while watching the downpour of snow piling over the hoods of parked vehicles, choking the sidewalk and gathering in the storm drains. Illuminated by street lights, it was something more perfect than beautiful. Absolutely silent, without a hint of wind, flakes swirled on their slow journey to the ground, landing without so much as a whisper.

A different kind of beauty than I had experienced in Arizona, Florida, or the cornfields of Missouri. But no less enchanting.

I settled into the chair and put my feet on the end table. I read my late fiancée's Bible for half an hour, taking selections from the books of Samuel and Matthew before my eyes grew heavy. I set the Bible back on the table and I prayed for a while.

At least, I thought it was prayer. I still wasn't entirely sure how that mysterious spiritual communication worked. I simply sat quietly, and in my mind I talked to God. I thanked Him for the workday. I thanked Him for my friends, and a warm place to sleep. I asked for safety for Lyle's mother.

Then I shut the blinds, I climbed beneath my covers. I

stretched out on the air mattress and thought of my dear Mia one last time as sleep overtook me like a cloud, unbroken by dreams or nightmares.

Near-perfect for nine hours...until the helicopters stormed in like a hurricane.

6

I sat bolt upright at the first rumble of distant rotors, a sound I would have recognized anywhere in the world. I was temporarily disoriented by the incongruence of that gathering thunder paired with my current surroundings.

Was Iowa a dream? Was I back in Afghanistan—or Africa?

No. I blinked the sleep away and recognized the room around me. The wood-paneled walls, scarred by nail holes from photographs and memorabilia long removed. The drooping ceiling fan I never turned on. The trio of windows shielded by blinds, the first kiss of a winter sunrise peaking beneath their edges.

And that thunder growing rapidly louder. I recognized the familiar churn of Army UH-60 Black Hawks, a distinct pound impossible to mistake. They roared in from my right, at least three of them. Even as I tumbled out of bed and reached my feet, the rotor wash passed near enough to Main Street to rattle the window panes in their frames. I yanked the blinds back and rocked my head just in time to see the gray underbelly of a Black Hawk pass immediately over Lyle's law office, turning and casting up a storm of dry snow from the street below. In a flash, it was gone, orbiting to the edge of town.

But the pound of rotors persisted, now joined by the rumble of heavy engines. Not jet engines but truck engines, another sound I recognized.

Deuce-and-a-half troop transports. Humvees.

What?

I dropped the blinds and hurried back into the room, tugging on my jeans and jamming my feet into my boots. All the junk I carry—keys, Victorinox Locksmith, Streamlight MacroStream—found its way into my pockets. I cinched my belt down. I snatched the Carhartt coat off the back of the chair.

Then I was headed down the steps, thundering to the bottom even as the pitch of the helicopter engines wound down behind Lyle's office.

The birds had landed. I thought I detected shouts but I couldn't be sure. The grind of the incoming vehicles was too loud. I reached the front door even as Lyle called out to me from his living suite in the back of the first floor. I ignored him and stepped out onto the sidewalk, a rush of icy air flooding my lungs as my boots punched through six inches of snow.

The street was covered in it. All the parked vehicles lay blanketed by thick layers. But storming down the middle of Main Street, snow exploding over thick military tires, was a heavy-duty truck painted in desert tan. Not a deuce-and-a-half as I initially guessed, but one of the US Army's newer FMTV trucks—the Family of Medium Tactical Vehicles, a series of troop transports and general-purpose trucks built on a universal chassis. In contrast to the long snout of the old deuce, the new FMTV had a flat nose and rode higher off the ground. It rumbled right past me with a storm of crushed snowflakes exploding over the sidewalk, continuing to the intersection of Main Street and Washington Avenue, where the truck pulled right beneath the single traffic signal and ground to a stop.

I stepped off the sidewalk and squinted in the sunrise, reading the letters stenciled onto the truck's door at a distance of fifty yards. *Iowa National Guard.* The truck's canvased rear shuddered. The rear flap tore open.

Then the troops exploded out, landing in the snow in twin stacks, rushing out toward the sidewalks with M4 rifles held across their chests...their bodies fully clothed in dark green Nuclear, Biological, and Chemical suits.

NBC. What the hell?

My gaze switched back up Main Street to the next intersection. Another FMTV sat there alongside a pair of Humvees. Two dozen more soldiers bailed out, all dressed in full NBC gear. Faces housed behind filtered masks, weapons at the ready as they dispensed automatically across downtown. The tactical dispersion was familiar to me—I knew what they were doing even before they finished assuming positions at each street corner and the mouth of every alley. In seconds the Iowa National Guardsmen had established a full tactical stranglehold of Main Street, moving from door to door and pounding with gloved fists.

It was so sudden—and so bizarre—that I should have been shocked. In consideration of the NBC suits, I should have been worried. Maybe I should have taken cover.

But I wasn't shocked, and I didn't take cover. The only

thing I felt was irrational anger. Despite the American flags printed on the trucks and the reasonable expectation that these guys were on the sides of liberty and justice, the operation unfolding before me felt like an invasion.

Those feelings only intensified when Schmuck appeared from the alley next to Millie's Place, and one of the soldiers kicked him out of the way, sending the cat flying.

"*Hey!*"

I addressed my shout to the first guy I saw who might have been an officer. It was impossible to tell with his uniform covered by the NBC suit, but he stood in the middle of the intersection of Main and Simmons Streets, directing the other soldiers with an outstretched arm. As I neared, I identified the subtle glimmer of twin silver bars on his collar beneath the mask.

A captain.

"What are you doing?" There was more than a little accusation in my tone. As voices rose from two blocks off Main Street in the residential district, carried by the icy still air, I knew I wasn't the only one confronting the madness.

"Sir, we need you to return to your residence and remain inside." The captain turned hard eyes on me, his mask systematically fogging and then clearing with each breath. His voice sounded a little robotic through the filter.

That sound brought back a flood of memories. They weren't all good memories.

"I'm not going anywhere until you explain this," I said. "Why are your men in NBC? What happened?"

"We're here by order of the governor. That's all you need to know at this time. Return to your residence, or we'll be forced to detain you."

With that the captain turned away, gesturing to a nearby

infantryman seated on the roof of a Humvee with his feet dangling through the gun turret. There was no machine gun in that turret, but there was a loudspeaker mounted to the roof of the Humvee, and on the captain's signal the infantryman hit a switch. A recording began to play. Easily carried by the cold air, it broadcasted between the downtown buildings.

"*Attention!* By order of the Governor of Iowa, this municipality is being placed under temporary emergency martial law. Please remain in your homes. Do not venture out, do not engage with National Guard personnel. Please remain calm. You are safe at this time."

I rocked my head in disbelief toward the infantryman. He gazed at me behind his mask, eyes a little wide. Face a little pale.

He was terrified—I could see it in his withdrawn posture. Barely old enough to hold a driver's license, let alone an automatic weapon, the kid noticed me staring and spoke with confidence I knew he didn't feel.

"Go back inside, sir! Captain's orders."

"He's not my captain," I muttered. Turning on my heel, I found Schmuck walking in circles outside Millie's Place, meowing at nobody as he struggled through the snow. I wasn't sure how or why he had vacated his warm bed inside Millie's kitchen, but with the snow riding up to his belly, he had to be freezing. Terrified, also.

Nobody in this town had ever kicked him before.

I scooped him up, pulling the cat inside my coat as I turned down the sidewalk. Not back toward Lyle's place, but farther down the street. Toward city hall, and the police station.

I found Jeter standing on the sidewalk outside his two-story police headquarters, a building that looked like a carbon copy of Lyle's law office. He was joined by another National Guard officer dressed in a full NBC suit—only in place of the twin bars I'd found on the captain's collar, this time I detected a silver leaf. It was the emblem of an Army 0-5. A lieutenant colonel.

Red-faced and with eyes bulging, old Jeter was giving the LTC a mouthful as I approached, seasoning his words with more than a little pepper.

"You can't just storm in here—"

"Sir! *Sir!*" the LTC cut him off with a raised hand, breathing hard through his mask. His stiff, squared posture reminded me of every officer I ever knew who ascended the ranks during the eighties and nineties.

Long-term soldiers, and dedicated servants of the public good. Generally.

"Mr. Jeter, I need you to calm down—"

"*Chief* Jeter. This is *my* town and you ain't gonna roll in here like a bunch of—"

"Chief Jeter, we're only trying to do our job. There's been an emergency. We're here by order of the governor. All the details will be communicated to your office shortly. Right now my men could really use your cooperation."

Before Jeter could answer, a car alarm blared from down the street. Everyone present looked down the sidewalk to see a soldier in full NBC gear walking backwards, beckoning with one hand. A Humvee engine churned. A chain yanked tight. Then a red sedan was jerked out of the snow, its bumper popping loose as the Humvee dragged it across the street.

"What the hell!" Jeter bellowed.

The LTC held up an apologetic hand. "They're just moving it."

"They're ripping the bumper off!"

"It was blocking the street. We have to get through."

Jeter whirled on the officer, face a bloody shade of crimson. "It was blocking the street because Ms. Cramer got *snowed in*. She was waiting for a tow truck. Are your men going to pay for that damage?"

"*Sir!*" the LTC shouted, finally losing his cool. "I'm going to ask you one more time to *return to your office*. If you do not remove yourself from this street, we *will* detain you."

Indignation erupted across Jeter's face. His hand dropped toward his hip...and his sidearm.

Not good.

I sprang forward, one arm cradling Schmuck while I caught Jeter by the elbow with the other.

"Rans! Stay calm. Just take a breath."

Jeter's angry eyes snapped toward me, then dropped instinctively to the bulge in my coat. Schmuck stuck his head out, meowing pitifully at the cold, or perhaps the noise. His voice clashed with the grumble of military chaos unfolding around us, and its pitiable weakness was just enough to bring Jeter back to earth.

He stopped. Closed his mouth. Swallowed.

Then he moved his hand away from his gun.

"Just go inside," I said. "I'm taking Schmuck to Lyle's place. He's cold. I'll be back."

I didn't move, raising both eyebrows. Waiting. The LTC hadn't moved either. Everybody seemed to be on full alert, gazes locked on Jeter. At last the chief jerked his elbow free of my grasp and turned toward his office door with a curse. I let him go and shot a look at the LTC.

But the officer wasn't waiting around to answer questions. He stepped off the sidewalk and shouted an order to one of his men.

"Get that road clear. Signal the Black Hawks. Move to the subdivisions."

I set off down the sidewalks with Schmuck in my arms, his plump body shivering against the cold. With every street I passed the noise of military activity grew louder. Trucks chugged between shops and homes. The recorded message blaring from the loudspeaker persisted, joined by the shouts of protesting civilians and insistent guardsmen. One of the helicopters took flight from the church parking lot behind Lyle's place and ripped overhead, nose down. Headed east.

Toward Prairie Junction's suburban neighborhoods.

I reached Lyle's office just as the door exploded open. Lyle rolled out in his wheelchair, pumping the wheels with his thick arms. His face was red in the cold, much like Jeter's, but less angry. He swept the streets and turned wide eyes on me.

"What happened?"

"I don't know, Lyle. It's the National Guard. They're placing the town under martial law."

"They're *what?*" Lyle responded with the abject disbelief typical of Americans who have spent their entire lives deep inside the land of the free. Maybe I'd seen too much military action. Maybe my mind was jaded by too many dumpster-fire civilizations overrun by the thunder of helicopters and machine guns.

Whatever the case, the situation wasn't so much shocking to me as deeply concerning.

"Let's get inside," I said. "Schmuck's cold."

Lyle shook his head. "I've got to get to my van. I can't get

Mama on the phone—it won't even ring. She'll be freaking out with these helicopters!"

"It's okay," I said. "We'll call her from my cell."

"Mason." Lyle put a hand on my arm, arresting my progress toward the door. "You're not listening. They're *all* down. Landlines, cell phones. Even the internet. It's all gone."

"What?"

"You can check for yourself. I've got to go."

Lyle fought with his wheelchair. I stopped him, turning sharply toward the church as a distant sound sent a lightning bolt of dread shooting through my veins.

Gunfire.

Pushing the door open, I grabbed Lyle's wheelchair by one handle and dragged him inside before he could argue. I placed Schmuck on a high-backed client chair, then I zipped my coat up.

"Stay here," I said. "Stay inside."

"Wait!" Lyle wheeled himself toward the door. "Where are you going?"

"To check on your mother," I said. "And to get some answers. Stay put, Lyle. I'll be back."

Getting to my truck was easier than it should have been. Avoiding Main Street, I routed down the narrow lane behind Lyle's law office, my footsteps light on the snow as I closed on Millie's Place.

The Iowa National Guard moved with the speed and precision of a unit that had seen combat—or at least deployment. But for all their agility, they were a long way from locking down Prairie Junction. They simply didn't have the manpower. With intersections secured and the Humvee armed with its loudspeaker making routes through the older neighborhoods adjacent to downtown, most of the streets were left necessarily unattended. I made it all the way to the alley next to Millie's Place without incident, finding my truck parked right where I'd left it. The cab, camper shell, and hood were all covered in snow.

But the tires were encased in quality snow chains, just as I'd told Lyle. I waited for the nearest guardsman standing at the street corner to turn his back, then I slipped up to my truck, unlocked the door, and eased inside. The door always shut with the heavy thunk of a closing tank hatch, so I opted to leave it cracked open as I pumped the gas, then primed the key.

This had to be quick. I wasn't sticking around to have a gun shoved into my face.

With a flick of the key the motor turned. The GMC coughed and I shut the door, my cover blown. The soldier at the street corner turned my way—I saw him through the top half of my window, not yet covered with snow. He held up a hand and advanced, but he was already too late.

Paciello's Custom Restorations had done one heck of a job with the refurbishment of my pickup. The inline-six rumbled straight to life, and I rocked the column shifter into reverse before releasing the clutch.

The truck lunged backward, snow sliding off the roof. I looked back through the camper shell's hatch, but the glass was frosted over. I couldn't see a thing.

Stepping on my brakes, I slid to a stop on Main Street. The soldier was running now, both hands on his rifle. Shouting at me.

I flatly ignored him, hitting the wipers to displace the blanket of windshield snow. It cascaded to the road, and then I was off. The soldier's masked face drew near to my passenger side window as I passed. My righthand rearview mirror clipped his arm.

Then I was gone. I reached the intersection where I had confronted the captain and wheeled right, skirting past the parked FMTV. The next street I entered was bereft of military personnel and I was able to accelerate to forty miles per hour as the tire chains smacked the asphalt, sending vibrations shooting through my spine and down my gunshot left thigh.

It had been three months since the nine-millimeter slug zipped into my leg, burying itself in two inches of muscle. In terms of mobility, I had recovered well. I could walk, I could drive, I could work.

But it still randomly hurt like crazy, especially in the cold. I turned up the truck's heat, then reached for the stereo built into the dash. It was a brand-new unit, installed by Arty Paciello and his people. Made to look like a factory original, the device was capable of Bluetooth, auxiliary connectivity, and all kinds of other things I didn't care about. I only ever used the FM radio, and I knew it worked.

Locked into a country music station I'd been enjoying over the past few weeks, the first voice I heard was that of Blake Shelton. He sang "Sangria", a song that always reminded me of good times with Mia in New Orleans. I twisted the tuner, searching for the next channel. I found a jazz station. A rap station. A political talk show featuring a screaming male voice that ranted about political deadlock in Washington.

But no local news. Nothing out of Waterloo, or even Des Moines. It both surprised and perplexed me, but just as I was about to switch from FM to AM, I topped a low hill and the edge of town stretched out before me.

There was a Methodist church and accompanying grave-yard to my left. A gas station and a Subway restaurant to my right. Parked in between was another FMTV, its reverse lights glowing as it eased toward the ditch, tires cut to the side. Two NBC-clad soldiers stood outside the truck, guiding it backwards until the tires almost dropped off the pavement.

Then the reverse lights clicked off. The wheels turned and I saw what was happening from fifty yards out—the heavy truck was about to pull directly across the two-lane. It was a roadblock in progress, and the gap between the FMTV's front bumper and the chain-link fence was only about twice as wide as my truck—and shrinking.

I downshifted from third to second and slammed on the gas. The GMC surged, the inline-six dumping impressive torque to the wheels as I laid on my horn. The blare had the desired effect—the FMTV's driver slammed instinctively on his brakes. He turned to look through his open side window. One of the soldiers on the street stepped forward to close the gap, lifting a hand and shaking his masked head.

I plowed on, wheeling left and exploding through the gap in a shower of snow. On the other side I up-shifted but kept the accelerator mashed to the floor, hurtling down the two-lane as blood surged through my chest.

This wasn't right. I knew it even as I looked into my rearview to find one of the soldiers angrily yanking his arm, directing the FMTV to close the gap.

What was happening? A total town lockdown? How did that make sense?

There could only be one rational reason for the National Guard to deploy to a place like this, and that would be to protect the inhabitants from a mortal threat. The first item to come to mind, of course, was the nuclear plant. That might explain the NBC suits.

Except, if there had been a problem at the plant resulting in potential radiation fallout as far as Prairie Junction, thereby necessitating the NBC suits, the soldiers shouldn't be locking civilians in their homes. They should be evacuating them—evacuating *everybody*. As quickly as possible.

Further, if there was a nuclear problem, where were the Geiger counters? I had observed nobody measuring for radiation contamination. I'd observed no specialized anti-radiation units on-site—only standard infantry clothed in NBC gear.

Maybe the radiation units were on the way. Maybe the National Guard was just the quick-reaction force, waiting for backup. But again, that didn't make sense. It takes time to deploy the National Guard, and *if* there was a problem at the nuclear plant large enough to trigger this sort of response...why wasn't I finding anything about it on the radio?

I shelved my thoughts as I retraced my memories of visiting Lyle's mother, calling up landmarks to signal each turn through the Iowa countryside. If ever there was an angel of a woman, it was certainly Ms. Molly Pritchard. Now in her early eighties, she was widowed and still lived alone, managing her rural country home with ease despite her age. She got around well. She gardened in the summer and knitted a lot in the fall. She kept chickens year-round and doted on them like children.

Most of all, she cooked. Better than anyone I'd ever known. Lyle visited his mother for dinner every Sunday afternoon, and I was always invited. It felt like an intrusion at first, but after an initial helping of Ms. Molly's chicken and dumplings, I stopped arguing. It wasn't like I was the only loner crowded around Ms. Molly's table. Maggie, her maid, often joined us. So did any number of friends and total strangers.

That was just the way Ms. Molly functioned. She was a saint. Kind and thoughtful, always happy to listen, but equally adept at sharing her own life stories. I enjoyed her company as much as Lyle or Jeter's, so it was natural for me to check on her in Lyle's absence. I could only hope that Ms. Molly's lack of a television, coupled with her rural address, ensured that she had been thus far insulated from this madness.

I reached the turnoff for the Pritchard farm and scanned a long dirt road choked with snow. Barbed-wire fences lined it on both sides, blocking out cow pastures. The house itself was early twentieth century in vintage, clad in white lapboard siding, two stories tall, with a wrap-around front porch. It sat on a slight rise with another hundred-acre Iowa field spilling out behind it. The battered Ford Ranger parked under an oak tree hadn't moved since I'd first met Ms. Molly. She didn't drive—Maggie ran all her errands and Lyle took her to church each Sunday morning. The property looked as peaceful as it ever did...but somehow, just a little too still.

I turned down the drive and bumped along its half-mile length. The closer I drew to the old house, the more I felt in my gut that something was wrong. No lights were visible through the front windows. No smoke rose from the iron-pipe chimney of the kitchen woodstove—an old-school contraption that Ms. Molly used daily.

Maybe it was just the cold weather. Maybe Ms. Molly was sleeping in, and her phone lines had been damaged by the weather.

Maybe...

I stopped the truck at the front porch and left it running. I climbed out, breath clouding in front of my face. I advanced to the front door and glanced across the side yard toward the chicken coop.

The chickens were still barricaded in their nightly roost. Ms. Molly hadn't let them out.

I knocked. Waited. When nobody responded, I knocked again, a little louder. I called out, "Ms. Molly? It's Mason Sharpe!"

Silence. I tried the door, but it was locked. I departed the house and circled around the side, toward the kitchen entrance. There was a barn out back, and a woodshed loaded with the split oak firewood that fed the kitchen stove. All was blanketed in snow, with no sign of any boot prints.

I reached the door. I tried the latch. It was unlocked. I pushed the door open and called into the kitchen.

"Ms. Molly! It's Mason. Lyle sent me to check on you."

I stepped into the kitchen and my anxiety spiked. It was icy cold. The stove was full of ashes. The overhead lights were dark, dirty dishes piled at random on the counter. As I advanced across the floor old habits from the Phoenix PD kicked in, and by sheer muscle memory I avoided the light switches, drawing my Streamlight MacroStream instead. I cast blinding light across the floor and noted a trail of dusty footprints—the kind Maggie would never tolerate.

"Mama sent her away... Said she wasn't feeling good."

Lyle's comment about Maggie's scheduled cleaning visit echoed through my mind as I proceeded to the parlor. It was also unoccupied. I crossed toward the front door. I passed the staircase and orbited into the living room.

Then I stopped cold. My chest tightened. The flashlight beam passed across a dark room and fell onto the couch—onto a familiar face, laid back awkwardly against a pile of pillows, one arm dangling toward the floor. Face purple and blue, swollen and contorted. Dry vomit running from the lips, coating the couch and the floor. Eyes wide and vacant.

It was Ms. Molly Pritchard. And she was dead.

8

I stood frozen in the cold, temporarily disabled. I took two steps forward toward the body, my initial investigator's desire to gain a better look at the body stopped short by a darker, harsher truth.

Those purple marks on her face. The contortion of her hands, the bloodshot eyes. That bile filling her throat and coating the floor.

I'd seen this before. Not in Iowa, but on the other side of the world. Dead bodies contorted by constricting muscles. Purple faces, bloodshot eyes. There was no possible way this could be...

Then another thought slammed home in my mind. *The NBC suits.*

Nuclear? No. Not hardly.

I turned from the room and left Ms. Molly where she lay. I rushed back out to the truck and climbed in, slamming the door. I sat for a minute in the warming rush of the pickup's heater, eyes burning as the image of Ms. Molly's corpse flooded my brain. I'd seen a lot of horrible things in my life. As a cop, as a soldier, as a starving orphan kid scrabbling on the streets of Phoenix. I'd seen more bodies than most morticians. I'd witnessed death, destruction, and carnage.

But something about that sweet old lady, twisted on the couch, drowned by her own vomit, hit harder than a barrage of artillery shells. It brought tears to my eyes before I could stop them. My stomach twisted as my knuckles whitened around the steering wheel.

And more than anything, it brought understanding—a realization of what it was all about. All those helicopters, trucks, and sprinting soldiers in NBC suits. They weren't evacuating the town and they weren't sweeping for radiation. No, they were *locking the town down*. Quarantining it.

This wasn't a nuclear disaster. This was a biological outbreak, and a bad one.

I shifted into reverse and pulled out of the yard. I didn't go back for Ms. Molly's body, as badly as I wanted to. Without knowing exactly what illness had brought her into an early grave I couldn't be sure how that disease was transmitted, or whether or not I'd already been exposed. Should it be an airborne virus, I was very likely infected. Regardless, there was no point in risking direct contact by recovering her body.

No. I had to get back to town. While remaining safely distanced from others, I needed to report this case to the applicable authorities. And then I had to fully isolate—and wait.

I drove back to Prairie Junction a lot slower than I had driven out, reaching the roadblock I had previously evaded and finding the FMTV completely blocking the street. I stopped ten yards away and waited while National Guardsmen jogged forward with rifles at the ready, looking good and pissed behind their NBC masks.

I kept the doors locked and windows up. When the first guy shouted for me to exit the vehicle, I simply looked at him. He was a kid. Maybe not yet only enough to buy beer. He looked terrified.

If I was right about what evil had claimed Ms. Molly's life, he had every reason to be.

"Where's your commanding officer?" I called through the window.

"Exit the vehicle, sir! We're placing you under detainment."

I scanned the lineup of soldiers. I didn't see any collar-pinned officer's insignia.

"Get me your NCO," I said.

The kid shouted again for me to exit the vehicle, brandishing his M4 as though he would actually use it. I snapped.

"*Do it,* soldier!"

That was enough to rattle him. He blinked. He turned from the vehicle and jogged to the back of the FMTV. A minute later he returned with an older man who might have been a sergeant. The guy rapped on the window.

"Shut off your engine and exit the vehicle."

I held his gaze. I didn't blink. Then I said the words that changed everything.

"I've been exposed."

THE SERGEANT LEFT me in my truck. He retreated and made several radio calls using his military-issued communications equipment. I sat in the idling pickup for twenty minutes, thinking about Ms. Molly and her chicken dumplings. Her knitting and her stories about the old days.

I wanted to call Lyle and tell him the news. He deserved to know, but when I checked my phone it still had no signal. The little bars were all gone, replaced by a gray X.

The phone towers were down, and I wondered if the National Guard was responsible. Curtailing communications might enflame local residents, but it was certainly a logical strategy in containing the spread of panic. A military strategy, no less.

At last a Humvee appeared on the road beyond the FMTV. A soldier stepped out, and I immediately knew by the way the other guardsmen deferred to him that he must be an officer. He approached the NCO and held a short conference. He looked to me and my truck. Then he returned to the Humvee and turned it around in the road. One of the guardsmen started up the FMTV and backed it up far enough to allow passage. The NCO approached my vehicle and pointed to the Humvee.

"Follow him. *Do not* exit your vehicle."

I simply nodded and shifted into gear. I followed the Humvee back into town, through the outskirts, past the churches and schools, across the north end of Main Street, and through a neighborhood. There were a *lot* more guardsmen on-site than there had been when I had departed town only an hour earlier. More helicopters roared overhead. Every major intersection was secure. Iowa State Patrol had joined the mix, their silver SUVs blinking with blue lights as they assisted with roadblocks.

The Humvee was allowed to pass through them all, as was I. We reached the northwestern corner of Prairie Junction, and I recognized the boundaries of Open Plains Community College. A small campus consisting of only half a dozen buildings, a soccer field, and a park, OPCC was nonetheless the pride and joy of Prairie Junction. Boasting a strong female student body, the crown jewel of the campus was the fifteen-hundred-seat basketball arena where the Lady Ravens played regular matches against regional competition.

The team was more than a college team. It was a true community team. Locals often wore Lady Ravens gear, and the arena was nearly always full on game nights. I had attended a handful of games myself, and enjoyed them. It was a great way to spend a Friday evening.

It was also where the Humvee was headed.

National Guardsmen in full NBC gear directed me to the back of the school parking lot. I stopped my truck, cut the engine, and awaited further directions. I could already see that the basketball arena was being converted into some manner of operations center. There was a white tent erected just outside the main entrance, and men and women in white lab gear worked behind tables with a variety of gear I didn't recognize. It looked medical. They were protected by armed guardsmen. A short line of locals, some of whom I *did* recognize, were lined up outside, feeding slowly through the tent.

I thought I knew what it was. I didn't like it.

"Step out of the vehicle, sir."

I turned to find one of the white-suited people standing just outside my truck. Looking more like someone out of a post-apocalyptic film than the soldiers in NBC gear, the doctor—I assumed he was a doctor—was covered head to toe with the white suit, the sleeves and pants legs actually duct-taped to his shoes and rubber gloves.

Face covered in a mask. Eyes wide with focus.

Not good.

I cut the engine and dumped the keys in the floorboard along with my Victorinox, phone, wallet, and Streamlight. I knew they would confiscate those items the moment I surrendered myself. I wasn't worried about local theft— Prairie Junction was a pretty harmless place.

At least...it had been.

I stepped out and shut the door. I kept my arms loose at my side. The doctor handed me an N-95 medical mask and I donned it. Then he extended a bottle of hand sanitizer and squirted an aggressive puddle into my palm. I slathered it on while the questions rained in. The *who, what, when, where, and how.*

I recounted every detail of Ms. Molly's frozen, purple body, remaining calm and didactive. Nobody took notes—it's hard to write in NBC gear—but somebody held a voice recorder. When I finished, the doctor stepped back.

Then he gestured toward the arena. "This way, sir."

I squinted, caught off guard. "Did you not hear me? I've been exposed."

"I understand," the doctor said.

"So you shouldn't be placing me in an arena with other people," I said. "Take me out into a field where I can camp in my truck. You can post a guard, if you want. I won't go anywhere."

The doctor shook his head. "I'm sorry, sir. By standing order of the governor, anyone found outside their home is to be detained together. The arena is the best we have."

"Is the governor a raging moron?" I asked.

I could see in the doctor's eyes that he agreed with me—or at least understood my point. But he didn't answer.

"It's an outbreak, isn't it?" I said. "Something nasty. I've seen it before. If I'm contaminated, and you put me in that arena, you're endangering everyone."

No answer. The doctor looked to the nearest guardsman. He stepped forward with rifle at the ready, keeping the muzzle pointed down but flicking the selector switch from safe to fire.

"Comply with the doctor, sir," the guardsman said. "We won't ask again."

There was no further point in arguing. I walked down sidewalks sheltered by the draping arms of hundred-year-old oak trees, escorted, with the doctor in the lead and the two guardsmen at my back. At the white tent my temperature was checked with a laser device. My mouth was swabbed. A vial of blood was drawn.

Nobody spoke, but I could see the truth in their eyes. They were terrified.

Then I was pushed through the double glass doors of the arena entrance, into the main concourse. The guardsmen led me past the snack bar, beyond the vending machines and the bathrooms, through a ground-level tunnel, and into the main arena. Bright lights blazed down from the ceiling, the angry-eyed logo of the Lady Ravens glaring down from either end of a polished basketball court. The basketball goals were spotless and glimmering. The floor was clear.

But the ranks of bleacher-style seats were not. I was only one of maybe fifty others, spread out around the court. All wearing N-95 medical masks. All keeping their distance.

All frozen in a mixture of disorientation and fear.

"You're not allowed to leave without permission," the guardsmen said. "Food and water are on the way. If you need a restroom, knock on the door. *Do not* remove your mask."

With that the two men retreated behind the steel doors of the tunnel. Those doors clapped shut with a bang.

And I was locked in.

9

As soon as the door closed I selected a vacant aisle that ran up one side of the arena and climbed all the way to the most empty section of bleachers I could find, positioning myself with my back to the wall. Besides the overhead lights, a series of two-foot-tall, rectangular windows framed the top of the wall around the entire perimeter of the oblong building, allowing swaths of daylight inside.

It was almost too bright. I leaned back against the desert tan blocks and folded my arms, surveying the people gathered in little knots throughout the arena. Some talking in low whispers. Some staring around with wide, disbelieving eyes.

I knew what they were thinking—it's the same thing every small-towner thinks when something unbelievable happens.

This can't be happening here. Not in Prairie Junction.

Normally, such denial is misguided. It has long been my experience that bad things can happen to anybody, anywhere. A rich zip code or a poor one, an urban metropolis or rural farming county. Fate is no respecter of rational or even reason. But for once, I had to agree with the undertone of confusion. What I'd seen in Ms. Molly's face, what I recognized from battlefields far away...it *shouldn't* be in Iowa. There was no rational reason for it.

Yet here it was—whatever it was. A virus of some sort, I guessed. Something highly infectious and very deadly. Something terrifying enough to justify the military lockdown of an entire rural community.

I inhaled a deep breath, briefly considering whether I was, in fact, infected. Whether these were the first of my last hours. It was possible, sure, but that reality is always possible. The next hour is never promised.

So I did the best thing I could do under the situation. I relaxed. I closed my eyes.

And I thought of Africa.

The mission out of Djibouti was an aggressive departure from my traditional military career. I had been stationed there for barely three weeks when the call came for a fire team of Rangers to deploy aboard a US Army CH-47 and fly west, deep into Ethiopia, where a World Health Organization team had fallen off the map. There were rumors of an outbreak. Whispers of that dreaded word—*Ebola*.

At the time, I hadn't really believed them. Another threat was boiling in the region—the threat of significant civil unrest. In Africa, unrest always means bloodshed, and the fear of such turmoil was the reason for my deployment to Djibouti in the first place. When the WHO team fell off the map, myself and my fireteam were tasked with escorting yet another WHO doctor for the rescue mission. I reasonably assumed that her colleagues' disappearance had more to do with the roving bands of genocidal militias than any outbreak of horrific disease.

I was wrong, and I was right. We'd landed at the epicenter of both threats and barely got out alive. The one survivor we recovered from that little mud hut died soon after we returned to base. The disease was Ebola, just as the WHO feared. A nasty strain of it that spread like wildfire.

Ironically, the scourge of that plague brought a quick and decisive end to the ethnic unrest. The roving militias disbanded. A few hundred died.

Then the pages of history turned and the world moved on, just as it always does.

But not in Iowa.

That was the part I couldn't wrap my mind around. I understood very little about the scientific nuances of deadly viruses, but one detail I did remember from the African mission was that all viruses have a preferred method of transmission. For Ebola, it's bodily fluids. Various flu viruses are often airborne. Other biological scourges are carried by animals.

But in all cases, they each begin somewhere, and then are transmitted someplace else via a logical, physical highway. Something you can trace, given enough information. Something that connects one dot on the map to another. The disease doesn't just pop up at random in an old lady's farmhouse, particularly when that old lady never *left* her farmhouse.

Had a local resident recently spent time in Africa, or perhaps another part of the third world where this dreadful scepter of death maintained a foothold?

Possibly. But if that were the case, that individual would have returned to Iowa via New York, or Atlanta, or Chicago, meaning that this outbreak could already be generating hotspots across the nation. Why hadn't I heard anything about it on the radio?

My thoughts were interrupted by a clamor at the entrance tunnel. My eyes opened and I looked down to see two NBC-suited guardsmen dragging in a tall character with gray hair. He was slender, and wiry. He was resisting with shoves and kicks.

He was also dressed from head to toe in Vietnam-era BDUs.

"I'm telling you!" Taggert screamed. "I know what this is all about! There's outsiders in town. I've found 'em last week. They're making a play for the nuclear plant. They—"

Taggert's words were cut short by the slam of metal doors. I actually heard the *thunk* of the latch. He cursed and tore off his N-95 mask. Proceeding to the door, he spent the next five minutes pounding on it, calling for the commander, threatening constitutional lawsuits, and even going so far as to promise violence.

It was that last threat that made me sit up. Casting a glance around the arena, I noted every eye fixed on Taggert, more than a few faces taut with fear. A mother held her children close. An elderly couple huddled together.

Taggert was scaring them all, and maybe not without reason. I pulled myself to my feet and shouted toward the tunnel.

"Taggert! Clay Taggert! Stop that nonsense. They're not letting you out."

The pounding paused only long enough for Taggert to launch an expletive. Then he was back at it, harder than ever. It sounded like he was kicking the door.

I could only imagine what conversations were being held

on the other side. Whatever the nature of our current illegal incarceration, an escalation of tensions would help nobody. I shouted again.

"Taggert! You sit down and calm down or I'm gonna put my boot up your ass."

It was a deliberately provocative comment. Taggert's pounding ceased. A moment later he appeared from our side of the tunnel, eyes blazing, face orbiting the arena until it landed on me. I stood motionless, waiting to see if he would lunge or take a breath.

"Just calm down," I said. "You're scaring people."

I sat back down on my bleacher, some fifty yards from the basketball court where Taggert stood. He eyeballed me a moment. Squinted. Then he seemed to recognize me.

"You're Jeter's friend," he said.

I didn't reply. Taggert reached for the handrail and started up the bleacher steps.

"Don't come up here," I said. "Pick your own spot and sit down."

Taggert ignored me, breaking into a jog. Despite his age he was in superb physical condition. He managed the steps easier than I had.

I waited until he'd reached the top of the bleachers, level with my position but still thirty feet to my right. I held up a hand and lowered my voice.

"Not another step. Put your mask back on."

Taggert swore. "Masks? Really? Weren't you military? You ought to know there ain't a danged thing this junk will do against radiation. Might as well put a paper bag over your head! It's K-19 all over again. You remember that? Them Ruskies sent a nuclear submarine to sea and they had a reactor problem. You know what they gave the sailors for protection? *Chem suits*. Like fishing waders. Ha! As if that would stop gamma rays—"

"Taggert," I snapped. "Lower your voice. You're gonna cause a panic."

He stopped, casting a glance around the perimeter of the arena and seeming to notice the others for the first time. His jaw sagged. He hesitated. He turned back and took another step.

"*Stop*," I hissed, hoping my voice wouldn't travel. "I like my space. Sit down right there. We can talk."

To my surprise, Taggert complied. Maybe because the opportunity to converse with somebody about his hair-brained theories was more appealing than getting into another confrontation. He sat and ducked his head, his voice dropping to a conspiratorial whisper.

"I *told* Jeter there was a problem. It's them outsiders—the ones I photographed. They got a hit on the nuke plant some-how. Now we're all bathing in radiation. They shouldn't be quarantining us, they should be evacuating these people. If I had any sense at all, I'd be back home in my bun—"

He stopped, catching himself. Our eyes met. He ran his tongue over his lips.

"Anyway. I came out here to warn the authorities—which was a waste of time. National Guard's just a bunch of feds these days. Another arm of the police state! You know what I'm talking about. You seen it first-hand, ain't you?"

I didn't answer. Taggert wiped his mouth with the back of his hand. He was sweating despite the chilly air of the arena. He scooted a little closer.

"*Stop*," I growled.

Taggert squinted, looking ready to object.

"For your own good," I said. "Please do not come any closer."

Confusion played across his face. Conflicted thoughts. I could see the gears turning in his eyes. He was processing, and I wondered if they were the crazed thoughts of a wild conspiracy theorist, or the more logical thoughts of a man who had simply seen and experienced too much.

Whatever the case, Taggert's next move surprised me a second time. He didn't say a word. He simply stood, turned, and departed. He retreated to his own corner of the upper bleachers and sat, bent over, a notebook spread across his lap, a pencil scratching away. He remained like that for the next hour, rocking a little back and forth, muttering to himself. Lost in his own world.

I sighed and ignored him. I watched as the NBC guardsmen carted in trays of sandwiches and carts full of bottled water. Neither Taggert nor myself approached the provisions. Everyone else was lined up, six feet apart, and slowly fed. As the meal concluded my mouth grew dryer by the second. I was thirsty—I would have paid good money for one of those bottles.

But I didn't want to risk getting near anyone. I simply waited, unsure what I was waiting for. My watch counted the hours as noontime passed and early afternoon set in.

Just after three p.m., something finally occurred...and it was the worst thing possible.

A woman began coughing.

10

T he cracking rasp of the coughs broke across the arena and echoed against the block walls. Random at first, but growing more frequent. The woman sat by herself, wrapped in a blanket. Shivering.

And hacking into her fist.

Forty minutes after the first cough the National Guard arrived, escorting two of the white-suited doctors. They consulted with the woman. Her temperature was checked. Then she was rapidly removed from the room.

I glanced left, noting that Taggert was no longer fixated on his notebook. He watched the proceedings instead. As the woman was escorted into the tunnel, Taggert's gaze snapped toward me. His eyes widened, then he stood.

Great.

I braced myself for his arrival, holding up a hand when he was twenty yards out. This time, Taggert didn't argue. He stopped frozen, fixated on me as though I were some type of lab specimen. He rocked his head and seemed to be sweeping my body.

I said nothing, knowing what was coming.

"It's biological, ain't it?" Taggert said at last. "It's a disease!"

"Keep your voice down." My tone was cold, although at this point there was little value in denial. Everyone in the arena must have had some inkling what this was about—and it had nothing to do with a nuclear plant.

"Did you see it?" Taggert pressed. "Are you infected?"

I hesitated. Then I nodded. "I could be. I'm not sure. You should stay back."

Taggert swore, scratching his left cheek. He looked less alarmed and more triumphantly fascinated, as though he'd just solved a complicated riddle and was still double-checking his work.

"That's why there's a quarantine," Taggert said. "That's why they're wearing the NBC suits. It's not nuclear, it's biologic. Some kind of plague! It's—"

His gaze snapped up. His mouth opened but his words froze. There was something freshly chaotic behind his concrete-colored eyes. Something revelatory.

"What?" I said. "It's what?"

Taggert shook his head. He retreated, and I stood and called after him. Taggert ignored me. He sat in his old spot and went to work with the pencil, tearing through pages and scratching notes.

I settled back onto my bleacher and watched him for the next three hours as the high-mounted windows grew dark, the daylight fading into black. There was something about his demeanor that had changed. I could tell he was processing, digging through ideas and growing increasingly agitated all the while. By six p.m. the rocking was replaced by irritated circular orbits, beginning at the waist and leading up to his chest. He tore a sheet of paper out of the notebook and wadded it up, hurling it to the ground. He ran one hand through his hair, knocking the BDU cap off and not seeming to notice.

Then he froze. He looked up. His eyes grew wide and he didn't blink. He lowered the notepad and stood.

"The compound," he whispered.

"What's that?"

Taggert didn't seem to hear. His mouth fell open. He repeated the singular phrase, now as a shout.

"The compound!"

Then he started running. Right down the bleachers, headed for the steps. Hat abandoned, notebook flapping at his side. I stood as he rushed past, two rows beneath me and turning at the aisle.

"Taggert!" I said. "What are you doing?"

It was too late. There was no stopping him. He reached the court and turned for the tunnel. I departed my perch and started down after him as his fists fell against the steel doors.

"It's the compound! I know what happened. You gotta let me out! I gotta see the governor. They're gonna attack!"

The commotion exploded out over the court and filled the arena. I reached the mouth of the tunnel just as many of the others reached their feet. A murmur of alarm filled the building. I turned the corner to find Taggert twenty yards ahead, pounding and screaming the same desperate statements over and over.

Then the lock clunked. The door opened. Taggert tried to throw himself ahead, but was met with the muzzle of an M4 rifle straight to the gut.

I instinctively fell back behind cover, orbiting out of the

tunnel. Taggert shouted, and a rough voice barked back at him—one of the guardsmen.

"*Calm down*. Don't make us restrain you!"

"It's the compound," Taggert repeated. "It's got to be! There's foreigners in the county. They must have found something. They're going to kill us all!"

"*Sir!* I won't tell you again."

A scuffling ensued. I risked a glance around the corner, half-expecting gunfire to erupt at any moment. Taggert was pressed against the wall. Guardsmen in NBC suits manhandled him. An NCO called orders.

Then two more men appeared through the doors. Dressed as the others in head-to-toe NBC gear, instead of rifles they wore pistols. SIG Sauer M17s, the current standard issue of the US Army, and the Iowa National Guard by proxy. Desert tan, clashing awkwardly with the dark green of the NBC suits.

"Shut up!" one of the newcomers snapped, driving his palm into Taggert's sternum. "Just shut up."

The two newcomers closed in. I remained at the end of the tunnel, my body sheltered by the turn. I leaned out just far enough to gain a partial view of the proceedings. I wasn't sure why I didn't step forward to engage. Maybe it was the knowledge that I could still be carrying a deadly illness.

Maybe it was the red flags popping up like fireworks in the dark recesses of my mind. Something wasn't right here, and it was bigger than Taggert's bizarre, paranoid behavior. I was inclined to wait. To listen.

"What are you talking about?" It was one of the newcomers again. He spoke in a growl.

"There's a compound," Taggert said. "Someplace outside

of town! Medical research. There's folks from overseas trolling around—terrorists! They're here in town—"

"*Shut up*," the new guy snarled. "You'll scare people."

Temporary silence. Taggert grunted as though he was struggling to recover his wind.

"We can take care of him, sir." It was one of the original soldiers who spoke. The guy I'd pegged as an NCO. By his use of the term "sir", I guessed the newcomer must be an officer.

"I'll speak with medical," the NCO said. "We'll get a sedative."

"You'll what—"

Taggert's objection was cut short by the blow of a rifle stock to his stomach. Even I winced as he doubled over, choking.

It wasn't one of the original soldiers who'd struck him. It was the second newcomer. The guy who, as yet, had remained quiet. He'd snatched the rifle from a nearby guardsman and struck Taggert before anyone could stop him.

"*Stop*," the officer snapped. "That's enough. We'll take it from here, Sergent. Get me some handcuffs. We're moving this man off-site."

"Sir, we're under orders—"

"And now you have new orders! Get the handcuffs. *Now.*"

The scuffle continued. Taggert was resisting arrest—or detainment. Or whatever this was.

With every second additional red flags popped up in my brain. I couldn't pinpoint why. This simply felt wrong. Not just the rough handling of Taggert, but the sudden decision to remove him from the arena.

Why? They'd left him here all day. He'd raved and

shouted before. He'd scared people before. According to the sergeant, standing orders required that these people remain on-site.

But now the officer was moving him. Only *after* the confrontation.

I didn't like it. I couldn't quite decide why, but as Taggert disappeared through the double doors along with the soldiers and the lock *thunked* into place, I decided I had played ball with my illegal detention long enough. I might still be infected. I might still be hours or days from a gruesome death.

In the meantime, I could better distance from the population by being outside a contained space, and while I was at it...I might as well find out what the heck was happening.

I returned to the top of the arena, as far as I could get from the overhead lights. I approached a darkened rectangular window, glancing over my shoulder to see if anyone was watching.

Everybody was focused on themselves, knotted together in tight little groups. Discussing. Worrying. Consumed by their own situation.

I consulted the window. Updates to the basketball arena had been installed over the years since its original construction in what I guessed to be the late sixties. The facility was clean and in perfect operational order, but there had never been any need to replace the windows. They were constructed of aluminum frames, hinged at the top, with a crank mechanism and a turn handle in one corner.

I tried the handle. It wasn't locked, but it was frozen by time. I wiggled it back and forth and leaned on it, gradually adding pressure as my breath grew hot behind the N-95 mask. I'd worn it all day and it was starting to feel claustrophobic, but on the off chance that I *was* infected with some nasty virus, I didn't want to risk an unrestricted sneeze. At least not until I was outside.

The handle still wouldn't budge. I pressed my full body weight against it, but the years had frozen the mechanism in place. I needed more than pressure. I needed torque.

I decided to kick it. Backing up along the top of the bleachers, I measured the handle's position three feet above the top seat. Well within reach of my right boot. I cast another glance around the arena, stepped back, then lunged forward.

The handle moved, all right. It broke off altogether, falling with a clatter to the aluminum bleachers. I staggered against the wall, my thigh throbbing as I broke my fall against my left leg. The flash of pain—and the certain knowledge that my cover was now thoroughly blown—angered me. I was tired of fooling around.

I was tired of being boxed up in this place against my will.

Regaining my feet, I twisted on my heel and kicked again. Not for the crank, but straight for the window pane. It was dusty and misted with age. It exploded in a shower of jagged shards, raining down the outside of the arena. Somebody called out to me, but I ignored them. I found my winter gloves inside an interior pocket of my Carhartt coat. I used them to clear away the shards and knock out more of the pane. Somebody called for the soldiers. I stuck my head through the hole and looked down.

From just beneath the roofline I was only about a twenty-foot drop from the ground. Subtracting the six feet two inches of my height, I figured I could handle a fourteen-foot drop into a blanket of snow.

I rolled my right leg out first. It was the most flexible. I lay on the base of the window frame, now clear of glass shards, then twisted to ease my left leg out—the one with the healing gunshot wound. From inside the arena the shout returned. A woman from across the court was screeching for the authorities, pointing and panicking as though I were about to set off a nuclear weapon.

A real peach.

I got both legs through and they fell against the exterior block walls. I eased my body out, descending until I hung from the window frame by my hands, feet dangling over the ground. All those lumber-tossing muscles I had developed over the past three months held me with ease. I twisted my neck to inspect the ground again. It was a ditch, mostly full of snow, with shards of glass glimmering beneath a nearby streetlight.

Good enough.

I dropped. The tan exterior of the block wall passed in a flash. I hit the snow and collapsed naturally into a ball, sinking twelve inches to the dirt beneath as fresh pain erupted from my left thigh. I bit back a groan and completed the roll, returning to my feet and staggering.

It's never like the movies. You take a bullet to the leg, and that junk sticks with you for a while. But despite the pain I was satisfied with my performance. I broke into a jog, turning away from the arena and darting across the adjacent parking lot. The nearest street was populated by Humvees and a pair of Iowa State Patrol cars. I didn't see any soldiers. I didn't see Taggert. A clear sky allowed for the light of a three-quarter moon to illuminate my path. I took cover behind a tree. I kneeled and turned, a full view of the arena entrance now visible.

I saw the soldiers—I saw Taggert. Two guardsmen in NBC gear escorted him by the elbows, driving him toward a waiting Humvee where two additional guardsmen stood waiting.

Only, these men didn't wear NBC gear. At least, not the full gear. Their hoods were down and their masks missing. They stood casually alongside the running vehicle, one of them smoking a cigarette, the other beckoning toward Taggert's escorts.

Both men wore rifles across their chests, complete with plate carriers and sidearms. Both men were...*wrong*, somehow. I couldn't put my finger on it. It was something to do with their bearing. The way they surveyed the surrounding landscape. The way they appeared casually relaxed but fully focused.

They didn't look like part-time infantry. They looked like highly trained commandos—like spec ops, or...

Surely not.

The thought occurred to me and I dismissed it. Taggert reached the rear of the Humvee. His escorts shoved him in. They climbed in after him. The doors slammed. I was back on my feet and jogging toward my parked GMC.

My theory was a loose one. It didn't really make sense. But I was ready to follow them and find out.

11

No one had bothered my truck. A fresh layer of snow lay heavy on the hood and roof, but despite the fact that I'd left it unlocked, my keys and personal effects remained in the floorboard. I climbed in. I pumped the gas pedal and started her up. The inline-six purred to life like a giant house cat, and I used the wipers to clear the windshield. I left the headlights off as I rumbled through the snow, back toward the street. I turned in behind the Humvee, giving the vehicle a two-hundred-yard lead but easily keeping it in sight by the twin glow of its tail lights.

I have a lot of experience with Humvees. I know all about their performance metrics, driving characteristics, and limitations. One of the worst limitations of a High Mobility Multipurpose Wheeled Vehicle comes in the form of visibility—or better put, *lack* of visibility. Particularly out the rear. With a solid rear hatch and no window, the driver is left with nothing but the limited scope of his sideview mirrors to monitor the road behind him. You could lose a semi-truck in that blind spot with ease, and I had a pretty good idea how to keep my GMC well within the ambiguity of that zone.

Another limitation of the Humvee is speed. Simply put, it doesn't have any. Despite the low gearing of my GMC, I kept pace with ease. I followed the vehicle straight out of town, noting with interest a torn patch of snow laced with wide and heavy ruts right at the end of Main Street. Clearly the location of another roadblock, but that roadblock had since been moved. The heavy ruts led straight north, away from downtown.

The security perimeter, I concluded, had been expanded well outside of town. What did that mean?

The Humvee rumbled on, selecting a two-lane that streaked through a collection of newer subdivisions on the outskirts of Prairie Junction. Still no roadblocks or check-points. When the Humvee's brake lights finally blazed, the heavy tread marks of the FMTV presumably placed on perimeter duty continued into the dark.

The Humvee, meanwhile, turned right. Off the road. Through an open metal gate, overhung by more hundred-year-old oak trees.

It was a park—or, better put, *the park*. Prairie Junction only had one outside the college campus. A sprawling field of eight or ten acres, complete with a fish pond, a play-ground, two pickleball courts, and plenty of picnic benches. It was a popular spot in summer, or so I was told. I'd arrived in Iowa as winter set in, and I'd only ever driven past the park while it lay deep in the clutches of winter.

Stepping on my own brakes, I eased to a stop on the edge of the two-lane. I cut the engine and pulled my parking brake. I shook a stick of gum out of a paper carton and gently slipped it between my teeth as the Humvee rumbled up the park's main road, two hundred yards from my position. I traced it between the trees. The vehicle rumbled into the parking lot. Finally it disappeared from view.

The alarm bells in the back of my mind weren't the least bit muted by the flush of sugary peppermint unleashed by the gum. I chewed methodically as I collected my pocket gear. I drew a pair of binoculars from the glove box and exited the truck, boots sinking in another twelve inches of snow.

I listened for the sounds of other military vehicles. For the hum of mobile heating units, the chug of diesel generators. Anything to mark the presence of an auxiliary camp, maybe a secondary detention facility.

There was nothing. The park was so perfectly silent that I could hear the distant rumble of the Humvee even as it wound farther away from my position.

I set off through the ditch, snow drifts rising almost up to my knees. I reached the far side and broke into a jog, icy air burning my lungs as I reached the tree line. I filtered through. I resisted the urge to draw my Streamlight, and relied on natural night vision coupled with the glow of the moon to guide me through a narrow patch of forest.

Up ahead, the location of the Humvee was marked by its twin headlights. The vehicle had pulled to a stop at the edge of the fish pond, which was frozen solid from one end to the other, just a sheet of dark ice. The Humvee's doors popped open. All four men dropped out. They were still several hundred yards away, but even from a distance I recognized the familiar bulky silhouette of full NBC gear.

They dragged Taggert out, pulling him into the headlights. Then one of them struck him hard across the face, knocking his head back. Taggert cried out and fell.

I broke into a run, my footfalls whispering soft in the snow. I exited the trees and reached the edge of the pickle-ball courts, using their six-foot chain-link perimeter as cover. I orbited the courts and sprinted to a concrete picnic table standing a hundred yards distant from the Humvee. Descending to my chest, I landed with a crunch of snow, bitter cold cascading through my body despite the warm folds of my Carhartt coat.

I didn't need the binoculars to understand what was happening, but I deployed them anyway for a better view. The Humvee headlights illuminated the scene perfectly—four men surrounding a fifth, that fifth man on his knees, the other four taking turns driving boots into his gut.

They were interrogating him. As I focused the binoculars a gentle wind swept up from the road, washing over my body and placing my target downwind of my position. I heard the voices but couldn't quite make out the words.

One of the guys leaned down low, close to Taggert's face, and snarled through his NBC mask. Taggert cursed and spat blood. The guy cuffed him across the back of the head, sending him crashing face-first into the snow.

I gritted my teeth, contemplating the math of one against four. I'd faced those odds before, and usually prevailed. Then again, I rarely engaged four heavily armed—and armored—soldiers with nothing more than a pocket knife.

The guardsmen withdrew from Taggert, stepping to the far side of the Humvee. I still couldn't hear anything, but judging by their body language I thought they were holding a conference. There was some debate—some tension. I zeroed the binoculars on the guy in the middle, just visible around the doorpost of the Humvee.

Behind his mask I could see almost nothing—only the

glint of his dark eyes, clouded by anger and the threat of violence. It was those eyes that once again ignited the confusion in my chest. The uncertainty.

This wasn't right. The visual data I viewed through the binoculars didn't mesh with my existing understanding of National Guardsmen. It wasn't that guardsmen aren't good soldiers—many of them are excellent, but they're also parttime. They don't grow as hard as full-timers. They don't master the bearing of relaxed but permanently alert career veterans.

By contrast, these guys were razor-sharp. Their very aura radiated the edge of men who had spent *years* down range. Years training. Years—

My thoughts were cut short as a consensus was reached. The guy in the middle flicked his hand and snapped an order. Then he turned and orbited the face of the Humvee. He approached Taggert, walking calm and easy, shoulders loose. Almost looking bored. He called out to Taggert, and the prisoner looked up from the ground, a question faced.

My stomach tightened, uncertainty and alarm building together. Warning me that the situation had somehow escalated.

But it happened so fast, there was nothing I could have done even if I'd taken my chances with the knife in my pocket. The soldier closed within two yards of Taggert. His right hand dropped to the SIG M17 holstered on his hip. The gun appeared in a flash, muzzle arcing upward even as dread washed my stomach in a tidal wave.

His finger dropped over the trigger. Taggert's eyes widened. Then the gun cracked—he shot Taggert right in the head.

12

Taggert's body collapsed in a spray of blood, his life extinguished long before his head landed in the snow. I choked on cold air and yanked my face up from the binoculars, the echoes of the gunshot fading across the pond. The soldier stood motionless with his arm extended, finger still curled around the trigger. He cocked his head with the posture of a man inspecting a dead animal.

Then he holstered the gun. Muttered something to his men. Two of them dragged Taggert up by the elbows, blood and brain matter coating the back of his skull. As I watched they hauled him through the open rear hatch of the Humvee. The final soldier kicked snow over the blood. All four men climbed back into the vehicle and the motor churned. I clawed my way to my feet as they reversed, slinging snow. I raced for the pickleball court as they turned back down the drive. This time the motor howled, and they surged toward the road. I threw myself back into the trees and ran with no thought of protecting my cover.

I had to get back to my truck. I had to get back on their

trail. Even as the gleam of my pickup's trim appeared in the moonlight, the Humvee reached the two-lane and turned— not toward me, but away from me. The engine rumbled again. They were racing away.

I reached my truck and threw myself in. I fired up the engine and dumped the clutch. My tires spun and the rear end of the truck fishtailed, slipping toward the ditch. The snow chains caught, and I reached the road. I gathered speed and shifted into third gear.

But I already knew I was too late. The Humvee wasn't fast, but it had at least a thirty-second head start on me. I reached the next intersection and found the crossing road covered in snow but rutted with the tracks of multiple passing vehicles. There was no sign of the Humvee, and I couldn't tell which way it had turned. Low hills and patches of light forest obscured my view on every side.

I picked a direction at random—right, out into the county. Someplace to hide a body. I drove for three miles, keeping my boot jammed into the accelerator.

I squealed to a stop when I topped a low rise and saw a roadblock half a mile ahead. It was another FMTV, pulled across the two-lane with lights blazing. A military tent was staked nearby. There was a generator and a mobile heating apparatus. Steam rose from a pipe jutting through the tent's roof.

But there was no Humvee. No body, no sign of Taggert's killers. Just the roadblock with endless expanses of pitch-black Iowa corn and soybean fields stretching beyond it.

Sitting with my foot jammed against the brake, white-hot anger boiled out of my gut. I cut the pickup's heater off and sat on the road with the engine running, teeth grinding, my gaze switching from the roadblock ahead to my rearview mirrors.

There was nobody behind me. Save for the roadblock I was completely alone, mind spinning as I replayed what had just happened. I closed my eyes and pictured Taggert kneeling in the snow, face bloodied by the violent interrogation of the guardsmen.

No—not guardsmen. I couldn't believe it. I'd seen soldiers go off the reservation plenty of times before. Stressful situations and the opportunity for unchecked violence is too much for some people. No unit, no matter how elite or how celebrated, is immune from collecting a few bad apples. A military criminal isn't a military criminal until he chooses to commit a crime. Sometimes, bad apples band together. Four of them climb into a Humvee in the middle of the night, drive into the desert, and rape an Afghani teenager.

I'd seen it before—but I didn't buy it now. Not because they were guardsmen, but because I didn't *believe* they were guardsmen at all. There were too many conflicting signals. Not just the behavior of the four men, or the way they carried themselves. The easy body language mixed with perpetual self-awareness, a hallmark of special operators hardened by action.

No, it was more than that. It was more even than the way they had beaten Taggert in the middle of that park, heedless of his cries. Most of all, it was the way their leader had stepped up to Taggert's helpless form, drawn his sidearm, and casually blown his brains out.

Execution style. Like he'd done it before. His men hadn't blinked, either—because they'd *seen* it before.

This wasn't new. They *weren't* National Guard.

So what, then? If they weren't Guard, who were they? And why had they killed Taggert?

The first question was impossible to answer with the information at hand, but the second question was simple enough. All I had to do was retrace the series of events that led to Taggert's death, reaching the second time he had pounded on the arena doors, demanding an exit.

Remembering what he had said—all those shouts about terrorism. About a *compound*.

Taggert was ignored the first time he pounded on the doors. But the second time? They responded in minutes. They interrogated him in the tunnel. They dragged him out and interrogated him again in the park. They held a conference and debated.

Then they executed him. Cold and quick. Without question.

Why? *Because Taggert knew something.*

Just as the thought occurred to me, a white-hot beam of light sliced from the nose of the FMTV and cut through my windshield, temporarily blinding me. The voice of a guardsman shouted through a loudspeaker, demanding that I exit my vehicle and identify myself.

I didn't exit my vehicle. I jerked the column shift into reverse and mashed the gas instead. The tires spun. I pulled to the edge of the ditch, then turned in the middle of the road. In another moment I was hurtling back toward Prairie Junction, leaving the roadblock behind. Blasting through stop signs and racing past the vacant fields. I was no longer worried about locating the rogue Humvee. In a county this large, this rural, and this dark, that vehicle could be anywhere. I would likely never find Taggert's body.

But I'd witnessed their crime. I may not have seen their

faces behind the NBC masks, but the body language of a hardened spec ops warrior is impossible to disguise—not from a guy like me, who had lived that life. Walked in those boots.

Yes, I would recognize any one of those four killers. I would find them again, and when I did, their murderous crusade would come to a permanent end. The mystery of this mess would be solved, once and for all.

I was going to crush this snake before it slithered another inch.

13

I returned to downtown Prairie Junction the same way I had departed it, sticking to darkened roads inside the expanded roadblocks. Orbiting around Main Street, I parked in the vacant lot of a local grocery store and cut the engine. I locked the doors this time, and kept my gear on me. I set off behind the grocery store and flipped over a low privacy fence, landing amid trees. I crossed a drainage ditch heavy with snow, building on my existing sweat as I slogged around the edge of the neighborhood.

Chief Ransom Jeter lived alone in the heart of town, within easy access of his police station. Another early twentieth-century style home, this one was square with square columns, a wide set of stairs, and both rocking chairs and a swing on the front porch.

It looked like a home from the Andy Griffith Show. I'd visited on a couple of occasions, joining Jeter on the porch to sip Irish coffee while we reminisced about wars gone by and enjoyed the winter cool. I wasn't sure why Jeter had taken such a shine to me. Our first interaction certainly shouldn't have placed me in his favor—he pulled me over after I conducted an illegal U-turn.

Maybe it was the shared military heritage. Maybe it was the simple chemistry of compatible personalities, or the fact that I indulged his stories. Whatever the case, we'd developed a casual friendship over the past three months, building mutual trust along with it.

Now that an ugly situation appeared ready to boil over, Jeter was the first man to consult.

I almost approached the front door directly, but then I thought better of it. I already knew by the muddy rear bumper of the Crown Victoria parked beneath the carport that Jeter was home. By the darkened windows, I guessed him to be asleep. It wasn't yet eight p.m., but I knew he'd had a long day of managing—or attempting to manage—the complete military takeover of his town. Likely quarantined to either his house or his police station, Jeter would have worked until he was ready to drop.

Now he was grabbing much-needed shut-eye—something any veteran would know to catch whenever he could. With the disaster unfolding across his little town, there was no telling what would happen next. No doubt Jeter was on edge.

It was better that I didn't bang on his door. I'd try something a little more subtle.

Orbiting the side of the house, I leaned low beneath the windows and circled the heat pump. I wasn't exactly sure which window was the bedroom—it wasn't like Jeter had given me a full tour of his house. I did know that the front room was a living room, and then there was a dining room and a kitchen. I figured the bedroom would be in the back.

Circling the heat pump, I approached a large window

that glimmered in the moonlight. With the street lamps far behind, I was cloaked in full darkness. I eased up to the window and squinted inside.

There were no blinds, only a pair of sheer curtains. Through the thin fabric I spied the familiar red numerals of an alarm clock, and the shadow of what might have been a bed.

Bingo.

I tapped on the glass. "Jeter!"

My voice was a low hiss. The window pane was old, wider at the bottom than the top as the lead-based glass had settled over time. A hallmark of old homes. The glass rattled in the frame, but there was no response from within.

I tried again, a little louder this time. "*Jeter!*"

The second try ignited movement from the darkness beyond. There was a grunt. A shadow rolled on the bed. I tapped again.

That did it. Jeter's feet hit the floor with a thump. A light snapped on—a tactically poor choice, but I cut Jeter some slack for being out of action for so long. Ducking into the shadows next to the window, I watched as his shirtless bulk crossed the window. A pistol flashed across the glass. I risked another call.

"Jeter, it's me!"

The window shrieked open, admitting the muzzle of a polished 1911 handgun along with an angry growl.

"Who's out there?"

"It's Mason Sharpe," I said. "Calm down, Jeter. Lower the gun!"

Jeter stuck his head out, gray hair a tangled mess, eyes a little wild. He wore nothing but boxer shorts. The handgun was already cocked, the safety disengaged. He pivoted the muzzle on me before I could stop him. I threw up both hands, backing away from the window.

"Easy! Don't shoot."

"Sharpe!" He said it as though his sleep-deprived mind were just waking up. "What are you doing out here? They told me they detained you!"

"They did. It's a long story. Listen, Jeter. We gotta talk. Right now."

Another slow blink. Jeter flicked the safety back on and finally lowered the gun. "Come around front. I'll put some clothes on."

I shook my head. "I don't want to come in. There's still a chance I'm infected."

That statement was enough to eradicate the rest of the sleepiness from Jeter's eyes. He recoiled a little, blanching. But he didn't shut the window.

"So you know," I said.

A long pause. Jeter nodded softly.

"They briefed me this morning. Not many details. They just said there had been a deadly outbreak of some kind— something really nasty. They're quarantining us to keep it from spreading. I didn't realize they were telling civilians."

"They're not. I figured it out on my own. I saw one of the victims."

"Victims?"

"Ms. Molly Pritchard...Lyle's mother."

A cascade of sadness crashed over Jeter like a waterfall. He groaned. "How could she have gotten sick? She never went nowhere!"

I'd been wondering the same thing myself. For the moment, that question would have to wait.

"I don't know, Jeter. All I can tell you is that somebody is lying. They put Taggert in the arena with me. He was screaming about terrorists—those Middle Eastern guys he saw."

"He's still hung up on that?" Jeter said.

"Not anymore. They shot him."

"What?"

I raised a hand, backtracked to my detainment at the arena and running through the highlights. Taggert's erratic behavior. His removal from the arena. My escape and pursuit. The park.

The gunshot.

By the time I concluded Jeter's face was cherry red. His hands tightened around the pistol until his knuckles turned white.

"Unbelievable!" he snarled. "Hold on, Sharpe. Let me get my uniform."

"Jeter! Wait. You can't do that."

My voice was just harsh enough to arrest his attention. He wheeled back. "Why not?"

I hesitated, slightly unwilling to launch into the second half of my thought process. It was all conjecture. Just an idea. I hate trafficking in unproven theories. It can be dangerous, especially in a volatile situation like this.

But given the circumstances, I wasn't sure I had any choice.

"I don't think those guys were National Guard," I said. "I think they're just wearing the uniform."

"What? Why?"

"I don't know. Could be any number of reasons."

"You're saying none of these people are legit?"

"Of course not. Most of them have to be. It's too many people. But clearly there's a subtext to this mess that we're all missing. Something about how it originated, or some*body* that stands at risk. An entity with a small private army willing to pose as National Guardsmen and execute potential witnesses."

"Sharpe..."

I raised my hand again. "Just listen to me, Jeter. Everyone ignored Taggert while he was screaming about a nuclear disaster. But the moment he started talking about a compound, about a terrorist threat, what happened? They appeared out of nowhere. They dragged him out to a park and shot him in the head. How does that make sense? There's only one logical conclusion—Taggert was onto something. There's somebody behind the curtain, and Taggert was a threat."

"Now you sound like a conspiracy theorist."

"So maybe I am. We've both been around a long time, Jeter. We've seen a lot of crap. You really think Reagan sent you to Grenada to rescue med students? There's *always* a bigger story."

Jeter pinched his lips together. I simply raised my eyebrows and waited. At last he sighed.

"Okay. So let's say you're right. What next? You want me to arrest somebody?"

"Definitely not. I couldn't tell you where to find them, and besides, if there's a legitimate biological threat circulating, you've got other priorities to attend to. I'll look into it. I just need Taggert's address."

"His address? Why?"

"He was a prepper, right? A survivalist."

A snort. "You look up *prepper* in the dictionary, you'll find his picture."

"So he'll have a compound of his own, then. Some kind of safe haven. A place where he kept gear...and notes."

Jeter thought about that. Then he nodded.

"Hold on a minute."

He shuffled off. I heard him speaking into a radio, communicating with a member of the Prairie Junction Police night shift—somebody barricaded at the police station, no doubt. I didn't think the guard would allow local cops to patrol so long as the town was placed under martial law. Seconds ticked by. Jeter returned with a scrap of notebook paper.

"Out Route Fifteen," he said. "Near the old feed mill. I've never been there myself... Knowing Taggert, you'd be well advised to proceed with caution."

"Don't worry," I said, accepting the notebook paper off the windowsill. It was printed with directions as well as an address—Jeter had thought ahead. "I know something about booby traps. I'll update you when I'm done."

I started to turn. Jeter opened his mouth as if he had a parting comment. Both of us were interrupted by the familiar growl of an Army Humvee. It roared up in front of the house, headlights blazing down the street. A door squealed open.

"Get down!" Jeter said.

I didn't need to be told twice. I took shelter behind the heat pump, squatting low with the notebook paper clutched in one hand. I listened, measuring the tempo of the footfalls.

Two men. Possibly three. Stealing a glance around the air conditioner, I looked out to the street to find a fourth man standing outside the Humvee.

I couldn't see his face—he wore a mask like all the others. But that body language rang familiar. That steady alertness. Never quite relaxed, always ready to strike. It was one of the men present at Taggert's execution, I was sure of it. A hardened soldier, trained to protect his country...and now hired to assault it.

I'm coming for you.

A heavy fist pounded on the door. Jeter called from inside the house, shouting for the visitor to wait. Floorboards creaked. The porch light flicked on, and the deadbolt slid. I held perfectly still and listened, shivering in the cold.

"Yeah?" Jeter's voice sounded a lot sleepier than it had only moments prior at the window. I hoped he wouldn't oversell it.

"Sorry to bother you, Chief. We thought you should know. One of the potentially infected citizens escaped from the arena—a Mr. Mason Sharpe. He's at large in the community. Have any of your men encountered him?"

"Encountered him? How could they? You've got us hogtied seven ways to Sunday!"

Well. That confirms my suspicions about the police force.

"We thought he might have stopped by the police station —maybe even your house."

"Why would he have done that? And why did you use the word *escaped*? You told me those people were housed at the arena of their own free will."

Nice re-direct, Jeter.

"The situation has developed, Chief. By order of the governor, we're now placing at-risk civilians under mandatory quarantine."

"By what, now? Why wasn't I notified?"

Jeter sounded genuinely pissed. He was a good guy, very easygoing and calm. He hadn't written me a ticket the day he pulled me over for that illegal U-turn. He almost never wrote tickets. He saw himself as a protector of the community, not a regulator of it.

But that was exactly the problem; his community was being threatened. The mama bear was coming out of him.

"You'll be advised as we are authorized to divulge details," the voice said. "Right now we need to be immediately alerted if your men encounter this missing civilian. There's a high probability he's infected. He could be contaminating the environment as we speak."

"Contaminating the environment with *what?*" Jeter demanded.

"You'll be advised as we are authorized to divulge."

That was too much. Jeter broke down into a stream of dog cursing. I backed away from the heat pump and slipped into the back yard. I flipped over another fence, navigated through a dormant grove of apple trees, and reached another street a block away.

In another sixty seconds I was back at my truck. I fired up the engine. I watched as the dark forms of the pseudo-guardsmen returned to the Humvee. They roared away. They never saw me.

I dropped the truck into gear and followed Jeter's handwritten directions toward Taggert's address.

14

I 've never known what to think of preppers. Any soldier who's spent any legitimate time in a war zone will tell you that there's more than a little logic to the prepper mentality. When the confetti hits the fan, the resulting carnage is both predictable and catastrophic. Any society, no matter how apparently stable, is really just a few grid failures and food shortages away from resorting to the barbarian tactics of cavemen armed with sticks. I'd seen it in Afghanistan. I'd seen it in Africa.

I prayed to God I would never see it in America, yet I knew it was possible. Taggert might be crazy. He wasn't entirely irrational.

On the other hand, I myself had never identified with the more cynical, paranoid spectrum of the preparedness community. Those people who isolate themselves from society, stacking up provisions and salivating over closets full of small arms and munitions until a person could be forgiven for thinking that they *hoped* for an apocalypse. That mindset I had always found to be toxic, and usually ignorant. Those who thirst for war are almost always the same people who have never experienced it.

Where Taggert fell on that spectrum was difficult to say. He *had* tasted war. He had also tasted plenty of other things, judging strictly on his behavior and mannerisms. Psychedelic drugs, I thought. Probably consumed to manage PTSD. But when improperly administered and subsequently abused, they can wreck a person's entire psyche, unleash hellish amounts of paranoia and depression...and even generate hallucinations.

Had Taggert been hallucinating when he tracked mysterious outsiders probing the community? I'd seen the pictures myself. I couldn't be sure whether they were legitimate or simply the product of a hard life expressing itself in bizarre, prejudiced forms.

One thing I knew for sure: Whether by intention or accident, Taggert had struck a chord with the wrong people. Those people had killed him for it. That by itself was enough to justify an investigation.

It was a nine-mile drive out of town to reach the turnoff to Taggert's property, which was exactly what I would have expected. A true survivalist wouldn't construct their bastion of safety too near to civilization. The feed plant Jeter mentioned stood at the edge of the road, a tall fence overgrown by dead vines, No Trespassing signs posted everywhere. The yard beyond was covered in snow, but the tall dry grass that protruded from the perfect white revealed the disuse of the place.

It was abandoned. Decaying. Forgotten.

An ideal spot to plant a hidden compound... Easily missed by anyone who drove by. Taggert's actual mailbox stood in front of the plant, easily mistaken for being the plant's mailbox. But upon further investigation, the street numbers on the gatepost of the plant's main entrance and the street number on the box didn't match.

It was a decoy mechanism.

Even though I knew what to look for I required two passes before I located the entrance drive. It dove off into the trees, well concealed by dead bushes and a low rise covered by snow. Taggert had learned a lot in Vietnam. He knew how to contour a man-made facility around the natural shapes and shadows of nature, shrinking into the morass just like his old adversary, the Vietcong, had done.

I turned onto the drive and kept the truck in low gear, slogging along through the snow as tree limbs closed over me. It was dark, my headlights providing the only illumination ahead as the tree cover blocked out the moon. I drove for another quarter mile, turning twice along the road before I abruptly reached a rusted steel cattle gate.

It crossed the road and met a steel post at the far side, where a chain held it closed. Another No Trespassing sign advised against entry. I bent my head and searched the trees.

It didn't take long to locate the cameras. There were two of them, well concealed but not perfectly so. The pair maintained a clear view not only of the front of my truck but of the rear, also.

For license plates, I thought. Taggert was hardcore.

I departed the truck, dropping into the snow. The icy bite of the night air stung my lungs as I opened the hatch of the camper shell and dug through my camping gear. A pair of bolt cutters lay inside a rubber bin, a product of an earlier collision with thugs in Arkansas...or maybe it had been Tampa.

I couldn't remember. This sort of thing was starting to become a habit.

The chain Taggert had used was thick. So was the lock. But unfortunately for him, the metal tabs holding the gate hinges to the gate itself were much thinner. My cutters snapped through them with the concentrated application of my log-rolling muscles. I twisted the cutters until the hinges broke off. Then I simply lifted the gate and dragged it back against the trees, still chained to the far gatepost.

You didn't think of everything, Tag.

I rumbled another half mile into the forest, noting additional cameras. More signs. What might have been a deer blind, or else simply a sniper blind.

Then at last I reached the house. It sat in a two-acre clearing, among tall grass bent by the snow, icicles hanging from the eves of the roof. Ranch in style, constructed of brick, with blank aluminum-framed windows and a wooden front door. No porch. No flower pots or yard decor. The drive led around the back, where I found a small patio with a barbecue grill and a couple of lawn chairs, both coated in snow. In the rutted yard a nineteen eighties model Isuzu Trooper sat on blocks, a giant tire leaned against it. Taggert's primary conveyance, whatever that might be, wasn't present.

That made sense. He'd been detained in town. His vehicle was likely parked near the police station.

I cut my engine and sat a while, listening for the rattle of chains. The scrape of toenails. A dull snarl. Anything that would signal the presence of a big, nasty dog—something a lot scarier than sniper blinds or hidden cameras.

I heard nothing, but I reached under my seat and produced a crooked tire iron anyway. I kept the iron riding next to my right leg as I stepped out of the truck. My left thigh burned in the cold, stiffening a little.

I ignored it. I surveyed the property and noted a small tool shed near the tree line. Nearby was a chicken coop, similar to Ms. Molly's coop, only this one was fully enclosed with chicken wire, and the door left open. No doubt the birds themselves were fast asleep.

Otherwise the place was empty...vacant. Almost too ordinary looking.

I approached the back door. I tried the knob. It was locked, and there was a deadbolt. I hesitated only a moment before inserting the edged tip of the tire iron into the gap and leveraging against it like a crowbar. In a few seconds I had it wiggled in deep enough to offer significant leverage. I shoved.

The doorframe splintered with a crash, and the door rocketed open. I stumbled, catching myself and brandishing the tire iron, again ready for a dog.

There was nothing. The house was empty, dark, and ice-cold. I deployed my Streamlight with my left hand and thumbed the switch. The first room was a mud room complete with a washer and dryer. Boots against one wall. Coats on a rack. Then came an ordinary kitchen with a humming fridge and a gas stove. A few dishes. A small table. One living room occupied by a couch and a coffee table, both way out of date in terms of style, and both dusty. A bathroom with a toothbrush and two towels. No pictures on the walls. No books, no TV, no newspapers. The first bedroom was empty and the second contained a single bed. No nightstand. Only a few clothes in the closet. A dresser with socks, underwear, an abandoned watch.

And that was it—that was the entire house. No personal

effects at all. The food in the pantry was so old that I didn't even recognize some of the outdated branding of familiar food companies. Dust coated everything. There was no fresh produce or anything spoilable in the fridge—just beer and unopened bottles of condiments.

And that toothbrush? It was brand new. Unused. The bristles were perfectly straight, and also dusty.

"What were you up to, Taggert?" I whispered to myself even as I already knew the answer. The house itself, just like the relocated mailbox next to the road, was a decoy. A stand-in, designed to look like it might just be Taggert's residence, but it really wasn't. As much a clue as all the peculiar things present were all the things *not* present.

Guns, for one thing. Not a single firearm in the entire place. No gun safe. No ammo.

What prepper sleeps without a gun?

The Trooper.

I set across the yard and entered the trees. The front bumper of the Trooper protruded out of the forest, a young sapling growing through the engine bay and reaching for the sky through the missing hood. The windshield was covered in snow on the outside, and as I scraped the snow away, I found that it was shielded by a sun deflector on the inside. So were the side windows—spray paint, it looked like.

Clever fox.

I stepped around to the back of the vehicle and tried the door. It was locked. I smashed the rear glass with the crook of my tire iron. It required two blows. I scanned my light through.

Oh, it had been an SUV at one point. But not anymore. The interior was gutted. The floor was gone. The roof of the vehicle no longer sheltered the passenger's compartment, but instead concealed a giant silver tube that protruded from the ground—a ventilation shaft.

I turned away from the Trooper and sifted through the forest. There was more junk—a lot of it. I found what I was looking for forty yards away, disguised as an abandoned fiberglass satellite dish. Not one of the new ones that are only a couple of feet across. This was one of the old-school dishes, six or eight feet across, lying face down in the dirt, ten yards inside the tree line. But when I looked back toward the house, I found a clear path running from a cleared spot next to the chicken coop—a parking spot, maybe—and into the trees. It wound right to my feet, then continued to my left.

It stopped at the edge of the satellite dish.

I kneeled, grabbing the edge of the dish and bracing myself to heave. Despite its apparent weight, the dish rocked upward with only moderate pressure. Hydraulic cylinders opened like the pistons of the hatch on my pickup's camper shell. A dark path opened beneath, constructed of concrete. Steps led six feet down, with a pull cord dangling from the underside of the dish to bring it back to earth.

My Streamlight flicked on again. It flooded the steps and the narrow concrete walkway at their base. Three feet wide, with concrete block walls rising on either side, the walkway became a tunnel only a yard beyond the bottom of the steps. That tunnel ran another yard through the packed Iowa dirt...

Straight into the back end of a yellow school bus completely buried beneath the forest, only its rear emergency door entrance visible.

I'd found the entrance to Taggert's true address.

15

The rear of the bus was still printed with the name of an Iowa county school district, but the windows had been replaced by plate steel, riveted and welded in place. I tried to force the door with my tire iron, but it wouldn't budge.

In the end I returned to my truck, located my lock picks, and resigned myself to doing things the old-fashioned way. The deadbolt required some time—it was nearly new and contained a complex tumbler system. I succeeded at length and tugged the door open, standing back in fear of a shotgun blast to the gut. An explosion of tear gas.

The dog I had feared.

Nothing happened. The door opened on greased hinges. Lights clicked on. I ducked my head and peered inside...to a whole other world.

I'd heard of people burying buses before. It's a cheap and relatively easy way to construct an underground bunker. You rent an excavator, dig out a giant trench, roll the bus in, and then cover it up. You leave access to the rear door. You run wiring and plumbing, if you like. It's a great storm shelter.

But whatever storms Clay Taggert had designed this place to weather, I seriously doubted they were the natural kind. It wasn't a single bus but *multiple* buses, all connected into a maze of hallway-like rooms, each forty feet long and about eight feet wide. The bus seats had all been removed, the windows covered in steel plates. Linoleum flooring had been laid throughout, with fluorescent lights riding the center of each bus's roofline. I walked down the entrance tunnel and found all the things missing in the decoy house outside—boots, jackets, gloves, random hand tools. A pump-action shotgun with a bandolier of shells. The next bus served as a hallway, intersecting the first bus like the top of a letter T, with four additional buses sticking out from its top. The walls of this hallway bus were hung with bookshelves and personal effects—photographs of Taggert in Vietnam, Taggert with a young wife and child leaning against a brand-new, mid-seventies-model station wagon. All looking very happy, very normal.

The pictures ceased around the mid-eighties, judging by the style of the woman's hair. The child was already gone. Something in both Taggert and his wife's faces had changed.

My stomach tightened and I inspected the first intersecting bus. It was a storage room, packed to the absolute brim with every imaginable form of dry food, medical supply, and utility tool known to mankind. Flour, rice, fifty-five-gallon drums of water, blankets, and even an outdated operating table. It was well organized and labeled, easily surveyable under the flickering overhead lights. Stocked for extreme disaster, no doubt, but I could tell by the cleanliness and various expiration dates printed on the canned and bottled food stores that Taggert kept his goods properly cycled.

I moved to the next bus and found a bunkhouse. Enough room for twenty people to sleep. Only one bed appeared used. The bus after that was a galley/living room combo. There was a television set, couches, bookshelves laden with both classics and modern paperbacks—most of them of the military and dystopian genre. The kitchen was all gas, but controls to an exterior generator were present behind a metal door. There was a sink, broad counter space, and a large table.

I stood at the entrance of the kitchen, staring over the dirty dishes in the sink and the random personal items cast across the floor and the coffee table. I couldn't deny an overwhelming wash of sadness. Whatever mental illness— coupled, perhaps, with some form of genuine prudence— had driven Taggert to live this way, the overwhelming loneliness of his existence was impossible to ignore. The number of beds in the bunkhouse confirmed that he'd prepared to assist others in the event of the apocalyptic scenario he so believed in, but it was also clear that Taggert was the only person ever to set foot in this bunker. He ate, slept, and lived in this place all by himself. Long days and longer nights that couldn't be differentiated without the presence of natural light, waging war with the demons of his military service and personal loss alike.

I understood it—deeply. Personally. And that understanding was enough for me to drop my head and say a silent prayer for Taggert.

God rest his soul.

The last bus was a bathhouse. Two shower stalls, two

sinks, two toilets. A tile floor and a water heater. Everything worked.

But still...something was missing. The bathhouse was only twenty feet deep, much shorter than the other bus-length rooms. I advanced to the end. I pulled a curtain aside and found another steel door, welded to its hinges with a deadbolt as before. I went back to work with the lock picks. Another few minutes trickled by. I managed to get it open, and readied my tire iron as before.

Then, at last, I hit the jackpot. The room that opened beyond the bathhouse filled the end of the final bus—twenty feet long by eight feet wide, with the same fluorescent lights hung from the ceiling. For the first ten feet the walls on either side were lined with wooden racks—and those racks were *packed* with firearms. Everything from AK-47s to AR-15 variants, a pair of M1As, multiple shotguns, hunting rifles, two AR-10s, and no less than twenty assorted handguns ranging in vintage from old M9 pistols to modern Glocks and SIGs. Beneath the racks were rows of dresser-style drawers, and those drawers were chock full of ammunition. Not thousands of rounds—tens of thousands, joined by small explosives and more than a few hand grenades.

My body tensed as I surveyed the collection. I wasn't surprised, but I was still a little impressed. Despite the proximity of the bathhouse and the resulting humidity, every gun was spotlessly clean and perfectly maintained. The ammo was well organized and labeled.

Clay Taggert was as ready as a man could be—but it wasn't the firearms that held my attention. It was the operations center that lay at the end of the room. Desks stood against both walls and the nose of the bus, with computers, satellite phones, a complete ham radio setup, camera gear, and multiple bulletin boards joining them.

It was the bulletin boards that put the *jackpot* in the room. They were plastered in photographs—still images predominantly of two things.

A pair of Middle Eastern men, and a blocky white building surrounded by a high chain-link fence.

I breathed deeper. I set the tire iron on the nearest desk. Then I settled into Taggert's chair, and went to work.

16

I emerged from the bunker two hours later. It was nearly midnight, and I was exhausted, but there was zero chance I was opting to stretch out on one of Taggert's bunks. The survey of his operations center had been enlightening—extremely so, but not in a reassuring way. Like a broken clock that's correct twice a day, Clay Taggert was a troubled man with a terrifying proclivity for spying on his neighbors. And yet, despite his craziness and paranoia...*he was right.*

I couldn't get into Taggert's computers, but I didn't need to. He kept hand-written logs of his activities, recording every event from brushing his teeth to staking out an intersection to watch for his targets. He noted times, dates, locations, durations, and even the weather. The logs were carefully organized, fanatically detailed, and in the end, overwhelmingly conclusive.

I took the logs along with half a dozen key photographs from the bulletin boards and returned to my truck. I rubbed my hands to keep warm while the engine slowly reached operating temperature. Outside an owl hooted. The moon had vanished and now the sky was pitch dark. Taggert's property felt suddenly very eerie—too quiet when the owl departed. Like a graveyard.

I shifted into gear and turned back for Prairie Junction.

The mental math for what I'd found inside the school bus bunker was neither complex nor dismissible. Regardless of his probable mental health issues or overt prejudices, Taggert's intel-gathering skills were beyond thorough, leaving me to wonder if his part in Vietnam had lain deep behind enemy lines. He knew what to look for, knew how to record it, and had some idea how to organize and interpret it. He just fell short with the critical next phase—what to *do* about it.

I didn't drive back toward town. Instead, I deliberately turned away from Prairie Junction, following the snow-rutted roads until I reached the inevitable roadblock that I had expected. It was part of the National Guard perimeter—a circle that, judging from my current distance from downtown, must be ten miles in diameter. It was a significant swath of land, cut off from the rest of the state...alone.

Approaching to within a hundred yards of the FMTV pulled across the road, I kept both hands on the wheel and left my brights on, forcing the trio of NBC-suited soldiers that jogged toward my truck to squint while I maintained clear views of their faces.

I didn't recognize anybody. The body language was tense but not overly prepared—they all ran at me together. Nobody stood back to provide cover fire or circled to either side to obtain a clear kill shot through my side windows.

No. These weren't Taggert's killers.

"Hey! Turn off your high beams!"

I shifted my left foot to the floor-mounted high-beam switch and tapped it off.

"Sorry about that," I said, keeping my window up.

"Where you coming from?"

"Open Plains Community College."

"Say what?"

"The basketball arena. I'm the guy who escaped."

That did the trick. The soldier's eyes temporarily widened behind his mask. His rifle rose into his shoulder.

"Don't move! Cut your engine."

I kept my hands on the wheel and left the engine running. The solider shouted to his counterpart, who reached for a radio. I spoke calmly through the glass.

"I want to see your commanding officer—whoever's in charge of the city."

"You're not going anywhere, sir. Turn your engine off!"

I didn't blink through the glass. "Do you know why you're here, kid?"

Long pause. The fear in his eyes told me that he did—or, at least, he had an inkling.

"I have critical information regarding public health. I want to see your CO. *Now.*"

He swallowed. One of his buddies shouted something. The soldier turned away and the three of them held a conference. At length the kid returned to my truck.

"Follow me," he said. "Stay in your vehicle. If you exit, we *will* fire."

"I understand."

I motioned for him to lead the way. One soldier started

up the FMTV blocking the road and backed it up. The guy I'd been talking to climbed into the driver's seat of a parked Humvee. It took a few moments for the glow plugs of the diesel engine to warm. When he started off down the street, I followed. We wove past the Prairie Junction elementary school and the bowling alley. We hit Main Street as fresh snowfall fluttered out of a darkening sky, vibrating and melting on the hood of my truck.

The Humvee halted in front of a large metal building with leafless bushes planted out front and a small parking lot populated by Humvees and State Patrol vehicles. It was Prairie Junction's city hall/community center/chamber of commerce. I'd driven past before but never been inside. The guardsman dismounted and held up his hand, again warning me to stay put.

I complied, cutting my engine off. The silence of the peaceful snowfall enshrouded me as he disappeared inside, and I couldn't help but think that his NBC suit was pretty much useless if he wasn't going to decontaminate it before entering a command center.

Rookie mistakes—he could be forgiven. How many special operations soldiers had real-world experience with a biological threat? Let alone infantry guardsmen.

The soldier returned ninety seconds later with one of his brethren, along with a woman in a full white lab suit complete with a hood. They approached my truck and the guardsman motioned for me to wind the window down. I complied.

"Name?" the woman said. He voice was tired, her eyes bloodshot.

"Mason Sharpe."

She tapped on an iPad with touch-screen-compliant rubber gloves. She asked my date of birth, social security number, height, and weight. Then she passed off the iPad and produced a plastic bag from the pocket of her lab suit. There was a swab inside.

Test kits had arrived.

"Tilt your head back."

I obliged. She rammed the swab so far up my nose I was convinced she was scrambling my brain stem. After several painful seconds, she retracted the swab and replaced it in the bag.

"Remain in your vehicle."

I relaxed in the seat. The guardsman remained on post while his buddy escorted the doctor inside. He kept glancing between the building and me.

"What's your name?" I asked.

He hesitated. "Private Welch, sir."

"Does your mama call you *Private*?"

I thought he may have smiled at that. It was difficult to tell behind the mask.

"My mama calls me Trav."

"It's a good name. Been in the Guard long?"

"Six months, sir."

Six months...and now this. Life is merciless.

"Take a breath, Trav. Obey your commanding officers. You'll be okay."

I shot him a wink. He nodded. Ten long minutes passed. Then the doctor stuck her head out the door and lifted her hood.

"He's negative."

Welch's shoulders visibly slumped in relief. He stepped back and beckoned.

"Follow me."

I pocketed my keys and rolled up the window. The pickup's heater had done wonders against the cold, but as soon as I stepped out the bite of Iowa winter returned. I followed Trav across the snow-covered parking lot to the entrance of the community center. Despite my negative test, the doctor handed me an N-95 before she allowed entry. I donned it without complaint, Taggert's files held beneath my left arm.

Then I was inside, and the moment I crossed the threshold, I felt like I'd dropped straight into a war zone. All the indicators were there—the ragged nerves, a vague sensation of chaos and uncertainty. Disorder, instability. The flailing legs of a first-response team struggling to find their footing as the situation on the ground developed by the minute.

I'd been in places like this before, plenty of times. Just not on US soil.

"Our ground commander is LTC Hughes," Trav said. "He'll see you now."

The doctor departed and Trav led me down a long hall past city offices and community rooms, all repurposed as command centers and dining halls. Guardsmen sat everywhere, some sleeping as they slumped against the wall, some shoveling down MREs. All looking strained and exhausted.

At the end of the hall Trav motioned to an open door and I turned the corner into an office marked by a silver name plate: MAYOR PETE SALTER. I knew the name. Pete played regular poker games with Jeter. I'd joined, on occasion.

But the man behind the desk wasn't Pete, it was the tall LTC I'd encountered on Main Street earlier that same day— the one who had talked Jeter off the ledge. Without his NBC gear he looked younger than I had expected. He sat slumped back in a chair, a pot roast MRE held in his hands, the gravy congealing atop cardboard meat. His cover lay on the desk next to him. His hair was salt and pepper, his uniform a little wrinkled.

He looked up when I entered. Trav stood at attention but didn't salute—not indoors.

"Mr. Mason Sharpe to see you, sir."

Hughes swept me head to foot. He licked his lips, then grunted.

"Have a seat, Mr. Sharpe." I moved for the chair across from him. Hughes turned back to Trav.

"We got any hot sauce around here?"

"I think we have Tabasco, sir."

"Grab it. This stuff's about as bland as my first wife's sense of humor. "

Trav scurried off. Hughes wiped his mouth and chugged from a can of Coca-Cola.

"You ever try an MRE, Mr. Sharpe?"

Only a few thousand of them.

"What do they taste like?" I said, deciding to hold my cards for the moment.

"Oh, you know. Like wood chips seasoned with pigeon crap."

Hughes didn't laugh. Neither did I. Trav brought the hot sauce and Hughes simply motioned for him to leave it on the desk and close the door behind him. The latch clicked. Hughes eyed me for a protracted moment. Then he grunted.

"So if you've never had MREs, what did they feed you in Afghanistan?"

I leaned back in my chair, Taggert's files resting on my lap. "You pulled my records."

"Of course I did. You wouldn't be sitting here if I hadn't."

"So you take me seriously."

"Enough to give you five minutes. I'm a busy man, Sergeant. Let's get to the point."

I dropped the files on his desk. "The point, sir, is that you have a real problem."

17

Hughes opened the file without a word. I allowed him to scan a few images and read the first two pages of Taggert's log before I began my briefing —short, sweet, and right to the point. Just the way I'd done it in Afghanistan.

"Clay Taggert was retired US Army. Vietnam war. I'm told it was rough on him. As you can see, he kept close tabs on the community. Those photographs are all date- and time-stamped for the last week leading up to your arrival. Taggert was tracking a pair of unknown individuals around the community—Middle Easterners, he thought. His logs detail their activity around town. They stayed in a hotel near the highway, and didn't appear to have any reason to be here, or so he claims. He was initially concerned about their interest in the nuclear plant. They visited that region on multiple occasions, but later in the logs he mentions a 'compound'...some other facility in the county. He didn't name it."

Hughes frowned. "What are you getting at?"

"You're facing a major biological outbreak, are you not?" I said.

Hughes didn't answer. I didn't expect him to.

"Clay Taggert suspected these men of ill intent. Now Clay Taggert is dead."

"Dead? He was infect—"

Hughes stopped himself, but what was the point? I already knew what this was about. The government could only sit on the truth so long.

"You could say that," I said. "Infected with a dose of lead to the brain."

"Excuse me?"

"He was shot. By men wearing *your* uniform."

That got Hughes's attention. His gaze snapped up.

"What?"

"I wasn't able to get names or ranks—all their patches were covered by the NBC suits—but it doesn't matter anyway. They aren't legitimate guardsmen. They're just borrowing the costume."

"How do you know that?"

"Because I saw it."

"First-hand?" His surprise was approaching disbelief.

"Right. At the city park. They shot him in the head, then carted his body off in a Humvee. I lost them on the roads. Then I went and checked out Taggert's place and found this stuff. Then I came to you."

Hughes dropped the file. He squinted. "Who are you?"

"You already know."

"No, I know who you *were*. I'm asking who you are now."

It was a simple question with a complicated answer. I decided to go with the highlights.

"I got out of the Army and spent some time as a cop. Now I'm nothing. I work at the local sawmill. I just live."

"And poke around civilian bunkers during a local crisis."

"Old skills die hard."

Hughes looked back at the file. He sucked his teeth. "You realize what this looks like?"

"A racist, crazy old war vet stalking random tourists. Probably lost tourists."

"Exactly."

"That's what I thought also. But then I saw this."

I leaned over the desk, shuffling through the photographs. I stopped on a closeup. It was shot from a distance with a telephoto lens. It featured one of two men Taggert had followed stopped at a gas station for a fresh tank of fuel. Dark hair, dark eyes, olive skin. A close-cropped beard. A jacket and jeans paired with black boots.

The jacket hung open. The grip of a handgun was visible. I tapped the photograph. Hughes snorted.

"You do realize this is Iowa, right? The preachers carry guns."

"Not the pistol, Colonel. The boots. Take a closer look."

Hughes did. He studied the image under the mayor's desk lamp. He frowned. Then his face went taut, and his gaze snapped up.

He saw—and he understood.

"Standard issue NATO boots," I said. "Probably donated by the US or the UK to the Lebanese Armed Forces to aid their fight against insurgencies. If you look on the heel you'll find the emblem of the LAF in place of the NATO seal. I've seen it before. Those boots were captured and dispersed amongst every extremist group from Beirut to Kabul. Hezbollah, Hamas, ISIS. You name it."

It was true. Many of the Taliban fighters I'd shot in Afghanistan wore NATO boots, usually stamped with the emblem of whatever military America or Europe had intended those boots to be worn by. It was the same with uniforms. With weapons. Even with MREs, sometimes.

These particular boots were emblazoned with the LAF symbol—golden branches bent around crossed swords and a cedar tree. Impossible to misidentify.

"Tourists don't wear NATO boots, Colonel," I said. "And legitimate Lebanese soldiers don't pop up in Iowa. Certainly not while packing heat."

Hughes bit his lip. He studied the photograph only a moment longer. Then he lifted a satellite phone and dialed somebody—a captain, apparently. Hughes addressed him as such, requesting a location for Clay Taggert, a local civilian detained at the basketball arena. Then he set the phone down and tapped the photos.

I let him think, not bothering to repeat that Taggert was dead. Hughes wanted to hear the story from his own men.

"Just to be clear," Hughes said. "You're saying that two unidentified Middle Eastern males are at large in this county, with possible ties to our current emergency?"

"Not at all. That's what Taggert is saying. I'm only conveying his opinion alongside news of his demise. Anybody willing to kill him must have something to hide."

"You realize how absurd this sounds? How..." he hesitated.

"Xenophobic?" I offered. Hughes didn't answer, and I understood why. I was well aware of how politically correct the US military had become. To presume that two unidentified males were terrorist threats simply because they *appeared* to be Middle Eastern was more than dangerous, it was potentially career-jeopardizing. And not without reason. I'd known thousands of Middle Easterners during the course of my military and police careers. The vast majority of them are golden people. America is a melting pot. Taggert had no legitimate reason to suspect these guys.

At least not until he saw the boots. And then somebody killed him.

"You have to investigate this," I said. "These two guys could be totally unrelated, but when Taggert started shouting about the compound, he was dragged out of the arena and murdered. The compound could be your linchpin."

"*What* compound?"

"I have no idea. I've only lived here a few months. If Taggert found it, I'm sure you can find it."

Hughes ran a hand over his face. He was about to answer. Then his mobile satellite phone rang, and he snatched it up.

"Hughes." Somebody on the other end spoke. I couldn't make out the words. The call lasted nearly three minutes. Hughes made a few "uhuh" sounds. He squinted. Then he hung up and faced me. He didn't say anything.

"What?"

"That was my ground commander at the college. He spoke with his men and checked in with state police. Apparently, Taggert was being escorted to an isolation facility when he broke free of his restraints and assaulted his escorts. He banged up one kid pretty bad. They shot him in self-defense."

I shook my head. "That's not what happened."

"That's what they say happened."

"*Who*?" I pressed. "Who says that?"

No answer. Hughes tapped the photographs. "State

police had a file on Taggert. Apparently, he's got quite the record with them. Sixteen reports of suspicious persons in the last twenty-four months. Seems they had a special file just to manage his complaints. None of them ever went anywhere—they say he was crazy."

"He was. But crazy people can still be right."

"Did you know he was treated for schizophrenia at the VA facility in Des Moines last year? They were pursuing a diagnosis when he checked himself out of care. Refused to be treated any further. He'd already been prescribed half a dozen psychological medications. Stuff for depression, anxiety. Some of it was pretty heavy."

"How do you know that?" I demanded.

"It was in the state police file."

I shook my head. "No it wasn't. No chance. Not unless they were launching a criminal investigation into Taggert himself. Do you have any idea how *hard* it is to get a warrant for those types of medical records? You don't order copies on impulse."

Hughes shrugged. "What do you want me to tell you? The state cops had them."

"And now you have them," I said. "Within minutes of placing a call asking about Taggert. Just like magic. Doesn't that seem strange to you?"

"What are you insinuating?"

"I'm not insinuating anything—I'm stating the obvious. Somebody wanted Taggert gone, and they laid their groundwork ahead of time to discredit his story. You've got killers posing as guardsmen, and somebody pulling strings from the shadows. If you don't take that seriously, you've got no business being in command here."

Hughes bristled, flipping the folder shut. I should have

known that threatening his ego was a bridge too far. Show me a senior military officer, and I'll show you a guy who doesn't like to be questioned—not by subordinates, and certainly not by random civilians. Hughes had worked hard for the silver leaves on his collar.

But Taggert had worked hard for the contents of that file, and now he was dead because of it. I didn't know what to believe at this point, but I knew what I'd seen. Taggert hadn't assaulted anyone. He'd been executed.

"Mr. Sharpe, the men under my command are the finest soldiers in the state of Iowa. I will insist that you do not defame—"

"I'm not talking about the men under your command, Colonel. I'm talking about the men *pretending* to be under your command. How many soldiers do you have here, anyway? Two hundred? It's a chaotic situation. Anybody with a uniform and an idea of how to behave like a soldier could exploit the chaos. I'm telling you that's what happened."

"And I'm telling *you*, Mr. Sharpe, that you need to leave crisis management to the professionals. I'm contacting the state police and turning you over to their care."

He reached for the phone. I jabbed a finger at the file.

"*Think*, Colonel. Those boots don't pop up at Goodwill. If there's even a chance, no matter how slim, that a militant terror organization is operating inside this county, you're obligated to investigate. I've faced biological threats before, first-hand. This isn't something you can sleep on. You need to filter your ranks and—"

"Welch!" Hughes shouted for his guardsman, and Trav appeared like an apparition.

"Please escort Mr. Sharpe to the lobby and hold him until the state police arrive."

There was no wiggle room in Hughes's tone. I wasn't sure if he was angry over my insinuations of his bad leadership, or simply too exhausted to manage one more problem. Whatever the case, Trav still held a rifle, and it was obvious that Hughes was finished with our discussion.

"You're making a mistake," I said.

Hughes shook his head. "No, Mr. Sharpe. I'm doing the best I can. Do the world a favor and stay out of our way."

18

Officer McFear of the Iowa State Patrol arrived twenty minutes later. I sat in the building's lobby, lifting my N-95 every thirty seconds to sip coffee while Trav stood by and watched through his NBC mask. He hadn't removed it during our entire interaction—not once. Not even after I tested negative for the as-yet-unnamed biological terror ripping through the community.

He was terrified. Maybe he had good reason to be.

McFear wore an ill-fitting uniform and an N-95 like mine. He flashed a badge and gave me a once-over with narrowed eyes, but he didn't ask my name. That was my first clue.

In the back of an unmarked jet-black government sedan I rode with my hands in my lap, coffee resting on my thigh. McFear had a partner, a big guy who bulged beneath a button-down shirt that appeared about a size too small. McFear drove, the big guy sat in the passenger seat.

Neither of them spoke as we turned down Main Street, the wipers gently dismissing a fluttering of snow as we passed the police station. Then Millie's Place. Then Lyle's office. All of them dead quiet, their windows black, nobody around. A sort of eerie stillness hung over downtown that penetrated the sedan. It radiated from the front seat, the two cops exchanging irregular glances, taking turns eyeballing me in the rearview mirror when they thought I wasn't looking.

McFear drove with his left hand riding the bottom of the steering wheel, his right hand free. The big guy rode with his right hand out of sight, pressed against the door. We turned west out of town, passing right by the entrance of Open Plains Community College and gaining speed on the snow-covered road.

"Not back to the arena, huh?" I asked.

No answer. I smiled.

"Did anybody fix that broken window? It was letting in a nasty draft."

McFear eyeballed me in the rearview mirror, but he didn't answer. I leaned back in my seat, rotating the coffee on my left knee. Slowly dropping my right hand off my lap.

"So how long you boys been with the State Patrol?"

McFear grunted. Something worked in his jaw—I thought it was gum at first. Then I smelled tobacco. He'd been swallowing. Now he lifted his mask and spat into a soda bottle.

"Six months," he said. "Kinda new."

"Is that right? You from the area?"

McFear met my gaze in the rearview. He didn't blink. "Born and raised."

"Must be nice to work in your home town."

"Real nice."

My gaze drifted to my window, marking the passage of

snow-covered fields in the dark. We were moving at maybe fifty miles per hour—I couldn't see the dash to confirm. At that speed, even with good snow tires, the sedan could stop in no less than two hundred feet. Probably twice that, assuming we didn't fly into the ditch.

Easy math.

My fingers touched the top of the Victorinox. The grip protruded from my pocket. I got a hand on it just as McFear's eyes twitched back to the rearview.

"Funny thing," I said, meeting his gaze. "I was a cop, once upon a time. I worked with tons of state police. And you know one thing they never do?"

McFear's gaze hardened. I never broke eye contact.

"Station new officers in their home towns."

McFear knew the game was up as the last words left my mouth. I saw the alarm bells clanging behind his eyes. I gave him just enough time to shift his foot to the brake pedal. By the time his face ratcheted toward his bulky companion, a curse exploding from behind his N-95, I already had the Victorinox out. The blade deployed with a practiced flick of my right thumb, locking with a snap. The big guy pivoted in his seat, the invisible handgun I had predicted flashing out from the far side of his right thigh. He swept up a black semi-automatic with an attached suppressor—*not* a cop's weapon. He fought to bring the gun around. McFear shouted for him to shoot.

He was ages too late. I unlatched my seatbelt and exploded out of the back seat, leading with the Victorinox. The long blade glimmered in the dash lights. The muzzle of the handgun arced toward me. The big guy's finger dropped for the trigger.

Then he took three inches of edged steel straight to his

left eye. A short-lived scream broke across the interior of the sedan. The pistol's muzzle dropped and a single shot cracked, the bullet zipping past my chest and slamming into the back door. The big guy twitched and jerked, one hand rising up to his face.

But I wasn't finished—this guy had wanted to murder me, and I would respond with equal force. I lunged out of the seat, driving with my right shoulder. The knife sank up to the hilt, plunging into his brain. I twisted.

Lights out.

The guy slumped. McFear shouted and the sedan's brakes locked. Barely three seconds had passed since the moment I deployed the knife, and already the interior of the car was a chaotic mess of spraying blood and flying arms. In a flash of white illuminated by yellow headlights, the road ahead rotated as the sedan launched into a spin. McFear had lost control. His knee was locked, driving his foot against the brakes. His left hand snatched against the bottom of the steering wheel as his right elbow shot backwards, fighting to strike me in the face.

I didn't give him the chance. I ducked, slashing with the knife. I caught him in the ribs. The sedan bucked as we left the blacktop. Dirt exploded over the hood. We were still spinning but not yet rolling thanks to the flat farmland on every side. I couldn't quite reach McFear's face due to his bulky buddy's fallen body. My shoulder collided with the front passenger's seat. I choked. The sedan slammed to a halt as mud and snow rained down. McFear shouted again, clawing for his gun.

I was finished being shot at. I powered off the floor and abandoned my attempt to lay his guts open, driving a punch to his jaw instead, fist closed around the knife. Bone crunched. McFear's right hand slammed against his fallen comrade's head, struggling to shove him off. The guy had fallen right atop McFear's sidearm. The weapon was temporarily inaccessible.

But McFear was no longer going for his own sidearm—even as he slammed sideways into the driver's side door post, his right hand fell to the console where his buddy's silenced semi-automatic lay. Even as I struggled for a better position in the rear floorboard, overextended and off-balance after my vicious right hook, McFear got the gun. He twisted in the seat, pulling his face and torso out of reach of my right arm. He clawed the gun up. He was sweeping the muzzle toward me, already squeezing off shots. One blew out the rear passenger's side window. The next zipped over my head.

Then I drove the Victorinox point-down into his thigh, all the way to the hilt. McFear screamed, the muzzle falling. His next shot struck his dead companion in the back. His leg jerked and I lost the knife. I fell into the floorboard, clawing for footing, slipping on blood. McFear continued to thrash. The gun cracked again, and the sedan's rear window exploded. My heart hammered, knowing his next shot would obliterate my spine.

Then my left hand found the reclining latch of his seat. It was a cheap sedan—most government models are. No power seats, only manual. A quick flip and a shove of my right shoulder drove the seat back forward, knocking McFear off balance. He fired into the back seat, the bullet zipping above my Carhartt coat. I powered out of the rear floorboard, twisting and driving the seat until McFear was pressed against the steering wheel. He struggled. I reached up with my left hand and caught the top of his seat belt—he was still wearing it. My right hand dropped around the bottom of the seat and I pressed the disconnect. The belt popped free. I wrapped both hands around it. He fired again, but he could no longer get a shot at the back seat. His next bullet zipped into the ceiling as I finally regained my knees. I loosened the belt once and yanked it upward.

Then I pulled, hard. Right around his neck. The belt dug in and McFear's shouts died in a desperate gurgle. He thrashed, fighting to break free, but his head was pinned against the seat back. He couldn't move. He wormed and fought to bring the gun around, but the weapon was still clasped in his right hand. There was no shot. He strained and I temporarily considered releasing the belt and going for his gun. Taking a chance on capturing my enemy alive.

No—it wasn't an option. I could release the belt and he could ratchet around. I'd seen it too many times before, a last desperate surge of adrenaline.

I closed my eyes. I gritted my teeth and pulled. McFear flailed. He jerked.

And then, at last, he fell very still.

19

I kicked my way out of the sedan's rear seat, falling onto torn ground mixed with snow. The car—a Dodge Charger—had never rolled. But modern Chargers are unibody cars, and bouncing through the ditch had been enough to twist that body. The front right wheel was buried in the ditch. The tail lights gleamed in the darkness.

Nobody inside moved.

Spitting blood—not my own blood—from my lips, I clawed my way to my feet and swayed for a moment. I was dizzy from the frantic action, and my left leg erupted in its perpetual, aching disagreement. I stared at McFear—or whoever he was—lying lifeless in the front seat, eyes bulging, and I didn't feel a thing.

Not because I was cold and dead inside. Not anymore. I felt nothing because I was still too confused to process a clear thought.

What the *hell* was happening?

I looked both ways down the two-lane but saw nothing save snow-swirled darkness. The wind that blew off the blacktop couldn't have been warmer than five or ten degrees. It battered my coat, slicing through my jeans, and left me with a decision to make.

To call the authorities...or not?

I wrenched the driver's door open, jarring McFear's body off balance. He flopped against the steering wheel, and I retrieved my Victorinox first, pulling it from his leg and wiping the blade on my own. Then I conducted a quick search of his pockets. I knew there had to be a radio—my phone was still without signal. As far as I knew, the cell towers were still down. McFear had to have a way of communicating with his bosses, and I found it hooked to his duty belt at the four o'clock position, just behind a holstered H&K USP.

Another indicator of his true colors: The H&K is a fine gun, but I've literally never encountered an American law enforcement department that issues them.

Drawing the radio, I adjusted the dial to increase the volume and keyed the call button twice. I waited, a fog of breath clouding my face. The radio screen blinked, but I didn't hear anything. Then I saw the earpiece in McFear's left year. Maybe Bluetooth. Not state trooper issue.

Removing the earpiece, I wiped it off and fit it into my own ear. I keyed the radio again.

"Bad copy, Michaels. We've got nothing but static."

The voice was direct. Male. American. Middle-aged. No discernable accent.

An everyman.

I raised the radio but didn't press the call key. My mind spun as I calculated a way to spin this. Should I pretend to be McFear/Michaels? How much could I say before they busted me?

Better question—what did I need?

Proof, Mason. You need proof.

I keyed the mic, ready with my best impersonation of the dead man's voice. He hadn't said much. I didn't have a lot to go on.

"We had a problem," I said. "Sharpe jumped us. It's a mess. What do you want done with the body?"

Long pause. I waited. When the speaker returned, his voice was just as cold and empty as before.

"He's down?"

"Confirmed."

"Hold, one."

Ice crept up my spine, and it wasn't from the bitter weather. I looked back to the two dead men and embraced the confirmation of what I already knew to be true—they weren't taking me to a detention center. They never had been.

This ride was meant to be my last.

"Is the vehicle compromised?" The speaker returned.

"It's bloody," I said. "Shattered windows."

"Right. I'm deploying backup to your position. Hang tight. ETA twenty minutes."

I lowered the radio, clenching my teeth. I looked back up the road and considered.

I didn't like the idea of "backup". There were too many ways that situation could turn against me, and with nothing but a couple of handguns and a knife at my disposal, there was almost a guarantee that I would be outgunned.

I needed an edge *now*. It was time to push the envelope.

"Sharpe knew about the compound," I said. "He knew the address. We're exposed."

I waited, holding my breath. The response was not what I hoped for.

"The compound?" Brief pause. "Who is this?"

Busted.

I looked back to the car, mind spinning. I evaluated my options, and then I got good and pissed. I remembered Taggert, crazed and distressed, just trying to sound the alarm. This whole mess—whatever this mess was—was shrouded by clouds of deceit and manipulation.

To hell with that.

"This is somebody you didn't count on," I said, dropping the affectation of Michaels's voice. "And that's a mistake you'll never survive."

The radio went silent. I waited, but after thirty seconds there was no reply. It was the smart move for whoever held the mic on the other end. They'd already said too much. The only thing left was to convert that backup team into a QRF team—and tell them to burn rubber.

I tossed the radio back into the floorboard and collected the H&K USP. I searched Michaels's body but found nothing in the way of identification. On closer inspection, his Iowa State Patrol ID was clearly a fake. So was the badge on his belt. In his pockets I found a can of chewing tobacco and a wallet with two hundred bucks cash, but no credit cards or driver's license.

This guy was covert. He'd come ready, and his buddy was just the same. Eighty-two dollars, cigarettes and a lighter in his pockets. No ID, no spare ammunition for the Smith and Wesson M&P Compact with the attached suppressor, its slide locked back on empty.

I tucked the USP into the oversized right pocket of my Carhartt, deliberating only a moment about what to do with the car. Then I rolled to the ground at the rear bumper. I used the awl on my Victorinox to punch multiple holes through the plastic gas tank. I allowed the pungent fuel to drain across the ground, tinting the snow a nasty yellow.

Then I stood up. I lit one of the dead guy's cigarettes, drawing on it just hard enough to build a strong cherry at the end of the stick. Then I stepped twenty feet away and tossed it beneath the car.

The rush of hot flames felt good on my face, warming my hands as a column of flame consumed the car's rear bumper. Clouds reached for the sky. The streams of gas still pouring from the tank ignited and carried the flame toward the gallons of fuel still remaining. I jogged backward.

When the car went up, the concussion was so strong I felt it in my chest. A heavy thud that coursed up my spine and carried across the empty Iowa plains.

A message.

20

I jogged the first mile across a snow-covered field, the burning sedan at my back as I reached a distant tree line. When I finally stepped into the shadows, I was too far away to make out details of the wreck site.

But I saw the headlights racing toward the column of fire —and I knew they were much too late.

Setting off through the trees, I was left without stars or cell phone to chart a course back toward town. It was so dark that I could barely see my hand in front of my face. I wanted to use my Streamlight, but until I was another mile or two farther out from the burning car, I wouldn't risk it. I couldn't be sure what surveillance measures were in place—I had no idea whom I was dealing with. Theoretically, a drone complete with an infrared camera could already be on my tail. I had experienced such menaces before, and they came at the behest of men who hid behind fake badges and nonexistent governmental authority.

No. I couldn't afford any additional risks. My best bet was to force-march my way back to civilization, relying on natural night vision and my own wits to guide me away from the carnage behind, and toward a haven someplace ahead. I wasn't headed back to Prairie Junction—not yet. I wasn't really certain *where* I was headed.

I just needed to find someplace warm and isolated where I could clear my head, organize the data at hand, and begin searching for a solution to this mess.

Half an hour of hard marching through empty, glass-flat fields passed before I saw the first lights on the horizon. They were yellow, and even from another mile of distance I knew they were much too high off the ground to be the lights of a house. I fixated on them nonetheless, bending forward and slogging ahead. The bitter Iowa cold, so much worse at night than it had been the day before, had long ago penetrated the barrier of my Carhartt coat, seeping into my very bones and closing around every individual strand of muscle. I could no longer feel my fingers or toes. My face burned and when I traced my tongue over my upper lip, I tasted frozen snot.

It was colder than cold. My only solace was a relative lack of wind, a rare thing in Iowa. I embraced the bitterness and focused on putting one foot ahead of the other, slogging through the snow that rose halfway up my shins, each foot post-holing through the blanket as the light on the horizon grew only very slowly larger.

It was a farm complex. A group of hundred-foot silos were marked by slowly flashing aviation security lights, their bases cloaked in shadow. I thought I made out a mainte- nance shed, also. Several gigantic tractors parked alongside combines and tilling equipment.

And one mobile office—a trailer-type building standing

on blocks a few feet above the yard, with dim lights glowing beyond the windows.

Bingo.

I accelerated, leaning against the throbbing burn of my left leg and the near-concrete numbness of both feet. I didn't shiver—I was too cold for that. My body was losing energy fast, leaving me with nothing but slow, burning breaths of subfreezing air.

I reached the yard. I staggered past the tractors, heedless of the bright yellow light I'd stumbled into. In the back of my mind I worried about a sniper—in the front of my mind I knew a sniper didn't matter. If the men from the radio had trailed me, they would have shot me with infrared by now.

I had to get inside. I had to get warm. It was the only thing that mattered.

I reached the door of the office trailer. It was locked—not with a deadbolt, simply with a thumb latch, which would have been easily defeatable with my lock picks under normal circumstances. These circumstances weren't normal. Even if I'd brought my picks from my GMC, I couldn't have used them. My fingers were too numb.

I stumbled off the concrete steps and turned for the tool shed. It was packed with all the usual junk I'd seen on farms in the South—only a lot bigger. Work benches, mammoth tractor tires, drums of oil and hydraulic fluid, a lot of rubber belts and nondescript parts. One UTV with a dusting of snow blown over its hood, an Iowa Hawkeyes sticker pasted to its tailgate.

And tools. Screwdrivers and massive wrenches. Hammers and a crowbar.

I returned to the door. I shoved the crowbar in. I inhaled

one long breath of miserable ice air. Then I threw my whole body into the bar, grunting and straining.

The latch broke. I slammed into the trailer's wall and nearly fell, only just catching myself on the door knob. I dropped the crowbar and wrenched the door open. The interior was pitch black. I clawed for a light switch and made it inside.

The floor was linoleum, creaking under my feet. The interior was dirty and utilitarian. I blinked in the glare of overhead fluorescents and pulled the door closed. I surveyed the interior to find battered metal desks and outdated computers. Work boots abandoned on the floor. A bathroom to one side. Rows of file cabinets.

And miracle upon miracles—a coffee maker.

HALF AN HOUR and two cups of coffee passed before I felt alive again. I found the climate controls to a gas heating system and cranked it to full blast, haunting the nearest floor vent until my fingers and toes thawed.

Besides the warmth, the caffeine in the coffee helped to clear my mind. It drove back the confused tangle of chaotic thoughts I always experienced following sudden, unexpected combat, and helped to simplify the questions at hand —the questions of what, exactly, was happening in that unmarked government sedan.

Whoever Michaels and his associate were, their mission was both obvious and simple. The ride out of town was meant to be a one-way ticket for me, and that left me with only one question: *Who* had set me up?

It could have been Hughes, the LTC back at city hall. If

true conspiracy was at play, it wasn't unthinkable that the scheme ran that deep. Hughes himself could be a fake—a thug posing as a guardsman...

But no. I didn't buy that. His body language and general behavior had all been legit. He *felt* like a career officer. He talked like one. He disregarded me like one. Maybe the problem had occurred when he contacted the state police—maybe that was where the enemy lay.

If that were the case, where did murderous thugs hiding behind fake badges and stolen uniforms intersect with the two unidentified men dressed in Lebanese Armed Forces boots? And *why* had Clay Taggert been murdered?

I breathed deep, a sudden wave of exhaustion that raw caffeine couldn't mute descending over me like a tidal wave. I blinked at a sprawling wall map of the surrounding county, fields and farm facilities marked with red ink and sticky notes, a layer of dust covering everything. I tried to think how long it had been since I'd last slept.

Had it been at Lyle's place, the previous day? I hadn't slept at the arena. I hadn't slept since seeing Taggert shot.

I have to rest. It was the next priority. I couldn't expect my abused mind to unravel this riddle running on so little energy. I needed eight hours of solid shut-eye, and a balanced meal.

Before I could enjoy either of those things, I needed a safe place to lie low. Safer than a farm facility that could be compromised as soon as sunrise—or, knowing farmers, *before* sunrise.

I advanced to the map. I set my coffee cup down and found my location, marked by a gold star and a note about corn storage. I traced roads back to Prairie Junction, the closest thing to a metropolis anywhere on the map. I tapped on Jeter's neighborhood, considering.

Then I shook my head—no good. Jeter's house was too close to the enemy. I traced my finger outside of town, down a long and lonely road. Straight to an empty spot on the backside of an abandoned feed factory. A middle-of-nowhere dot, lost in the woods.

Good enough for Clay Taggert. Good enough for me.

Abandoning my coffee cup on the nearest metal desk, I collected a pen and a notepad to record the route. I accessed an unlocked key locker and sifted past keys branded with John Deere and Masterlock logos until I found another sort of logo—the one I was looking for.

Kawasaki.

I palmed the keys, shut the locker, and headed for the UTV with the Hawkeyes sticker.

21

I slept like a dead man. Spread out on one of Taggert's bunk beds with a fully loaded AR-15 resting next to me and a propane heater pumping waves of glorious warmth down the length of the school bus bunker. I didn't remember dreaming. I wasn't aware of the passage of time. I simply closed my eyes and faded from existence for hours... too many hours.

When I finally opened my eyes and checked my watch, it was two p.m. in the afternoon. With no windows to mark the sunrise, twelve full hours had raced by.

I swung my legs onto the steel floor and rubbed my eyes, taking my time to slowly wake up with the rifle cradled across my lap. I looked to the locked bunker door and listened for sounds from the outside.

All was absolutely silent, like a graveyard. Even the hum of the propane heater had cut off, and when I touched the metal frame of the bunk bed, it was icy cold.

Coffee. More coffee.

I clawed my way out of bed, my legs and spine as stiff as

boards. Aching pain ripped through my left leg, a reminder that healing bullet wounds *do not* like to be cold. But despite the discomfort, my toes felt present and accounted for inside my merino wool socks. My fingers all flexed on command.

I was alive.

Unlocking the door, I stepped into the intersecting bus and glanced either way. Everything was exactly as I had left it the night before. I passed down the length of the "hall-way", inspecting each intersecting bunker and finding nothing out of place. I reached the kitchen/living bus and ducked inside, resting the rifle against the counter.

There was a coffee pot and a five-gallon bucket filled with cans of dark roast. I dumped an ample portion into the filter, filled the reservoir, and flicked it on. The machine burbled while I returned to the heater controls and reset the timer for three hours. A few seconds later, welcome warmth whispered from the floor vents while coffee dripped into the pot.

I found powdered eggs, powdered milk, and canned beans-n-sausage to make breakfast with. It wasn't a particularly appetizing mix, but it cooked quickly over a gas stove and the protein count was right. I sat at Taggert's kitchen table and ate in silence while allowing my still-sleepy mind to wander at will.

There was something vaguely haunting about the inside of the bunker. It wasn't the first bunker I'd visited, and in hindsight they all felt a little eerie. Knowing that Clay Taggert had passed into eternity couldn't have helped. It felt disrespectful to be there, almost as though I was intruding.

I finished my meal and my third cup of coffee, washed up, then departed the living area bus for the bathhouse. I skipped the shower stalls and accessed the door beyond, ducking into Taggert's gun room/office with the AR-15 cradled in one arm. I ran my tongue over my teeth and inspected the racks of firearms, my gaze passing on to the U-shaped desk with the map of the county. The computers. The notepads.

The ham radio.

I settled into the desk chair and rested the rifle next to me. I pulled every desk drawer and checked each notepad for a record of Taggert's computer password, but found none. Closing my eyes, I replayed the file of information I'd passed off to Hughes from memory.

The compound.

It was the one piece of intelligence that returned to my mind over and over again. Such a vague term, and yet a vaguely sinister one. What had Taggert meant by *compound*, anyway? Some might call his underground network of school buses a compound. Others might envision a military facility, or a group of plywood buildings constructed way out in the sticks by religious extremists.

There were a hundred possible definitions, but the context of my problem narrowed those options considerably. I clicked open a pen and scratched a list onto a legal pad, noting every piece of data which I had already confirmed.

> *Rogue actors posing as military/law enforcement.*
> *State, possibly federal government calling shots.*
> *Cell towers and communications shut down.*
> *Unknown persons in LAF boots.*
> *Biological threat at play—possibly deadly virus?*

I circled the last note, the one about a virus. It was the

crux of the issue, the fulcrum. All other points orbited around the question of *what* emergency the sleepy farming community of Prairie Junction was facing. Every other element of this disaster sprang from that single question. It was the epicenter of the problem.

If I didn't know what the threat was, I couldn't expect to understand how a shadowy group of killers acting from the shadows played a part in the aftermath—and I was determined to solve that mystery. Determined to rip back the shadows, expose the truth, and root them out one at a time.

Not for me. For Clay Taggert. Because crazy or unstable, backwards or paranoid, he had served his country with distinction. He hadn't deserved an execution.

I tapped the pen over the circled item, twisting it over in my mind and approaching from every possible angle, only to reach the same conclusion each time. I simply didn't know enough—not enough about the situation, about the context, or about the nature of viral, deadly diseases. I was way, way outside my depth on this. I needed intel. I needed expertise.

I needed help.

I turned slowly to the ham radio. It sat on the desk, a thick cable disappearing into the ceiling of the bus and no doubt connecting to a tall antenna mounted high in a pine tree. It was an impressive and thoughtful setup, but I wasn't thinking about the mechanics of Taggert's preparations.

My mind was traveling back in time six years. Not back to the jungles of Africa, but back to Camp Lemonnier in Djibouti City. Back to the days following my near-death experience in Ethiopia. Long nights at the mess hall. Escapes into Djibouti's capital for dinners by the ocean, full glasses of red wine, late-night cigarettes at the Atlantic Hotel.

Not alone.

I swallowed. Not because they were painful memories—quite the opposite. They were simply archived memories. Relegated to deep places in my psyche, surrendered to the passage of time and the progress of change. An old version of Mason Sharpe, multiple times updated and reinvented.

Changed by another woman.

Realizing I had drifted off, I shook my head to clear it. I lifted a hand to the ham radio's headset and slid it over my tangled, dirty hair. I powered the unit on and spent a few minutes reviewing the controls. I'd used ham before, very briefly, also in Africa. I knew something about the protocol and the society of mostly civilian enthusiasts who manned units around the globe. It was an impressive network—an impressive technology, really. While the marvel of modern cellular and internet communication had failed me, Taggert's forethought in installing a radio system kept me covered. I could still communicate with anyone from Chicago to Dubai.

Flipping open the radio log book resting on the table, I scanned hundreds of communications entries recorded over the past several years, each identified by a ham radio call sign and some by nicknames. Taggert kept up steady communication with a half dozen individuals scattered from New Mexico to Morrocco. With a twist in my gut, I realized that this—not Prairie Junction—was his true community.

I settled on a frequency and thumbed the mic, reading off Taggert's call sign from the logbook.

"CQ, CQ, CQ. This is Kilo Zero Tango Whiskey Tango calling CQ and standing by. Anybody copy? Over."

I waited. Nothing but static filled the headset. I adjusted the frequency and tried again.

"Kilo Zero Tango Whiskey Tango. Calling CQ and standing by. Anybody out there?"

"Copy that, Kilo Zero. You've got Victor Echo Niner Charlie Charlie Zulu, live from New Brunswick. How copy?"

The voice was boisterous and good-natured. I hadn't expected the wash of relief that coursed through my body at the sound of another human—a human not presently intent on killing me. I relaxed into the chair and adjusted the headset.

"Good copy, Victor Echo Niner. How's the weather up there?"

"Bitter cold, bitter cold. Where are you calling from?"

"Prairie Junction, Iowa," I said. "Ever visited?"

I waited, listening intently for any shift in tone. Any hitch in breathing—an indicator that word of Iowa's present distress had leaked to the national news.

But Victor Echo Niner remained perfectly relaxed in his reply.

"That's a negative. Spent some time in Minnesota. That's not too far, right?"

"Not too far." I leaned forward, clicking my pen. "Listen, Victor. I've got a pretty big favor to ask. You gonna be around the radio today?"

A laugh. "There's two meters of snow in my front yard. I'm gonna be around the radio all month."

"Right. So here's the thing. Our local communications are down. I need to get in touch with a friend. I'm hoping you could look her up for me and give her a call."

"You can't email?"

"Everything's down. Phones, internet. It's a mess."

"Blizzard, eh?"

"Something like that. I really need to speak to her."

"Well, I can help with that. What's her number?"

I hesitated. "That's the thing... I don't know. It's been a few years. I'll need you to find it."

"Oh, mysterious. Shoot straight with me, Kilo Zero. This is all on the up and up?"

"Perfectly. She's just an old friend."

"Okie-dokie. What do you know?"

I gave him the name. I gave him what details I remembered—last city of residence, occupation, title. Places she might have moved to. Jobs she might have taken.

Every word out of my mouth unearthed another distant memory. The smell of shampoo in the shower. The touch of skin to skin at the Atlantic Hotel's swimming pool.

It brought a lump to my throat. A strange uneasiness... like a mixture of eagerness and uncertainty. Excitement and guilt.

"Got it, Kilo Zero. I'll do what I can. Stay by the mic."

I peeled the headset off and sat staring at the radio a while, still lost in something between conscious thought and confused reflection. I pictured Djibouti. I saw the beaches, the late-night bars, the dancing haze of inebriation.

The years long, long since passed.

Then I shook my head. I ran a hand through my hair. I stood and turned for the door.

I needed a shower.

22

Victor Echo Niner called back exactly two hours later. After scrubbing myself beneath the drizzling water pressure of Taggert's shower, I borrowed a t-shirt from one of his lockers and redonned my jeans and boots. I found a toothbrush and deodorant in his storage room—brand new in the packaging. Taggert really had been ready for anything.

Back in the office I scrambled for the headset as the light flashed, indicating an incoming call.

"This is Victor Echo Niner Charlie Charlie Zulu, calling for Kilo Zero Tango Whiskey Tango. Do you copy? Over."

"Victor Echo Niner Charlie Charlie Zulu, this is Kilo Zero Tango Whisky Tango. I copy. Got you loud and clear."

"Sweet, Kilo Zero. I've got some good news for you. Took some work, but I found your lady friend. Had to leave a message with her office. I mentioned the name you gave me and she called right back. I've got her now."

Deep in my chest my heart rate quickened. I hadn't

expected the reaction, and I swallowed in temporary hesitation —not just at the thought of hearing that voice after so many years, but also because of the uncertain logistics of the situation. What I wanted to discuss I didn't really want to discuss over public radio waves. And yet, what choice did I have?

"So...uhm..." Victor Echo hesitated. "You want me to just put her on speaker?"

"Roger that, Victor Echo. Ready when you are."

A brief pause. Victor Echo cleared his throat.

"All right, ma'am. I've got you online with Kilo Zero—err. Mr. Mason Sharpe. You can go ahead."

"Thank you, John."

Dr. Evelyn Landry's voice crackled through the speakers, distorted by distance and the overlay of multiple communication technologies, but absolutely impossible to misidentify. That gentle sweetness blended with an undertone of Brooklyn toughness. Six years had passed since Djibouti— six long years—and they had aged me well more than a decade.

Evelyn's voice hadn't aged a day.

"Can you hear me, Mason?"

I mashed the call button. "Copy—I mean...yes. I can hear you."

Pause. I wasn't sure what to say. Suddenly, I felt tongue-tied. I swallowed water and shook my head.

Focus.

"It's...been a while," Evelyn said. She seemed equally caught off guard. "How are you?"

I opened my mouth. I stopped. I wasn't sure what to say —where to begin. I wasn't sure if I *wanted* to begin. It was a monolith of a story, all those rough-and-tumble moments that had transpired since I last saw Evelyn at the Atlantic Hotel.

Looking back over her shoulder—hiding tears. Withholding rage.

Not now, Mason.

"I'm good," I said. "We should catch up. Listen... I'm calling to ask a favor."

Pause. When her voice returned Evelyn sounded more tentative than before.

"Okay."

"Are you still working with infectious diseases?"

The question was enough to kill the hesitation in her tone. Evelyn transitioned easily into a business tone. "Yes. No longer with the WHO, though. I transferred Stateside. I'm in Washington. What's up?"

I ran a hand through my freshly washed hair and considered for only a moment longer before jumping right in. The public radio waves couldn't be helped. Victor Echo listening in couldn't be helped. I started at the beginning, with the moment Iowa National Guardsmen stormed into Prairie Junction. I skated over some of the violent parts. I focused on the key points, finishing with a summation question.

"I guess what I'm asking is...what do you know?"

The radio crackled. I thought I heard Victor Echo curse. Then Evelyn returned.

"They've locked the town down?"

My stomach sank with the question. It was the worst possible answer—an answer that confirmed what I most feared. Evelyn knew nothing about the situation in Prairie Junction. And if she was in government, working with infectious diseases, she certainly should have.

"National Guard," I said. "With some other players sprinkled in. That's another story."

"You saw a body?" Evelyn pressed.

I confirmed, describing the condition of Ms. Molly's corpse with as much detail as I could recall. Even over the distant crackle of the radio, I could tell that the entire tenor of our conversation had shifted. Evelyn's voice was as tense as a bowstring when she responded.

"Where are you now?"

"Not important," I said. "I'm around."

"You're safely isolated?"

"I am. I also tested negative last night...for whatever that's worth."

"It's worth nothing until I know what's happening. *Don't move.* Stay right where you are. Mr. John, I'll call you back."

Then Evelyn's voice terminated. Victor Echo grunted apologetically.

"She, uh, hung up."

Right.

I leaned back in the seat. I scratched one stubbled cheek and contemplated a shave.

Mostly...I contemplated Evelyn.

"You want me to...hang around?"

I sat up. I mashed the call button. "Negative, Victor Echo. I appreciate everything. Just give me a buzz when she calls back, okay?"

"You got it, buddy. You...uhm. You stay safe, okay?"

"Wilco. Kilo Zero Tango Whiskey Tango, out."

I pulled off the headset and stood, staring a while at the unit. Trying not to make the focus of my thoughts Djibouti... and all the jumbled events that led up to the moment that

Evelyn Landry walked out of that hotel. Her voice brought it all back.

Focus, Mason. You don't have time to sit around.

I pushed the chair aside and started at the far end of the U-shaped desk, ready to make yet another search of Taggert's cluttered office cave. I went from one drawer to the next, shifting books and magazines aside, digging past pens and flipping through notepads. I strongly suspected that anything of real value would be contained on one of the two locked laptops—but even if I was right, there was no use bellyaching about it. I couldn't access those computers. I needed to focus on the attainable data.

I had circled past the radio and was almost at the other end of the U, standing beneath a bulletin board still pinned with notes, photographs, and random clutter when I noticed the single sheet of paper that had slid off the desk and down the interior wall of the bus. As I leaned close and clicked my Streamlight on, a bright pool of blue spilled into the gap. It highlighted the paper. I thought I saw a note, but I couldn't reach it.

Grasping the end of the desk, I pulled. It slid two inches out from the wall, screeching on the metal floor. I dropped to my knees and reached into the gap. I tugged the paper out.

It was a print-off—a satellite image, it seemed, pulled from one of those online mapping software. Google Earth, perhaps. Printed in black and white, the picture was a little pixelated. I thought it depicted a large building, or several buildings constructed together. Flat-topped. Covered in snow. Surrounded by trees and maybe a fence.

An address was printed inside a display bubble near a computer cursor—a street number, a county road...and a city.

2212 County Road 77. Prairie Junction.

Written beneath the image in bad handwriting was a single word, followed by a question mark.

Compound?

My heart rate spiked again, but this time for a very different reason. I rushed to the map on the wall and traced it with one finger, locating the county road—then immediately jumping to a red pushpin marking the road about sixteen miles as the crow flies from my current position. On the far side of town, way out in a forested patch surrounded by more endless cornfields. But still inside Prairie Junction's endless city limits.

Bingo.

I tapped the spot. I memorized the layout of roads between myself and that point. Then I grabbed my Carhartt and turned for the door.

I wasn't sitting around waiting for Evelyn to call back. I could touch base with Victor Echo on my return. There was work to do.

It was time to determine just what sort of *compound* had driven Clay Taggert into such a panic.

23

The UTV I'd borrowed from the farming outpost still had better than a half tank of fuel, and locked into four-wheel drive it managed the snowy highways with ease, but it wasn't very fast. Topping out at twenty, maybe twenty-five miles per hour, the little engine sounded like a cross between a lawnmower and an incoming A-10 Warthog.

I needed my truck back. I would take the UTV to town and leave the keys in the seat. The good people of Prairie Junction would return it to its owner. I would liberate my truck—hopefully without drama.

Then I was headed out County Road 77...toward the compound.

The plastic windshield on the UTV did its best with the bitter wind, but I was still freezing cold by the time I reached the outskirts of Prairie Junction, fully forty-five minutes after departing Taggert's bunker. I'd passed no National Guard troops along the way, although I had spotted an FMTV parked across an intersection a thousand yards across a cornfield. They had spotted me too—I knew because one guy lifted an arm in an attention-grabbing wave.

I ignored him and rumbled on, passing a closed produce stand and the local flea market before I pulled the UTV onto salt-covered gravel alongside a Dairy Queen. I parked behind the building. I cut the motor and left the keys in the ignition.

Then I shoved my numb hands into my pockets and set off toward downtown, cursing myself for the coin flip in St. Louis that had sent my dumbass *north* right into the onset of winter.

I was an Arizona boy. I wasn't bred for the chill, let alone the bitter cold, and Afghanistan had nothing on Iowa when it came to bitter cold.

The streets of downtown Prairie Junction were totally vacant, leaving the place looking and feeling like a ghost town. With fresh snow piled over parked vehicles and the windows of restaurants and businesses dark, it was easy for me to slip down alleys and back streets all the way to the heart of town.

Main Street wasn't empty. Multiple National Guard Humvees and one FMTV sat along the curbs. A retired farm supply warehouse turned wedding venue had been seized as a sort of downtown troop headquarters. It sat three blocks south of the parallel parking spot where I'd left my GMC. The truck still sat there, just outside the parking lot of city hall, where additional Humvees and state patrol vehicles lined up against icy curbs.

But I saw no soldiers—not outside. It was too cold.

I stuck to the buildings as long as I could, only stepping out onto the open sidewalk at the last possible moment. From there I broke into a sprint, pounding through the ankle-deep snow on my way to the truck. I flipped my key out as I neared the rear bumper. I scanned city hall's parking lot for indicators of resistance, and saw none. I made it inside the truck and closed the door, pumping the accelerator. Twisting the key.

That gem of an inline-six struggled for only a moment before coughing to life. It ran rough at first, as brutally cold as my own bones. I rubbed my hands together and hit the wipers. They dumped snow off the sides of the windshield. I scanned left, back to city hall.

A pair of National Guardsmen stood there, not wearing NBC gear but both wearing N-95 masks. They squinted at me. One seemed to say something to the other. I dropped the shifter into first gear. One of the soldiers held up a hand, stepping off the sidewalk.

But I was already gone, snow chains grabbing the blacktop as I surged back onto the two-lane. I reached second gear. I turned west by memory.

And headed for the compound.

I DIDN'T ENCOUNTER a roadblock on my way to the compound, and deep in my psyche I knew that meant something. The address was a long way from downtown—more than the five-mile radius I had estimated the roadblocks to encircle. That could only mean that I had been wrong about the size of the roadblocks, or else their perimeter had been expanded...again.

I filed the information away in the back of my mind and proceeded to my target, noting each passing landmark and the gradual shift in landscape as I progressed. There's a bizarre sort of voice a location can project. Innate and without breath, it's remarkable what a story the subliminal vibe of a place can tell you if you pay attention.

Dirty sidewalks speak of age and neglect. Covered windows speak of secrets and mistrust. The age of vehicles, the condition of flower beds and fountains, the display of branding—or lack of branding—all speak to a deeper truth. A subtext that's easily missed or ignored, but worth taking a second look at.

The subtext of the facility marked by Taggert's red pushpin broadcasted the story of concealed activity just behind the towering oak trees that lined the property.

It was almost dark by the time I arrived. I parked my truck half a mile away, behind another monolithic John Deere tractor, itself parked at the edge of a cornfield. Green blended with green, and I took my backpack from the floorboard on my way out. All my key essentials were inside— binoculars, camo paint, even bolt cutters. I didn't bother with the paint. It wouldn't do much good in a winter wonderland. I wished I had white clothes instead of dark blue jeans and the pitch-black Carhartt coat. The best I could do was stick close to the trees, hoping to blend with their darkened trunks as the last light of another short winter day faded toward South Dakota.

I penetrated the forest well south of the facility's entrance—or where I judged the entrance to be based on Taggert's map and satellite printout. I wasn't going to risk driving any closer. On my feet, amid a blanket of rotting foliage covered in snow, I moved as silent as a deer between the trees, not slowing until the vague glimmer of lights caught my eye from three hundred yards away.

I descended behind a red oak, falling to one knee and

deploying the binoculars. The oncoming lights were head-lights—a single Humvee, growling through the trees in a perfectly straight line, perpendicular to the intersecting county road to my left.

It was the access drive, I decided. The Humvee would pass me in another ten seconds. I returned to my feet and launched into a steady jog, weaving amid the shadows and circling behind the trees. By the time I closed within fifty yards of the Humvee it had crossed in front of my position and continued eastward into the forest. I turned to follow it, jogging parallel to the access drive and quickly losing ground on the Humvee. Its tail lights dimmed to red specs in the forest ahead as the last of the sunlight vanished, the air growing colder by the minute.

Then the Humvee halted. I saw it from three hundred yards and kept up my pace. I closed half the distance and observed other lights marking the spot where the vehicle had stopped—security lights, yellow in color, glaring down on the vehicle. I wove right. I dropped to my knee behind a hickory tree and produced the binoculars again.

It wasn't a checkpoint—it was a full guardhouse. Ten feet square, with concrete walls at its base and windows mounted above them, the building was painted pure white to match the surrounding snow. At its back it connected with a twelve-foot chain-link fence topped with curled razor wire. That fence shot out in both directions, streaking into the trees and marked periodically by additional security lamps mounted low on the fence posts.

The Humvee had stopped directly next to the guard-house, and as I focused the binoculars I noted a man in a full biological protection suit handing something through the driver's side window of the vehicle. The guy standing guard at the gate nodded once. A buzzer rang.

Then a pair of twelve-foot-high metal gates, also painted white, swung open in front of the Humvee. The brake lights flashed. The vehicle rumbled through, and the gates swung closed again.

The guy in the bio suit retreated into the guardhouse, closing a door and raising his hood. The gates shut, and the buzzer rang again. All fell deathly silent.

And I knew in my very bones two things at once. First, this *was* the compound Taggert had mentioned.

And second: Everything about it was wrong.

24

The first red flags were the corporate signs mounted to the gates—there weren't any. There weren't any signs mounted to the guardhouse, either, or any visible identifying patches on the guard's bio suit.

The suit itself was another red flag. It was nondescript, similar in style to the military NBC suits now in such vogue around Prairie Junction, and yet totally different. It was white, for a start, not green. I might have thought that made it a medical uniform, not a military one. But the cut and design of the outfit held more in common with the suffo-cating gear I wore into Ethiopia.

Also, the guy in the guard shack was most definitely *not* a medical professional. Not a doctor. This guy was a solider, likely a private contractor. He wore a full chest rig with addi-tional magazines and an AR-15 pattern rifle held in a two-point sling. A drop holster clung to his right thigh, only momentarily visible as he disappeared into the guardhouse.

And all of it—the rifle, the chest rig, the holster and the gun it contained—were winter patterned. Either spray-painted or ceramic-coated. Regardless, it was a very intentional blend of pure white and splotchy brown.

Cold forest colors. Winter camouflage, something not even the National Guard was using.

A third red flag. A giant one.

What on earth was so secretive that most of Prairie Junction knew nothing about its existence, and so sensitive that it required the security of multiple heavily armed commandos in environment-matching camo gear?

I had an idea. I didn't want to assume. I decided to take a closer look instead.

As I approached the fence I looked both ways for any indicator of what entity laid claim to the property, and still saw nothing. No branding. No logos. What I *did* see were periodic plastic tags, posted every twenty feet along the fence. Yellow in color with black letters and a black lightning bolt—a warning that the fence was electrified. The sight of them brought to mind memories of St. Louis and a similar fence enclosing a criminal mastermind's private property. Those tags were fakes—his fence was not actually electrified.

Somehow, I thought these tags were perfectly legit. This fence was very legitimately electrified—the forest and undergrowth on either side was cut way back to prevent an unintentional grounding of the current. This place was the real deal.

I closed to within twenty yards of the guardhouse and descended back to one knee behind another red oak, listening. In the frozen stillness of the forest, every distant noise rang as clear and sharp as a gunshot across water. I detected the distant rumblings of Humvee engines, mixed with undiscernible shouts from far beyond the fence.

I couldn't see any lights. I didn't notice any movement. At least, not from beyond the guardhouse. That structure was fully illuminated by the fluorescents burning inside. Two men were silhouetted, both dressed in head-to-toe bio suits and tactical gear, but neither wearing a mask.

I lifted the binoculars. One man turned, and my gut tightened.

It was one of Taggert's killers—I was certain of it. The body language I had identified from the park was all there, that relaxed confidence and perpetual readiness. The hallmarks of special operations matched with the icy eyes of a cold-blooded killer. The guy slouched against a desk with the rubber bio hood pulled back over his shoulder blades, the mask laid aside, his hair a tangled mess. A row of monitor screens ran the length of the desk in front of him, their backs turned to me. He sipped coffee and surveyed them, muttering occasional comments to the second man who manned a nearby computer. Another figure radiating the hallmarks of a special operations commando.

I watched for two minutes, then withdrew into the shadows behind the tree to contemplate. It was more than a guardhouse, it was a surveillance center. That much was clear. I hadn't observed any cameras on the way in, and clearly, they hadn't observed me either.

But they must be there. Taggert's killer sat like an eagle with a view of the complex—or compound. It was a private security perch, which likely made him a private security contractor. Not current military, but ex-military, now trading the extensive skillset that he developed on Uncle Sam's dime for his own profit.

All well and good; plenty of retired soldiers do that. It was the last fact that my logical train of thought produced which made this guy a bad guy—the fact that he had a homicide to answer for.

I considered my options for only a moment, one hand dropping to the small of my back where the H&K USP I'd taken from the burned-out sedan remained tucked next to my spine. The glass of the guard shack didn't appear bullet-proof. I could engage both men and take them out with a pair of headshots long before they reached their rifles. I could also neutralize one and disable the other, leaving him alive for an interrogation.

But no. There was a better, much less bloody way to handle this situation. I wanted to develop the context before resorting to gunfire. I wanted a look at those security moni-tors—but to do that, I needed the pair of killers inside lured out of the shack.

My gaze drifted back across the forest, beyond the shack. Back to the fence.

I had an idea. I returned to my feet and vanished into the darkness.

———

25

The jog back to my truck was quicker than my incursion had been. I presumed that my original path had circumvented any hidden cameras in the forest, so I retraced that route. I reached the truck and circled directly to the passenger seat. The tire iron I'd used to break into Taggert's fake home lay in the floorboard, icy to the touch. Beneath the camper shell in the bed of the truck I dug through plastic camping bins until I located the second component of my planned distraction apparatus—a pair of heavy-duty jumper cables.

The last item I found in my campsite cooking bin. It was a bottle of lighter fluid, nearly full and uncompromised by the brutal temperatures thanks to its petroleum composition. I tucked the bottle beneath one arm and wove through the forest for a third time, closing to within three hundred yards of the guard shack, then turning east—toward the fence.

The yellow tags clipped to the fence advertised—or

threatened—a pulsing electric shock of ten thousand volts, which was far beyond the rated capacity of the twelve-volt jumper cables curled over my shoulder. I selected a spot with a pair of birch trees standing only ten yards outside the fence. I checked again for cameras, and didn't see any. I stepped closer to the fence, closing to within reach of the jumper cables.

I stopped when I heard it. The regular two-second-interval *snap* of ten thousand volts surging through the fence. Not a constant, direct current, but an alternating one that could be timed by that audible click.

I kneeled, turning the tire iron crook upward and shoving the pointed end into the ground a full ten inches. I connected one end of each jumper cable line to the crooked top, then stood and dispensed the lighter fluid in a wide pattern all over the snowy blanket surrounding my makeshift metal stake. I emptied the entire bottle, then tossed it into the snow. I looked over my shoulder, back toward the guardhouse. I approached the fence and breathed deep, grasping the remaining clamp ends of both the black and red jumper cable.

They were insulated—but not *that* insulated.

I timed the clicks. I developed a tempo in my head, like the tap of a solid kick drum. I moved my body with it. I made myself one with the rhythm.

Then I opened both clamps, waited for the click, and snapped them over the bare fence wire. The moment their copper jaws closed I threw myself backward, bracing for that next click. It sounded as I landed in the snow, louder than the last, and immediately followed by a dull buzzing. Then a stench of burning rubber.

I didn't wait to see what would happen next—I scrambled back to my feet and sprinted into the trees as sparks exploded from the jumper cables at both ends, the fence grounding against the tire iron, the jumper cables quickly melting down under the pulsing blasts of ten thousand volts.

I made it fifty yards into tree cover and looked back just as those cascading sparks ignited the lake of lighter fluid swimming atop a basin of snow. In a flash the blue of electrical flames mixed with the hot orange of burning lighter fluid, igniting the night in a golden inferno directly adjacent to the fence.

It was better than beautiful—it was brighter, hotter, and quicker than I hoped it would be. The fence had shorted out, and nobody within the vicinity would have to wonder why.

I shrank into the shadows and drew the H&K as I started back toward the guardhouse. No alarm sounded—these guys were smarter than that. By the time I passed deep enough into the trees to view the lights of the gate complex, I could already see one of Taggert's killers departing the guardhouse.

He ran with his head down, an AR-15 rifle held into his shoulder with its weapon light slicing through the forest. Behind him his buddy followed a little slower, his own rifle sweeping wider swaths closer to the guardhouse.

"Fire!" the lead man called. "Fire on the fence! Radio QRF."

QRF. It was an odd thing to say. He didn't call for a fire-fighting team. He didn't call for emergency services.

He called for the quick-reaction force, something only a military guy would want. It told me a lot about both the men I was now watching and the men who lay on the far side of that fence, but for the moment I shelved that information in favor of the more immediate problem—getting to the guard house.

The second guy spoke into a radio, still standing back while Taggert's killer rushed toward the flames. I measured the swaths of his weapon light and detected another pattern —a steady tempo.

Rookie mistake.

I departed the shadows and circled left. In five seconds I had closed well within reach of his light, but there was no chance of being discovered by it. The path of the beam was too predictable. I ducked behind trees as necessary. I moved all the way to his four o'clock position and glided through the snow as swift and silent as an arrow.

By the time he detected movement and first began to break his search pattern, I was already on him. I grasped the H&K by its slide and slammed the butt into his temple, full force. His eyes rolled back in his head. His body collapsed like a house of cards. I grabbed the rifle on its way down and mashed the release buttons on the quick-detach sling. The H&K slid into my coat pocket. I flipped the weapon light off and snatched up his radio.

Then I abandoned him in the snow and headed for the guardhouse. I reached the door just as a crackle of voices over the radio signaled the incoming QRF—ETA, thirty seconds.

Inside the shack I descended to my knees, concealing the bulk of my body beneath the windows. I held the rifle into my shoulder and swept the contents of wall-to-wall desks. There was a coffee maker, a microwave, and a mini fridge. A small gun locker and two desk chairs.

Then the computer monitors—six of them, all of them ultrawide, all displaying multiple black and white, night-vision-enabled views of the property surrounding me...and the facility within.

Clay Taggert was right to call this place a compound—it was the perfect term. Consisting of multiple rectangular buildings arranged together with connecting hallways and skywalks, the total size of the facility had to be fifteen or twenty thousand square feet. A parking lot lay mostly empty, occupied by a handful of personal vehicles and a trio of Humvees—one of them headed this way.

The front door looked more like the entrance of a top-secret military facility than a civilian place of business. It was armored, without any windows. Another guardhouse stood there. Camera angles indicated high posts dotted across the complex, almost all of them looking inward—watching the facility. Most of the buildings featured only narrow windows, like the kind you see at a prison.

It was austere. It was colorless, styleless, bland. It *reeked* of government design.

And here it stood, right in the middle of nowhere, Iowa. *What?*

"Colbert! Where are you?"

The radio in my lap crackled, and I recognized the voice. It was Taggert's killer—not one of the men who kidnapped him, but the guy who'd actually pulled the trigger. I looked back toward the door, and I could still see the glow of the distant fire reflected off a cloudy sky. I figured the source of that fire must have been discovered by then.

I was right.

"It's jumper cables! Somebody shorted out the fence. Colbert, do you copy?"

I wanted to radio back. I wanted to psych him out, to tell him just what a walking dead man he was. I resisted—I needed every second I could get.

Drawing my phone, I noted that I was still without cell phone signal, but a little bubble popped up notifying me of a nearby secured Wi-Fi signal. The name was just a series of random letters and numbers, nothing identifiable, but it wasn't difficult to assume that the signal came from either the guardhouse or the complex beyond.

So it seemed that not *everyone* was without internet. That was useful information.

I tabbed to the phone's camera and began snapping pictures of each monitor screen, recording their black and white displays from one end to the other. I snapped photos of the guardhouse's interior and was just turning back to the door when another shout burst through the radio.

"Man down, man down! Missing his rifle—we've got an armed tango on-site."

Terrific.

I pocketed the phone and shouldered the rifle. I turned for the door. I was halfway there when an explosion of head-lights signaled the arrival of the QRF Humvee. My radio exploded with communication—a voice shouted for the gate to be opened. I reached quickly to the wall and smacked a switch, killing the lights inside the guardhouse. I looked out into the trees and identified the sweeping blaze of a weapon light—the weapon light of Taggert's killer.

Then that light blinked off, and the next radio call sent a chill up my spine.

"Switch to NVGs! He's in the guard house."

The radio call was answered in a split second by the termination of the Humvee's headlights. In an instant the surrounding forest was consumed by thick shadow. I lost everyone—but I had to assume they hadn't lost me.

Time to split.

I rotated the rifle and thumbed the selector switch. I'd been wrong in my initial identification—it wasn't an AR-15. At least, not a civilian model. This was a full-fledged military-issue M4A1 equipped with a standard issue "fun switch".

Full auto. Let's dance, boys!

I swung out of the guardhouse and lit up the night with a jerk of the rifle's trigger, firing from the hip and not really aiming. I simply pointed the rifle toward the joined gates, sending a hail of lead pinging against the Humvee and slicing through the night. The storm of cover fire was enough to send the QRF scrambling for cover, shouts and temporary pandemonium overcoming the battlefield as the rifle locked back over an empty magazine.

I slung it down. I turned and sprinted into the trees even as the crack of another rifle engaged me from the direction of my rigged electrical fire. Bullets whispered over my head and zipped into the hardwood. I drew the H&K and hurtled on, ducking and weaving, not so much as flinching as a buzzing ricochet whined over my head.

The shots were close—but not close enough. Night vision or not, the shooter couldn't overcome the forest, and I zigged and zagged at random. In another ten seconds I was so far out of range that the gunfire ceased. I circled wide, keeping up a steady loping pace until I eventually reached the two-lane.

It was snowing again. I ran through a swirl of giant flakes, my left thigh throbbing and my lungs burning as I headed for my pickup. I could still hear the distant shouts—I could see the lights of the guardhouse as they flashed back on.

But I was long gone. I reached the GMC and fired up the engine, keeping the lights off. In another five seconds I was pointed southeast—headed back for Taggert's bunker with a pocket full of evidence.

26

There's something about surviving a gunfight—especially a gunfight wherein I took the enemy by complete surprise, outmaneuvering them on wit and skill alone—which really ignites my appetite. With a nearly euphoric sense of *got you* churning through my body, I was simply ravenous as I parked the GMC behind Taggert's decoy house.

The snowfall had increased to a heavy shower, but inside the school buses the air was still and warm. I peeled off my coat and made my way to the living trailer where I opened two cans of clam chowder and grilled Texas toast in a cast iron skillet. Taggert had an old-fashioned turntable on hand with a Merle Haggard record pre-loaded—the first song was "Okie from Muscogee", an anti-hippy, Vietnam-era track. The opening lines were strong enough for me to pause over my soup pot, casting another slow look around Taggert's living quarters. Stopping over all the pictures and personal effects.

Suddenly not feeling quite so elated.

I switched the turntable off and ate in silence, polishing off both cans of soup and three slices of toast, washed down with warm Dr. Pepper. I scrubbed all the dishes and cleaned the kitchen, stacking some of Taggert's mail—mostly prepper and gun magazines—before I headed to the bath house to wash the GSR off my face. The M4 I'd fired outside the guardhouse was a direct impingement weapon—it ejected a ton of gas alongside spent casings, leaving my face feeling vaguely greasy. Only once I was clean did I finally venture back into the office space, settling into Taggert's chair and drawing out my phone. I surveyed the photos I had taken from the interior of the guardhouse, zooming on each surveillance screen. Without the risk of being shot in the head, I was able to relax and take my time with each snapshot. I noticed things I hadn't before.

Things like the utilitarian pair of nondescript, window-less vans parked at the rear of the parking lot. The signs posted next to the entrance—not readable, but recognizable by their bold letters as warning signs. The ventilation stacks rising from the roof of one building. The abject lack of land-scaping or exterior facilities—no picnic tables. No fountain or dormant flower beds.

The place was entirely utilitarian. Nothing was particularly wrong with that, but there was something beyond the drifts of snow and the bitter wind that made the place feel... very cold. Very clinical.

Somehow sinister.

I was working my way through the photographs for a second time when a light flashed on the ham radio set. I absently lifted the headset, not putting it on but simply placing one ear cup alongside my head. I flipped the switch to activate the audio.

"—Niner Charlie Charlie Zulu, calling for Kilo Zero Tango Whiskey Tango. Do you copy? Over."

I laid the phone down and donned the headset. I keyed the mic.

"Good copy, Victor Echo. This is Kilo Zero Tango Whiskey Tango—I have you loud and clear. What's up?"

"Geez, Kilo Zero. Where you been? I've been calling every twenty minutes!"

I checked my wristwatch. It was nearly nine p.m. My last communication with the New Brunswick radio enthusiast had been...at five thirty? Something like that.

"I was distracted," I said. "What's up?"

"Your lady friend called back. She was real distressed, real urgent. She said for me to call her as soon as I got ahold of you."

"Okay. I can talk now."

"You're not listening, Kilo Zero. That was two hours ago. She called again and said she had booked a flight. She wants you to call her from Des Moines."

"Des Moines? What?"

"She's flying to Iowa, man. I don't know what you two are involved in, but she sounded all kinds of stressed out. She said you can't interact with anyone—not under any circumstances. Wear a mask if you've got one. Drive to Des Moines and text her when you're there. As soon as she lands she'll call you."

"Wait—she's flying *now*?"

"She called me from Dulles two hours ago. Said she had a connecting flight in Chicago and would arrive in Des Moines around midnight. I'm telling you, Kilo. She's really wound up!"

My mind spun. I checked my watch again, then looked to

the regional map Taggert had spread across one wall. It depicted all of Iowa with a little of each adjacent state fading to the map's edges. Our location was marked with another red push pin.

I couldn't be sure how far away Des Moines lay. By rough estimates, at least three hours' drive. Evelyn would land before I arrived.

"Good copy, Victor Echo. Ready for the number."

He gave me Evelyn's phone number. I saved it into my phone and called it back to him twice. Then I prepared to sign off.

"Hey, Kilo!"

"Yeah?"

"You...you be careful, man. I'm gonna be praying for you."

That brought on a smile. "Thank you, Victor. Kilo Zero, out."

I switched off the unit. I peeled off the headset. I looked to the phone and the programmed number—it was the first time I'd read her name in six years.

And she's coming here.

It wasn't the reaction I expected from Evelyn, and even as vague anticipation surged my bloodstream I knew—it couldn't be a good thing.

I took the H&K, took my phone and my coat. I headed for my truck.

27
_____

Thanks to the expansion of the National Guard perimeter, I hadn't been forced to circumvent a roadblock since the morning I went to check on Ms. Molly. But a three-hour trip to Des Moines, I knew, was certain to bring me back into contact with the quarantine line no matter how large it had become.

I was right. I found the National Guardsmen sixteen miles south of downtown, staked out at the intersection of two county roads only half a mile from the four-lane state highway that would carry me to Iowa's capital. Two FMTVs blocked the intersecting county road, while the gap between their front bumpers was filled by a pair of Humvees, completely sealing off my path. Joining the vehicles was a tent, a generator, and several security lights mounted to high poles that illuminated the entire intersection.

This wasn't a short-term post, but a long-term anchor, and even from a mile out with my headlights switched off, I could see the soldiers stationed outside their vehicles, bracing in the bitter cold to ensure an effective lockdown.

I stepped on the brakes, checking my phone again and still finding no signal. Tapping one hand against my knee, I swept the horizon and considered my options.

If my truck was four-wheel drive, I might have taken my chances with a frozen cornfield. Even with two-wheel drive, circumventing the roadblock via the surrounding open farmland could be a viable option. But it was also an option that might leave me stranded, buried up to my axles in snow and dirt, subject to arrest and detainment.

No. I couldn't leave the road. I had to find a way through the same intersection the National Guard was busy blocking, and to accomplish that, I needed to use my head.

Dropping out of my truck, I circled to the back and let down the tailgate. Digging through the contents of my camping containers a second time, I sifted past cooking utensils, tent stakes, a hammock, and a propane camp stove. All items unused for the duration of my stay in Iowa, all relatively harmless in the hands of an ordinary camper...but I had cut my teeth in the art of the bivouac amid Afghani mountains.

I selected the camp stove. It was fed by a sixteen-ounce metal cylinder packed with pressurized propane. Again, relatively harmless when used responsibly. There were two spare propane cylinders rolling around in the bottom of the camping bin, both full. I removed them also and retreated ten yards off the road. I set the camp stove in the snow, cranked the gas up, and flicked a match with my numb fingers to light the burner heads.

The resulting rush of warmth felt good on my skin. I adjusted the gas flow until blue flames rose above the cooking grill, hot enough to melt nearby snow. I toed the stove with my boot to ensure that it was stable.

Then I placed both spare propane cylinders like tea kettles right on top of the cooking burners. I jogged back to my truck, slid behind the wheel, and rumbled a half mile down the road with my headlights still switched off. Well outside the security lights of the checkpoint, I positioned my truck right in the middle of the road, straddling a dashed yellow line.

Then I looked back over one shoulder, chewing my lip. I could barely see the glimmer of fire from the camp stove—and only because I was looking for it. I calculated the seconds that had elapsed, and estimated the temperature of the compressed propane.

Like any other gas, propane expands when it's heated. Inside the confines of the steel cylinders, the gas was technically a liquid, but that liquid would also expand, hence why the good people at the propane-filling company only loaded each cylinder to eighty or eighty-five percent capacity. It was a safety margin to allow for the natural fluctuation in seasonal temperatures.

But that safety margin didn't allow for direct application of thirty-five-hundred-degree cooking flames. Steel can only take so much pressure. Given enough heat, enough time—

My thoughts terminated with an ear-splitting blast—the rupture of both propane cylinders at once, joined immediately by a plume of orange flame as the liberated gas ignited. It was better than I'd hoped for—both louder and brighter. The windows trembled in my pickup's doors and the cornfields were temporarily illuminated for three hundred yards in every direction. Snow and dirt hurtled into the air.

I twisted back to my windshield, dropping my truck into first gear and fixating on the roadblock. The response was delayed—the guards on sentry duty seemed disoriented.

Additional guardsmen emerged from their tent. The flames died down. My truck was safe again amid a blanket of shadow.

Then the boys and girls of the Iowa National Guard ran for their Humvees. They mounted up. Engines fired and headlights blazed. Even as the propane bonfire in my rearview mirrors faded to black, the guardsmen were on their way. I waited until they were two hundred yards out, their high beams ready to expose my position.

Then I dumped the clutch and floored the accelerator. I roared down the middle of the two-lane county road, driving straight toward the oncoming grills of the twin Humvees. They hurtled toward me using both lanes, engines howling. I flicked my lights on and mashed the high beam switch in my floorboard, instantly blinding them.

It was more than enough. The guardsmen inside those Humvees had been trained in combat, but not in psychological warfare. The shock of the propane blast mixed with the sudden appearance of blinding light blazing toward them was enough to override their military training, sending them instead into a spiral of self-preservation seasoned by high school driver's ed.

The soldier to my left broke first, yanking his Humvee to the right to avoid a head-on collision. I killed my lights and hurtled ahead. A gap opened between the two vehicles, and I raced through at sixty miles per hour. Five hundred yards beyond, the pair of FMTVs guarding the intersection stood twenty feet apart, a gap in their defenses beckoning me onward.

One soldier shouted. Another ran for the cab of the nearest FMTV. Both were far too late. I rushed through the gap without so much as a scratch across my pickup's brand-new paint. I cleared the roadblock and didn't let off the gas as I blazed onto a split state highway and turned southwest for Des Moines.

Looking into my rearview, I saw nothing but empty blackness. No sign of the heavy military vehicles. No sign of the soldiers who operated them.

I couldn't resist a dry grin.

Nearly thirty miles passed beneath the GMC's tires before cell service finally returned. Two bars and a little data. I accessed my GPS and routed for a truck stop outside the city. I texted the number Victor Echo had given me, but received no response. The roads were empty and I passed no cops.

So I set the windshield wipers to a steady thump and leaned back in my seat...trying not to think about Evelyn.

It was all my fault, as were all my failed "relationships" prior to Mia. In truth, I didn't even feel right calling the nine-day fling in Africa a relationship, but that very question was the problem that had brought the whole thing crashing down.

After landing at Camp Lemonnier in Djibouti City—and giving the Army pilot a piece of my mind that he would never forget—I lost Evelyn on the crowded tarmac. The chaotic machinations of a military base had swallowed her whole, a tidal wave of bio-suited medical personnel rushing my team into a tent for inspection and isolation.

The bodies were recovered. The disease was medically diagnosed. I spent three days under careful observation before finally being released to the real world...and when I was, I found a card resting on the pillow of my cot back at my barracks.

Call me.

That was it. Just two words. I flipped the card over and found the bold blue logo of the WHO coupled with a name —Dr. Evelyn H. Landry, MD, Virologist.

I did call her. We met for coffee. She wanted to thank me for my efforts in the jungle...and as so often happens in desolate, lonely corners of the world where two young and lonely people collide and like what they see, that thanks spilled into something more.

Nine days. Nine wonderful, slow days, coupled with eight equally exquisite nights spent at the Atlantic Hotel with a sweeping view of the Gulf of Aden. We were both on leave. We both enjoyed the local cuisine and cheesy eighties movies. We danced at a nearby nightclub and lay on the beach to stargaze.

We talked. We drank. We laughed a lot. And yes...we spent a lot of time tangled in the sheets. It was my M.O. at the time. I wasn't a player, but I was a soldier. I was young. I was single and eligible.

In hindsight I could barely fathom how impossibly dumb I'd been. I could still remember the way Evelyn's green eyes shone on the dance floor—all the stories she told about back home in Pennsylvania, her parents and her goofy little dachshund dog with only one ear. Her aspirations of working in the government sector, fighting diseases around the world. Her dreams of a house by the lake where she could practice her poetry and watch the sunsets.

I should have known what was happening. I should have understood that one man's careless fling was another girl's developing romance. But I didn't, and by the time the issue came to a verbal head at the terminus of Evelyn's leave, I was caught off guard. She was smarter than me—she saw the disconnect first.

I could still hear her voice, tentative and soft. "What...do you think this is?"

It was a fair question, but a question I was too immature to face with the seriousness it deserved. I freaked out instead. I stalled.

Then I chose the worst possible response—a juvenile joke.

"Booty in Djibouti?"

Evelyn sat stunned. She didn't speak. She didn't blink.

She simply got up, a tear glimmering at the corner of her eye. She stormed out, leaving most of her things.

And that was the last time I ever saw her.

It had been years since I'd replayed those memories. A good man would have recognized potential and gone after her. A growing man would have at least learned from his mistake and curtailed future flings.

A stupid kid—which was all I really was—leaned into his foolishness and restricted any female interaction to a regimented forty-eight-hour period. No exceptions.

At least...not until Phoenix, four years later. Not until Mia, and the whirlwind night that turned my entire life on its head.

And now?

I startled as my phone buzzed. Just seeing Evelyn's name on the screen was enough to accelerate my heartbeat. It was a text message, not a phone call. I flicked my thumb to open it.

> Just landed. Meet at Walmart on 14th
> Street. Park in the back. DO NOT get out of
> your vehicle. I will come to you.

That was all. No undercurrent barbs. No vague references to the past. All business.

Six years, Mason. Grow up.

I found the Walmart in my GPS and re-routed accordingly. It added ten minutes to my drive. I kept the radio off and both hands on the wheel, pulling into the rear of the parking lot and backing into a space where I maintained a full view of my surroundings. I kept the H&K next to my leg. I cut the ignition and listened to the engine tick as it cooled.

The snowfall had ceased, leaving a light dusting over the empty parking lot. It was very peaceful, very calm.

I texted:

> Green and white 1967 GMC pickup. Back
> corner of parking lot.

Evelyn texted back a thumbs-up emoji. No other response. I leaned back in my seat and ran a hand over my face, scrubbing unshaven beard stubble. I looked to myself in the rearview mirror, a sudden wave of self-consciousness overcoming me. Why hadn't I shaved? At least combed my hair or found a hat? I looked like a total bum.

I shuffled through the glove box, hoping I had stowed a comb amongst the napkins, plastic forks, and random rest stop maps. Junk spilled into the floorboard. I didn't find anything.

I almost jumped out of my skin when a sharp rap rang against my window. Snatching up the H&K, I pivoted toward the door.

Evelyn stood outside. I recognized her by her bright green eyes and strawberry-blonde hair swept back into a ponytail. An N-95 mask covered her face. She wore jeans and a heavy sweater.

"*Don't move*," she said. "Stay in the truck. I'll be right back."

28

Evelyn returned to a parked Toyota RAV4 Hybrid, its near-silent electric motor partly to blame for how easily she had snuck up on me.

The other part? More stupidity.

I lowered the H&K and waited while Evelyn dug through the open rear hatch. She produced a black bag and began unwrapping medical supplies. I observed another lengthy swab but barely registered its importance.

I couldn't look away from her. The concrete in my stomach had hardened into a weight that kept me pressed down in my seat. My mouth was suddenly dry. I didn't know what to do with my hands.

I felt like a kid again. A moron.

Evelyn returned to the window. She made a rolling motion with one hand.

"Just far enough for me to swab you."

I worked the hand crank. The window glided down, and I rolled my head back in compliance. Evelyn completed the swab with practiced ease, then motioned for me to roll the window up as she returned to the Toyota. She was gone for nearly fifteen minutes, leaving me seated with the H&K in my lap.

At last she reappeared at my door, shoulders relaxed in obvious relief. She peeled the mask off, displaced strands of strawberry disrupted by the wind. Our gazes locked, and the breath froze in my lungs.

She hadn't aged a day. She looked *exactly* as I remembered her in Djibouti.

"You should be in the clear," she said.

In the clear of what?

It was the first mission-centric thought I'd processed since her arrival. I sat in the truck just staring, and long seconds trickled past as neither of us blinked. Finally Evelyn flushed, breaking eye contact first.

"Come on... We need to talk."

I cut my engine and followed her to the Toyota, the H&K sliding into the small of my back. She shut the SUV's rear hatch with the press of a key fob, and I slid into the front passenger's seat. The leather was warm—the whole cabin was warm. Evelyn's petite frame glided behind the wheel and she closed the door, peeling medical gloves off.

As I closed my door I smelled vanilla and lilacs, and the scent ripped my mind straight back to Africa. To that fragrant shampoo Evelyn used—and still used, it seemed. It wasn't overpowering, just overwhelming. Enough so to leave me temporarily tongue-tied.

Evelyn broke the silence for me. "So. Had any booty lately?"

Blood surged into my face, and I looked away, rubbing my stubbled face again. Searching for words.

"About that... I..."

She hit me in the arm—not hard, but definitely harder than she could have.

"Relax, moron. It's a joke. How are you?"

I looked up. She was smiling now, but the smile didn't quite reach those emerald-green eyes. Flushed with cold, her hair paler than I remembered, she looked like a European princess.

I hesitated a beat, unsure how to respond. Usually when people ask how I've been, I'm forced to assume they've looked me up. That they read the headlines from back in Phoenix. But given the context of Evelyn's expedited departure from wherever she called home, that seemed unlikely.

"I'm good," I said. "I'm doing good. How are you?"

A slow nod. She sat with the gloves wadded up on one thigh, staring and not blinking.

"I'm good," she said. "Anything you need out of your truck?"

"What do you mean?"

"We're headed north—and you're riding with me. Grab your stuff."

I paused again. She made a rolling motion with one finger. "Let's go, soldier."

That jarred me loose. I returned to the truck to collect my backpack—the only thing I really needed. Everything else essential was already in my pockets or the small of my back. I locked the truck and took the keys. Tossed the backpack in the Toyota's floorboard and peeled off my coat—Evelyn had the climate control turned way up. Then I was back in the front seat, she shifted into drive, and we were off. I glanced to the full-color display spread across the SUV's dash and found a GPS arrow guiding us north. Destination: Prairie Junction.

"We'll have to catch up later," Evelyn said, punching the gas as we hit the highway. "There's a lot of ground we need to cover—a lot you need to know. But for the moment, I'll ask the questions. Take it from the top, every detail."

I forced my mind back into operational gear—mission-focused. I recounted again for Evelyn the events that had transpired since the Iowa National Guard had placed Prairie Junction under martial law, and this time I didn't spare any details. I described Clay Taggert's role in the chaos, his resulting death, and what actions I'd taken since then... including the pair of self-defense killings inside that unmarked government sedan.

Evelyn didn't so much as blink at the violence. She set the Toyota's cruise at a healthy eighty miles per hour and we raced northeast out of Des Moines. When I reached my description of the suspect facility—Taggert's "compound"—I glanced sideways to read her reaction.

There wasn't so much as a flinch.

"That's everything I know," I said. "I'm not aware of any fatalities other than Ms. Molly—virus fatalities, I mean."

"And you don't know who patient zero is?" Evelyn asked.

"You mean the first to get sick? No idea. The first I encountered was Ms. Molly—which is still bothering me. She lived alone. She never went anywhere. Her housekeeper checked on her a couple days ago and reported to her son that Ms. Molly wasn't feeling well, meaning that she must have already been sick. Again...I can't imagine how."

"There's always a trail," Evelyn said. "Sometimes it's hard to identify. Regardless, we've got a bigger problem—the problem of why my office wasn't notified the millisecond this crisis was born."

Reference to her professional capacity reminded me of a

question I had forgotten to ask—a question that might explain why she had flown out to Iowa so suddenly.

"What *is* your office, by the way?"

Evelyn motioned dismissively to the console of the Toyota. I glanced down to find an ID badge. It was blue and white with *Centers for Disease Control* printed above Evelyn's name and photograph.

Her department? *Office of Laboratory Science and Safety.* Her job title? *Assistant Director of Laboratory Safety and Compliance.*

"It's not just us," Evelyn continued. "Nobody knows."

"What do you mean, nobody?"

"I mean that CNN thinks there's been some kind of environmental accident in Prairie Junction. Like a chemical spill. That's the story out of the governor's office—that's how they're explaining the National Guard deployment, the roadblocks, the NBC gear."

"They're covering it up?"

"Quite effectively. The weather and Prairie Junction's natural isolation is helping. This story hasn't reached headline status yet. Just footnote reporting."

"That's hard to believe."

"Well, it's true. And heads will roll for it, believe me. But before we pin blame we've got to get control of the leak."

A dull chill ran up my spine. I wasn't sure why—it was spontaneous. It was something about the way Evelyn said the word *leak.* The natural undercurrent of sinister focus in her tone. Maybe a hint of fear.

"What do you mean by *leak?*" I said.

Evelyn met my gaze. She didn't blink.

"What do you know about gain-of-function research?"

29

"Assume nothing."

It was my gut reaction to her question. I had heard the term *gain of function* before, and had some vague idea what it meant, but with two and a half hours left on our drive, I figured we had time for Evelyn to give me a crash course.

"Okay, well...it's kind of like biological war gaming. In the Army, did you ever imagine scenarios where the enemy acquired a bigger, more destructive weapon? Like...a bigger bomb. Or a nerve agent."

"Sure. All the time."

"Gain of function research is the scientific version of that. The enemy is the disease—any disease. Smallpox, influenza variants...whatever."

"Okay..."

"Gain-of-function research is all about asking the question—*What would happen if the disease mutated into something stronger?* Specifically, something we don't yet understand how to combat, or treat."

"Just like the Army," I said. "You establish a scenario, then craft a response."

"Right. At least, that's the idea. But the problem is, there's no way to predict a virus's mutation on paper alone. You have to...well. Arm the enemy."

I squinted. "You mean—"

"Deliberately mutate the disease," she said. "Deliberately make it stronger—more potent. Give it a special attribute, or *function*, that we're not yet able to control. Then we can study the effects and develop better medications and vaccines, just in case we ever need them. That's what gain of function is all about."

I considered. I already had a terrible idea where this story was headed.

"That sounds dangerous," I said.

"It is. Very dangerous, and also controversial. All it takes is one mistake, and a heavily armed, viral enemy that we don't yet understand leaks into society. In the blink of an eye we could be facing a pandemic of cataclysmic proportions."

And that's what happened here.

The reality of what I had faced in Prairie Junction hit me like a fist to the gut, hard enough to silence the emotional discomfort and awkwardness I experienced when Evelyn first appeared outside my window. I saw it plainly. I connected the dots.

I *did not* like the picture.

"What's the facility?" I said. "What did Taggert uncover?"

Evelyn's hands tightened around the wheel. "It's a lab—specifically, a Biosafety Level Three research facility operated by the private corporation Coleus Biotech. They're a government contractor paired with the National Institute of Health, mostly studying obscure, innocuous diseases."

"But?" I pressed. I knew there was a but coming.

"But I did some digging while I was waiting for my plane. Made some phone calls." She glanced toward me. "The lab was upgraded to Biosafety Level Three status only six months ago. They were granted authority to perform advanced gain-of-function research."

There it is.

The tingle in my spine turned to a dull chill despite the heated seats. I sat back, remembering Ms. Molly, the overbearing application of National Guardsmen in Prairie Junction, the secrecy, and the panic.

It all made sense...and yet none of it made sense. What about Taggert's murder? The nondescript security contractors posing as guardsmen and state police? If there had been a leak, why on earth had the CDC not been notified? Why was the lab in the woods so concealed, so unmarked?

I'd lived in Prairie Junction for three months. I knew almost everybody. I understood the simplicities of the local economy. A major medical research facility had *never* been mentioned.

"They're killing people," I said. "They killed Taggert and they wanted to kill me—likely for the same reason. They're hiding something. Everybody is hiding something, not just from the locals but from the country. From people like *you*."

I poked a finger at the ID badge.

"I know," Evelyn said simply.

"You gotta call somebody. Your bosses—the White House. Somebody who can bust through the fog and get to the truth. If this thing is even half as serious as—"

"Why do you think I'm here?" Evelyn's voice snapped with sudden strain. "I *know* how serious this is better than anyone. And I've already made calls. I rang every phone off the hook at our headquarters in Atlanta. It's the middle of the night. Most officers are off work. We'll get things moving, but I shouldn't have to tell you what an absolute bog a government agency can be. They move in slow motion, even during an emergency."

"And in the meantime?"

"In the meantime, they're going to answer to me," Evelyn said. "And you're going to be there to make sure I don't get shot in the head."

30

I passed most of the next two hours in near silence. Evelyn was on and off phone calls, mostly speaking to her headquarters in Atlanta, or the secondary office in Washington DC where she apparently worked. The tone of her voice carried an undercurrent of authority that left me thinking she had advanced quite a way up the chain of command since our last meeting.

That didn't surprise me. Between the buzzes and the hangovers, the dancing and the dream-state late nights, I recalled her sharing aspirations of transferring out of the field and into the administrative offices of the WHO or the CDC, where the "real decisions were made."

"They need somebody with practical experience," she said. "Somebody who actually understands the impact of these policies on the ground."

I remembered the comment, because it reflected an opinion that myself and my fellow Rangers often shared. We had plenty of experience with highly educated but practically ignorant bureaucrats in ivory towers who made decisions without concern for the wisdom of the men and women in the trenches. Those being shot at. Those treating viral outbreaks in the jungles of Africa.

People like Evelyn.

Mashing a button on the LCD screen, Evelyn hung up with somebody from Washington and shook her head in disgust. She ran one hand through her hair and I couldn't help but watch her out of the corner of my eye. I noted the vague trace of silver near her temples—an intrusion I'd recognized in my own hair over the past couple of years.

It looked a lot better on her than it looked on me.

"No luck?" I asked.

"They're moving," she said. "Just very slowly. Whoever is bottling this thing up has done one heck of a job. Nobody actually believes there's a problem."

"They haven't contacted the lab directly?"

A snort. "They *tried*. They're getting an answering machine—closed for weather. Apparently, there's a blizzard coming."

"They're not closed," I said. "At least, they weren't a few hours ago. The security cameras displayed plenty of action."

"That's why we're going to knock on the front door."

I grunted. Sucked my teeth. Evelyn glanced sideways.

"Is that a problem?"

"Not for me," I said. "And not for you."

"That's all I'm concerned about."

She took an exit off the highway. We were on two-lanes now, reaching Prairie Junction's outskirts. A half a mile ahead I marked the same roadblock that I had circumvented with the help of a repurposed camp stove. Two FMTVs parked across the road with a pair of Humvees filling the gap between their noses. This time, they weren't budging.

I opened my mouth. Evelyn held up a hand. "Leave this to me."

She reached for the badge.

NOBODY ARGUED with Evelyn's ID card. They made some radio calls. They demanded my ID, and when they read my name on the Arizona driver's license some predictable consternation resulted.

In the end they agreed to let us through. LTC Hughes wanted Evelyn to report to city hall. She took our IDs back and wound her window up. The FMTV backed off the road. A Humvee pulled out to lead the way.

Evelyn mashed the gas and raced right past the much slower military vehicle, fading quickly into the darkness. Not headed for city hall, but for the Coleus Biotech laboratory. The Humvee flashed its lights but was quickly lost in the darkness. Evelyn drove with both hands on the wheel, blazing around the outskirts of town.

"They're gonna resent that," I said.

A soft snort. "I'll blame it on you."

I glanced to the LCD display. The GPS mounted into the Toyota's dash was still operating from satellite signal alone. Our destination was only nine minutes away, and the miles passed a lot quicker under the nimble SUV than they had beneath my truck.

"Listen," I said. "I'll need you to stay close. You can't allow them to pull you into a room without me."

She glanced sideways. There was no defiance in her gaze. No fear, either.

"Are you armed?" she asked.

"Yes, but they'll have metal detectors. I won't be able to get inside with a weapon. Not unless you brought me a fancy government ID."

It was a joke—another lame attempt at humor that fell flat. We rode in silence until the turnoff, passing the stretch of shoulder where I'd parked the GMC during my incursion only seven hours prior. The light snow shower had ceased, and the tire ruts left by my truck were still visible. But despite the stillness of the frozen winter air, the Toyota's headlights reflected off low-hanging, dark clouds with every bounce over the rough road.

Not a single star was visible. The dead stalks of corn protruding through the blanket of snow in every endless field didn't so much as flinch under a winter breeze. I'd only been in Iowa a few months, but I knew the signs. A blizzard was indeed coming.

We reached the turnoff. Evelyn slowed to a near stop. I twisted in the seat and drew the H&K, press-checking to ensure a round was chambered and ready. Evelyn saw the move and tensed. Her mouth fell open.

I cut her short. "They killed a man. They would have killed me. If I give you the word, you duck behind that wheel and don't get up for anything. Okay?"

No answer. The first hint of uncertainty compromised the focus in her gaze.

"Okay?" I repeated.

A brief nod. I concealed the H&K between the door and my right leg, out of sight but still held in my steady right hand. Evelyn turned off the two-lane and onto the drive. The Toyota's tires churned through the snow. We passed into the trees and this time I did notice the cameras—multiple units mounted on steel poles, not the least bit concealed. All focused on the road.

"Slow," I said.

Evelyn eased back on the accelerator. I swept the surrounding trees, looking southward toward the point on the fence where I'd set the fire. I couldn't see anything—it was too dark. I momentarily considered whether any of the guards had recognized me during my incursion, but I didn't think so. Not unless I had missed a camera inside the guardhouse that might have recorded my face.

The two guys who had attempted to murder me in the government sedan weren't available as witnesses. Taggert's killer and his accompanying thugs had never seen me.

Yet there was still the possibility that my face, perhaps copied from my driver's license file, had been broadcast among these thugs after I escaped the arena. They'd come looking for me by name at Jeter's house, after all. The fact that they'd disabled the cell towers and internet lines proved that whoever I was dealing with, they weren't short on resources or influence.

The first interaction at the guardhouse would tell the story, and I decided I was ready to roll those dice. But as it turned out, we never got that far. The headlights of the Toyota spilled over the gate and the guardhouse, security LEDs glaring down from tall posts, those little yellow signs warning of electrocution.

And then Evelyn stepped on the brakes, because jogging out of the guardhouse was one of the security detail. Dressed in the same white bio suit as before, but not wearing a hood or mask. Grasping an M4A1 rifle with his right hand, holding his left hand toward the Toyota in a clear *"stop"* motion.

I glanced right. I glanced left. Just outside of the pool of

security lights I detected movement in both directions—
shooters in the forest, covering the vehicle. We'd only just
arrived, and already they had us pinned.

The H&K pressed next to my thigh might as well have
been a soda straw and a spit wad.

"Your bosses know you're here?" I asked.

A short nod from Evelyn.

"Good," I said. "Here we go."

The Toyota rolled to a stop and the guy standing in front
of us lowered his hand. He held the rifle in low-ready. He
glared through the darkness.

Then he approached the driver's window.

31

"Ma'am, we need you to turn around. This is a secure area."

The speaker with the rifle wasn't a face I recognized, but his bearing and general disposition was the same as Taggert's murder team's. Ex-military, definitely. Maybe special operations, or maybe post-military trained in the art of advanced security tactics. All the indicators were there: The way he held himself, the way he stood back from the vehicle with the rifle only a twitch away from dumping bullets into the door panel. His gear wasn't standard infantry gear, it was pro gear. A Glock 19 with a Trijicon RMR red-dot sight. A Benchmade Infidel clipped to his chest rig above three magazines for the AR, all secured by quick-detach elastic bands.

There was even a CAT tourniquet strapped to his left leg, a sure sign of somebody who understood the real dangers of close-quarter combat.

"I need to speak with your commanding officer," Evelyn said, unfazed. "Immediately."

She produced her badge, flipping it out for the guard's inspection. His gaze passed over it and something behind his eyes flashed. But he didn't approach, and he didn't reach for the ID. Instead he bent to look beneath the roof line. He stared at me.

And he *didn't* ask who I was.

Stepping two paces back, the guy dipped his head toward the radio mounted on his shoulder and spoke into it. I couldn't make out the words. I couldn't make out the response, either—he wore an earpiece.

Then he approached again.

"Ma'am, you have to turn around. This area is secured. Please consult the National Guard command post in Prairie Junction for further questions."

Something in Evelyn's back turned rigid. It was a subtle movement, a barely detectable flinch, as though her spinal cord had turned to steel. I recognized the signal from Djibouti, from that tenth-floor room in the Atlanta Hotel when my gut-shot of a joke didn't land.

I wouldn't have taken a million dollars to stand in that guard's boots.

"You listen very carefully," Evenly said, her usually melodic voice reduced to a monotone knife edge. "You get back inside that shack and you get your boss on the phone. You tell him that an assistant director with the CDC regulations division is on-site, and I *will* be allowed entry, or you can all punch your tickets to grand jury trials. Am I clear?"

The guard hesitated only a moment longer. I noticed him glancing over the hood of the SUV, farther into the trees to my right. I thought I knew why—the fire team leader was out there, probably lying behind a precision rifle, calling the shots in more ways than one.

"One moment," the guy growled. He turned for the guard house.

I watched him go, my gaze flicking into the impenetrable shadows as I calculated the angles. We were sitting ducks at the gate. If Taggert's murderers wanted to bloody their hands a second time, all they would require was the briefest twitch of two trigger fingers.

But no—they wouldn't shoot. They couldn't afford to. I could tell by the guard's strained face as he spoke to his boss on a telephone. When he reappeared at the Toyota's window, I correctly guessed his announcement.

"You see that Humvee?" The guard pointed through the gate as the tail lights of the military vehicle flashed to life. Evelyn nodded.

"Stay right on his bumper. Do not divert for any reason. He'll take you to the director."

The director.

I checked my watch. It was well past midnight, and yet "the director", whoever that might be, was in their office and willing to meet with Evelyn.

Why? *Because they need to know what she knows.*

Evelyn rolled the window up. The guard returned to the guardhouse, his hard face fixed on us as he mashed the gate button. The twin steel barricades swung back and I glanced again to the shadows. Then to the Humvee.

"Here's what happens next," I said. "They'll take us to the facility. They'll stay right on us for the entire visit. You'll jump through some security hoops and meet the director. They won't show you anything."

"They won't have to," Evelyn said. "I know what questions to ask. We'll be at the bottom of this thing inside of five minutes."

Right. Because they'll tell the truth.

I thought it, I didn't say it. Evelyn already understood the situation. She drove up a long, pencil-straight drive between tall, snow-covered hardwoods. The Humvee led the way, diesel fumes pouring from its tailpipe. I noted security cameras staring down from tall steel poles, bright orange lights lining our path, keeping us fully illuminated.

And then I saw the facility—Taggert's compound. It sat far enough back from the gate to be invisible behind the trees, but when the forest finally parted, the resulting property was larger than it had appeared on satellite imagery. The sprawling parking lot was there, covered in white like everything else. The complex itself stood three floors high, blocky and white with strips of dark glass windows—like a seventies office structure, only this place looked no older than a few years.

There was no sign. No flag poles planted out front. No pavilion or portico. Just a pair of heavy, windowless doors framed by polished steel, a short walkway connecting the entrance to the parking lot. The Humvee pulled just beyond the doors and stopped. I glanced right, sweeping the ground floor. The only thing visible was a cluster of simple white block letters—the only indicator of what organization lay beyond those doors.

COLEUS BIOTECH — LAB 04.

Evelyn shifted into park. I watched as another white-suited contractor departed the Humvee with a rifle held across his chest. He stared over the top of an N-95 mask—not looking at Evelyn. Looking at me.

I stared right back, not blinking.

"No matter what happens, they *do not* separate us." I faced Evelyn. "If I give a shout, you hit the deck. Immediately. Understand?"

A trace of uncertainty crossed Evelyn's brilliant eyes, but she didn't argue. She simply unbuckled her seatbelt. I followed suit, slipping the H&K out of my waistband and sliding it beneath the seat alongside my Victorinox.

I wanted to keep both items, but the metal detectors I had predicted wouldn't allow it. Either weapon might give the security force a reason to cancel Evelyn's visit—or attempt to separate us. If things turned sideways, I would simply have to improvise.

We stepped into the bitter cold. The guard led us to the door, tugging two additional N-95 masks out of his cargo pocket before allowing entry.

"Wear these."

It wasn't a request. We donned the masks. The guard turned to the door and nodded once to an invisible camera. A lock buzzed. He pushed through.

It was warmer inside—but not much. Bleak, hospital-style floors stretched out beyond a row of horseshoe metal detectors. Half a dozen additional contractors were on-site, all dressed the same, in white bio suits and N-95 masks.

Like that's going to do any good, I thought.

If Evelyn was right about this place—if a supercharged strain of some unthinkably evil virus had leaked—we were all dead men walking.

We submitted to the security check. Evelyn was stripped of a metal pen and two hair clips from her purse. My Streamlight MacroStream, which wasn't a weapon but was made of metal, was taken also. They scanned our IDs at a computer.

Nobody said a word, and throughout the entire process at least two men stood back with rifles at the ready—their gazes fixed not on Evelyn, but on me.

I stared right back, comfortable with the discomfort. They knew who I was, all right. In that way, they had me at an advantage. But I didn't need to know *who* they were to know exactly *what* they were.

The hallway beyond the security checkpoint was sterile, adding to the hospital vibe. Continued white floors, white walls, and metal doors secured by electronic locks. At the end we reached an elevator. Our escort flashed a key card and the doors rolled open. He selected the third floor.

Executive level.

We rode up in silence. At the third floor the white tile was replaced by carpet—cheap, industrial carpet, but an indicator of the office floor nonetheless. The lights dimmed, less harsh than the hallway below. Our escort led us through a lobby occupied by cheap waiting room furniture. We reached a final entrance—twin glass panels tinted pitch black. No identifying name plate.

He scanned a card once more. The lock buzzed. We made eye contact, and I saw the warning in his face.

I simply shoved past him, stepping into a wide executive office with windows overlooking the winter wonderland parking lot outside. A pair of couches faced a coffee table. A row of bookshelves were laden with thick, boring-looking medical books. There was just one desk, wide and polished, bare save for a computer. Behind it sat a single man, rail thin and taller than I was. Bald-headed. Clad in an immaculate business suit and an N-95 mask. He rose from the chair like an apparition, looking first to me, then to Evelyn. Finally to our escort.

A long moment passed. Then a short nod from the man in the suit. Our escort retreated into the lobby. The glass doors closed.

Then the rail-thin man approached. When he spoke his voice carried just a hint of a German accent—long subdued by years of life in America.

"Welcome, Dr. Landry. I'm so glad you've come."

32

D r. Simon Müller—I assumed his identity based on the nameplate resting on the desk—did not extend a hand. He simply ducked his head, body bending like a very skinny blade of grass in the wind, and motioned to the pair of chairs in front of his desk.

Evelyn helped herself to a seat. I remained standing just a beat longer than was necessary, locking eyes with Müller. Transmitting a silent threat.

Then I sat, draping one leg across the other, hands folded in my lap. Content to let Evelyn take the lead.

"This isn't a social call, Dr. Müller. I'm here to find out just what the hell is happening at your lab, and why my agency hasn't been notified."

Evelyn's voice cut like a scalpel. Müller didn't so much as blink as he settled into his chair, most of his face concealed behind the mask. There was something...*off* about him. Something odd. I thought it was his nearly colorless eyes, at first.

Then I noticed that his baldness extended beneath his

scalp. He had no eyebrows—no eyelashes. His skin was pale. He looked like he hadn't set foot outside in decades.

"Forgive me, Dr. Landry—"

"*Assistant Director*," Evelyn corrected him. "AD, if you like."

Smart woman. I almost smiled. I kept my gaze frozen on Müller instead.

"Of course," Müller said. "My mistake. I was only just informed of your unannounced visit. I must say I am surprised. The CDC usually notifies us in advance."

"This isn't a regular inspection, Doctor, and you know it. What happened? And why wasn't the CDC informed?"

Müller seemed to stall. I wondered if he was going to deny it.

How could he? It was the middle of the night and here he was at his office, surrounded by bio-suited bodyguards and a town under full martial law. This hesitation wasn't a stall for denial, but a stall for calculated confession.

"I do apologize, Madam Assistant Director. The situation is quite fluid. I gave directions for my own AD to notify your office... I suppose that courtesy must have been lost in the shuffle."

"Notifying government regulators of a potentially catastrophic lab leak isn't a courtesy, Doctor. It's mandated by federal law."

"Lab leak?" Müller squinted in feigned confusion. I didn't buy it for a second. "Who said anything about a lab leak?"

"Don't be coy with me," Evelyn said. "At least one woman is dead, and others are reported sick."

"Dead? Where?"

"In *Prairie Junction*."

More produced confusion. Müller shook his head.

"Madam AD, I don't know what to tell you. There's been no lab leak here. All our research materials are completely secure."

"Is that right? So why the martial law? Why the lockdown?"

"In Prairie Junction?"

"In the *entire county*."

Müller shrugged. "I really couldn't tell you. I read on the news that there was an environmental disaster...potentially something to do with the nuclear plant. The governor issued the order for martial law—that's why I'm here, in fact. I elected to remain at this facility for the duration of the crisis, just in case I was needed. During a time of emergency, I'm sure you can understand how crucial proper leadership can be."

Unbelievable. I almost wanted to laugh.

"Director Müller, may I remind you that lying to a federal regulator is also a crime," Evelyn said.

The director snorted. He leaned back and folded his arms. "Please don't insult me. I take the security of the work we perform at this facility as seriously as anyone. I can assure you, whatever crisis the governor and the National Guard are managing, we know nothing of it."

"If that's the case," I said, joining the conversation for the first time, "then why are the National Guard performing nasal swab tests? Why are all their men dressed in full bio hazard gear? Why is there a dead woman with all the symptoms of a violent viral illness? Why did *your men* drag an innocent civilian out of town and execute him?"

My tone sizzled with anger. I glared at Müller until he

had no choice but to blink. He folded his arms, twitching a little but not looking away.

"You must be Mr. Sharpe," he said, voice cold.

I said nothing.

"My security personnel ran a background check on you. Seems you've been stirring up quite the fuss in Prairie Junction...what with your baseless accusations and rampaging behavior."

I wasn't amused, but I did smile. "Oh you can bank on it, Mr. Müller. I haven't even *started* rampaging. How about you answer my questions?"

Müller folded his arms. He grunted. "My grandfather served in the war. *Zweiter Weltkrieg,* we call it. He wasn't a Nazi...just a simple machinist swept up in a tidal wave of madness."

I didn't answer. Müller leaned forward, inspecting me as though I were a lab rat, or a dot of liquid under a microscope.

"I have long been fascinated with the psychological fallout of the battlefield. It interests me so much, I almost surrendered my career in biology to pursue it. Alas, in this brave new world the dollar is the ultimate dictator. There is so little money in psychology. Still, I maintain a personal interest. I can only imagine what horrors you must have seen in Afghanistan, Mr. Sharpe. In...*Africa.* The sorts of things that keep you awake at night, no doubt."

My jaw tightened. "I'm not the only one awake in the middle of the night, jackass."

A tilt of his head. "No. I suppose you're not."

The room fell silent. Evelyn tensed. I felt her at my elbow. I knew she was about to speak—but Müller spoke first, and this time I knew he was smiling behind his mask. I could see it in the cold crinkle around his eyes.

"Was it worse in Phoenix, Mr. Sharpe? Did she really die in your arms?"

I exploded out of the chair. Müller followed me, Evelyn only a split second behind. I was already circling the desk as the director shouted to the door.

"*Security!*"

The door exploded open just as my right hand closed around Müller's throat. I rammed him straight past his spinning desk chair, across the industrial carpet and against those heavily tinted plate glass windows. He was tall but he wasn't heavy. I powered him onto his toes with ease, not stopping until his shoulder blades collided with the window.

Müller choked. The guard behind me shouted. Evelyn called my name.

I tuned it all out. I ripped my mask off with my free hand, then I ripped Müller's away. I leaned close, snarling into his face.

"You wanna play games, Director? Let's play. I've got all kinds of lessons I can teach you in psychology."

Müller's eyes bulged. Behind me, boots pounded the ground. A rifle barrel swept over my shoulder, the muzzle zeroed on my skull. Outside the office additional voices shouted. More boots thumped through the door.

"Drop him!" the guard shouted.

I ignored him. I stared deep into Müller's eyes.

"You can't lie your way out of this mess. I know what you've done. And you better believe, before I'm finished, the world will know just as much."

I squeezed. Müller choked, his wide, eyelash-less eyes bulging.

"*Drop him!*"

I released the director just as heavy hands closed over my shoulders. Multiple men yanked me back. Müller fell. I didn't fight as they threw me against the desk, wrenched my hands behind my back and secured them with zip cuffs.

"*Mason!*" Evelyn's voice finally broke through the fog. One of the guards planted my face into the desktop. A radio crackled.

But I remained perfectly calm, no longer feeling any need to fight back. Whether or not Müller was smart enough to believe me, I'd made him a promise.

My rampaging behavior was just getting started.

33

They frog-marched me back to the waiting Toyota, Evelyn following behind and demanding that I be released while the guards—and Müller—flatly ignored her. In the bitter cold the guard from the metal detectors closed behind my back, his rank breath flooding my nostrils as he spoke only inches from my ear.

"Thanks for the visit, Mr. Sharpe." He snapped a knife open and slashed the zip cuffs. "Don't come back."

The plastic cuffs dropped from my wrists. At the door Evelyn was still shouting threats. Nobody cared.

"I want my flashlight," I said.

"What?"

"At the metal detectors. You're holding my property."

He snorted. He tugged his mask aside with one finger and spat into the snow. Then he shouted over his shoulder, and one of his guys brought my MacroStream along with Evelyn's pen and hair clips. She stomped around the nose of the Toyota, red-faced as she mashed the key fob. We both got in. We both slammed our doors. The engine purred to life as the Humvee ahead of us started with a chugging growl.

Neither of us spoke until we were back on the two-lane, windshield wipers thumping against a gathering snowfall. Then Evelyn broke the silence with an enraged shout.

"What was that?"

I relaxed into my seat, gently massaging my wrist where the zip ties had bit into my flesh. I glanced into my rearview mirror.

I saw nothing but blank highway—for now.

"Mason!" Her knuckles turned white around the wheel. Her face was still bright crimson. "Are you out of your mind? You just committed assault!"

"So let him call the cops," I said. "The local chief is a drinking buddy. I'm sure he'd be fascinated by the story I have to tell."

Evelyn spun on me, her jaw locked. She breathed a curse, and I knew she wasn't cursing at me.

What had transpired at the lab wasn't what she expected, but it was exactly what I expected. I'd traveled this road many times before. I knew the director would deflect, shift on his feet, and bog Evelyn down with bureaucratic denial. His knowledge of my military background and personal history wasn't surprising, either. Anyone could Google my name and find that news story printed by *The Arizona Republic*. Anyone could know that Mia had died in my arms. A wise man would have known better than to throw that fact in my face.

But even when Müller did, I could have taken the barb without blinking. I *chose* to launch myself out of that chair. I *wanted* him to know just how crazy I could be.

It was the quickest way to alter the status quo. To get the sludge moving—and uncover the truth.

"...I swear, the moment I get my boss on the phone they're gonna sweep down on Müller's ass like hawks." I realized Evelyn was talking again and I broke my gaze away from the rearview mirror. I glanced left to find her practically fuming behind the wheel, boiling like a volcano ready to erupt.

"We'll shut the entire place down," Evelyn said. "I'll drag him out in handcuffs if half of what we suspect is true."

I wanted to laugh but I respected Evelyn too much to audibly mock her. Her naivete wasn't born of stupidity, but a simple lack of experience beyond the outer bands of law and order.

"So call your bosses," I said. "Deploy the cavalry."

Evelyn reached for her phone. She glanced once at the screen. Dropped it.

"No signal," I said. "They've shut down all the cell towers around here. All the internet, too. Every form of communication. They don't want *anyone* talking about what's happening inside this county, and thanks to the National Guard and the weather, they're getting their wish."

"You can't honestly believe they control the National Guard—"

"They don't need to. They only need to control the governor, which is very believable. A trunk full of campaign cash would do the job. I haven't the first inkling what's really going on here, but you can bet that lab is at the heart of it, and you can bet that *something* we know is a threat. That's why Müller met with us. It's why he met with *me*. He needed to know what we knew—and who we told."

"And now?" Evelyn said.

I looked into the rearview mirror. The snowfall was rapidly thickening. Joined by howling wind and decreasing visibility, the forecasted blizzard was underway. In another twenty or thirty minutes the roads might no longer be drivable.

And yet I could see the pair of headlights—distant behind us. Easy to miss in the swirling snow and passing streetlights, but I didn't miss them. Neither did I misunderstand them.

And now they'll try to kill us, I thought. *They'll run us into the woods and leave our bodies buried in the snow.*

Or at least...they would try.

"And now we go to ground," I said, answering Evelyn's question. "We buy time and get through the weather. Then we find a working phone or internet service and contact your people. We rain fire and brimstone on these thugs."

Evelyn was already shaking her head before I even finished the sentence. "No. No, we get back to Prairie Junction now. Find the National Guard command. They'll have satellite phones."

We'll never make it there.

I was looking into the rearview mirror again. Even as the swirling snowfall thickened, the lights drew closer—just close enough to remain visible through the gathering storm, which meant we were also visible to them.

It was a tail, all right. Not a Humvee. Something lighter and faster, able to wrangle the icy roads. My gaze switched to the Toyota's GPS display, and I reverse-pinched two fingers across the screen to reveal a map of the area. Prairie Junction and the questionable safe haven of city hall still ten or more miles distant...but between us and downtown lay another option. A much better one.

"Stop the car," I said.

"What?"

"Put on the brakes." I reached beneath the seat and found the H&K. "Do it."

Evelyn hit the brakes. The Toyota slid to a stop, briefly breaking traction on the slick roads. It was all-wheel drive with quality, all-weather tires but those tires lacked snow chains. I hit the locks and reached for the door handle.

"Switch seats. Move now."

Outside the Toyota the wind blasted my face, so strong it knocked me backward against the side of the SUV. I caught myself and dug my toes in. Evelyn shouted. I shut the door and pulled myself to the back of the vehicle using the empty roof rack as a handrail. I stared into the snow-clogged darkness and noted the headlights, flicking suddenly dark two hundred yards down the road.

I flipped the pistol in my left hand, grabbing it by the slide. Clutching it with one numb, burning hand.

Then I smashed the butt of the gun into the Toyota's passenger side tail light, hard enough to shatter the plastic and the LED bulb behind. I repeated the blow, busting the second bulb. The tail light went dark, and I hurried to the driver's side of the vehicle. I bashed a second time. The fully loaded magazine worked like a battering ram, the pistol's butt smashing straight through the tinted plastic.

Then I was headed for the driver's door, piling in and slamming it. I dumped the gun into the console and shifted into drive. I mashed the gas, easy at first and gathering speed as the tires regained traction. The wind pounded our windows, the windshield wipers beating at full speed but failing to displace the fog of snow. It was a full-blown blizzard now, drifts of snow piling on the road and obscuring the view ahead. I didn't need to be an expert in winter weather to know that we had zero chance of making it back to Prairie Junction—we'd be doing good to make it half that far.

"What are you doing?" Evelyn demanded. "Are you out of your mind? This is a rental!"

"They're following us," I said flatly, looking into the rearview mirror. I still thought I saw the flicker of headlights a hundred yards back, but the swirl of whitened darkness was growing too thick to be sure. I mashed the gas, pushing us up to forty miles per hour. It felt like suicidal speed amid the driving wind, but I needed the distance.

There was a turn coming—two miles. If we could make it that far...

"Why are they following us?" Evelyn's voice grew taut. She looked over one shoulder. I pushed her back into her seat with my free arm.

"Because we're the only ones who know—and if they can tie up the loose ends they have a prayer of surviving this mess. Fasten your seatbelt!"

The angry flush of Evelyn's cheeks faded to a chalky white as she struggled with the belt. I put both hands on the wheel and counter-steered as the next gust of wind drove us sideways through a turn. Visibility faded to barely twenty yards, my high beams reflecting off the swirling snow like a wall of white. I switched to low beams and used the GPS to map each turn. Plowing deeper into the county. Guiding the SUV to the middle of the road and leaning low beneath the windshield to mark the path ahead.

A collision with an oncoming vehicle could be catastrophic, but sliding off the road into a snow-filled ditch would end this escape before it began.

"How far to town?" Evelyn said.

"We'll never make it to town. There's a spot closer. Hold on!"

I mashed the gas to power through a turn. The hybrid engine surged. I checked the mirror again and now saw nothing but blackness. Our headlights played across a reflective stop sign and I swung into the left turn early, ready for the Toyota to slide. It did, but the all-wheel drive helped to keep us on the blacktop. We cruised down another arrow-straight Iowa county road, bumping over double-yellow line reflectors buried beneath the snow.

It was pitch black, and the crosswind now became an alternating tail wind that struck us from one corner and then the other, pushing us toward the ditch. At one gust we slid fully five feet, and Evelyn shouted. She clutched the A-pillar grip, eyes wide as I wrestled us back toward the middle of the road.

How much farther? I didn't know. I couldn't pinpoint my exact destination on the GPS map. I couldn't recall the address—I'd only ever been to my destination one time.

I needed landmarks, but leaning low beneath the windshield and looking ahead, I couldn't see a thing. Just darkness and blasting snow, wind beating on the SUV as the drifts grew taller around the wheels. We were lurching along, slipping a little at regular intervals.

The Toyota was losing traction. The snow was thickening, packing out the tire treads and compromising traction. When it reached the axles we would be stranded.

I took a risk and floored the accelerator. The Toyota spun up to fifty miles per hour. Evelyn called my name but I didn't answer. My heart thumped and I stared ahead.

Another mile. Get me another mile.

The GPS screen was lagging, the satellite signal obscured

by the storm. I marked our distance traveled by the odometer, checking the dash-mounted compass to confirm direction. I knew we were in the right vicinity. I knew we were close.

But in weather like this a matter of yards, not miles, could be the difference between life and death. The Toyota's exterior thermometer read negative fifteen degrees. At that temperature I estimated that we would last only a couple of hours after the engine choked off. We'd last even less if we became lost in the woods.

"Mason! There's a curve—"

I saw it coming as a flash of yellow warning signs and pulled the wheel. The Toyota hurtled on, the front bumper plowing through a drift of snow. I felt us sliding again, losing traction. I tapped the brakes to bleed off speed. My wheels were cut hard to the right, but we weren't turning. We plowed ahead, straight for one of the warning signs. The brakes locked and the ABS failed to engage. I released the pedal then pumped it again. Our back end swung wide.

Then we hit the edge of the road. I felt it as the driver's side tires skipped onto the shoulder. We leaned and I wrenched the wheels desperately to the left to avoid a roll. It was too late—just enough speed and momentum remained to rock us into a gentle tumble. We swung slowly left, striking a road sign. The metal post folded. Then we landed into a snow drift with an explosion of white and the driver's side window shattered. My shoulder struck the door pillar and the breath exploded out of my lungs. The engine coughed, then choked out as an emergency message played across the LCD screen.

*WRECK DETECTED — DIALING EMERGENCY
SERVICES.*

I didn't wait for the call to fail. I clawed my way out of my
seat belt and caught the H&K as it fell across my lap. Evelyn
hung above me, choking on her seatbelt and clawing at the
release. She couldn't it get free.

"Stay still!" I said. "I'll get you!"

My Victorinox lay on the upturned side of the console. I
drove my foot into the inside of the driver's door, powering
up out of my seat. I snapped the blade open and slashed
Evelyn's belt. She fell out with a grunt, landing in my arms.

Her body was light in my grasp, the sweet fragrance of
vanilla and lilac shampoo filling my nostrils as her head
crashed against my chest.

"Find your feet," I said. "We escape through the back
hatch."

"Mason!" Evelyn choked. "We can't go out there. It's
freez—"

"We'll freeze if we stay! There's a place not far from here.
Come on!"

I pushed Evelyn between the front captain's chairs. I
folded the knife closed and jammed the H&K into my coat
pocket. Then I was following her over the back seat, into the
cramped rear cargo hold where her luggage lay upturned
against the windows.

"Stand back!"

I rolled the closed knife in my hand. I slammed the butt
of it into the rear glass—once, twice. The pane shattered on
the third blow, little cubes of glass sticking to a thick layer of
sagging tint. I used my coat sleeve to clear the mess away,

continuing to smash as a bitter blast of deathly air exploded through the gap.

Snow swirled around my face. I choked on the burn of the cold, so frigid that it turned the moisture on my lips to instant ice.

"Come on!"

I grasped Evelyn by the hand. I ducked through the hole, my coat shielding me from the remaining glass shards. She wriggled out behind me and we fell into the ditch—snow rising up to my waist.

I struggled back to my feet and exchanged the Victorinox for the MacroStream, flicking it to full power. I scanned the emptiness around me but couldn't even see the road—I only saw white. Wading ahead, the drifts grew a little shallower as we departed the ditch and reached the blacktop. Evelyn choked and struggled behind me. I curled my left arm and shouted over my shoulder.

"Get on my back! *Quick!*"

Evelyn didn't argue. She stuck her leg through my curled arm and reached over my shoulder to pull herself onto my back. Then we were off, powering up onto the road. I turned instinctively out of the wind, the MacroStream clamped in my teeth as my ears burned with the cold. I saw the turn. I waded ahead at a sloppy half-jog, fighting for every step. Praying for one more. Evelyn clung close, face pressed into the rough exterior of my coat.

I made it through the turn. I looked up into the pitch-black sky, sweeping the trees with the MacroStream clamped in my mouth.

And then I saw it—a red blink. A distant light, mounted high above an abandoned feed mill, there to protect low-flying planes from accidental collision.

A beacon of salvation.

34

We made it to Taggert's bunker without a moment to spare. Fighting through waist-deep snow drifts, I circled his house and found the abandoned Isuzu Trooper first, then retraced the path to the upturned satellite dish by memory. It was nearly buried under the blanket of frozen precipitation. I fell over it before I actually saw it. I dropped Evelyn and struck my knees.

I got it open with the aid of the hydraulic cylinders mounted beneath it. I guided Evelyn ahead, down the steps and into the entrance shaft. I pulled the dish back to the ground with the dangling tether rope, blocking out the howl of the wind as I slumped to the floor, gasping for breath.

I couldn't feel my face. I couldn't feel my fingers. Every breath triggered ice picks of pain in my lungs, so sharp they felt like they were slicing straight into my spine.

On the concrete next to me Evelyn huddled, still shivering as she clutched herself. Her nose was beet red, her hair frozen stiff. She looked a little like a cartoon character stumbling out of a deep freezer. It was almost enough to make me laugh at the both of us.

Almost.

I pulled myself to my feet and reached out a hand. "Come on. Let's get you warm."

The lights inside Taggert's bunker still ran. Within seconds I had the gas heating system cranked up, pumping hot air into the living room bus as I guided Evelyn to a couch. She collapsed, still holding herself. I found blankets in a wall locker—one of them was electric. I plugged it in and wrapped it around her shoulders, settling onto the couch next to her. Evelyn leaned into me, resting her head on my chest and bunching her body into a ball beneath my arm.

I stiffened, momentarily awkward. Then I pulled her close. I held her and we both melted into the electric blanket for a long twenty minutes, only coming back to life by degrees—one Fahrenheit bubble at a time—while the blizzard above us hummed like a distant ceiling fan. Barely audible. A dying memory.

The ice on my nose melted. My lungs defrosted. I breathed a little more easily, and Evelyn's body relaxed. After a long time she lifted her head. She swallowed and swept her surroundings, seeming to examine the bunker for the first time.

"Where...where are we?" she whispered.

"His house," I said simply.

"Whose house?"

I looked down into her green eyes, bloodshot and dry from the biting wind.

I said, "The man they murdered."

I MADE coffee while Evelyn remained on the couch, still shivering in random little shudders but looking a little more alive by the second. The snow had melted out of her hair, leaving her face shining with what looked like sweat. She took the coffee with eager hands and buried her face in the mug, slurping long and slow. She squinted. Wiped her mouth and looked up.

"Honey?"

I smiled. "I remembered."

Evelyn looked away and set the cup on the coffee table. I sipped my own coffee, bitter and black, then looked over my shoulder toward the bunker entrance.

I'd locked the door of the hallway bus. By now, the upturned satellite dish should be completely covered in snow. Our footprints would be erased, concealing our path even if the wrecked Toyota was discovered.

And still, I couldn't quite relax. Not just yet.

"I'll be back."

I departed the living quarters and headed for Taggert's office. Once past the bathhouse, I stopped at the gun rack and set my coffee down. I didn't reach for an AR-15 this time, opting for a Zastava PAP M90 Serbian-built AK-74 instead. I wanted something that would punch hard, straight through ice, metal...and even light body armor.

Taggert had equipped the rifle with a two-point sling, spray-painting the barrel, receiver, and redwood furniture a mottled pattern of brown and white, perfect for the snowy conditions outside. He'd mounted an optic rail, also, using the M90's built-in receiver rail mount. An Aimpoint PRO rode the rail—a decent red-dot optic, and judging simply by the immaculate conditioning of the rifle, I took a risk and assumed the optic to be zeroed.

The magazine was loaded. I racked a round into the chamber, set the safety, and drew a spare magazine from the shelf beneath the rifle rack. Only then did I turn for the U-shaped desks.

The ham radio hummed to life with a click of the power switch. The light flashed. I adjusted the dial, holding the headset to my ear to listen for a clear signal.

Nothing—only a lot of static. I tilted my head back and imagined the radio antenna towering high above the bunker. It could be frozen over by now, or broken by the wind.

So we were without communication, then. It was bad news, but considering our heavily concealed, heavily armed and weather-safe position, I was content to count my blessings. I closed my eyes and breathed a prayer of gratitude, then returned to the living room bus where Evelyn's gaze immediately caught on the rifle.

"Where did that come from?"

I jabbed a thumb over my shoulder. "Gun room. I checked the radio...no good. We're snowed in."

Evelyn made no comment. I leaned the rifle against the wall and went to work in the kitchenette, opening fresh cans of soup and slicing apples for a side. Evelyn sat on the couch and simply watched as I worked. My gaze traveled to the record player and I wanted to turn it on, but somehow the noise felt intrusive.

Maybe the gentle rush of the wind several feet above was ambiance enough.

Setting a bowl for each of us on the coffee table, I popped an apple slice into my mouth and went to the fridge to see what Taggert kept in the way of beverages. Not to my surprise, the collection was entirely alcoholic. I selected a pair of beers and returned to my seat. Setting the food down, I found myself ducking my head out of habit—a relatively new habit.

Another prayer of thanks. It was good to be alive.

"You pray?" Evelyn's voice was gentle, the bowl of soup cooling in her lap. I looked up, a steaming spoon halfway to my lips.

"I do. Why?"

She shrugged. "I don't remember that."

Our gazes locked and held. Something deep in my gut twisted. Not pain—not sorrow. Maybe just a little awkwardness.

I lowered the spoon and sat back on the couch. I sipped beer. Evelyn didn't seem to have an appetite either.

"It's been a long six years," I said at last.

A nod. "Yeah. It has."

She fiddled with her spoon. I set the beer down, resting my forearms on my knees.

"I'm sorry, Evelyn."

"About what?"

"About Djibouti. About the way things ended. You deserved a lot better."

To my surprise, Evelyn smiled. Just a little.

"I did," she said. "But in your defense...it *was* booty in Djibouti."

She shrugged awkwardly, bashful gaze avoiding mine, one thumbnail picking at her beer bottle. I somehow sensed that the ball was back in my court.

Was she waiting for an extended apology? Perhaps for me to better explain myself?

No. We were grown adults. We were well beyond that.

So I cut loose with a low whistle, shaking my head in admiration. "Yes, it *was*," I said.

Evelyn flushed. For a split second, I thought I'd miscalculated. Then she laughed—a hearty, melodic sound that began in her gut and filled the room. Warmer than the hot air pouring through the heat pump vents.

"You're such an asshole." She flipped me off. I lifted my beer. We both chugged.

And the awkwardness melted like snow under the sun.

"I really should have thanked you," Evelyn said, relaxing into her couch. "Settling down would have killed my career. I left Djibouti and got in with the CDC. Continued my studies and really advanced in virology. A change was just what I needed."

"I guess you returned to the States?" I asked.

"Yeah. Atlanta, for a while. CDC headquarters. When I took the assistant director job they sent me to DC. Been there ever since. Bought a little condo...got a cat."

She chuckled, a little more self-consciously than before. I simply sat, not the least bit judgmental of the simple life. In more ways than one, it was a lot more stable than my own.

"What about you?" Evelyn said. "You got out, I take it."

I grunted. "Yeah. Not long after Djibouti."

"And then?" It was a simple question, but the look in her eyes left me thinking it might be loaded. Evelyn had heard every word Müller said at the lab—that barb about Mia. I knew she had to be curious.

"I went back to Phoenix," I said. "Became a cop. Advanced to detective."

She nodded. Didn't comment. I felt the gap in my story hanging over us both, and I set down my beer with a sigh.

"Her name was Mia. She was a school teacher."

Evelyn said nothing. I swallowed, my throat turning dry. I realized it had been months—maybe a lot longer—since I recounted this story.

"She...uh. She was killed," I said. "School shooting. Senseless thing."

I swigged beer, using the raised bottle as an excuse to brush my cheek. I hoped she didn't notice.

"I'm so sorry," Evelyn whispered. "I'm sure she was amazing."

I looked up, somehow caught off guard by the tenderness in her tone.

"She was," I said. "She really was."

Evelyn smiled. The moment lingered. I shook myself out of it.

"So...did you...?" I trailed off. Evelyn didn't leave me hanging.

"Oh, yeah. A guy from Atlanta. We also met in a bar, actually. A juice bar." She laughed, but there wasn't much humor in her tone. "He was a big-time runner—fanatical about health stuff, hence the juices. He would never have a beer, but...I don't know. He made me laugh. It was good. We got married, actually."

I tensed, glancing to her left hand even though I already knew there wasn't a ring. Evelyn caught me looking and flicked her hand, chugging beer.

"You know what they say about runners?" she said.

"What's that?"

"They get around."

She laughed. I joined in, even though I didn't much feel it.

"I'm sorry," I said.

She shrugged. "I should have seen it coming. Lesson learned, I guess."

Her gaze drifted away, but mine didn't. I looked across the room and the woman I saw felt braver than most of the Rangers I'd charged into battle with. The absolute lack of bitterness in her voice, the open forgiveness was astounding. It was superhuman.

I thought I recognized it.

"You pray too, don't you?" I said.

Evelyn smiled, and this time the warmth reached her eyes. Just a little.

"All the time."

She lifted her beer. Our bottles touched with a soft clink. We both sat back and drank in silence for twenty minutes.

It had been years since I'd felt so not alone.

35

It was the smell that woke me. So faint I thought it was a part of my dream, but as my eyes flickered open I knew it couldn't be.

I'd been dreaming of Djibouti. Of a sunrise beach, the haze of a hangover still clouding my mind as I walked along the shoreline, hand in hand with Evelyn.

There was no gas in that memory—no acrid smell of propane. But when I inhaled again the odor was impossible to miss. It flowed through the bunkhouse bus, vaguely sour on my tongue. Just a hint at first, yet growing stronger.

I rolled upright on the bunk, automatically planting my feet into my boots. My gear remained in my pockets, the AK-74 leaned against the bed next to me. I didn't reach for the light switch—I palmed my Streamlight instead, sweeping the beam toward the half-open door at the end of the bus.

I couldn't actually *see* the gas—it was colorless. But I could see the displaced dust on the floor, pushed aside by a current rushing through the doorway.

"Evelyn!" I called, whipping the beam toward the bunk

across from me. It fell across her face as she squinted, recoiling beneath her blanket. I hurried across the aisle. I shook her shoulder.

"Evelyn! Wake up!"

Her eyes opened. She rolled her head. "What—"

"Shh!" I held a finger to my face. "Get dressed. We've got to move."

Evelyn blinked the sleep away. I moved to the door, leaning out and shining my light down the hall.

The smell of propane was stronger—noticeably so. I pointed the light toward the kitchen, recalling the gas stove. I didn't think the smell was flowing from the kitchen. My gut warned me of a different story.

Regardless, the next step would be the same.

I looked back to find Evelyn zipping up her coat, feet planted in the same winter dress boots she'd worn since Des Moines. Her nose wrinkled, and I knew she smelled it also. Panic crossed her face.

"Stay calm," I said. "We're headed out. Stay close and breathe normal. It's heavier than air—it'll sink to the floor first."

Evelyn nodded. I led the way out of the bunkhouse, the rifle held at my side, its spare magazine jammed into my Carhartt coat pocket. With every step toward the hallway bus, the smell grew stronger. We passed the kitchen and I noted that the door was closed—Evelyn must have shut it, meaning that the gas was unlikely to be coming from the stove. We passed beneath the primary ventilation shaft—the one connecting to that vent box beneath the Isuzu Trooper —and a rush of icy stickiness cascaded down my neck.

I looked up. I sniffed once. Then I reached for Evelyn.

"*Move!*"

I found her hand and pulled her into the hallway. We rushed past the shoe racks, past the photographs. I accelerated to a run, all the way to the door that led into the concrete entrance tunnel. I hit the latch and shoved it open —the hinges were frozen; they resisted. We barged through as the subtle hiss grew louder behind me, the smell so strong I wanted to choke.

In the concrete tunnel the temperature dropped eighty degrees in the blink of an eye. I gasped on sub-zero air and kicked the door closed. I could still smell propane. I rushed up the steps into the blackness beneath the upturned satellite dish, Evelyn's hand still grasped in mine. I held the rifle beneath my arm and pressed my shoulder against the underside of the dish.

It wouldn't move—it was laden with God only knew how many inches of fresh snow. I released Evelyn's hand and advanced up the steps, placing my shoulder against it. I pressed again, that stench of the gas growing stronger by the millisecond.

The satellite dish shifted, then groaned upward an inch under the combined strength of the twin hydraulic cylinders and my own muscle. Early morning sunlight leaked through the gap, and I advanced another step up the concrete stairs, leaning low. Putting my back into it, leveraging every log-rolling, lumber-tossing muscle I'd developed while working with Paul.

Snow crunched. Ice cracked. The cylinders shifted another inch. I bunched my legs and forced upward, giving it everything I had.

The dish lifted, exploding out of the snow with a rush of bitter air and a brighter flash of sunlight. I rocketed upward like a mushroom popping out of the ground, almost falling. I caught myself on the edge of the tunnel. I reached back for Evelyn, heart hammering.

"Come on!"

She caught my hand. We exploded upward, rolling out from underneath the half-open dish and landing in a field of powdery fresh snow, nothing but cold and bright white closing around us on all sides.

Then a sickening rush. A moment of pure silence. A flash of heat.

And the gas went off like an atom bomb.

36

The blast was so strong it blew the satellite dish right off its hydraulic lift mechanism, blasting the fiberglass in two as it shot thirty feet into the sky. A column of fire exploded from the mouth of the bunker entrance, instantly melting the snow on every side and singeing my face.

I wriggled backward, dragging Evelyn with me as the blaze quickly receded, the initial surge of gas consumed by a fire now starving for oxygen. Rolling onto my stomach I clawed for the rifle, instinctively knowing what I would find in the open lot behind Taggert's decoy home.

I wasn't wrong. The vehicle was a RAM three-quarter-ton pickup, jet black, sporting a bull bar and elevated suspension. The four men gathered outside of it all wore white winter camouflage, rifles held across chest rigs loaded with spare magazines and armor plates. They were more of the security contractors from the Coleus facility, and there was no time to wonder how they had traced us here. Whether they located the wrecked Toyota and spread out to search the surrounding countryside, or whether they had located Taggert's property records and simply guessed as to where we might hide—it didn't matter.

The exploding satellite dish entrance had caught their attention. Their gazes—and their rifles—swept toward it. Toward *me*.

And straight into my line of fire.

I smacked the AK's selector lever off *safe* and clamped down on the trigger, delivering a string of white-hot gunfire ripping across the snow. The first guy fell with a bloodcurdling scream, taking one bullet to his hip and another to his gut, just beneath his plate carrier. Crimson sprayed the snow as his three buddies broke for cover, sprinting into the trees.

I rolled to my feet, finding Evelyn huddled in the snow, her jacket smoldering from a slow burn. Grabbing her arm I yanked her up and broke for the sheltered end of the decoy house. Gunshots cracked behind us—a mix of AR-15 rifles and the pop of a single handgun, likely from the guy I'd gut-shot. We reached the end of the house with bullets slicing the air just over our heads—a deathly whine that kicked my battlefield instincts into overdrive.

"Are you hurt?" I shouted.

Evelyn slid to her knees at the base of the house, flinching as the next stream of gunfire sent pulverized brick blasting over our position.

"Evelyn!" I kneeled beside her, grabbing her shoulder. I shook her and she looked up, eyes wide.

"Are you okay?" My voice softened despite the gunfire. She blinked hard, breathing too fast. She swallowed. Then nodded.

"I...I think so."

I reached into my coat pocket, producing the H&K USP. I pressed it into her hand.

"Do you know how to use this?"

Another hesitation. "Not really."

"It's easy. Just point and pull the trigger. Keep pulling until the threat goes down. Okay?"

"Wait. Where are you going?"

"To draw them away." I returned to my feet, rocking out the AK magazine to check the load. I wasn't sure how many rounds I had fired—maybe six?

I ratcheted the magazine back into place and offered Evelyn a reassuring smile.

"Stay calm," I said. "I'll be back."

Then I pulled the rifle into my shoulder. I turned for the corner of the house and listened to the near-perfect silence of a pause in the gunfire—only broken by the groans of the wounded guy lying between the bunker entrance and the RAM pickup.

Here goes nothing.

I lurched out from behind the house, starting into the forest as an immediate storm of gunfire unloaded on my position. Bullets whistled over my head and zipped into hardwood tree trunks. Branches snapped and snow rained over my shoulders. I slid into cover behind a large hickory and breathed easily, rifle at the ready. My brain worked like a sonar system, mapping the source of each burst of gunfire. Tracing them to their individual points of cover or concealment, spread in a semi-circle around the still-burning entrance of the bunker.

I stole a glance and noticed that the parked Isuzu Trooper—no doubt the point of entry for both the gas and the flame that ignited it—was also burning. The first man who caught my eye was the wounded gunman now propped against the front wheel of the RAM. He sat in a pool of blood, his lap saturated with more of the same as he managed a SIG P320 pistol with a trembling right hand.

An easy target, but not worth giving away my position. He would bleed out in another two or three minutes.

I swept the forest, regulating each breath. Three men were spread somewhere amid the frozen trees. I looked for footprints or blood trails but saw nothing. I leaned a little farther from behind the hickory.

The next burst of gunfire nearly took my head off. It exploded from a thicket of brush caked with ice and snow, fifty yards into the forest behind the burning Isuzu. I tracked the position with my AK as I fell into a crouch, and then I engaged. A stream of five rounds exploded from the snow-camoed rifle, ripping through the brush and turning the AR's muzzle flash to ashen blackness with another scream.

Not waiting to see if he would pop back up, I executed on an opportunity to obtain better cover, sprinting through a crackle of gunfire off my right shoulder and from directly ahead. My lungs burned, my fingers numb around the rifle's grip. With each stride the healing gunshot wound in my left thigh burned, sending throbbing pain into my own pelvis. Bullets zipped through the trees and I slid around a corner, mapping the first starburst I found and dumping my magazine. One steel casing after another spat from the AK's ejection port, raining across the snow as I leveraged my new firing position against an exposed enemy. It wasn't the guy I'd shot behind the brush—this was Survivor Number Two, and a spray of blood against red oak trunks and the exposure of a limp arm in the snow confirmed his death.

I dumped the magazine and reached for my reload,

sliding back into cover. From the thicket where I'd engaged Survivor Number One a low groan broke the frozen stillness —a cry for help.

But Survivor Number Three didn't answer. I scanned the forest, reviewing my mental sonar map. Hadn't Number Three fired from my twelve o'clock position? Maybe one o'clock, but I saw no sign of him. All was still, horrifically empty and hauntingly quiet.

I shouldered the AK, its fresh magazine locked and loaded. *Thirty rounds.* More than enough to finish off Survivor Number One and send Survivor Number Three hurtling into eternity...

But first I had to find him.

Dropping into a low crouch, I identified a gap in the brush between my current tree and the next hardwood. It offered a more or less clear line of fire from my former twelve o'clock position. I breathed deep and weighed the odds of locating my enemy versus the risk of being shot.

I thought of Evelyn hiding at the end of the house, helpless save for a weapon she wasn't trained to use. The decision was easy—I had to flush him out.

Launching out from behind the hickory, I sprinted for my selected birch tree with everything I had in me, crossing the channel of death in the blink of an eye. Sure enough, halfway there, the fire rained in—but not from the direction I had predicted. The bullets whizzed in from my *new* twelve o'clock position, my former nine o'clock position. The channel of death I was sprinting across was no longer my chief concern—now I was running straight into the gunfire, forcing me to slide behind the birch tree instead of circling it. Bullets chewed off the bark and sent shards zipping into my neck while alarm bells clanged in my brain.

Exposed! You're exposed!

It was Survivor Number One—the one I had winged behind that thicket covered with ice and snow. His position lay forty yards behind me, and while I was confident that he couldn't actually see me thanks to the cover of snowy brush, my position still left me vulnerable to his raking gunfire. I rolled to the snow and brought my rifle to bear just as he joined the fight, shaky and unaimed shots ripping over my head and slamming into the birch.

My sights aligned. I opened fire on him again, emptying half the mag and shredding the brush as snow cascaded down.

His rifle fell silent. A river of blood streamed out over the snow. I worked my way back to my feet, careful not to expose myself to my lone remaining enemy.

But when I circled the birch, rifle up, and swept the trees I found nothing. He had faded into the forest again, a white-and-brown blob in a world of white and brown.

Now it was cat and mouse.

37

I moved left—out of the forest, back toward the house. It may or may not have been the tactically ideal move, but given Evelyn's position it was my only choice. Drawing the fight toward her was dangerous but offering my enemy a chance to get between us was potentially mortal.

Crossing over my former path, I mapped a trail of blood and looked down to find my left hand coated in crimson. I rolled it and exposed a clean palm—it was a cut on the back of my hand, maybe from a bullet, maybe from the brush. I ignored it and swept the yard behind the decoy house.

Flames from the bunker entrance had dissipated. The Isuzu still burned. My gun sites settled over the wounded guy leaned against the RAM's front wheel, but there was no need to fire.

He was dead, bled out just as I expected.

I lowered my body closer to the ground. As I crept along, my legs postholed as deep as twelve inches with each stride. The snow now appeared like the landscape of a war zone,

with rifle casings, blood, and footprints scattered everywhere. I looked to the corner of the house where I'd left
Evelyn, but I couldn't see her. I pivoted toward my enemy's
last known position, but I couldn't see him either. There was
too much brush clogging the forest floor.

Maneuver, Sharpe. Get on top of him!

I escalated my pace, slogging through the snow from
cover to cover, always sweeping the trees. Behind me the
Isuzu crackled, but the air in front of me was so perfectly
still I thought I would have heard a chipmunk sneeze. I
chased shadows with the muzzle of the AK, mapping out
every irregularity in the forest. Any shape or feature that
defied the natural patterns of nature. I orbited the half-moon
perimeter of the yard behind the decoy house and glanced
left to check on Evelyn a second time. I could now see her.
She was dug in behind the house's AC unit, the H&K
clutched in both hands.

Then the gunfire resumed in a flash of thunder, erupting
from a point in the forest thirty yards ahead at my two
o'clock position. Bullets zipped past my face as I lunged for
shelter behind another hickory tree, this time not bothering
to slide to my knees but keeping the rifle up. I wheeled
around the tree and returned fire, three quick shots into the
shadows. Muzzle flash responded and the hickory's bark
exploded into my face. I departed cover and raced left, firing
again toward the starburst. Closing the distance. Forcing him
to pivot right—the most awkward angle for a right-handed
shooter to swing quickly.

Hopefully he was right-handed.

The zip and whine of hot lead whistled past my legs.
One round tore my jeans and may have sliced flesh. I

couldn't feel it in the mix of bitter cold and surging adrenaline. I had already cut the distance between us in half, dancing through a thicket of saplings as small dead limbs rained over my head. I spun behind the next tree, and then I drew a bead on him. He was dug in behind a rotting log, shrouded by thick underbrush and squeezing off shots even as he scrambled to trace my trajectory. His muzzle pivoted. I aimed and fired, sending four more rounds ripping through the brush.

He rolled right—and only just in time. Dirt and snow exploded from my gunfire. I lost sight of him behind a pair of red oaks. I ran—bolting for the spot, swinging left to cut him off before he reached his feet. I fired again, spraying that side of the tree. The AK hammered, and I remembered I was running low on ammunition. Half a dozen shots, not more. And then—

It didn't matter. The stun grenade came rocketing out from between the trees only a moment before it clapped like thunder. I saw it coming and had just enough time to duck before the blinding white light erased my vision. My ears rang and I stumbled back. I kept firing, spraying the trees. The AK thunked over an empty chamber.

Then I saw him, lunging out from between the trees with his rifle held by the hand guard like a club. Also out of ammo, it seemed. I saw the weapon arcing toward me and I ducked. I swung the hardwood stock upward, aiming to strike him in the ribcage. I missed, dizziness overcoming me as my body fought to regain equilibrium. I lunged again, one leg sinking into an invisible hole beneath the blanket of snow. He slammed his rifle butt into my shoulder and I toppled, hurtling sideways into the snow. It closed around me like laser-cut foam in a firearm case. My head struck the dirt, breath exploded from my lungs. I clawed at the rifle, fighting to bring it around. To use the sharp, angled muzzle break as a spear.

He pivoted over me, thumbing the elastic retention strap on his chest rig. Drawing a magazine. Rotating his rifle to slam it into the receiver. It played out in slow motion and I saw his face—it was the face of a Coleus Biotech guard. A mask of ugliness, cloaked in a bloodthirsty sneer.

I lunged with the AK, bursting off the ground in one final, desperate attempt to bring him down. To get on top. To extend the fight.

And then his face disappeared in a spray of blood, jawbone and then cheekbone simply evaporating right before my eyes. Even as I reached my feet the gunshots rained in at a rate approaching full auto. They zipped into trees and one of them glanced off his chest rig. Another struck his shoulder. A third slammed into the hand guard of the AK that I thrust like a lance. I hit the deck again as the shots kept coming. Taggert's murderer fell to his knees, blood running from his face like a waterfall. I saw it with my head rocked sideways, ear pressed into the snow. Ten, twelve shots. The gun smoke was thick in my nostrils. The shooter collapsed right onto my body, blood and battle gear sinking into the snow.

I tasted his sweat and choked, gasping for air. The gunshots fell silent. I bunched my arms and shoved, pushing the corpse upward and to the side. Clawing my way out of the snow and spitting blood.

Evelyn stood ten feet to my left, eyes as wide as silver dollars, the H&K shaking like a leaf in her clutched hands, its slide locked back over an empty magazine. She looked to the body and her mouth fell open. The gun fell from her hands and she stumbled back. She didn't make a sound.

I pulled myself off the ground and caught her as she started to sway. Tears filled her eyes and I pulled her close.

She didn't say a thing. She just dry-heaved, and I held her.

38

I placed Evelyn in the passenger seat of the RAM pickup while I scavenged the battlefield. The vehicle had survived the firefight without a scratch, sustaining only minor blood spray from one of the earlier casualties. I moved from body to body, stripping away every firearm, every magazine of ammunition, any useful tactical gear and —most importantly—all forms of communication and identification.

I collected three AR-15s in total, all chambered in the ubiquitous 5.56 with twelve-point-five-inch barrels. The guy who'd bled out had carried a breaching shotgun. They all carried sidearms—two P320s and two Glock 17s. There were knives, binoculars, combat gloves.

I stacked everything in the rear seat of the RAM, where I also found bottled water, beef jerky, and a tool bag—likely the tool bag they had used to reroute raw propane from Taggert's fuel tank into his ventilation shaft.

It was a nifty little scheme—a supersized version of my trick with the camp stove and the propane cylinders. Having survived the death trap, I couldn't deny being somewhat professionally impressed by it. Taggert's bunker was history, cooked from the inside out.

I shut the rear door and found Evelyn seated sideways in the front passenger seat, the door standing open, her feet resting on the running board. She'd found a package of cigarettes and was busy dragging on one. The butts of two others lay in the snow beneath her.

"You still smoke?" Evelyn's voice trembled as she exhaled a cloud of gray, her gaze fixed on the ground.

"No," I said.

"Me neither." Evelyn's hand shook as she inhaled another deep drag. I couldn't be sure in the biting cold, but I thought the pale of her face was turning a little green. I placed a gentle hand on her arm. She didn't look up. She looked out at the woods, staring at nothing, and shook her head.

"I've worked in a half dozen war zones. But never...never done that."

"It hits us all differently," I said. "You did the right thing."

A slow nod. A swallow. One more drag on the smoke. "I know."

I cast a glance over my shoulder, back toward the battlefield, and then into the sky. It was early morning, the sky broken by scattered clouds. I guessed that we must have slept no longer than six hours. The blizzard had blown through, but the sunlight brought very little warmth. It was still brutally cold—and we were still relatively exposed.

The bad guys had found us once. They could find us again. We needed to move.

"You see any keys?" I asked.

Evelyn jabbed a thumb over her shoulder. "In the console."

"Good. Let's roll."

I got the truck started and found it already locked into four-wheel drive. The giant Hemi diesel chugged, the tires crushing through snow as I backed away from Taggert's bunker, allowing the dead mercenary to fall from the pickup's front wheel.

I didn't look back—I didn't regret what I had done. The bodies would still be there, frozen stiff, whenever the authorities finally got to the bottom of this thing. In the meantime, we needed to navigate away from the action before reinforcements arrived—*if* they arrived.

The question all hung on how desperate Müller—or whoever stood at the top of this evil pyramid—might be. His willingness to send a heavily armed hit squad out into the woods to murder two sleeping nobodies was indicative of ample desperation.

"What now?" Evelyn's voice had calmed a bit. She abandoned the cigarette pack in the pickup's console and stared dead ahead as I wrestled the RAM to the end of Taggert's drive. It was no easy chore—the snow was nearly two feet deep in places. The heavy tires spun.

Luckily, the truck was built from the factory for rugged conditions, and the elevated aftermarket suspension certainly didn't hurt. At the end of the driveway I found the intersecting county road completely obscured by pure white drifts. I stepped on the brakes and looked both ways, breathing deep.

And considering the core question: *Why?*

It was the fulcrum of this entire screwed-up situation. Clearly, there had been some manner of biological leak from the Coleus facility. There was no other rational way to explain the sudden outbreak of a rare virus so close to a research center dedicated to studying that very virus. It was basic logic.

So the question remained—*why?* Why were Müller and his team of gunfighters so hell-bent on erasing anyone and everyone who wanted to pin the blame on them? A leak might shut them down, sure. It might terminate their contract. It might result in civil liability and congressional hearings.

But it wouldn't result in jail time—not like charges of homicide would. And yet the team of white-suited contractors so willing to pose as National Guardsmen or Iowa State Patrol, happy to shoot a man in the head or cook a pair of sleeping witnesses like holiday chickens, seemed perfectly willing to risk such eventualities. They seemed *eager* to kill—aggressive in their methods.

Almost as though their backs were against a wall...or *somebody's* back was, anyway. The boss's, perhaps. Müller's. Or Müller's boss's.

So what then? What was I missing?

I looked to Evelyn. She waited expectantly for an answer, still appearing a little shaken but coming around just like I knew she would. She was a professional, a veteran of some of the world's worst hellholes.

She knew how to handle this. The iron was returning to her bloodstream even as our gazes locked.

"Food," I said. "We start with food."

"And then?"

My hands tightened around the leather-wrapped steering wheel. "And then we're going to rip this thing apart limb from limb."

39

I was no longer worried about roadblocks. My plan was to remain well inside them. Once we hit the pavement the RAM ran well, barging through the snow at forty miles per hour while I kept an eye on the engine temperature gauge just to make sure we didn't blow any gaskets.

The roads were now familiar. The visibility excellent, in contrast to the night prior. I turned away from the Coleus Biotech lab, turned away from downtown Prairie Junction, and headed way out into the fields, mapping each turn by memory, tracking the strips of reliable blacktop by the gentle dips of the ditches on either side of them.

None of the roads had been plowed. None seemed to have been traversed, either. We barged ahead through a desolate wasteland of white so perfectly still, so totally natural that if I'd tried, I probably could have tricked my mind into expecting herds of buffalo, maybe hunted by bands of Sioux warriors on horseback, exploding over the horizon at any moment.

It was peaceful. It was vacant. It was the edge of the

world until I finally turned a corner and spotted a yellow dot on the far side of a sweeping field, growing gradually brighter as we drew nearer, until a full farmhouse was visible. Two stories tall, late nineteenth century in vintage, complete with a windmill and a barn and a chicken coop.

Across the road sat a giant metal building—a sawmill, with heaps of logs stacked on every side. Paul Schroder's little patch of the prairie.

"What's this?" Trepidation underscored Evelyn's voice. I held up a calming hand.

"It's a friend."

We made it only halfway up the driveway before my "friend" appeared on his front porch, a double-barrel shotgun swinging into his shoulder as he shouted something unintelligible. Evelyn screamed and ducked beneath the dash. I laid on the brakes, snow exploding onto the RAM's hood. Wrenching the door open, I popped out on the running board, waving a hand.

"Paul! Put the gun down—it's Mason!"

From the front porch Paul leaned forward, squinting beneath his felt hat. He lowered the gun a little. From the second floor of his farmhouse a small red head poked out of an open window, flashing a toothy grin. One of Paul's six offspring.

"Mason?" Paul challenged.

"Right!"

"What are you driving?"

"Long story. Look, can we come in?"

Paul seemed to regain his senses. The double-barrel dropped. He beckoned on. "Yeah, yeah. Get up here! Breakfast's almost ready."

I dropped back into the RAM to find Evelyn still

crouched beneath the dash. She shot me an accusatory look. I could only shrug.

"It's been a rough few days around here."

I parked the truck behind the house, well out of sight of the road. Evelyn remained sheltered behind the vehicle until Paul appeared on the back porch, the shotgun now gone, a corn-cob pipe poking from the corner of his mouth.

"They told me they locked you up!" he called. "What happened?"

I repeated my earlier dismissal. "Long story, Paul."

"Who's your lady friend?"

I turned to Evelyn, offering a reassuring nod. She circled the nose of the RAM, seeming to collect herself.

"Evelyn Landry," she said, forcing a smile. I noticed that she dropped the *doctor* from her name, and I thought I knew why. Under the circumstances, the honorific might trigger too many questions.

Paul grunted, "Pleasure," ducking his head. He blew a cloud of gray, his hardened Iowa face seemingly unperturbed by the brutal cold. Then one of his kids shouted about pancakes from beyond the screen door, and Paul snapped back to the present.

"Right. Well, you guys come on in. I hope you're hungry —we got plenty."

PAUL MAY NOT HAVE EXPECTED company, but his wife Judy had certainly cooked enough food to feed guests. Crowded around his picnic-style dining room table, I rubbed elbows with a grubby-faced six-year-old dressed in hand-me-down overalls, a pair of blond-headed twelve-year-old twins seated across from me and chattering endlessly about the newest album from the hottest new pop artist.

Nobody seemed the least surprised—or put out—by our unexpected arrival. Judy served fresh pancakes, thick-sliced bacon, hash browns, and as much milk as anyone wanted to drink. Paul sat at the head of the table, kicked back with a coffee mug in one hand, randomly shouting at a kid who was throwing food, or tousling the head of another eager to report on the latest episode of his favorite Disney show.

It was chaos, the kids bubbling over with energy, but there was a lot of warmth around that table—a lot of love. I packed down a stack of pancakes layered with bacon and maple syrup, the survival euphoria once again coursing through my body and unleashing ravenous hunger. Evelyn was initially caught off guard by the boisterous new environment, but quickly adapted. She'd experienced crowded family homes before, all across the world. Pretty soon she was chattering with the kids and devouring her own meal.

It made me happy watching her—the shine of her eyes, the returning warmth in her cheeks. With each bite she looked a little more alive, a little more invigorated. A little more like herself.

"Do you work for my daddy?"

The kid sitting across from me couldn't have been older than four, strands of brown hair hanging down into his eyes, face smeared with syrup. He stared at me through wide brown eyes stolen directly from his mother, a blue plastic spoon clutched in one hand.

"I do," I said.

"My daddy says the logs at his work are big enough to smash a man like a bug. You ever get smashed?"

I laughed, pushing my plate back. "Not so far."

"You ever seen a man smashed?"

I hesitated, thoughts of the bloodshed at Taggert's place rushing through my mind. I forced a smile.

"No, buddy. Your daddy keeps us safe."

That seemed to satisfy him. He returned to his potatoes, and I glanced down the length of the table and found Paul watching me. He tilted his head toward the door, and I nodded.

"You ruffians clean up, now!" Paul barked. "Simon Says in twenty minutes—don't be late!"

The kids giggled and scrambled for the dishes. I rose from the table and thanked Judy for the meal. I brought my coffee mug as Evelyn shot me a silent question.

"Give me five," I mouthed. She nodded and resumed her one-sided conversation with a barefoot two-year-old who hadn't stopped blabbing in ten minutes.

Paul led me into a living room at the front of the house, closing a pair of glass doors to isolate the noise. The place featured multiple armchairs, a bank of windows overlooking the front yard, and more books than many school libraries. They lined heavy oak shelves, floor to ceiling, old volumes and new. There wasn't a TV—only a coffee table holding a humidor.

Paul withdrew a can of pipe tobacco and offered me the spare pipe resting on a shelf. I politely declined. The smell of Evelyn's cigarettes back at Taggert's place had awakened long-dormant cravings. Pipe tobacco isn't the same, but I didn't want to play with fire.

Paul sat. He sparked up his pipe and puffed a few clouds, clicking the stem against his teeth. He sipped coffee. Then he faced me.

"What's happening, Mason? I went to town yesterday

and they got that place locked down like Fort Knox—won't let nobody go nowhere. The telephone lines have been down for two days. School has been canceled all week. I tried riding out to Waterloo and got turned back at gunpoint. Them Army guys got the roads sealed off!"

"I know," I said.

Paul cocked an eyebrow. I evaluated, sipping my own coffee. It wasn't a question of whether I could trust Paul—I knew I could. Explicitly.

I was simply still unpacking the problem for myself.

"There's been a medical emergency," I said. "I'm still working out the details. Your family is safe, but you need to keep them here. Don't go back into town until you get the all-clear from the authorities."

A snort. "Authorities? More like *bullies*. I tried to see Jeter. They've got him bottled up."

"Yeah. I'm working on it."

Paul dragged on the pipe. Blew through his teeth. "And the lady?"

I hesitated only a moment longer. "She's helping. She's a doctor."

Paul thumped ash from his pipe. He swirled his coffee, seeming to suddenly relax. No more questions—he was a simple guy. He looked after his family and took life one day at a time.

I'd always enjoyed that about Paul.

"Well, you just tell me what you need. You're welcome to stay here as long as you like."

I thanked him. I looked into my mug, picturing the dead men back at Taggert's bunker. Müller's icy eyes as he spat one lie after another back at the compound. Ms. Molly's swollen face. The swarms of troops converging on Prairie

Junction, the authorities from someplace deep in the stratosphere pulling strings and peddling lies.

An environmental emergency? No. Not hardly. So what was I missing? What could Müller, or his bosses, possibly be protecting?

The answer was just out of reach. I could feel it, but with each strain of my exhausted mind, I came up short. There were still too many gaps in the puzzle...and I knew where I needed to go to fill them.

"Actually, Paul. Do you have a map?"

40

The explosive cheers and rampant giggles rising from the family room at the commencement of a Simon Says tournament filtered through the glass doors as Evelyn and I gathered around the coffee table, shifting the humidor aside and spreading out Paul's yellowed map of the county. The date printed in the corner read 1987. The paper was crinkled with age, worn and heavily marked by pencil and various illegible notes.

But the details were all there. Prairie Junction, its expansive city limits spreading way out into the county. I held a sharpened pencil, kneeling next to the table and pointing to a spot northwest of town, deep in a patch of forest.

"This is Taggert's place," I said. I moved the pencil northwest. "And this is the lab—here, on the northern edge of the forest."

Evelyn leaned close. I traced the pencil in a wide circle around Prairie Junction, sketching a pair of little X's. The first lay at the intersection I had breached on my way to Ms.

Molly's, the day this mess began. The second lay at the road-block I had evaded using the camping stove bomb.

I wasn't aware of any other roadblocks, but I could guess. Drawing little circles, I mapped out a perimeter all the way around down, each hypothetical roadblock situated at a key intersection. Cutting Prairie Junction off from the world.

"The X's mark the known roadblocks," I said. "They're all situated between twelve and fifteen miles outside the city, encompassing the forest and the lab. If we assume the pattern is repeated, these roadblocks would continue around the southern side of town...like this."

I marked again, tracing circles this time. Evelyn followed my logic and nodded.

"Okay...so..."

I looked up. "So it doesn't make sense. Not given what we know."

Evelyn squinted. I tapped the map.

"This isn't a quarantine barricade, it's a tactical military barricade. Exactly what I would do if I wanted to lock down an entire city using trucks and ground troops. You secure the intersections, you seize the heart of town, and you *kill* communication. All of it. The internet, the phones, the smoke signals. You silence the populace and control the flow of information."

"They're resisting a panic," Evelyn said.

I shook my head. "Put yourself in their shoes, Evelyn. Pretend this was Africa, and you're in charge of containing an outbreak. Do you restrict the flow of the population? Certainly. But the flow of *information?* The flow of *communication?* No way. You need all the communication you can get. You need to know as much as possible—you need everyone to know as much as possible. It's your only lifeline."

Evelyn chewed her lip. She studied the map. I set the pencil down.

"They're not containing, Evelyn. They're concealing. They're barricading the media and preventing anyone who lives here from leaking information to the outside world. They're weaponizing the National Guard not as a safety mechanism, but a *control* mechanism. Now we have to ask *why.*"

She looked up. "You still think it was a lab leak?"

"I think it started with a lab leak. Whatever disease killed Ms. Molly undoubtedly traces back to the Coleus facility. But it's got to be bigger than that. Those guys in the forest today —the guys at the bunker. They came there to erase us. To silence us, the same way they silenced Taggert. Cold-blooded murder, without a second thought. There's only one rational reason a company—a large, American company operating in the heart of the civilized world—would resort to madness that extreme."

"There's a deeper secret," Evelyn said. "Something really ugly."

I nodded. "Something worse than an accident, and some-body a lot more powerful than Müller who's trying to cover it up. We're talking about a *really* big fish, the kind of player who could weaponize the National Guard and pull the plug on local cell towers and internet providers."

"A politician?" Evelyn arched both eyebrows. I gave a noncommittal tilt with my head.

"Maybe. Most of the power in this country actually lies with the bureaucrats. All the three-letter agencies and the lifers who run them. We won't know for sure until we dig deeper, and to do that—" I extended the pencil, circling that spot in the forest northwest of Taggert's bunker, "—we need another look at the lab. Everything traces back to it, like the core of a spider web. It's the epicenter of their security, and clearly their operational headquarters. We've got to go back."

Evelyn's gaze flashed. "Go *back?*"

"Go back and get inside. Not to waste time with Müller, but to find actual, actionable intelligence. Figure out who the big fish is, and what they're hiding."

"Shouldn't we contact the FBI? The military?"

"How? We don't have any communication."

"We'd have to slip through a roadblock, like you did before. Get to a bigger town and contact Washington."

I shook my head. "I slipped past them the first time because they weren't ready. The second time I arranged a distraction, and they fell for it. They won't take the bait a second time, and even if they did and we somehow managed to contact Washington, what then? How long before the government kicks into gear? Remember, the government is *already* involved. Coleus has successfully leveraged the National Guard—and presumably the governor of Iowa—into assisting in their isolation scheme. They've convinced the media that this is nothing more than an environmental scare. They even managed to isolate the CDC. You called your bosses, and nobody has shown up. Why do you think that is?"

I raised my eyebrows. Evelyn folded her arms and peered at the map. I could see the conflict in her eyes—the unwillingness to accept that the world was really so corruptible.

"I'll jump the chain of command," she said. "I'll run this right to the top. I'll reach out to my contacts on Capitol Hill —our oversight and funding committees. *Somebody* will respond."

"Of course," I said. "Eventually somebody will have to. But Coleus *knows* that." I jabbed the map with one finger, pointing to the lab. "All these measures—the National Guard, the disabled communications, the media blackout—they're all short term. The weather may have bought them time, but that advantage is now gone. Coleus's window of opportunity to conceal the truth is rapidly closing. By tomorrow afternoon it may be closed whether you call your bosses or not. That's why they're scrambling to cover their asses now. It's why they deployed a hit team into a blizzard to murder us. There's something important, something *critical* going down at that lab. Every second that passes, evidence is evaporating."

I kept my finger resting on the map, already knowing what came next. Already knowing my next step.

I just didn't know whether or not Evelyn would play ball. I could completely understand if she backed out—if she opposed the rash action I had in mind. She was an educated, civilized woman. She was part of the law and order mechanism that I seemed to be drifting further outside of with each passing day.

But I needed her—and I needed her to reach that conclusion herself.

"You want to bust in," she said. "You want to raid the lab."

"Expeditiously."

"And you need me."

"My medical knowledge terminates at battlefield trauma management. I know nothing about virology. I wouldn't know what to look for."

Evelyn chewed her lip, gazing absently at the circled spot on the map. I waited, slipping my hands into my pockets. At last she looked up.

"You knew, didn't you? When we flew into that village in Africa. You knew we were headed into a firestorm."

I nodded. "You develop a sixth sense after a while. You know when something is wrong."

"And now?" She raised both eyebrows, eyes open and honest. "What does your sixth sense tell you about this?"

"That they're hiding something horrific. And we're running out of time to catch them."

One more glance at the map. Then Evelyn reached for her coat.

"I'm sold. Let's go."

41

The RAM was low on fuel. Paul topped us off out of the big diesel tank he used to fill his tractor and the sawmills. He didn't ask questions about where we were headed next, or whether we would return. As I circled for the driver's door, Paul called my name.

"Mason."

"Yeah?" I looked back over one shoulder.

"Do I need to move my family?" There was a deep, icy concern in his eyes that defied his easygoing nature. I'd seen him stressed before. I'd never seen him like this.

"Keep them close, Paul. Stay in the house. We'll clear this up soon."

Paul tipped his hat. Then he started back toward the farmhouse, trailed by a big fluffy Great Pyrenees dog.

I climbed into the RAM and started the engine. A moment later warm air rushed into the floorboard. I locked us into drive and turned for the road.

"What's the game plan?" Evelyn's voice was edgy with tension, but not with panic. I glanced sideways and found her sitting upright in the seat, gaze fixated ahead, breathing easily.

All those years of medical service in so many impoverished, war-torn places were paying off. She was focused, zeroed in. I felt confident in counting on her.

I felt good having her close.

"We need access to their files," I said. "I assume those will be digital. You would know better than me where to look. I can provide cover while you do the searching."

"There will be computers in the actual laboratories," Evelyn said. "If they're cooking up something off the books, I can find it there. It may take some time."

"You'll have time. We just gotta get inside."

"Yeah...about that. They have an electric fence."

I chewed the inside of one cheek, mapping out the complex in my mind and evaluating each option. I pictured the pair of heavy steel gates. The security infrastructure. The cameras and the glass doors securing access.

There were plenty of ways I could sneak in. After bypassing the fence, I would simply need to avoid the security cameras, at least until I reached the laboratory. After that, things would get complicated. There would be security and surveillance systems in every hall. It would be impossible to move without detection and resulting conflict.

Adding Evelyn to that mix would further complicate everything. She wasn't trained in covert movement. She had no experience in tactical activity of any sort. Even if we defeated the fence, it would only be a matter of time until we were discovered.

All of which left me with Option B—the more direct approach. The *damn the torpedoes, full steam ahead* method.

The strategy that would most certainly result in gunfire, but also seemed the most likely to succeed.

I had killed two men posing as Iowa state cops, and four more at Taggert's bunker. How many mercenaries remained?

I ran the numbers. I glanced right across the cabin.

"Do you trust me?" I asked.

Evelyn met my gaze. Those beautiful pools of bright green were wide but calm, like the surface of still water. She didn't say a thing.

She simply nodded.

I STOPPED the RAM on the same road shoulder where I'd parked my GMC the previous night—the first time I had reconnoitered the compound. Piling out into the shin-deep snow, I looked through a fog of my own breath into the forest, gazing toward the Coleus lab.

Despite the midday sun, the forest was cloaked in shadow, the air perfectly still. So far removed from the bitter winds and pounding blast of only a few hours prior, the bone-chilling silence of the place was somehow even more disconcerting.

It was a pregnant emptiness. A toneless tone that reinforced every instinctual fear I'd already felt.

"Back seat," I said, tilting my head.

Evelyn piled out and met me at the rear passenger's door of the RAM. The pile of captured gear lay strewn across the seat and the back floorboard, the snow that had coated it now melted away. I sifted past the rifles and spare magazines, locating a pair of plate carrier vests, the largest of which was too small for me, and the smallest of which was too large for Evelyn. I handed the carrier off to her and she slid it on anyway, tearing the heavy AR-15 magazines out and tossing them back into the truck. I kept my magazines in, filling the one slot that was empty and cinching the chest rig's straps as tight as they would go. I added a belt holster with a SIG P320 and a spare magazine. I sifted through the rifles and located what appeared to be the cleanest.

It featured an Aimpoint Comp M4 and a Surefire weapon light. The magazine was half empty, so I swapped it out. I sifted through the mess once more and found a Glock 17.

"Here."

I extended the weapon toward Evelyn. She stared at it a moment, then shook her head.

"I'm a doctor, Mason. I help people. I don't shoot at them."

"These people might shoot at you."

"Yeah, well...that's what you're here for." She circled to the front passenger's seat. I dropped the Glock into the back seat and shut the door.

Back in the front seat, the moment I forced the bulky chest rig behind the steering wheel I experienced an overwhelming sense of déjà vu—almost nostalgia, but it's difficult to feel nostalgia over combat memories. The RAM was a great deal more comfortable than a Humvee, but the muscled stance of the vehicle took my mind right back to Afghanistan.

To planting my foot into an accelerator, listening to a different sort of diesel engine surge, and rushing toward the sound of the guns.

"You ready for this?" I asked.

Evelyn sat next to me, breathing a little more rapidly. Her

face was pale with the cold, her eyes permanently frozen open. One hand clenched around the RAM's armrest. The other drummed against her knee.

I knew she was deliberating. I understood why. I gave her a moment longer to back out.

Then she nodded. "Let's do it."

I ratcheted the RAM into drive. Powering out of the snow, we struck the road again. The heavy tires crushed along for half a mile before reaching the turnoff for the lab. Unlike the other snow-covered roads we had plowed through on the way out to Paul's place, this turnoff was heavily rutted by previous tire marks—some of them, no doubt, belonging to this same truck. I laid on the brakes and leaned forward to look beneath the windshield, down the arrow-straight road cutting between the trees.

"Here goes nothing," I muttered.

Then I planted my boot into the accelerator. Four wheels grabbed the asphalt. We launched into the trees and quickly accelerated. I kept both hands on the wheel, snow erupting on every side as we hit thirty miles per hour. The trees and the post-mounted cameras flashed by on every side. I flicked the truck's headlights to high beams, paving a bright pathway beneath the shadow of the tree cover. In another three seconds the lights of the guard house shone between the hardwoods, growing brighter until I could clearly see the twin steel gates barring access to the compound.

Those gates were closed. The guardhouse was shut. I didn't see an occupant. I glanced once to Evelyn and saw her pressed back in her seat, feet jammed against the floorboard. She closed her eyes and nodded again.

I punched the gas and rocketed straight for the gate.

42

W e hit the gate at forty-seven miles per hour, and despite the solid steel construction and thick wire, the twin doors buckled backward and erupted around the pickup's bull bar. Metal screamed against metal and I looked left to the guardhouse as it blinked past.

It was empty—lights shone but nobody was home. In a flash we cleared the gates, steel buckling and wire folding as an audible alarm screamed from an invisible loudspeaker. The truck remained planted to the road, only losing a quarter of its speed before my foot slammed into the floor again. Four tires caught. The big engine surged and we hurtled over one twisted half of a gate.

Then we were bounding up the drive and toward the parking lot. I muscled the wheel around, the pickup's rear end fishtailing as the trees vanished and the facility came into view. The building's windows were tinted pitch black, the parking lot covered in the same snow that blanketed the rest of the county. Only two vehicles were present—another

4x4 pickup and a Jaguar sedan. Both sat near the main entrance, and just beyond them a pair of white-suited mercenaries guarded the door, scrambling backward as we thundered toward them.

"There!" Evelyn said.

"I see them. Get down!"

She ducked beneath the dash as I kept my foot buried in the accelerator. The popping whisper of suppressed 5.56 rifles signaled the engagement of the enemy. I detected their muzzle flash as they took cover around the corner of the lab's entrance. The RAM's windshield shattered as a bullet blew the rearview mirror away. I ducked beneath the wheel and guided the truck onward—straight for the muzzle flash.

We blew past the other pickup. Additional rounds slammed into our front end and a cloud of radiator vapor erupted from underneath the hood. Warning lights flashed across the pickup's digital display. I braced my left foot against the floorboard, tensing for impact.

Then we smashed into the side of the building's tunnel entrance, blowing through brick and glass and hurtling onward, back into the parking lot and straight into the mercenaries dug in beyond the far wall. A bloodcurdling scream ripped through the air as our right tire crunched over something organic. I slammed chest-first into the wheel, the breath vacating my lungs as my foot found the brake.

We finally reached a jolting stop and I clawed for the door handle. My seat belt was off. My right hand closed around the grip of the rifle and I flicked the selector switch to fire as I fell into the packed snow outside.

I circled the nose of the truck to find the first mercenary clawing his way backward on his ass, his left leg brutally twisted. His rifle was tangled in its sling, but even as I appeared around the bent bull bar he clawed for a pistol.

I shot him twice in the face then swung right, instinctively searching for the second guy. I found him lying in the snow behind the RAM's front right wheel, his entire torso obliterated by the heavy tire. Our gazes locked and for a long, brutal moment, I saw the abject fear in his eyes.

Then his soul departed his body. He slumped into the snow, and I rushed back to my door.

"Come on! We're going in."

Evelyn's door was blocked by the collapsed mass of brick wall just outside the truck, so she clambered over the console and grasped my hand on her way through my door. I led the way around the tailgate, rifle at the ready as I swept the shattered entrance.

It was dark inside—darker than it should have been in the middle of the day. Every third fluorescent fixture glowed just brightly enough to provide security illumination, but the others were dark. Glass littered the floor. The lobby beyond was empty. I saw the horseshoe metal detectors but no further guards—no additional personnel of any kind.

This is wrong.

The message from my sixth sense registered in my brain as I fast-walked over the glass, thumbing the pressure switch on the Surefire and dumping hot-white light across the lobby.

"Keep your hand on my belt," I said. "If you see something, say something!"

Evelyn's fingers closed around my belt at the base of my spine. I slowed at the lobby entrance and swept the light around the room, confirming an absence of combatants. All was dark, everything was still. Just like this place was shut down—but it shouldn't have been. It had been alive with guards and personnel the night prior.

What happened?

"Elevator to your left," Evelyn said. "Stairs next to it. The lab will be on the second floor."

I led the way to the stairwell, snatching the door open and jabbing the rifle in first.

No answer. No sound. More of the same dim security lights as before.

Wrong. This is wrong.

We started up the steps. I slowed to the pace of Evelyn's shorter legs, clearing each flight of stairs with my finger on the trigger and my back bent. We reached the second floor and I kicked the door open. The hallway beyond was nearly thick with shadows, rows of tall metal doors labeled with numbers, the floor paved in industrial tile. I twisted left, weapon light flashing across a row of laboratory windows. I stepped out from the stairwell.

Then the gunfire began—a hail of rapid shots that exploded off the walls. I snatched my body back as bullets tore into the drywall next to me and slammed into the metal doorframe. Evelyn shouted. I regained my footing and thrust the rifle around the corner, returning fire with a quartet of shots. Brass pinged against the tile and the other shooter fell silent.

"Wait for my signal!" I pushed Evelyn's hand off my belt and spun outward, finger tight around the trigger.

The hallway was empty. The intersecting hallway twenty yards away was empty, shattered glass from a laboratory window sprinkling the tile. Brass rifle casings joined the glass—ejections from whoever had opened fire on us. But as before, I saw no one.

I rushed to the next intersection, using the Surefire in selective blasts. I inspected the floor for blood but found none. Bullet holes—my bullet holes—decorated the far wall. I turned both ways down the intersecting hallway, finding offices to my right.

To my left stood another elevator and another stairwell —but again, no people. No security. No sign of Müller.

"That's the lab!"

I looked back to see Evelyn poking her head into the hall. She pointed, and I redirected my attention to the bank of windows covering the room at the core of the second floor. It was a lab, all right. A massive one. Housed behind a secure access door, illuminated only by security fluorescents, the space was a hundred feet deep and three times that long. Rows of shelves and banks of work spaces filled the interior. I recognized microscopes and medical freezers. The remaining equipment was totally alien to me.

"Go!" I called.

Evelyn sprinted from the stairwell as I dropped into a crouch to secure the intersection. She reached the door and tried the latch—it was locked.

"Mason!"

I closed on the door and motioned her back. Three shots from the rifle decimated the locking mechanism. I tore the door open and ushered Evelyn in. Turning my back, I kept the rifle up and looked both ways down the hall. Back to the stairwell. Back to the elevator shaft.

My heart was hammering, but not with physical stress. Every honed battlefield instinct was screaming in my head. It was all I could think about, a flurry of red flags that nearly clogged my vision.

What was happening here? Where had everyone gone?

The previous night this place had been locked down like Area 51, the epicenter of the problem. Now it was empty. Resistance was minimal.

"Evelyn?" I called without turning my face away from the hall. Behind me I heard Evelyn running, muttering to herself, glass objects clinking and shifting, computer keyboards clacking.

"All the computers are locked! I'll take the hard drives."

"Hurry! We need to move."

"Five minutes. Give me five minutes!"

Inside a close quarters combat zone five minutes feels like an eternity. I moved from the door back to the intersection of hallways, sweeping the light and tracing dirty footprints on the floor. They led away from the fallen brass to the stairwell door. I trailed them, reaching the door and yanking it back. I led with the rifle and cleared both upward and downward.

The footprints vanished on the rough concrete. I listened but couldn't hear anything.

"Dear God..."

Evelyn's voice reached me through the shattered window. I looked into the lab, finding her standing over a desk, poring over an open binder. Her mouth hung open, hands frozen on the page.

Then I heard another sound, a distant rumble. A whirring. A coughing howl that heralded the ignition of a jet engine, followed by a *whap whap whap* of rotor blades. I tilted my head up toward the ceiling, one last puzzle piece sliding into the gap in my mind. Filling the void.

And finally, I understood.

"Evelyn!"

Her face snapped up, and I sprinted. I made it to the lab entrance and hurtled inside, still shouting her name.

"We're going! We're going now!"

She straightened over the desk, confusion clouding her face, mouth still hanging open. I grabbed her arm.

"Wait! I'm not done."

"Take it! *Move!*"

She grabbed the binder. We reached the hallway, my rifle held in one hand while I dragged her along with the other. I looked both ways, first to the intersection and then to my right—a long hallway terminated by tinted windows.

"*Come on!*"

I exploded out of the doorway, Evelyn stumbling behind. Overhead the rotor blades grew to a hurricane pitch, then started to fade. The helicopter was taking off, departing the roof. We were a hundred yards from the end of the building —then eighty. I lifted the rifle and opened fire, dumping half a magazine through the reinforced, tinted glass. It spider-webbed with cracks. The next string of shots turned those cracks into an avalanche of shards. I kept running. Evelyn's feet slid across the slick tile.

"Mason, what are you—"

She never finished. We reached the window and I wrenched her forward. She screamed and fought.

"*Go!*"

Then I leapt from the second-floor hallway, exploding through the window and hurling us both into the frigid blackness outside. We arced away from the building and the world descended into slow motion. My lungs burned with the bitter air. My fingers tightened around Evelyn's arms. She screamed. The snow-covered ground raced toward us. We landed in a crush of freezing white, air exploding from my lungs as Evelyn shrieked in pain. I tumbled over her, shoulder slamming into the hard ground eighteen inches beneath our fluffy landing pad.

Then I was back on my feet, head pounding and knees throbbing as I pulled Evelyn out of the snow. She clung to the binder, screaming about her leg. I twisted and picked her up, pulling her body close. I sprinted for the cover of trees a hundred yards distant. I looked up and noted the blinking tail lights of the chopper vanishing into the midday sun.

I made it halfway—and then the building behind me erupted into a chest-crushing blast of fire and fury.

43

The second time we struck the ground even harder than the first. The blast wave took me clean off my feet, flinging me like a rag doll back into the snow. I lost my hold on Evelyn. I rolled as the clouded sky overhead flashed with brilliant bright orange—as radiant as a sunrise, the flush of heat so immediate and all-consuming that it singed the unshaven beard stubble on my face and instantly melted the surface of the snow around me.

Then that light was gone, blocked by a tsunami of white and black pushed out from the building and now washing over me in an instant. I gasped for air, flailing. Then I was swamped, fully buried in the blink of an eye. I choked on snow. I tasted dirt. I clawed and writhed as the ear-splitting roar of the bomb faded across Iowa.

I was suffocating. The weight of the snow and the evaporating oxygen in my lungs completely negated any concern for the deathly cold. I kicked and struggled, half-digging and half-swimming. My foot found the ground and I powered upward.

I'd lost the rifle. So much more importantly, I had lost Evelyn. I completed a leap and returned to the surface, gasping for air as I landed on a half-melted mound of filthy black snow. I began sinking again, my gaze blinded by blazing orange. All around me lay debris from the detonated building—twisted metal, cubes of black glass, a nearly unscathed office chair.

"Evelyn!"

I twisted in the snow, instinctively clawing for the last place I remembered her falling. Disoriented by the blast, with ears still ringing, I couldn't be sure if my guess was even close to accurate.

But I did know she was suffocating—drowning, rather—beneath an avalanche of crushing snow and debris. I went in head first, scooping with both arms and wriggling down. It was a lot harder to descend than it had been to climb. The snow was compressed by the blast pressure and loaded with twisted building materials. My palm tore on a jagged chunk of metal. I choked on grit and clawed the mud.

I still hadn't reached her. I flailed, digging and twisting. My heart hammered. Total panic overtook me in a tidal wave, even more overwhelming than the blast of snow.

No, God. Please. Not again.

I thrashed. I shouted her name. I returned to my feet in chest-deep snow and scanned the perimeter. I found my original point of entry, now a torn gopher hole of black and white. I remembered how we had hurtled across the yard in those split seconds before the bomb went off—Evelyn held in my arms, flying forward as I fell...

I marked one more spot and I dove. Clawing downward, I dug like a crazed dog, thrashing with all four limbs. I shoved past a chunk of shelving. I tore a coffee pot out of the way. I struck dirt and tunneled just above it, nearly hyperventilating with desperation. Pleading. *Needing.*

Then I touched a shoe. It twisted in the snow. I thought it jerked. I lunged forward and pulled, feeling a leg. Now I knew the leg was thrashing. Hope surged in my chest and I burrowed deeper. Reaching up the leg to a knee—finding another leg.

Then I pulled.

Evelyn emerged from the snow as a thrashing, muddy mass, still clinging to her binder. I fell backward onto the ground and struggled back to my knees, grabbing her by the shoulders and lifting her face out of the dirt.

Evelyn's skin was nearly blackened by soot, her eyes wide as she gasped for breath. She coughed up snow and I lifted her arms. The binder fell to the ground. She leaned forward and vomited over my knees, body quaking. As soon as her throat was clear she gasped for air. Her face pivoted upward, blinking hard.

We stared at each other a long moment in perfect silence, the stench of vomit and smoke swirling into a wicked cocktail all around us. Then, in unison, we both looked toward the building.

The lab was simply gone—reduced to a smoldering heap of rubble, with flames and smoke still rising from the core. We kneeled in the dirt fifty yards away, close enough to feel the irregular wash of heat as it pulsed from the already dying blaze. Still far enough away for a shiver of reality to rip up my spine.

We'd come within a hair's breadth of certain death...

And I knew: My sixth sense was right. This was more than something worth killing to conceal. It was something worth going to war over.

44

T he RAM pickup was history—so was the Jaguar. Both vehicles sat much too close to the blast. The RAM now lay on its side, the Jag on its roof. Both burned, sending columns of black smoke reaching for the night sky.

The third vehicle—the pickup that had sat a little deeper in the parking lot, farthest from the building—had mostly survived. It was a mid-2000s Ford FX4 with a coat rack sticking from its windshield, and burning lab books resting on its hood.

Good enough.

I led Evelyn out of the snow, the AR-15 lost somewhere in the wreckage behind me, and reached for the SIG P320 instead. With each step across the parking lot I swept the tree line and peered into the midday sky, now clouded by black smoke.

The chopper was long gone. So were the surviving mercenaries. Nothing was left save the stench of burning everything and one very decimated laboratory.

Destroyed evidence. I had been right when I warned Evelyn that we were running out of time—I just didn't realize how right I was. Not until it was almost too late.

Evelyn shivered despite the heat of the fire, scrubbing vomit from her mouth. She stared at the ashen mess with something between horror and survivor's euphoria covering her face while I tried the Ford's door handle.

It was locked. I drew my Victorinox and sent the heel of the knife smashing into the automotive glass. It required three blows to shatter it. Then I reached through and mashed the electronic lock switch. The door opened.

"Come on," I said. "Climb in."

Evelyn didn't require a second invitation. She circled the nose of the pickup and climbed into the passenger side front seat while I climbed onto the step rail to reach the coat rack. It took some effort to remove it from the busted windshield. Spiderweb cracks ran to the A-pillars, a hole the size of a bowling ball blown right through the middle. I threw the coat rack aside and looked back to the burning building, sudden rage mixing with the blast daze still clouding my mind.

It was unbelievable. And yet, perfectly logical. Evidence of the *thing* we came here to find now lay smoldering to ash in the middle of nowhere, Iowa.

I swept cubes of glass out of the truck's driver's seat and snapped my Victorinox open. The Ford's ignition wiring harness was clipped beneath the dash. I tore it free and spent some time mapping out the terminus of each brightly colored wire before I began to cut and strip. Minutes dragged past—it's always a lot slower than it appears in the movies, especially on a modern vehicle. Luckily, the truck was old enough to still have a standard key-turn ignition system, something I understood. With some patience, I got the dash display turned on. A minute later, the starter choked, then turned over. The truck was a gas burner, but still took some time to start in the bitter cold. My fingers were nearly wooden with stiffness before the engine finally rumbled to life. I twisted together the necessary wires and piled in, slamming the door.

Evelyn cranked the heat up to max. The air pumping into the floorboards and out of the defroster was cold, but would warm. I looked through a filthy windshield at the smoky mess and simply shook my head.

I wasn't sure if more shocked or horrified, but one thing was certain—I was good and pissed off.

I dropped the truck into four-high and shifted into drive. The tires weren't as beefy as the shoes on the bomb-blasted RAM, but they did the job. I got us turned around in the parking lot and headed back through the shattered gate. I kept the SIG ready, resting on my thigh as I swept the forest.

No one engaged us. We reached the terminus of the drive and I stopped at the road. It wasn't until we had sat there a second, the pumping climate control just beginning to warm, that Evelyn finally spoke.

"What the hell?"

I glanced right at her smoke-blackened face. Her eyebrows were singed, now crinkled into a disbelieving scowl. She stared at me, unblinking, and repeated the question, voice rising to a shout.

"What the hell, Mason? *What the hell?*"

I simply grunted. There was nothing to say. I turned us onto the road and powered into the snow, keeping our speed in the mid-thirties to minimize the bone-freezing effects of the air pouring through the busted window and windshield.

The engine thermometer rose to operating temperatures and my blood began to thaw. It became easier to breathe. Evelyn cursed again and slammed her hand into the binder lying in her lap.

"Are they out of their minds? This is America! We don't blow stuff up!"

The blatant naivete in her words should have irritated me—or at least sponsored a laugh. Instead it added to the warmth in my chest, somehow comforting in the face of abject destruction. I'd grown so accustomed to the worst humanity has to offer that I stopped interpreting evil in terms of borders and flags. I'd lost faith in the concept of "that doesn't happen here".

Evelyn's disbelief reflected a sense of idyllic security that felt precious to me. Worth protecting.

"They were covering their tracks," I said. "But this isn't over. Tell me you found something."

Evelyn looked back to the binder. She snorted, flicking the cover open.

"Oh, I found something. You're not gonna freaking *believe* this." She tore through pages, nearly ripping them across their three-ring restraints before she reached a line in the middle of the righthand page. I glanced away from the road just long enough to note a long list of log entries, written in black pen. Dates, times, notes. Signatures.

"It's the access log book," Evelyn said. "Every specialist, doctor, scientist, or lab assistant who entered the facility. When they arrived, when they left, and what they were working on. It's a security protocol, so that everybody is on the same page. That's why it's kept as a physical book."

"And?"

"And most of it is perfectly ordinary. December fourteenth, Doctor Keith Chattley, check-in nine fifty-two a.m., check-out twelve thirty-eight p.m. Project code Alpha two-two-zero. Subject: H5N1. That's Avian Influenza—bird flu. The NIH sponsors studies to investigate possible mutations which would allow transmissions to humans."

"NIH?"

"National Institute of Health. The government organization responsible for medical research."

Evelyn waved her hand as if the question annoyed her. I motioned for her to continue.

"January fourth, Doctor Kim Finch. Project code Charlie three-nine-three. Subject, ZIKV. That's Zika virus. January fifth, Doctor Chattley again. Back to H5N1. January sixth, Doctor S. Stevens, subject MTB—tuberculosis. January seventh, Doctor Finch, subject HIV. January tenth, Doctor Faulk, subject *B. anthracis*. Anthrax."

Evelyn looked up from the log, shaking her head in disbelief. I glanced right—I didn't get it.

"You're going to have to explain."

"They're testing half a dozen different major diseases inside of the same week!"

"And?"

"And that's unheard of. You don't do that. With a lab this size, they should be running experiments on not more than two, *maybe* three diseases at any given time. There would be a leading research scientist for each project. Lab and research assistants for each team with lab access split into shifts—maybe days. But six, seven different diseases under the same roof? Checking in and out with no obvious pattern or schedule? It's madness. It's begging for an accident."

We reached an intersection bound by snow and I blew right through the stop sign. With the sky glowing bright with a welcome winter sun, I could see for miles across the corn-fields we blew through. I didn't need directions.

My route was now very familiar.

"What are you telling me?" I said.

"I'm telling you that they're either criminally dumb, or else they have deliberately cooked the books."

"A smoke screen?"

"Exactly."

"So what could they be hiding? Could they fraudulently record fake projects to exploit government funding?"

Even as I suggested it I didn't really believe it. Fraud of that level might be jail-worthy, but it still didn't feel nasty enough to justify rampant homicide, to say nothing of Coleus Biotech bombing their own building.

Evelyn simply shook her head, still tracing pages. She squinted and stopped at random. Tapping entries with her index finger, then ripping to the next page. Stopping again.

At last she looked up. "There's these irregular entries for a subject labeled merely as 'X_1'. I thought it was an error at first. Bad handwriting. But I've counted it nine times over the last six weeks—lengthy, all-day research sessions. Same doctor every time. *T. Hutchins.*"

"What's X_1?"

"I have no idea. I've never seen that code."

"A special project?"

"Maybe."

"An *illegal* project?" I glanced right again. Evelyn's face hardened. She dug through the truck's console and found a pen. As I rumbled farther southward, she marked each instance of the X_1 code. By the time we reached the outskirts of Prairie Junction she had tallied a total.

"Sixty-two studies, ranging back to the start of the log on June first of last year."

"Too many to be an error."

"Too vague to be legitimate." She smacked the binder closed, jaw working. Fuming, but also processing. I watched her from the driver's seat, gliding to a halt at a stop sign on the outskirts of town. Despite her disheveled hair, smoke-blasted face, and clothes sodden with melted snow, there was something about the gleam in her eyes that hit me deep in my chest.

It was magnetic. It awakened feelings I hadn't experienced since...

"I need a phone," Evelyn said. "A phone that *works*. I need contact with Atlanta. And also—" She turned to face me. Her shoulders tensed. "I need to see a body."

I sat with one hand on the wheel, the other grasping the SIG. I measured the conviction in her face and knew what she was thinking. It was a request—but really more of an order.

And I was completely okay with that. I dropped my foot off the brake.

"We'll start with the National Guard," I said. "Get your CDC badge ready."

45

I plowed straight into the heart of Prairie Junction, no longer concerned about confronting the guardsmen that guarded the town in full NBC gear, and no longer concerned about whether Lieutenant Colonel Hughes was legitimate or dirty. I thought he was legitimate. I was pretty certain that I had already eradicated all the scum hiding amid his ranks, and any that remained...well...

The SIG was chambered and ready.

I pulled the Ford right up to city hall, blowing past a Humvee and a National Guardsman who scrambled to block my path. I threw the truck into park and pulled the wires to cut the engine off. I checked my watch.

It was approaching one p.m., and city hall was bustling with activity. I recognized one of Jeter's officers behind the misted glass of the front entrance. Scanning the parking lot, I also noted Jeter's patrol car—that exhausted Chevy Caprice that he refused to part with.

"Let me do the talking," I said. "These guys are jumpy. We'll get you a phone—then we'll talk about the bodies."

Evelyn reached for the door handle. I put a hand on her shoulder.

"Evelyn."

She looked back.

"I witnessed at least one person coughing in the arena. I don't know how bad it may have gotten. We're back in the mix, now."

Evelyn nodded. I didn't need to lecture her about the realities of bio hazard—she understood better than anyone. I reached for my own door handle and was immediately confronted by the muzzle of an M4 rifle, thrust through my busted window at the behest of a National Guardsman in full NBC gear.

"Don't move!" he shouted. "Take your hand off that weapon!"

I glanced down, remembering the SIG. I raised both hands.

"Get Jeter," I said.

"Huh?"

"The police chief! *Get him.*"

The guardsman thumbed his chest-mounted radio. A voice crackled. He called for Jeter. I kept my hands up, the SIG remaining in my lap as further soldiers exploded through city hall's main entrance. They encircled the truck. Jeter appeared a minute later, wrapped in nothing more than the same light hoody he'd worn at Millie's Place the night before this madness broke loose—that blue and gold emblem of the American Gridiron league printed across his chest.

"Mason?" he shouted through the hole in the windshield.

"It's me."

"What are you doing, kid?"

"Trying not to get shot. Tell them to calm down."

Jeter snapped at the guardsmen in charge. The guardsmen snapped back. Nobody would move from their weapons until I agreed to set the SIG on the pickup's dash. Then at last our doors were yanked open. Both Evelyn and I were hauled out. They manhandled me across the parking lot—not toward city hall, but toward a mobile command post parked several slots down from my truck. A white-suited doctor waited there. Evelyn and I were lined up outside the trailer and subjected to aggressive nasal swabbing while the guardsmen stood back with rifles at the ready. Jeter shook his head apologetically. I waved a hand in dismissal, too cold to be angry. Evelyn edged closer to me, and before I could stop myself I wrapped an arm around her shoulders. She leaned in, shivering, the captured binder held beneath one arm. Five brutal minutes dragged by. Nobody moved.

Then at last the trailer door swung open, and the medical guy stuck his head out.

"I think they're clear."

You think? What does that mean?

"Can we go inside now?" I directed the question at Jeter. He snarled at the guardsmen and they reluctantly stood down. Together we marched for the promised warmth of city hall, but even inside its brick walls it was still cold. Jeter ordered his officer to fetch hot coffee. I rubbed Evelyn's arm and continued to hold her close.

The coffee came so hot it burned my throat. I chugged it anyway, breathing fog and stretching my numb fingers. Whatever the temperature was outside, it was considerably colder than when this entire mess began. The last vestiges of winter were striking Iowa with a vengeance.

"Where have you been?" Jeter demanded. "I've been looking for you."

Dark circles hung beneath his eyes. His hair was disheveled beneath the City of Prairie Junction Police Department ball cap he wore. He looked like he hadn't slept since our last interaction.

"You got a satellite phone?" I asked.

Jeter squinted. "The Guard has them."

"Get them. And get that colonel. We've got a huge problem."

46

E velyn took possession of a sat phone after flashing her CDC badge. Then she barricaded herself in the city secretary's office while Jeter escorted me into the mayor's office, which was unoccupied. Four minutes later LTC Hughes arrived, barging in and sweeping angry eyes over the pair of us sitting in front of his borrowed desk.

"What now, Chief? What's he doing here?"

I pointed to the chair. "Sit. And listen."

Maybe it was something in my face. Maybe the LTC was simply too tired to pull rank on a civilian. Regardless, he complied. One of his NCOs brought more coffee. I chugged it as before.

Then I began. I detailed everything, from the moment Taggert was shot to the moment the Coleus Lab exploded. I explained Evelyn's identity and involvement. I described her findings in the binder, and detailed our theories of their meaning.

"You've got a level-three bio lab right in your back yard.

They just blew that place to scrap metal, and now they're gone, leaving a mountain of questions behind."

During the course of my story neither Jeter nor the LTC interrupted once. Both grew increasingly tense, Jeter's mouth falling open as I reached the description of the laboratory.

"*Where?*" Jeter demanded.

"You got a map?"

The LTC tore through the mayor's drawers. He produced a folding map of the county and spread it across the desk. I found the location of the lab and tapped it.

"There."

Jeter shook his head. "No, no. That's a data center. Like, an offsite computer storage facility. For cellular providers, I think."

"Maybe that's what they told you. They lied. It's a BSL-Three research lab—or it was. Now it's ashes and God only knows what manner of pathogens."

Jeter turned disbelieving eyes on me, then glared at the LTC.

"Did you know about this?" Jeter said.

The colonel kept his gaze on the map, glowering so darkly I half-expected the paper to burst into flames. He spoke through his teeth.

"Not a word. They told us this was a rare influenza outbreak—something to secure. That's what we've been testing for."

"*I think.*"

The white-suited doctor's words from only minutes before returned to my mind. Suddenly, they made sense.

"So you still don't know what this thing is?" I asked. "What virus you're dealing with?"

Hughes settled into his chair. He looked at Jeter a long moment. Then he shook his head.

"No. We don't. We've had minimal communication from Des Moines. The orders are all the same—secure and wait."

"How many people are dead?" I asked.

"Three so far. Half a dozen more sick. The quarantine seems to have curtailed any further infections."

Now it was my turn to pause. I looked back at the map and pictured the Coleus facility, implementing LTC Hughes's information into my investigation.

An unknown illness. A ground commander kept in the dark. A governor's office stalling for time.

The fresh variables failed to change the solution I'd already reached. The core value that remained constant in my mind, like the foundation of this entire puzzle.

"Somebody way up the chain is pulling strings," I said. "Somebody with a *lot* of leverage. Enough to lock this place down, to cut communications, to keep you in the dark."

"We take our orders directly from Des Moines," Hughes said.

"The governor?" I raised both eyebrows. Hughes flushed. I knew he wouldn't answer—it was career suicide if he was wrong. He changed the subject instead.

"You say these people infiltrated my men?" Hughes said.

"At least once, yes."

"And they fled in a *helicopter?*"

"Correct. A doctor named Müller and at least a couple of his mercenary men. I can't imagine how they think they're going to wriggle out of this. They probably assume both myself and Dr. Landry were killed in the blast. Now they'll spin a new story about what happened to the lab."

"This is insanity," Hughes said.

"Complete insanity, which should scare the crap out of you. That facility must have cost millions to construct. They wrecked it without a second thought. We need to be asking *why?* What are they hiding?"

Before anyone could answer the door burst open. Evelyn appeared, sat phone in hand, her gaze icy cold. She looked to me and nodded once.

"I connected with Atlanta. The CDC is deploying a full bio control team. They should be here within eight to ten hours."

Backup on the way. That was good, but my gut told me it wasn't good enough.

"Who were the three people that died?" I directed the question at Hughes. This time, the LTC didn't hesitate.

"One male who turned up at the local urgent care clinic. One female found in her house on the outskirts of town. And the old lady at the farm—the one you found."

"Ms. Molly."

"Right."

"Where are the bodies?" Evelyn said.

"I'm sorry?"

"The bodies." Evelyn's voice hardened. "I need to see them. *Now.*"

47

Our first trip wasn't to the city morgue, it was to the crash site of Evelyn's rental SUV. We rode in a Humvee—myself, Evelyn, Jeter, and Hughes. The LTC drove, hurtling through the snow-bound streets while barking into his radio.

He was deploying men to the site of the bio lab. He wanted a complete perimeter around the property. Nobody was allowed to enter beyond the electrified fence, not under any circumstances. Hughes placed calls to higher command in Des Moines. He attempted to reach the governor, but the governor couldn't be reached—he was attending the dedication of a hospital wing named in his honor.

The LTC hung up with a curse and pulled the Humvee off the road at the site of the overturned Toyota RAV4. I piled out, enduring the cold and digging through the already busted rear glass of the SUV to locate Evelyn's medical bag —the one loaded with all her mobile testing equipment. Then we were back on the road, returning to downtown and the city morgue. I rode in the back alongside Jeter. Despite the unheated interior of the Humvee—little more than a steel box—he still wore nothing more than the arena football hoody.

Jeter sat glowering out the window, lips pinched together. I couldn't tell if he looked more angry or afraid. There was disbelief in his eyes, that vague sort of shell-shock small-town people feel when the unthinkable lands on their doorstep.

I couldn't blame him. In my bones I knew that this thing was far from over, that there was another curve ball coming at lightning speed. I could only hope to identify it before it was too late to swing.

The morgue was a squat, windowless brick building. The parking lot, like the rest of Prairie Junction, was clogged with snow, but the National Guard had plowed enough of it out of the way to allow access to the main entrance. They had also established a completed perimeter around the property with additional Humvees and one FMTV serving as both a roadblock and a guardhouse. Hughes's men deployed in NBC suits to stop our vehicle.

As soon as they recognized their commanding officer, they backed the FMTV off the road and we pulled into the parking lot. Evelyn dropped out first, dragging her bag on her way to the door.

"Wait!" Hughes called. "We should escort you."

Evelyn placed the bag on the snow and unzipped the top. She was shivering in the biting cold as she produced a rubber lab coat, complete with hood and wrist-length sleeves. She added gloves and a mask. Then she began slogging toward the morgue again.

"Stay put," she called over her shoulder. "Give me twenty minutes!"

Jeter, Hughes and I remained in the Humvee as Evelyn reached the door and was admitted by the NBC-suited guardsmen inside. I watched as the metal doors clapped shut behind her. A minute dragged by, but neither Hughes nor Jeter spoke.

We all just sat, enduring the cold. Waiting. And I wondered: *Who was first?*

The thought returned to my mind, and I took a moment to ponder it again. To evaluate this mess not in terms of a spider web, but a chain of dominos.

Who was the first victim? How had that person connected with a lab leak? And how on earth had that leak led to Ms. Molly—all alone in her little farmhouse?

It still didn't make sense. Of all the citizens of Prairie Junction, Ms. Molly should have been one of the most secure from an evil such as this. She never went anywhere— she only socialized with very few people. She certainly shouldn't have had any contact with anyone from Coleus Biotech.

"You said three people died?" I questioned.

Hughes grunted.

"Do you have dossiers?"

"They're in my office. "

"Radio your men. I want to know."

Hughes flushed with irritation, but he made the call. Minutes ticked by. I fixated on the morgue door through the misting Humvee window. I prayed for Evelyn's safety. Despite her lab gear and training, she had little more idea what she was walking into than I did.

Project X1. What was it?

"Base to command. We have the dossiers on the victims. What do you need to know?"

Hughes shot me a questioning look. I remained relaxed, thinking slowly.

"Skip Ms. Molly," I said. "I want to know about the other two. Where they lived and worked. What their last forty-eight hours looked like. Who they may have interacted with."

"We already asked those questions," Hughes said.

"So you should have the information," I spoke through my teeth. "I don't. I want to."

Hughes radioed back. When the voice of his guardsman returned, I heard papers shuffling.

"Victim number two is Oliver Peters Junior. Age fifty-one, Caucasian. Native of Iowa. Lived at 121 Oak Street in Prairie Junction. Place of employment was 1707 State Highway 15, Prairie Junction. It looks to be...uh..."

"A service station," Jeter broke in. "A twenty-four-hour convenience store. Ollie inherited it from his old man. He... was a good guy."

I glanced left and thought I saw tears in Jeter's eyes.

"Where was he found?" I asked. Hughes relayed the question.

"He walked into the local clinic...uh...Prairie Junction Urgent Care. Reported difficulty breathing, vomiting, swelling of the face and airways. He died shortly thereafter. Two members of the urgent care staff are now sick."

I bit my lip. The paper shuffling resumed. "Victim number three is Margarita Pérez Torres. Age forty-two, Mexican-American. Looks like she immigrated as a child. Lived at 114 Magnolia Street, Apartment 3. Prairie Junction. Place of employment isn't listed...just says *self-employed*."

"Where was she found?" I said.

"At her apartment. Looks like the property manager

checked on her after the town was locked down. Ms. Torres was already deceased at that time. Same general symptoms as Mr. Peters. The apartment manager is now sick as well."

I glanced at Jeter. He was frowning, lips moving silently. He looked up and shook his head.

"I don't know her."

I turned back to Hughes. "To clarify, we still don't know who patient zero was?"

Hughes shook his head. "We don't. The autopsy people were supposed to be estimating time of death."

"Do you have an update?"

Hughes asked. The radio fell silent for almost a minute. At last the voice of his subordinate returned.

"I just called the morticians. They can't be sure who patient zero was, but they think it was the first victim—the old lady. Margaret J. Pritchard."

"Wait. What?" I squinted.

"You found her yourself," Hughes said. "She could have been dead a while."

"I realize that. But I found her hours *after* you were deployed to lock down the town. And if you didn't know about her, then she couldn't have been the reason you were ordered to deploy."

Hughes blinked. I saw the revelation on his face like a parting curtain, followed an instant later by a flush of red as the implication of the timeline struck him.

"Somebody was pulling strings from the start," I said. "There was another trigger. Some event that necessitated immediate and aggressive response, even before people appeared sick."

"What was it?" Jeter barked the question as though he held Hughes personally responsible for the entire situation.

The old police chief's eyes were still red. I understood his pain.

"How should I know?" Hughes said. "You think I gave the order? I follow orders, Chief!"

"So who pulls *your* strings?" Jeter snarled.

Hughes came out of his seat. He twisted toward the back of the Humvee, teeth clenched. Before he could speak the front passenger's door of the Humvee snapped open. We all started as Evelyn appeared out of nowhere, stripped of her lab gear but carrying a clipboard. She piled in. She slammed the door, breathing hard and shivering. The vehicle's cabin fell still, the only sound the continued chug of the diesel engine. All eyes fixated on Evelyn.

Everyone waited.

Evelyn rubbed her hands together, breath clouding in front of her face. She leaned close to the dash to capture what pitiful warmth churned in from the engine. Seconds ticked by.

At last I broke the silence. "Evelyn?"

She turned to face the three of us, and when she did an ice pick of dread gouged through my gut. Her bright green eyes were wide, consumed by strain. She didn't even try to hide it.

"It's Ebola," she whispered. "An unrecognized strain...a function-enhanced virus."

48

The ice pick twisted, and my body went cold from the inside out. I locked gazes with Evelyn and saw something I'd never seen before, not even as bullets ripped past our heads in war-torn Africa.

It was honest, genuine terror.

"What do you mean it's Ebola?" Hughes demanded. "Like that stuff in Africa?"

"No, Colonel." Evelyn turned to the officer. "Worse than that. It's a modified virus. A deliberate mutation."

Hughes squinted. "What does that mean?"

"It means they monkeyed with the formula!" Evelyn broke into a sudden shout, slamming her gloves into her lap. "It means they performed illegal, undocumented gain-of-function research on the Ebola virus, testing and modifying its attributes, and *somehow* the disease leaked."

"Illegal?" Jeter joined the conversation. "Like terrorism?"

Terrorism. The twist in my gut tightened. I blinked, a puzzle piece rising from the void in the back of my mind and clicking into place. I saw it—even as Evelyn continued to snap angry, abrupt sentences, explaining to Jeter the nuances of medical research regulation and how her office had been kept in the dark. Hughes interrupted with barked questions of his own—demands for details on contagiousness, transmission, incubation period. All things Evelyn didn't and couldn't possibly know. How could anyone know? This was literally a brand-new disease.

They were pertinent questions, but my mind had already skipped far ahead of them. Or, rather, far *behind* them. Back to my original meeting with Taggert at Millie's Place. The crazed ranting. The *photographs.*

And then Ms. Molly.

"Maggie!" I snapped. "Maggie Pérez Torres!"

The conversation in the Humvee cut short. Hughes wheeled on me.

"What?"

I snapped my fingers. "Get your man on the radio. Ask him if Margarita Pérez Torres ever went by *Maggie.*"

Hughes frowned in confusion.

"*Do it!*"

The LTC thumbed his radio. We waited for the response. It took a minute to come, but when it did, it came as the affirmative.

"Uh...yeah. Yeah. The property manager called her Maggie when she reported finding Ms. Torres in her apartment."

I snapped my fingers again. I wheeled on Jeter.

"It's Maggie, Jeter. We knew her as *Maggie.*"

"Maggie? Maggie who?"

"Maggie Torres. She ran a cleaning business. Remember? She drove a yellow van."

A light clicked on behind Jeter's eyes. "Right! Maggie. I spoke to her before. She cleaned city hall on occasion."

"She also cleaned *Ms. Molly's house*," I said. "Lyle hired her to help his mother. They were good friends. Maggie would sometimes stay for dinner."

"So they're linked?" Evelyn broke in. "Maggie could have infected Ms. Molly."

"No." I shook my head. "It was the other way around. Ms. Molly infected Maggie."

"Huh?" Hughes squinted, but my mind was already racing ahead—or rather, racing back to the question that had baffled me from day one. How a woman who lived all by herself in the middle of nowhere could have contracted such a rare disease.

A twenty-four-hour convenience store owner. A woman in the middle of nowhere.

"We need guns and NBC suits," I said, pivoting toward Hughes. "We've got to get to Ms. Molly's place—*now*."

"What?"

"Patient zero, Hughes. It wasn't Ms. Molly, but I know who it was—and I know what Müller was hiding."

49

Hughes wanted more information. They all did. I wasn't sharing. I measured and contrasted the picture in my mind, manipulating the visual and challenging it with every slice of relevant information I knew. Everything I had learned from the compound, from Müller and his men, from Evelyn.

From *Taggert*.

We didn't have time for me to explain every detail. Most likely, we didn't have any time at all. I got the Humvee rolling in the end. We roared up to city hall where Hughes obtained the NBC suits, but he refused to arm anyone. I met Jeter at the back of his sagging Chevy Caprice. Without comment he dug into his glove box and passed me a worn Beretta 96 with fifteen rounds of nine millimeter housed in the box magazine.

"Keep it covered," he whispered.

I chambered the weapon and slid it into the small of my back. Then I donned the US Army-issue NBC suit Hughes brought me. Jeter, Evelyn, and the LTC himself did the same.

Four additional guardsmen appeared with rifles in hand and mounted up in another Humvee. I met Evelyn's gaze and saw the fear again.

She had more reason to be terrified than any of us. She understood just how ugly this disease could be. For my part, I didn't need the details. In my mind the reality was clear enough.

And so was the target.

Hughes drove. I took shotgun, my mental map guiding us as I directed him out of town. The Humvees bounded over rough, frozen roads, snow exploding from the front tires. We arrived at the same FMTV barricade I had originally circumvented to check on Lyle's mother, and I was surprised to note that it hadn't been relocated beyond the Pritchard farm. Hughes shouted at the sentries, and they moved the truck. Then we hurtled on, diesel engines surging.

We reached Ms. Molly's old farmhouse just as the sun transitioned from midday blaze to early afternoon glow. The driveway was blocked by a barricade of sawhorses marked with official "DO NOT ENTER" signs, but the National Guard troops who accompanied us quickly displaced that barrier. Then the Humvee jolted over the busted dirt driveway. I surveyed the same wraparound porch, the same woodshed and parked Ford Ranger. The chicken coop. The barn.

"What are we looking for?" Hughes said. His voice was taut, laced with anger at my refusal to give details.

"Bodies," I said. "And possibly armed militants. Tell your men to be ready."

Hughes shot me a look, then he bailed out of the Humvee and I followed, pulling the NBC mask over my face and donning the hood. The rubber did little to block out the cold, and I strained to draw air through the filter. A deluge of déjà vu from training days at Fort Moore—then called Fort Benning—not to mention the mission out of Djibouti cascaded through my weary mind. I turned to see Evelyn falling in behind me. She donned a similar mask and our gazes locked.

I knew the same memories were hitting her. I nodded in reassurance.

"Spread out and search!" Hughes called. "Be advised, armed militants may be on-site."

The National Guardsmen required no further instruction. The Army had trained them well—they knew how to seize a position and clear a property. They dispersed and began with the old farmhouse, entering through the front while two men covered the back. Hughes stood by with his radio, barking orders through his mask.

I departed the Humvee and circled the house, Evelyn and Jeter slogging along behind in their ill-fitting NBC suits. I checked the abandoned Ford Ranger, scrubbing snow from one window. I found nothing but an empty bench seat and long-abandoned soda cans in the floorboard. Then I inspected the chicken coop, circling to the back and pulling the pins from the access door Ms. Molly used to collect eggs.

Jeter stood back, one hand on the sidearm now strapped to the exterior of his NBC suit. The hinges groaned. The door swung back.

And then the ice pick returned, plunging into my gut.

Ms. Molly's chickens were there, all right. The electric heater mounted to the roof of the coup blazed down, pumping enough warmth to drive the thermometer on the wall into the mid-sixties, Fahrenheit. There was food in the dish and water in a trough.

But the birds were dead, all sixteen of them. They lay on their sides, contorted and stiff, beaks frozen open. Eyes bulging and red.

I glanced to Evelyn. She approached the coup and shone a flashlight over the tangled corpses. Then she turned to me, and I knew what she was thinking.

The virus is trans-species.

I shoved the door closed, dropping the pin back into the latch with my gloved hand. I glanced to the house to see lights flashing on behind second-floor windows. Guardsmen had reached the back porch and were now searching the storm cellar.

So far, they reported nothing.

I pivoted my attention toward the barn. I glanced once at Jeter and nodded. He unsnapped the retention strap on his sidearm. I opened my suit just long enough to access the Beretta. The safety snapped off and I deployed the Macro-Stream alongside the handgun. I rested my shooting hand across my left wrist.

Then I started through the snow. I reached the barn door and stood off to one side, dropping my finger across the trigger. I tilted my head for Evelyn to stand back. She didn't need to be told twice. I indicated for Jeter to approach the giant rolling door. It was constructed of wood, resting on metal rails ten feet overhead. He pulled a chain free of the doorpost. I looked to the end of the chain and noted that the padlock hanging there was already unlocked.

I nodded again. Jeter pushed the door. It rumbled and rattled, rolling backward. I stepped forward automatically, sweeping right, with the MacroStream dumping five hundred lumens over a dusty barn interior. I tightened my trigger finger, ready to squeeze off that first lengthy, double-action shot. I stepped across dusty orange dirt littered with ancient straw, clearing a tangled mess of farm equipment on one side, a row of livestock stalls on the other, twin overhead haylofts split by the same aisle I now stepped into.

It was too much to cover with a single weapon, but Jeter's decades-old Army Ranger skills hadn't left him. He advanced with his sidearm pointed at the hayloft, covering me from overhead and allowing me to clear the ground. We moved in unison, advancing down the middle aisle as I swung the handgun right, sweeping the light over a rusted Massey Ferguson tractor. Two plows. A stack of fertilizer. A workbench littered with rusted tools. An anvil and a propane-powered forge.

But no humans. I pivoted left to clear the first livestock stall. It was empty save for more dry straw and packed dirt. The next was the same. Jeter held back at the middle of the room to maintain the best position to cover both hay lofts. I passed the workbench and cleared a storage room full of animal medicines and tractor parts. I cleared the third stall. I advanced to the fourth as my chest tightened.

There were boot prints on the floor outside the final stall's door. Scraping through the dust, displacing the straw. They were too big to be Ms. Molly's shoes. Too big to be Maggie's shoes. Lyle was wheelchair-bound. I had never before set foot in this place.

I reached the entrance of the fourth stall, and unlike the first three, I found the rolling door cracked open by an inch. An electrical cord ran through the gap. A wash of vague warmth penetrated the thick folds of my NBC suit, joined by a dim orange glow. I saw it through the bars of the stall's upper walls, and my finger constricted around the trigger. I reached out with the toe of my boot and grabbed the end of the door. I shoved it back.

The door rolled easily on well-constructed rails, rumbling backward to review the interior. My MacroStream blazed inside, joined by the beaming orange glow of a large electric space heater. Both lights revealed the same thing at once.

Twin bodies, both lying in pools of dry vomit. Both contorted. Both stiff and half-frozen with mouths hanging open and eyes swollen and bloodshot. Both middle-aged males, Middle Eastern in appearance.

They were Clay Taggert's missing outsiders—I knew it by the cut of their NATO-issued leather boots, stamped with the gold leaf emblem of the Lebanese Armed Forces.

50

"Jeter!" I shouted without turning away from the grizzly scene. Jeter's boots pounded toward me while I remained in the doorframe, blocking the entrance.

I didn't advance—I didn't need to. I could see everything right from the door. In addition to the two bodies and the heater, there were blankets. Two duffel bags, torn open, with clothing and personal items scattered around. A camping stove, dirty cooking pots, empty soup cans and crushed eggshells. A pair of holsters, but no handguns.

And a black vinyl backpack, lying empty on the floor, white letters stitched to the outside.

Coleus Biotech.

Jeter and Evelyn rushed in beside me, both breathing hard through their masks. They surveyed the scene and Jeter swore. Evelyn tried to push through the door and I blocked her.

"Don't. We already know how they died."

"Who are they?" Jeter demanded.

I turned away from the bodies, meeting his gaze.

"Best guess?" I said. "They're exactly who Taggert said they were. They're terrorists."

HUGHES'S MEN arrived to search the barn, and I returned to the snowbound landscape outside, naturally migrating toward the open sunlight. I lowered my gun and lifted my mask, inhaling welcome fresh air.

"Mason! Don't do that. The virus could be airborne."

Evelyn rushed from the barn. Jeter wasn't far behind. The old cop looked dazed and disoriented, staring through his NBC mask as the guardsmen rushed by. Hughes shouted orders. Radios crackled.

And I stood between the barn and the chicken coop, gazing across the barnyard and retracing the events in my mind. I saw it now—the full picture. It was crystal clear and even more horrific than I had initially estimated.

A secret worth going to war over.

LTC Hughes appeared from the barn, marching through the snow with the aggression of someone who couldn't decide if he were more pissed or terrified.

"Who are they?" He shouted the question, pointing back at the barn.

"Just who I told you they were the first night we met. They're foreign nationals, likely from the Levant. Equipped with stolen NATO-issue boots."

Hughes's widened eyes told the physiological story of the

fear coursing through his blood—the realization that he had missed something huge.

"It was a break-in, Colonel," I said. "That was the first domino to fall. Whoever these guys are, they came to Prairie Junction to raid the Coleus Biotech facility. They knew it contained something special—something particularly potent, and off the books. They broke in and something went sideways. They accidentally infected themselves, after which they fled down State Highway 15, back toward Prairie Junction, where they must have run out of gas. They stopped at Ollie Peters's service station to fill up and buy those cans of soup you saw in the stall. That's how Ollie was infected. Then they needed an obscure place to hide, and they found one at the Pritchard farm."

I turned away from the chicken coop, facing Hughes. "They infected Ms. Molly. They infected these chickens when they raided the eggs. Lyle told me that Maggie stopped by to clean the house, but Ms. Molly sent her away—said she wasn't feeling well. Likely, she had a gun to her head. She wouldn't even let Maggie inside, but Maggie was still infected."

Hughes stood stunned. He looked back at the barn. Back at me. His mouth hung open.

"How...can you prove that?"

"Wrong question, Colonel. What you need to be asking is *what happened next?* There's a Coleus Biotech backpack in that stall, and it's empty. So are their holsters. Somebody came here after they died—presumably their bosses or partners. Whatever they stole from Coleus is now missing, meaning that—"

"There could be an attack," Hughes said.

I simply nodded.

He blanched. He froze only a moment longer.

Then he was gone, shouting at his men, barking into a radio, demanding a sat phone. I stood motionless and watched the chaos unfold, my own heart thumping as I estimated the timeline. I swept the yard again, squinting at the tracks in the snow.

Not all of them were Humvee tracks.

"They came after the blizzard," I said. "We're twelve or more hours behind."

"They could be anywhere," Jeter said. "Fool Taggert! I thought he was just being racist."

"He was," I said. "Which I won't defend. His personal instincts may have been prejudiced, but in this case I think it was his battlefield instinct that told the truth. He was tracking a mortal threat."

Jeter swore. Evelyn drew near, lowering her voice.

"If half of what you say is true, Ollie Peters, Ms. Molly, Maggie—all these people were infected with only minor contact. You could already be infected. *Please* put your mask on."

I looked down. Her eyes were pleading behind her semi-fogged mask lens. I simply nodded and re-donned the NBC mask. I didn't think it would matter—whatever invisible highway this Frankenstein disease used to transmit itself from one unsuspecting host to the next, at this stage I was either infected or I wasn't. I really couldn't afford to worry either way.

The only thing that mattered was the hunt. Half a decade later and now on the far side of the globe, I was chasing terrorists again.

"We need the FBI," I said. "Homeland Security, the CDC —everybody we can get."

"And *Müller*," Evelyn snarled. "Somebody from Coleus is going to answer for this."

I simply nodded. There was no point in stating the obvious—that Müller was long gone, and that Coleus would lawyer up and stonewall the world. In fact, the stonewalling had already begun. Coleus had weaponized the National Guard and leaned on the governor to conceal this thing from the start—to buy time for their hired mercenaries to capture the terrorists and eliminate the witnesses.

A desperate, last-ditch attempt to prevent their illegal research from being exposed. And a failed attempt, in the end.

My best and only option at this stage was to step into the boots of those mercenaries, and assume their mission. To find whoever had stolen the virus, and gun them down before they could unleash it on unsuspecting millions.

And to do that, I really needed to step into a further pair of boots—the captured NATO boots of the terrorist enemy. I needed to imagine myself as a psychopathic killer with a backpack full of black death.

Where would I strike?

"Let's get back to city hall," I said. "I need another map."

51

The city hall we returned to was altogether unlike the city hall we had departed from only sixty minutes prior. With the clock grinding past one in the afternoon, a literal army swirled around the makeshift National Guard headquarters. Hughes roared the Humvee into the parking lot and stomped on the brakes at the front entrance. As before, he, Jeter, and myself stood back from the others until Evelyn had swabbed us. She swabbed herself also. She tested for the standard Ebola virus, which we all knew might or might not reveal the variant strain— even assuming incubation had progressed far enough to trigger a test at all.

We were all negative. We stripped out of the NBC suits and donned double N-95 masks instead.

"Standard Ebola is spread via body fluids," Evelyn said. "Keep your spit to yourself."

Yes, but this isn't standard.

I thought it, I didn't say it. There was no point. Inside the command post Hughes went to work directing his men, and

I couldn't deny that I admired the bulldog he became. In seconds he locked down not only the city hall but the bulk of Prairie Junction twice as tight as it had been since he arrived. Nobody was allowed outdoors. No vehicles were allowed on the streets for any reason short of mortal emergency. A detachment of ten guardsmen was deployed to the Pritchard farm with orders to lock the entire place down—and to stay far away from the buildings.

Washington was notified via satellite phone. I expected Hughes to know why the cell and internet towers were down, but he didn't. It was a mystery his men had fought to solve since arriving. In the meantime, the sat phones punched through. FBI field offices across the region sprang into action. Homeland Security, the NSA, the Pentagon, the CDC, the NIH—even the Department of Transportation was notified. The mission was brutally clear. Every measure had to be taken to constrict any possible transfer of the pathogen to a major metropolis.

Chicago was the obvious target. Minneapolis, Kansas City, and St. Louis were all easy drives. But with a twelve-plus hours' head start, the enemy could be anywhere. They could have reached Nashville, Dallas, Atlanta, or maybe even Washington.

And that was assuming they drove. They might have boarded an aircraft, in which case they could already be in Europe. They might have accidentally infected themselves while collecting the virus, and even now spreading the virus in every bathroom, airport terminal, and restaurant they passed through.

There was no way to know. There were too many variables. The best we could do was to hurtle ahead—to *find them* at any cost.

"We should focus on most likely targets first," I said. "Then work outward. Let's find a map."

Evelyn, Jeter and I found ourselves the odd people out as the National Guard crashed around under Hughes's orders. We barricaded ourselves into the city secretary's office and rooted around until we finally uncovered a multi-state atlas stored in a closet. It featured every major artery in the Midwest. It was also, unfortunately, about twenty years out of date. But without internet to access a digital map, it was our best option.

I flipped to a page that displayed all of Iowa joined by at least half of every state it bordered. Situated in the northeastern corner of the Hawkeye State, Prairie Junction was closest to Wisconsin, Minnesota, and Illinois, making Madison, Milwaukee, Minneapolis, and Chicago the closest major cities. Rockford looked pretty big, too.

"Assume it's not airborne," I said, looking to Evelyn. "How do these guys weaponize the virus?"

Evelyn stood with her arms folded while she considered.

"The pathogen is almost certainly in liquid form. Depending on its potency, skin contact could be enough. Injection would be most effective. Ingestion could also work."

"So they could poison a water supply? Like a water tower?"

"In theory. The virus would dilute pretty quickly in that much water. It might not be effective. A more logical strategy would be a contained water source. Something relatively small...or at least smaller than a water tower."

I looked back to the map. Jeter shifted on his feet next to the secretary's desk. The man absolutely could not stand still.

LOGAN RYLES

"We gotta move, Mason. We need people in the air."

"It won't do any good to be in the air if we don't know where to go."

"So we just gonna stare at a map?"

I pondered. Shook my head. "No. You're right. We need more evidence...some kind of lead."

"Such as?"

I closed my eyes and breathed deep. It wasn't easy through the dual N-95 masks. I again placed myself in the boots of the bad guys. I imagined what their original plan must have been, back before everything went haywire.

They would break into the Coleus Biotech lab. Steal the pathogen. Run for cover. Rendezvous with their bosses...or maybe execute the attack on their own.

The problem came when one of the terrorists dropped a vial, or opened the wrong jar, or whatever other incident occasioned the transmission of the pathogen. Then they had to lie low. They frantically called for help even as Müller discovered the security breach and sprang into action. He called his own bosses. The National Guard was deployed. The mercenaries were hired.

The coverup began even while the terrorists lay gasping for their last breaths in Ms. Molly's barn. Even while Müller and his invisible associates had locked down the whole of Prairie Junction, *somebody* had snuck in.

Somebody who knew about the stolen virus and was on the side of terror. Somebody who would finish the job. Somebody who had turned up at the barn, recovered the pathogen, and then simply drove away.

Drove away.

My head popped up. My eyes snapped open. "There was no car."

Jeter frowned. "Huh?"

"There was no car at Ms. Molly's place. No vehicle at all. The dead guys in the barn must have driven something to Ollie's service station, then on to the Pritchard farm. There's no way they walked that distance. But there was no car when we arrived on the property."

"So?" Evelyn said.

"So whoever took the pathogen and the handguns must also have taken the *car*. The National Guard never extended their roadblock to enclose the Pritchard Farm. The backup terrorists could have simply driven away in the same vehicle the original terrorists arrived in. Taggert described it as a small, black import SUV. They might still be using it."

Jeter snapped his fingers. I pivoted toward him. "Did Ollie have security cameras at his place?"

"I dunno. Maybe?"

"Send an officer to check. Make sure he's wearing protective gear. If we can get that license plate, we may have something."

Jeter was already headed for the door. I looked back to the map. I could feel Evelyn's tension radiating off her body like heat waves.

"Mason...if they dispense this stuff into a crowd..."

"I know."

"We're not talking about thousands. We're talking about millions. A global pandemic."

I looked up. The fear I'd seen in Evelyn's gaze before was matched with raw, unfettered energy. The desire to sink her teeth in.

I felt the same.

"It'll never happen," I said. "We're going to catch these guys."

52

"It was a rental!" Jeter exploded into the secretary's office with a sat phone clenched in one hand, his wrinkled face alive with triumph. "We got a clear picture from Ollie's outdoor cameras. Black Honda HRV, Tennessee license plate, registration links to a national rental company."

"Have you called the rental company yet?" I asked.

"Yeah. Got one of my officers on the line with them now. He—hold on, hold on." Jeter raised a finger. He lifted the phone to his ear and listened, squinting.

"What?" Jeter said. "Are you kidding me? You tell them we don't have *time* for a warrant. Do they understand the situation? We need this now!"

Jeter's face darkened from cherry to maroon as he alternated between listening, arguing, and simply cursing his officer. Within thirty seconds I knew he would never get anywhere.

"Give me the phone," Evelyn said, extending a hand. "I

know somebody at the FBI. He may have a back door with the rental company."

Jeter clung on only a moment longer. Then he passed her the phone. It was an Iridium model sat phone, several years old. No web search functions. Just a keypad.

Evelyn stared at the device a moment, thumb hesitating over the keypad. Then she commenced to mash numbers, apparently from memory. I recognized a 202 area code—Washington DC.

The phone rang. Evelyn held it to her ear. She wouldn't meet my gaze. After an extended moment, a man's voice crackled on the other end. I couldn't quite make out the words.

"Alex... It's Evie."

Long pause. Evelyn glanced sideways at me and flushed. She turned her back.

"I'm...I'm good. I... Look, I'm sorry to call you this way. I need a favor. It's an emergency."

I still couldn't make out the speaker's words, but it wasn't difficult to detect his change in tone. It became dry. Mechanical. Evelyn relayed the situation. She made her ask. The crackle of the voice rose in disbelief. Evelyn reinforced the desperation of her need. The extremity of the emergency.

Apparently, whatever department of the FBI this guy worked at, he hadn't yet been notified of the situation in Iowa. In the end Evelyn won him over anyway. He hung up first. She lowered the phone.

"He's going to try." She looked back over one shoulder, green eyes suddenly distant. I simply nodded, guessing and not needing to confirm. I stepped out into the hallway and shouted for Hughes. He appeared on the third call, sweaty despite the chill of the building. I beckoned him into the secretary's office. Within seconds I had him updated.

"You called the FBI?" he asked.

"Indirectly," I said. "We've got somebody working on the rental company, but apparently the Bureau isn't yet talking to itself. He had no idea about the potential attack."

Hughes's gaze turned hard, but he didn't say anything. I figured a man like him who'd worked in government for as many years as it takes to reach lieutenant colonel understood exactly how infuriating bureaucracy could be.

"We'll reach out to our own FBI contacts," he said. "They'll implement roadblocks. If these guys are using that vehicle, we'll have every cop and traffic camera in the country hunting for them. Keep me updated."

Hughes ducked out again. We stared at the map and counted the minutes waiting for Special Agent Alex to call back. I noted Evelyn picking at her fingernails, absentmindedly raising them to her face before remembering that she was double-masked and dropping her hand again.

It was something else I remembered from Djibouti—Evelyn biting her nails. It only happened once, just before "the talk" that ended with my bad joke and her embarrassed exit. In hindsight I should have known how tense she was. How focused, how stressed.

That conversation *meant* something to her, more than it had to me. Apparently, her brief phone call with Alex had meant something also. Maybe more than it meant to him.

"You got guns, Jeter?" I broke the silence for my own sake as much as anyone's.

"We got a locker back at the police station. A couple AR-15s, plenty of handguns."

"What about a vehicle? Something fast with four-wheel drive."

A hesitation. "I think one of my boys drives a Dodge Durango. It's got a V8. Why?"

I fixated on the map. "Because if we find a target, I'm going after it."

"Me too." I looked up. Evelyn's gaze locked on mine. The hurt had faded a little. She looked winded—but still very much in the fight.

"Whall heck. Never let it be said that Ransom Jeter denied the call of duty. I'll phone my boy."

Jeter shuffled off to find another sat phone. The stillness he left behind was somehow even more uncomfortable.

"He's my ex," Evelyn said. "The one I divorced."

"I wasn't asking, Evelyn."

"I know. I just...wanted you to know."

Our gazes met, but I didn't say anything. I remembered what she said about her ex being a passionate runner...how he *got around.*

It made me want to punch him. Maybe I really wanted to punch myself.

I looked away, still unsure what to say. Before I could think of something, the Iridium phone chimed. Evelyn turned her head and mashed the button. There was no speaker function. She held the device to her ear.

"Yes? Okay...uhuh...right."

Evelyn scrambled around the secretary's desk, scraping junk aside and locating a pen. She began writing on the back of an envelope. I read the words as the voice in her ear continued to crackle.

Rented in Chicago on 2/7. Abdul Muhammad, Virginia DL. Due back 2/13, Madison.

Evelyn lowered the pen. She listened a moment longer. The room was so quiet I could now hear Alex's words.

"...all I have. We'll keep searching."

"Thank you, Alex. This helps."

Long pause. Neither one of them spoke.

Then Alex said, "Are you safe?"

Evelyn glanced my way. She swallowed. "Yeah...yeah, I'm good."

Another long pause. I felt like an intruder barging in on a sensitive moment.

Alex's next words shattered that paradigm into a million pieces.

"Well, good. Give me a ring when you're back in DC. We should grab a bite."

Evelyn turned scarlet, color rising out of her neck and consuming her face. She mumbled something unintelligible and hung up the phone, quickly turning her back to me.

I stood awkwardly behind, trying to ignore her twitching shoulders. Every barely audible sniff sent blades of pain ripping through my chest. I could still see the color rising up her neck—the same color I'd witnessed in Djibouti, although I hadn't understood it the first time.

Morons, I thought. But I didn't voice my disgust—not at myself, nor at Alex. I knew it wouldn't help.

"I'll get Hughes," I said softly.

Evelyn simply nodded. I left the room and located the LTC. I handed him the envelope and he scanned it. Then he was back on his own sat phone, communicating with the FBI —the *other* part of the FBI. Dialing Homeland Security. Informing his contacts at the Pentagon.

It was actionable intelligence. With a little luck, the car might be found. And yet I knew that wasn't enough—this was chess, not checkers. We were still behind the target. We needed to be ahead of them.

I returned to the secretary's office to find Evelyn leaning over the map. Her eyes were still puffy but she had collected herself. She tapped Madison.

"The car was scheduled to be returned in Madison on February thirteenth," she said.

"Tomorrow," I added, checking my watch.

"Isn't that odd?"

"What do you mean?"

"It was rented in Chicago, then driven to Iowa. Then scheduled to be returned in Madison. Wouldn't you expect them to return the car where they rented it? So they could fly out of O'Hare?"

I studied the map, and then I saw what Evelyn saw. The subtext. The hint of a clue.

"Unless you were planning to fly out of Madison," I said.

"Which you would do if you were in a hurry. And if Madison lay nearest to your target."

A chill ripped down my spine. I shouted for Hughes. He bustled in a moment later, hanging up another sat phone.

"The FBI's got teams headed to O'Hare and all the major regional cities," Hughes said. "They're also deploying an investigatory team to Prairie Junction. ETA, two hours."

I shook my head, tapping the map. "Too little too late. The target is somewhere near Madison. They'll drop the car at the airport and fly out immediately afterward. Didn't you tell the FBI about the car?"

"Of course I did. They said they'd look into it."

Look into it. I wanted to bust noses.

"You have internet access?" I demanded.

"We have satellite internet. Why?"

"We need data on all public gatherings and major events in the greater Madison region for the next three days. Any place with high population density and low security. That's where they'll strike."

"The FBI will cover that. They're running profiles now."

I breathed a curse. "The FBI didn't know this threat *existed* two hours ago. Pardon me if I'm unwilling to disengage."

Hughes gritted his teeth, but I didn't think I was the subject of his frustration. I pressed my request.

"Where are your computers?"

"My people are using the internet to interface with command in Des Moines. We don't have latitude to run Google searches."

"Are you kidding me?" I knew he wasn't. I still needed him to hear the disbelief in my voice.

Hughes flushed a little. Then he turned for the door. "I'll see what I can do."

The LTC departed the room before I could press him any further. I bit back another disgusted curse and returned to the map, studying Wisconsin. Studying all the possible routes that rental car could have taken out of Prairie Junction toward Madison.

There weren't many. But where was the target?

I needed that freaking computer.

"I got the Durango!" I looked up just in time to see Jeter barging in, waving a set of car keys. "We can hit the station for guns. You got a target?"

I shook my head. Looked back to the map. "We're thinking Madison—"

I stopped. I looked back to Jeter where he stood in the doorway. The Prairie Junction Police Department hat sat cocked back over a crown of salt and pepper hair, and despite the chill, Jeter's hot nature left him dripping in sweat. It ran down his neck. It stained the top of his hoodie.

That blue and yellow hoodie, emblazoned with the skull inside the old-school leather helmet, letters bent beneath it.

AMERICAN GRIDIRON — Inaugural Season.
Yard by Bloody Yard.

My heart lurched. I grabbed Jeter by the shoulder.
"Turn around!"

Jeter blinked in confusion, but Evelyn understood. She circled the table and spun Jeter around, exposing the back of the hoodie. It was also blue, also printed with a yellow heading, followed by two long columns of white text—like a rock band tour schedule, with dates on the left and cities on the right.

Only, this wasn't a rock band schedule. It was an exhibition football game schedule. Eight teams. Ten weeks of regular season games, culminating in a bracketed, direct elimination playoff of two rounds.

February 5th — Semi Finals: Miami, Florida.
February 12th — Finals: Madison, Wisconsin.

"Couldn't get tickets. The dern thing was sold out!"

Jeter's comments on the exhibition championship replayed through my mind like a gunshot. I looked to Evelyn.

Then we both bolted for the door.

53

J eter may have been slow on the initial uptake, but by the time we exploded through Hughes's operation center and crashed for the city hall's main entrance, he was catching on. He shouted that he would drive. Hughes met us in the lobby, a laptop under his arm as he babbled about federal internet access restrictions.

I ignored him—I had neither the time nor the patience to wrangle through the layers of bureaucratic red tape that enshrouded the LTC like a mummy. Outside the building a surge of bitter air burned my windpipe. The Dodge Durango Jeter had promised sat in the snow, exhaust burbling from dual tailpipes as the windshield fogged over.

"Jump in!" Jeter shouted, circling the Durango.

The vehicle was a late model, jet black with a matching leather interior. The seats were heated. The climate control ran at full blast. Jeter jammed us into reverse and the Durango hurtled backward toward the street. He was muttering curses the entire time, pulling the wheel to turn us back toward Prairie Junction.

"You really think it's the ball game?"

"I don't know, Jeter. It's just a guess, but it's logical. How many tickets were sold for the semi-finals games?"

"I don't know. They sold out."

"So how big were the stadiums?" Evelyn interjected.

"They're not stadiums—they play in modified arenas. Maybe twenty thousand?"

Twenty thousand people. From all over America, or at least all over the Midwest. Crowded into a tight, enclosed space where transmission would run wild through the packed, boisterous bodies. If incubation was as slow as even eight hours, many of those people would be loaded aboard flights to their hometowns before the first symptoms kicked in. Passing through airports, spreading the virus from sea to shining sea.

Before anyone knew what had happened, the scourge of modified Ebola would run rampant. So much worse than a car bomb or even a suitcase nuke—the kind of thing that could bring the entire nation crashing into the abyss.

"There are a thousand possible targets," Evelyn said. "They could be headed straight to O'Hare...or someplace on the east coast."

"If they are, there's nothing we can do about it," I said. "The FBI will have to catch this. Their rental car was scheduled to be returned in Madison. The American Gridiron is still a relatively new league—security measures will be weaker than they might be at an NFL game or a major concert. It's a subtle target the FBI might overlook."

It was my last statement which rang truest in my own ears—the logical argument which most supported my growing belief that the American Gridiron game could be the target. While the FBI and Homeland Security zeroed in on airports and major cities, my gut told me that anyone smart enough to identify and steal a modified virus was smart enough to avoid the usual federal dragnets.

To select a more subtle, vulnerable point of attack.

"Gun locker in the back," Jeter said, slamming on his brakes in front of the police station. "Let's hurry!"

I followed Jeter inside, leaving Evelyn in the car to work her satellite phone, communicating mostly with her superiors in Atlanta.

Bracing them for the prospect of an unspeakable horror.

The police station was bright with fluorescent glow, only a few officers on station behind desks piled high with paperwork. Most of those officers worked satellite phones issued by the National Guard, interfacing—or attempting to interface—with Hughes's soldiers. One stood as Jeter entered, lowering a phone and shouting across the room.

"Chief! What the hell is going on? Bob Skyler says there was an explosion out by his grain silo."

Jeter ignored the question. I ignored it also. We barged through the desks and down the hall, past Jeter's office, the lunch room, and the officer lounge. We reached a back room where Jeter unlocked a wooden door with a key—the key was kept in the door. In the room beyond I expected to find safes or at least locking rifle racks.

I should have known better. This was small-town Iowa— the AR-15s sat coated in dust on a rack alongside Mossberg 500 shotguns. Ammunition was stacked in baskets on the shelves beneath. Handguns and body armor were piled on a long dining room table stained by grease and cleaning solvents.

"Gear up!" Jeter said.

I didn't need a second invitation. I began with Kevlar

body armor, followed by a Glock 17 loaded with eighteen-plus-one rounds of nine-millimeter concealed by my Carhartt coat, a spare magazine dropped into the coat's giant pocket. I bypassed a Taser but took two pairs of handcuffs, both dumped into the same pocket. One AR and ninety rounds of 5.56 ammunition completed the setup. Jeter took a rifle also, and two cans of tear gas. I grabbed a Glock 19 on impulse for Evelyn—she might not want it, but I felt better knowing she was armed. She had some recent experience with handguns.

Then we were barging back through the police station as the cop hung up his sat phone and shouted again.

"Chief! We—"

"Keep it locked down, Bucky!" Jeter cut him off. "Everybody stays home. You see anyone suspicious, you freaking put them on their ass. Understand?"

"Well...okay. What—"

Bucky never got the chance for further comment. We were back outside, and this time I cut Jeter off on his path to the driver's seat.

"You drive too slow, old man."

Jeter cursed but didn't argue. We tossed the rifles in the back. I adjusted the driver's seat and ratcheted the shifter into drive. The Durango's dash illuminated in red and blue, already locked into four-high. I spun the wheel and pointed us north by the dash-mounted compass.

"We need Route 18 through Monona," Jeter said. "It's two hours to Madison."

Let's make it ninety minutes.

I hit Main Street and cleared the last intersection. My boot rammed into the accelerator, and the giant V8 thundered.

54

Jeter's cell phone finally regained signal thirty-two miles northeast of Prairie Junction, some eighteen miles outside the last National Guard checkpoint, where the soldiers on station stood back and waved us straight through. I guessed that LTC Hughes must have radioed ahead—finally cutting some red tape for a change.

With signal restored, Jeter went to work using his smartphone to source phone numbers for Evelyn, which she dialed with her sat phone. Most of the people she spoke to seemed to have already been notified of the emergency at hand—possibly by Evelyn herself during previous calls. As a deputy director, Evelyn wanted updates on the response. She wanted to ensure that anyone and everyone involved was advised of the latest situation on the ground.

Basically, she wanted to feel like she was making a difference, even if there was very little any of us could do at this stage. Not unless and until we ran down that rental car in Madison.

"Call the Wisconsin State Police," I said, jerking my

head at Jeter. He did, but I wasn't sure if it mattered. The WSP seemed caught off guard when Jeter called to demand that the American Gridiron final be immediately canceled under concern of a terrorist strike. They didn't believe him. They promised to run the tip up the chain, but I knew the game would never be called off. Not because they were bad cops, but because no city official in his right mind would cancel a major cash-cow event based on the crazed demands of a caller nobody had ever heard of.

The FBI hadn't yet notified the Wisconsin state government—or, if they had, that notification hadn't yet trickled down to the Madison city level. Maybe it was nobody's fault. Maybe it was just the way of the world. But within the next eight hours, the question of who was to blame might never matter. In the end, the whole nation might pay the price.

It was four p.m. as we exploded across the Wisconsin state lane. The weather was turning nasty again, clouds of gray slowly overtaking us from behind as the winter sun began to set. Traffic thickened and we raced across the Mississippi River, passing into the town of Prairie du Chien where I was forced to lay on my brakes. Snowflakes bounced off the windshield and my chest tightened.

"I can't believe this." Evelyn's voice whispered from the back seat. I glanced into the mirror. She wasn't speaking on the sat phone any longer. The device lay in her lap, her eyes staring at the back of Jeter's seat. She looked up, meeting my gaze. Her face flushed.

"Do you know what this means? Coleus Biotech was *deliberately* conducting gain-of-function research on Ebola. Off the books and outside the scope of governmental oversight. We're talking about an *unthinkable* breach of research protocol, to say nothing of extreme illegality. I just can't believe it!"

"Believe it, honey," Jeter growled. "How much money you reckon there is in an effective Ebola vaccine?"

Evelyn snorted. She shook her head, eyes still wide. "Hundreds of millions?"

"Well, there you go. If there's a pot of gold, there's somebody dirty enough to do anything for it."

"But there's a *process*," Evelyn snapped. "If they wanted to research Ebola they could have done so under proper oversight."

"And that would have extended their research by years," I said. "Maybe decades. Jeter's right. This was a cash grab, plain and simple. The fact that they were willing—and able —to deploy mercenaries to cover their tracks tells you that there's a major player someplace up the chain. Somebody powerful enough to shut down cell phone towers and manipulate the Iowa National Guard. Somebody who couldn't afford for a terrorist break-in to expose Coleus's illegal research."

"I'm gonna find him," Evelyn snarled. "I'm gonna rip his freaking throat out."

Jeter and I exchanged a glance. Neither of us spoke— neither of us stated the obvious. But I knew we were both thinking the same.

Assuming you live that long.

I redirected my attention through the windshield and tightened my grip around the wheel. With the plains of Iowa behind us, we raced along an open highway surrounded by lightly forested, southern Wisconsin hills. Green signs advertised Fennimore, then Dodgeville. With the cruise locked at eighty miles per hour and the windshield wipers thumping to displace growing snowfall, I turned again to Jeter.

"When is kickoff?"

"Six thirty," Jeter said. "They're opening with a concert, though. Some classic rock band."

I looked to the clock built into the Durango's dash. We were still in Central Time. It was four forty-two and visibility was dropping by the second. I looked again into the rearview mirror and could no longer see the horizon. The sun had faded as a bank of clouds obscured the highway in blackness, that ever-present swirl of snow thickening by the minute. I knew I needed to slow down. I knew I couldn't afford to.

"How we gonna play this?" Jeter said. "They'll never let us through armed."

"We start with security," I said. "We notify them of the threat and try to gain entry."

"Then we just...search for Middle Easterners?" The discomfort in Evelyn's voice was obvious, and not unfounded.

"We search for anybody who's not where they should be," I said. "Anybody who's tampering or evading security. We secure concession stands first, then move to the arena."

"And if we find them?" Evelyn said.

"We neutralize them," I said. "Whatever it takes."

55

"Ladies and gentlemen, welcome to beautiful Madison, Wisconsin, and welcome to the inaugural championship showdown of the American Gridiron Arena League!"

Jeter located the local sports radio channel as we finally reached Madison. We'd lost time on the highway. Snowfall thickened until visibility faded to barely fifty feet. I ran the Durango's headlights on low beams as the vague glow of distant skyscraper lights broke through the shadows far ahead. I couldn't see the buildings. I couldn't see the billboards as the dash-mounted GPS led us eastward on Highway 18. Madison itself sat to our left, sandwiched on a bridge of dirt between Lake Monona and Lake Mendota. The arena—a brand-new facility constructed for minor league hockey and touring concerts—sat on the eastern shore of Lake Mendota in the suburb of Maple Bluff. Our only options to reach the arena were either to cut straight through downtown Madison or else to circle around the entire metro area, sticking to highways.

Glancing back at the clock, I knew we were running out of time. Kickoff was in barely forty minutes, but I didn't trust the narrow streets of a downtown mired by traffic lights. My gut said to stick to the highway. The radio broadcast—live from the arena—assured me that nobody was dropping dead just yet.

But it could already be too late.

"I'll do the talking," Jeter said. "The badge will help."

I had less faith in the power of Jeter's small-town credentials, but I didn't argue. I kept my gaze sweeping the streets as we exited the highway and dropped into the outskirts of Madison. I didn't actually expect to see the black Honda HRV from Ollie Peters's security camera recording, but despite the odds stacked against the probability of pinning a terrorist in this place, an instinct tingling up my spine told me that I wasn't wrong.

I'd experienced this feeling before—several dozen times, all across the desolate mountain ranges of Afghanistan, and once more on the tarmac of Camp Lemonnier outside Djibouti City. It was electric, supercharging my nerves and bringing my body to full alert. It was the sensation that I was deathly close to the enemy, growing closer with every rotation of the Durango's tires.

It wasn't a comfort in rural Afghanistan or Africa. It was much less a comfort in a crowded American city.

"There!" Jeter pointed, but I could already see the arena. It was lit up like Times Square on New Year's Eve—slicing strobe lights, flashing blue and yellow LEDs. The snow swirled thickly outside the Durango, but it wasn't enough to obscure a parking lot packed to the brim with vehicles. I noted plenty of Wisconsin license plates, but they were far from dominant. Minnesota, Iowa, Illinois, Michigan, Indiana

—even Texas was represented. My stomach tightened as that electric feeling ratcheted up a notch, turning my knuckles white around the wheel. I spun into the parking lot and raced down the first aisle, headed for the entrance of the arena.

"Get your badge ready," I said.

Jeter already had his wallet out. The badge itself was a generic gold metal shield stamped with the name CITY OF PRAIRIE JUNCTION, joined in the wallet by a police identification card printed with Jeter's photograph. Neither item looked very authoritative. Certainly, I had never heard of Prairie Junction before I rolled onto Main Street three months prior.

Madison City police, dressed like Eskimos, appeared from a mobile command building at the terminus of the parking lot. Horseshoe metal detectors stood there, along with a waist-high temporary metal fence that marked off an entrance channel toward the arena.

There were no other people. The sidewalk lay thick with gathering snowdrifts. But behind the arena's glass doors, the crowd was packed close together beneath those flashing blue and yellow lights. Even before I lowered the Durango's window I could hear the pounding music.

"We're all sold out!" the first Madison cop shouted over the wind, his voice heavy with a Wisconsin accent. "You'll have to catch it on TV."

Jeter shoved his arm across my chest.

"Ransom Jeter, Chief of Police, Prairie Junction, Iowa. I need to speak to your commanding officer!"

The Madison cop squinted at the ID. He seemed confused.

"Sir, the arena is sold out. You'll have to leave!"

"This isn't about the game! There's a terrorist on the loose."

"What?" The officer ducked his head to make eye contact with Jeter. His ears were covered by thick, fluffy muffs. I yanked them off and screamed through the window.

"*Terrorists!* There may be an attack!"

That got him. The cop blanched. He looked back to Jeter's outstretched ID, but seemed no less confused. Jeter cut in again, hitting him with the high points. The cop held up a hand.

"Wait here! I'll get my commanding officer."

He turned for the trailer. I buzzed the window up, already shivering. The humidity in Madison was much worse than Iowa. Every breath of wind sliced right to my bone marrow despite the heavy Carhartt coat.

"He ain't listening," Jeter snarled.

I said nothing, my gaze surveying the arena entrance and the tangle of bodies visible just beyond a row of glass doors.

What was I looking for? Should I open fire into a ceiling and send them all screaming for their vehicles?

It might save their lives—assuming they weren't already infected. But there was also a chance that the attack had nothing to do with Madison or the football game. The terrorists could be halfway to Los Angeles by now.

"Mason!" Evelyn's voice crackled with tension from the back seat. I looked over my shoulder. She pointed through her window, across the parking lot. I squinted through a screen of snow blown sideways by the growing wind. I saw the line of cars, but couldn't make out any details. They sat at the front edge of the parking lot, nearest to the waist-high fence.

"What?"

"*Look.* Black SUV!"

Then the snow parted. I caught a glimpse beneath bright yellow parking lot lights—a row of cars parked tightly beneath a sign, already buried up to their bumpers in snow. The nearest car was jet black, a small SUV with a silver *H* logo inside a box. The model letters read *HRV*. The license plate was blue and white—Tennessee.

And the sign posted above the vehicle read *Vendor Parking*.

My heart lurched. That electric feeling tingling up my spine supercharged to a lightning bolt. I saw the Madison cops returning through the swirl of windy white, but I was no longer interested in explaining. I would leave that to Jeter and Evelyn.

I simply shoved the Durango's door open. I exploded into the parking lot, sinking up to my ankles in snow.

And I hurtled toward the arena.

56

The horseshoe metal detectors lit up like Christmas trees, blaring an alarm as I hurtled through with the Glock 17 concealed beneath my coat. I hadn't bothered with the rifle. I knew the entire arena would panic the moment an unknown man with an AR-15 barged in, which might only escalate the terrorists' timeline of attack. My only thought was to get inside—to begin clearing the twenty-thousand-odd faces packed into this dish-shaped building.

Searching for what? I had no idea. A needle in a haystack, really. A very lethal needle.

But I had to try.

I reached the glass doors even as the cops shouted for me to stop. I ignored them and barged through, stepping instantly into a wash of warm air and a blare of classic rock music. The opening band was on stage—I couldn't see them beyond a wide concourse that stretched out to either side, reaching slowly around the curve of the building. Packed tight around me a swarm of spectators stood in long lines before concession counters.

There was food—hotdogs and nachos. Bagged chips and cotton candy. Drinks ranged from water to soda to beer. And hundreds upon hundreds of people, pressed together, laughing and shouting, some dancing to the music.

My hands turned cold and I swept the concession booths, still unsure what I was looking for. My battlefield instincts from the far side of the world naturally narrowed in on a mental image of a Middle Eastern man with dark eyes and a black beard, even as my twenty-first-century ethics objected to blatant stereotyping. Most of the faces I saw behind the concession counters looked like average Americans of every race and creed, each dressed in a matching food services uniform, while many of the patrons crowded up to the counters wore football jerseys, either orange and white or blue and black.

The doors exploded open behind me and the Madison cops barged in alongside Jeter and Evelyn. I tensed, ready to sprint into the crowd, but one glance at the police officers' faces and I knew they weren't coming for me. They had blanched, their wide eyes cast around the room as one of them held Evelyn's sat phone to his ear, grunting "uhuh" every few seconds as somebody on the other end of the line barked information.

Maybe he was speaking to the FBI. Or maybe the state police had decided to take our tip seriously. Whatever the case, it didn't matter. I was here. I was going to engage.

"I'm going right!" I shouted. "You circle left."

Jeter nodded and turned away. Just as I broke from the doors, Evelyn closed in next to me, grabbing my arm. I looked down to find her fingers clamped around my coat sleeve.

Our gazes locked, but she didn't say a thing. She didn't have to. I plowed through the crowd, making room for us both. Jersey-wearing fans shouted obscenities as I barged ahead, still sweeping the faces behind the concession counters as the classic rock song exploding through every passing tunnel reached a natural crescendo. With each face I passed, I fixated on their eyes. I measured their body language. Searching for those undeniable physiological giveaways that betray a person of any ethnicity.

Suspicious glances, trembling hands. Abrupt behavior that defied the natural rhythm of surrounding activity.

We passed another entrance tunnel as the crowd erupted into rowdy cheers. The music ceased—strobe lights blazed blue and yellow. A voice boomed over loudspeakers.

"Are you folks ready to see some *real* American football?"

The building trembled with the response. Feet pounded, and voices lifted together in a raucous, unintelligible roar. The loudspeaker thundered again with a subsequent announcement.

"Ladies and gentlemen, I give you your Eastern Conference champions: *the Baltimore Wraiths!*"

Blue lights blinked. I pressed ahead past the tunnel as the crowds migrated toward their seats. My heart thundered —I knew we were out of time. I charged ahead anyway, around the next curve to the backside of the building, where a row of service doors offered access to the storage and mechanical rooms beneath the arena seats. A knot of custodians and arena employees in blue jackets loitered outside, one dragging on a vape pen. Another texting on his cell phone. They looked up as Evelyn and I broke out of the last of the crowd. Most appeared confused. A few simply disinterested.

But not one. He stood at the back of the crowd, a ball cap pulled low over his long hair. He wore gray cotton work pants and the same blue jacket embroidered with the arena logo. He wasn't Middle Eastern—he was white. Early twenties in age, a scraggly beard concealing a thin face.

And unlike the others, he wore rubber gloves. He pushed a cart laden with soda fountain CO_2 canisters. He made eye contact with me as I burst past the last tunnel, and when our gazes locked, I felt it.

He was all wrong. Everything about him, from his stance to the ill-fitting uniform to the ice-cold look in his eyes. I'd seen that look a few thousand times before, and would recognize it anywhere.

It was the detached stare of brainwashed radicalization —of nervous focus, edgy paranoia.

I don't know what he saw in my eyes, but it was enough to push his paranoia into full-blown panic. His spine stiffened. He accelerated, turning left toward the nearest service door. I raised a hand and shouted down the concourse.

"*Stop!*"

He didn't stop. He shoved the cart straight into the pressure latch of a metal door, barging through. I sprinted to follow, jerking free of Evelyn. My right hand swept the coat back, closing around the Glock. The guy disappeared and I shoved the arena employees aside, reaching the door just as it slammed closed. A lock snapped into place as I collided with the pressure latch. Looking through a narrow window pane, I stared into wide eyes, sweat glistening on his skin.

Then he was gone, and I body-slammed the door. It

wouldn't budge. I moved to the next door but it was already locked.

"Keys!" I shouted. "Who has the keys?"

Evelyn had caught up as the arena workers stared in confused deadlock, the vape pen halfway to one guy's lips, his friend with the cell phone standing with his mouth hanging slack.

No time.

I drew the Glock. Somebody gasped. Three rounds obliterated the narrow window pane and I punched my fist through, slicing skin on jagged, glistening edges. I reached the interior latch, slamming my fist against the pressure bar.

The lock disengaged. I shoved through, Evelyn right on my heels. I entered a wide concrete hallway illuminated by flickering fluorescent lights. Storage closets lined the interior wall, and the hallway curved to my right beneath the stair-stepped concrete underside of the arena stands. I could actually feel the vibrations of pounding feet from overhead, mixed with the dull and distant roar of the crowd. I looked right, sweeping out of the door and raising the Glock.

Then the gunfire erupted like a storm.

57

Muzzle flash blazed from just around the curve of the hallway, a bright orange starlight matched with the crazed pop of a handgun. Bullets ricocheted off the concrete block wall only inches from my head, unleashing a maelstrom of shrapnel. I instinctively dove for the floor, returning fire one-handed.

The Glock popped, brass ejecting back toward the doors. I felt Evelyn behind me and shoved with my free arm, frantic to push her body out of the line of fire. My bullets ripped toward the curve in the hallway and the returning gunfire ceased. Footsteps pounded and wheels squeaked. I hauled myself back to my knees and crossed the hallway to the shelter of the wall's curvature.

Evelyn remained crouched just inside the door, breathing hard through her mouth. One hand gripped the wall, the other clutched her Prairie Junction PD Glock 19. Its muzzle shivered like a leaf in the wind.

"Are you hurt?" I kept my voice low.

Evelyn shook her head.

"Finger off the trigger," I said. "Take a long, slow breath."

Evelyn removed her finger from the trigger and inhaled once. Swallowed.

I lifted my own weapon to eye level and risked a lean away from the wall. I didn't see anyone. I couldn't hear anything either—nothing save the incessant roar of the crowd as the announcer read off the names of a starting offensive lineup.

"Stay put," I said. "Tell Jeter we've made contact."

Evelyn shook her head. She straightened from her crouch, the Glock steady in her hands.

"You don't know what to look for. I'm coming."

I wanted to argue. I wanted to push her back into the concourse and lock her out of the hallway, to see her running as far from this place as possible.

But there was no point now. I wasn't retreating—I couldn't expect Evelyn to retreat, either.

"Stay low," I said. "Confirm your target before you fire."

Two quick nods. I swung out from the wall and circled left, breaking into a jog. I could only see ten or fifteen yards ahead at any point—the continued curve of the hallway was sharper than the larger, exterior concourse. With every stride I expected to step into the gaping mouth of a handgun muzzle.

Instead I found only blank concrete, shivering under the pound of twenty thousand feet packed tightly overhead. The roar of the crowd reached a perfect crescendo, then paused in breathless silence.

It was the kick-off—the ball was in the air.

Then the thunder returned, louder than ever. The announcer's voice blared from the loudspeaker. I tuned it all out as we reached another bank of doors—bathrooms and staff lockers. I moved instinctively to the men's room and kicked the door back, rushing ahead with the Glock.

A bank of mirrors flashed me with the muzzle of my own weapon. I flinched, catching myself just in time before I fired. I cleared three stalls and a bank of sinks. Two showers and a row of lockers. I returned to the hallway with the blood rushing in my ears.

Move, Sharpe! You're taking too long.

"It's clear!" Evelyn emerged from the ladies' room, face streaming with sweat despite the chill.

"Every stall?" I asked.

She nodded. I wheeled left and broke into a faster jog down the hallway, sacrificing tactical security in favor of speed. With every step my heart thumped harder, visions of gunfire exploding into my face flashing across my mind. The storm of noise from the stands overhead reached an explosive climax as cannon fire thundered over the loudspeaker, temporarily bringing me to a scraping halt.

"Touchdown Wraiths!"

Sweat dripped from my face. The hallway had narrowed, nothing but locked utility closets and electrical panels breaking the endless gray block walls. I sensed that we had circled to the end of the oblong arena—the curvature had sharpened. We were rounding a corner. In another fifty yards we would be headed back down the far side of the building. I *still* hadn't seen the white male pushing the cart loaded with CO_2 canisters.

But within another yard, he saw me. The gunfire resumed as a chattering blare—not handgun fire this time, but something faster and nastier. A submachine gun, blazing not only from ahead but also from above my position. I skidded to a halt and fought backward as bullets ricocheted off the concrete floor and slammed into the matching concrete ceiling. Just as I regained cover a shriek exploded from behind. I whirled to find Evelyn stumbling backward, grasping her upper right arm with her left hand. Her fingers were coated crimson, a trail of the same splashed across the floor.

"Evelyn!" I scrambled backward, grabbing her by the shoulder and pulling her into the shelter of the curving wall. I lifted the Glock and blindly returned fire, dumping rounds toward the ceiling. My bullets pinged off metal and somebody grunted. I could barely hear any of it over my ringing ears and the roar of the crowd.

"Where are you hit?" I spun back to Evelyn. She peeled her hand away from her upper right arm, revealing a hole in her jacket that oozed with blood.

"My arm," she gasped. "It's okay...it just grazed me."

"Can you manage the bleeding?"

Evelyn gripped the wound, instinctively adding pressure. She nodded. "I'm good."

I squeezed her shoulder, then eased forward again. Leaning out from the wall, I peered around the curve. There was a ladder mounted to the hallway wall. It led into an unlocked metal cage, disappearing into the ceiling. The sign next to the cage read "ROOF ACCESS". The padlock that had held the cage closed lay on the floor, broken in half next to a pair of bolt cutters and the same cart I had seen loaded with soda fountain CO_2 canisters.

The canisters were now gone. So was the guy who had pushed them. Blood splashed the concrete at the bottom of the ladder amid a field of fallen nine-millimeter brass casings.

"Hang tight," I said. "When Jeter gets here, tell him I'm on the roof."

I swung out from the protection of the wall and hurtled past the base of the ladder, deliberately flashing my arm beneath the cage.

The result was instantaneous—a storm of semi-automatic gunfire exploding down the ladder shaft, striking the concrete and ricocheting into the walls. I danced back from the bullets and readied my Glock. I measured the breaks in the fire, then swung out and jammed my gun up. I unleashed a string of six return shots.

Nothing—and nobody—answered them. Brass rained over the concrete and metal clanged overhead like the rapport of steel targets at the firing range. I dug the Macro-Stream from my pocket and switched it to full power. I waited another beat, then leaned beneath the cage and shone the beam upward.

The ladder shaft was fifty, maybe eighty yards tall. It led through a concrete tunnel illuminated by dim yellow lights, all the way to a steel hatch with the words "ROOF ACCESS" repeated in red stencil paint.

The terrorist was gone. The shaft was empty.

He'd made it to the roof.

58

V oices thundered in unison as I started up the shaft, the MacroStream clamped in my teeth, the Glock grasped in my right hand. Every step up the ladder ignited pain in my throbbing left thigh, the bullet wound from St. Louis reminding me just how badly I wanted to avoid being shot again. I wasn't sure how many rounds remained in the Glock—maybe six or eight. I would dump every one of them straight up the shaft if that hatch so much as twitched.

Halfway up the ladder I knew I was traveling through the nosebleeds of the arena stands. The roar of voices burst through narrow ventilation grates mounted at intervals on either side of the concrete shaft, admitting also the stench of sweat, the sweet buttery odor of popcorn, and the distant flash of lights. The announcer proclaimed about an injury— a total knockout, it seemed. One of the Baltimore players was being carted off the field, and the rival fans actually cheered in raucous delight, sounding more like the spectators of a boxing match than a football game.

I climbed on, muscles straining, head beginning to pound. I glanced down only once to see blank concrete below—still no sign of Jeter. No sign of backup.

I was on my own.

I reached the hatch and paused for only a moment to catch my breath. Through the thick metal I recognized another sound—a swirling howl. A bitter blast.

It was the blizzard outside, beating on the roof of the arena, promising blinding gusts of snow and bone-chilling cold. I pressed my back against the rear of the tunnel, pinning myself in place and freeing my hands. I dropped the pistol magazine to inspect the load—five rounds remained. I replaced the mag with my fully loaded spare, then checked my pockets. Two useless pairs of handcuffs...nothing more.

I planted my free hand beneath the hatch. I pushed upward, lifting the lid only a crack before the gunshots rained in, pinging off the metal and whizzing into the night. I flinched, dropping it again and counting my breaths, then I shoved upward with everything I had.

The terrorist ahead of me had already cleared the snow atop the hatch. All I had to do was bull my way through the forty-odd pounds of the hatch itself, and if three months of slinging lumber had done anything, they had hardened my upper body muscles. The hatch exploded back on its hinges, landing with a snow-muted clunk as a howl of wind ripped across the tunnel mouth, blasting my face with brutal cold. I choked and clawed upward, ducking as the gunfire resumed. Bullets tore just over my head, some pinging off the hatch while most zipped into the empty Wisconsin night. I thought they were coming from my left, but I couldn't be sure.

I decided to roll the dice and return fire, jamming the muzzle of the Glock over the lip of the tunnel and dumping half a dozen rounds in the general direction of my adversary. Brass rained over my head and the gunshots faded.

I listened. I waited a beat. No response from the roof.

Dropping the Glock's mag one last time, I thumbed the final five rounds from my original magazine and topped off the new one. I slammed it home again, discarding the empty spare and breathing evenly. Concentrating on an even heartbeat.

Readying myself.

Here goes nothing.

I sprang through the top of the tunnel and into the bitter wrath of the wind. It hit me from my left side, nearly knocking me off balance before I even found my footing. A cyclone of swirled snow collided with my face and chest, obscuring my view. I found a handrail and braced myself, swinging the pistol left and dropping into a crouch.

I couldn't see anything beyond ten yards—it was all just blackness and cold. A walkway streaked out across the roof of the arena, protected by waist-high metal rails. I noted a splash of crimson beneath a brief application of my Macro-Stream, matched with a rapidly filling footprint. I marked a path down the walkway, toward the middle of the arena.

Then I followed, grasping the MacroStream with my left hand but leaving the light off. I glanced to either side and barely made out the gently curving roof of the arena beneath the obscured security lights mounted to the sides of the walkway. It dropped off on both sides, the pitch growing increasingly sharp as it reached the arena's edges. All that space was piled thick with drifts of white, torn and marred by the wind, frozen solid under the clutches of Wisconsin winter.

But the blood remained—only barely visible as a splash

here, a splash there. I noted a smear of it along the handrail. Somebody was wounded. Judging by the volume of blood it wasn't a mortal wound, but it was enough to leave a trail that struck out dead over the center of the arena.

Where was he going?

I didn't have time to wonder. The next chatter of gunfire was accompanied by the piercing blast of weapon light. It broke through the darkness and spotlighted my face as I dove for the ground. Bullets pinged off the walkway railings and one cut the back of my coat—I felt it as a whizzing tug, then it was gone. Lying prone with snow up to my shoulders I marked the muzzle flash from twenty yards to my left and returned fire. My own rounds pinged off metal and the weapon light died only a second after I caught sight of an intersecting walkway streaking off to my left.

I was back on my feet. I dashed through the snow, lungs so frozen every breath felt like the bite of a shotgun blast straight into my chest. I reached the intersection of the walkway and pivoted left in the darkness. I saw the flash of the weapon light igniting again, spotlighting my former position. It marked my target like a beacon, and I opened fire on him. A scream ripped across the rooftop. The weapon light fell to the walkway and I flicked on the MacroStream in time to see a geyser of blood exploding into the air, blasted sideways by the wind.

I pivoted right, toward the center of the arena roof. I kept the MacroStream on, cutting a swath of illumination through the blizzard. The next gust of wind sent me stumbling backwards, catching myself on the handrail. I directed the flashlight at a metal cage sheltered by a subsequent metal roof standing eight feet off the walkway. HVAC equipment stood clustered inside—massive, industrial units, each the size of minivans. The chain-link fence surrounding them was breached by an open gate. I detected a flash of movement inside—the shift of a metal cylinder. It was one of the soda fountain CO_2 cylinders I'd seen before, and it was joined by a face—the face of the man who had carried that cylinder. He was ducking behind a unit, pulling the cylinder along with him.

Then I understood—and just as I understood, the next terrorist hurtled in from my blind side, slamming into my shoulder with a bullish roar and sending us both crashing to the walkway with a shudder of vibrating metal. The Glock flew out of my hand, vanishing into the darkness as I landed on my left shoulder, pain exploding through my chest. The wind left my lungs in a frigid burst. I rolled onto my back and found the guy straddling me like a cat, teeth bared in the dim security lights, a knife flashing out of his waistband. He lunged downward.

I caught his right forearm with both hands and forced him back, stopping the plunging blade two inches from my throat. He heaved, dropping his bodyweight against the knife even as snow ripped between our faces, obscuring his hate-filled eyes.

He was white, like the other guy. He looked American. A scraggly beard bent in the wind. He was strong, also—gym muscles bulged beneath a thin jacket as he crushed down on me. But gym muscles are no match for the body mass developed by weeks of rolling half-ton pine logs. I heaved, thrusting upward as though I were completing a bench press. He flailed, feet scraping on the metal walkway. I felt him losing balance. I rolled hard left and slammed him into the walkway's railing. The air left his lungs in a raw choke. I slammed him again and drove the knife to the left, allowing it to plunge into the snow above my shoulder.

Then I was rolling over him. He flailed with the knife and the flat of the blade scraped harmlessly past my cheek. I landed on top and kneed him in the gut. He choked.

Then I heard the gunfire again, popping hot from the HVAC cage someplace to my right. A voice screamed and I recognized it.

The break in my focus was temporary, but it was enough. The terrorist released his knife with his right hand and slammed his fist into my jaw. I saw stars and I choked. Evelyn shouted again from the entrance of the roof access tunnel, and more gunfire exploded to my right. Then Jeter shouted through the wind, "*Mason!*"

"HVAC!" I called, again flailing to block the knife as it swept upward toward my face. "They're pumping the virus into the HVAC!"

From beneath me the terrorist's eyes flashed. He grinned, exposing perfectly straight white teeth. He pressed upward with the knife, driving the blade toward my eye.

"*Allahu Akbar!*" he hissed.

The Arabic phrase carried an east coast accent as it zipped through my mind like a bullet—a common refrain from Muslim prayers, and the appropriated battle cry of radicalized extremists. I'd heard it in Afghanistan. I'd heard it in Africa. The fact that the man pinned beneath me was American didn't matter a whit—I knew what he meant. I knew what poison had entered his mind, consuming his humanity, driving him to a place of such total hatred that he was ready and willing to exterminate his own people.

But not today.

I heaved, digging deep into every reserve of strength I

could tap. I grabbed his hands and snatched hard left, wrenching the knife point away from my face and toward his own. I broke his grip with a brutal twist of my sawmill-hardened shoulders. His eyes widened as the knife point dropped downward, dangling over his throat. I gritted my teeth. I heaved upward, extending my arms and raising my body.

Then I dropped. I crushed down with every ounce of bodyweight, every pound of muscle. I snapped his defenses like walls of twigs and drove the knife up to its hilt, straight into his throat. He choked, blood spurting from a carotid artery and spraying my face. His body retched as nerves took over. The blade penetrated his spinal cord, and then the light vanished from behind his eyes. His mouth fell open and didn't close.

He died under the bitter bite of the Wisconsin cold.

I twisted, jerking the knife free. I fell sideways onto the walkway, gasping for air as my frozen muscles quaked. I grabbed the rail. I hauled myself back to my knees as Jeter hurtled past—lumbering like a charging bull as his faithful 1911 barked at the HVAC cage. Evelyn was just behind him, her face washed pale, the Glock held up. From behind the chain link, muzzle flash marked return fire—the chattering snarl of a submachine gun.

Jeter twitched. He jerked sideways, agony consuming his face. He toppled even as the terrorist emerged from inside the cage—the white guy I'd seen from the concourse. He wielded a SIG MPX. He was struggling with the charging handle, yanking at the bolt. Jeter struck the walkway with his 1911 locked back over an empty chamber. Evelyn stood exposed. The terrorist flat-palmed the side of his weapon— the bolt was jammed over a stove-piped nine-millimeter casing.

He slung it down. I reached my feet. I looked but I couldn't find my Glock. Evelyn opened fire, arms shaking. Her bullets flew wide. I closed to within ten yards of her position as the terrorist reached beneath his jacket. I envisioned another weapon—a handgun.

What I saw was infinitely worse. A small handgrip connected to a wire. A single ignition button topped by a red safety cover. His thumb flipped the cover off as I reached Evelyn. She was still firing—her next round struck the terrorist in the shoulder as he stumbled onto the walkway. He dropped the detonator handgrip and nearly fell.

I hit Evelyn. I launched off the platform, arms wrapped around her stomach, heaving us both over the walkway railing. We struck the sloping, snow-covered roof of the arena. We slid. I flailed for footing. The edge raced toward us.

Then the suicide vest detonated with a thunder crack of orange fire. The roof shuddered. Shards of railing and platform and chain link exploded into the air.

We passed over the edge of the arena and plummeted into the dark.

59

I never felt the landing. The flash of the passing arena wall was lost in a blurred memory of blazing orange. Of gunfire.

But not from the roof, and not from Wisconsin. By the time we made impact with the hard ground fifty feet below and darkness consumed me, I was already envisioning Phoenix. The elementary school. The hiss of bullets ripping down a tiled hallway.

And Mia...crumpled against the wall, extending a hand toward the muzzle of a shotgun. Literally protecting her young students with her own body.

It's truly radical the way moments like that sear into your memory. I could lose my truck keys within seconds of laying them down, but every color, every smell, every vibrant and visceral sensation of that moment at Harris Morrison Elementary was etched in granite into my very consciousness. It was part of me, and always would be. If I lived to a hundred. If I married a good woman and enjoyed a dozen grandchildren. If I traveled the world and witnessed all the best concerts, all the greatest Super Bowls, a thousand watercolored sunsets.

Nothing would override it or replace it. The dominant undertone was regret—if I'd just been a little bit faster. A little quicker on the draw. Somehow, some way, closing that distance with just a second to spare.

It was the regret that enshrined those memories. The horror. I saw it all as the safety switch flicked upward from the top of that detonator handgrip—a device I was all too familiar with from other horrible memories overseas. As I launched myself off the platform like a lunging track sprinter, visions of Mia crumbled against the wall were replaced by flashes of Evelyn standing fully exposed on the walkway, unleashing shots and missing. Panic overwhelming her body as the wind blew her sideways and the driving snow blinded her.

I saw the shotgun rise. I saw Mia lift a hand. I saw the terrorist stumble, flailing for his fallen detonator. I saw the fear clouding Evelyn's face.

And then I hit her, throwing us both off the edge. Because I *wasn't* going to be a moment late for a second time. As we left the roof I twisted, placing her body atop mine. Turning my back to the ground. Clamping her close and smelling the vanilla-lilac of her shampoo—a scent that brought the Atlantic Hotel storming back.

Another granite memory. Another flash of the visceral, the permanent.

And then blackness.

60

I saw the lights next. Not the bright, white lights people with near-death experiences recount. These were red lights, blinking from the ether, burning my gaze. They weren't pleasant. I cringed and recoiled. Pressure descended onto my arms, and a distorted voice called through the darkness.

I couldn't discern the words. They joined the thunder trapped inside my skull, a pounding that made me gasp. I tasted cold and bitter air. My mouth was dry. My face burned.

If this was death, it wasn't Heaven. Was I...in the other place?

"Mason! *Mason.* Please wake up."

The voice was soft. Kind. Pleading.

I blinked hard and the world swirled overhead. The red lights clarified, shining through a windshield. I was inside a vehicle. The lights shone from the side of a fire truck. I was on my back.

Ambulance?

The hand closed around my arm again. Another squeeze. Then the voice returned.

"Mason...it's me."

Mia?

My head twisted. My vision clarified. I looked over the top of an oxygen mask to the bench seat running next to me. And then I saw her. Not Mia...no. Even as I blinked the fog away, Mia faded into the stony cold of the moment I would never forget. She was replaced by a paler face. Brighter hair. Brilliant green eyes, skin streaked with dirt and blood and trails of tears. One arm wrapped in a sling. The other reaching out to clutch my hand.

"Can you hear me?"

My lips parted and my mouth flooded with oxygen. I couldn't speak, but I didn't need to. Our gazes locked and vivid relief passed across Evelyn's face. She smiled, tears in her eyes.

Then another face joined her—a paramedic wearing an N-95 mask. He ushered her aside and clicked on a pen light. He did the thing with my eyes, holding my eyelids open and doing his best to blind me. He grunted.

"Can you hear me, sir?" he repeated Evelyn's question, but I couldn't answer through the mask. He removed it from my face and I panted on raw air.

"Slow down, now. Take it easy. Can you feel your toes?"

I blinked. I wiggled my toes.

All present and accounted for. My head still thundered, though.

"What happened?" I whispered.

The paramedic snorted. He probed my chest and shoulders. He rolled my head and inspected my skull. Muttered a curse.

"What happened, Mr. Sharpe, is you totaled a Lexus."

I blinked. I saw the side of the arena hurtling past, Evelyn clutched to my chest. I remembered the flash of fire as the suicide vest detonated.

And then...darkness.

"Wait," I hissed. "The virus?"

The paramedic said nothing. He simply replaced the mask on my face and clicked his pen light off. Then he was gone, and I fought to sit up. I made it only two inches before blinding pain exploded through my back and ribcage—lancing, shooting pain, stronger than the headache. I collapsed with a shout.

Evelyn appeared at my side, hand on my shoulder. She was still crying.

"Lie still...don't move. You're okay."

The ambulance shuddered again, sagging on its suspension. A bulky form appeared at the foot of my gurney. I looked over the oxygen mask to recognize the now all too familiar green rubber of a military NBC suit. The soldier wearing it peeled his mask off, exposing disheveled gray hair and a hard, wrinkled face.

It was Lieutenant Colonel Hughes of the Iowa National Guard. He stepped to my left side and looked down, silent. His face was cherry red from the kiss of the weather, snow dusting his NBC suit. Bags hung beneath his eyes. Wrinkles cut his cheeks.

But he nodded once.

"Well done, Sergeant."

I lifted my own aching arm. I removed my oxygen mask for the second time and ran a dry tongue over my dry lips.

"Did we make it in time?" I asked.

Hughes grunted. "With about six seconds to spare. The

virus was held inside a capsule attached to a can of soda fountain CO_2...like a giant aerosol can. They had it set on a timer to dispense into the HVAC return. It would have pumped through the roof vents. Likely infected everybody. When the dumbass clacked himself off, the suicide vest blew the mechanism apart. The virus sprayed across the roof."

My heart thundered. I started to sit up again, the panic returning.

"It dispensed?"

The LTC nodded. "Yeah. But outside the arena, in the cold. Viruses don't like the cold. Apparently Ebola in particular is inactivated by sub-freezing temperatures. It's no longer infectious, in other words."

Evelyn squeezed my hand. "That's right."

"Washington sent teams," Hughes continued. "The whole city is on lockdown. They've quarantined everyone inside the arena—including you, actually. We might all be dead by sunrise, but if you hadn't gone up onto that roof... America would be over."

I sagged back onto the gurney, not feeling like much of a hero. It turned out that arriving with seconds to spare still left you feeling like a fool—overcome by how close you had danced to the edge of the abyss.

"How did you get here so quickly?" I asked.

Hughes glanced down. "Your buddy called us after you found the rental car. He phoned me from the arena."

"Jeter?" I managed.

A nod, but no further comment. Dread sank its claws around my gut.

"Is he..."

Hughes swallowed. He shook his head.

"He didn't make it. Shot through the chest. I'm sorry."

I slumped into the gurney. My eyes stung, but I couldn't cry. My vision simply blurred. I was vaguely aware of Hughes re-donning his NBC mask and stepping out of the ambulance. I lay staring up at a blurry ambulance and thought of Jeter on the roof.

Jeter at Millie's Place. Jeter at the pool hall. All his stories and old pictures. His raucous laugh. His giant heart.

I'd been a few seconds late after all.

Next to me Evelyn descended onto one knee. Her face drew next to mine. One gentle hand stroked my forehead, displacing sweaty, half-frozen hair. I tilted my face, and our gazes locked.

She was crying. Her lips quivered. We stared at each other for what may have been a minute or could have been ten. I looked past the fear, the exhaustion, the trauma in her face. I looked deep.

I saw Africa. I saw a hotel by the beach. I saw long, late nights wrapped in cigarette smoke and fueled by alcohol. I smelled vanilla and lilacs. I touched her hand and her fingers closed around mine.

Then Evelyn leaned low. Our lips touched. I wrapped my aching right arm around her back and pulled her close. I kissed her like I'd only ever kissed two women in my life.

Not a moment too soon.

61

They moved me from the ambulance to a Madison hospital. I was locked inside, put under guard of a Wisconsin National Guardsman in full NBC gear. I wasn't allowed to see Evelyn for six days.

According to the TV in my room, practically the entire city was placed under lockdown. Six confirmed cases of modified Ebola virus were being treated by the best virologists in the country. Everyone present at the arena was under strict quarantine. The facility itself was placed under government control and was scheduled for a full, industrial decontamination...whatever that meant.

Prairie Junction made the news, also. Finally. The entire story was spreading across the country like...well. A virus. The FBI was on the ground. Dr. Müller had been arrested in Chicago attempting to flee the country. His suitcase was packed with a fake passport and thirty-six thousand dollars in cash. According to the talking heads on major news networks, Müller had lawyered up and was demanding a deal.

He claimed that bigger fish were indeed available for capture. He was eager to spill the tea...but only for the right price.

I watched the story unfold with something between disgust and resigned acceptance of humanity's natural evil, but whatever I felt, I felt no surprise. No disbelief. I'd journeyed from Phoenix to Afghanistan to Africa. I'd learned all about the depravity of powerful men with a profit to make or a dictatorship to seize. It was an educational experience.

But in a lot of ways, the two years I'd spent wandering America since Mia's death had been even more eye-opening. I'd learned that in many ways, the Land of the Free was the home of the corrupt. The conniving. The exploitative.

At this point, I wasn't sure if anything would ever surprise me again.

On the seventh day after the defunct terrorist attack, I was finally released from Madison. The guard was removed from my room. Discharge papers were issued. I tugged my dirty jeans and torn Carhartt coat on, limping downstairs with a mandatory N-95 mask stretched across my face, smelling of antibiotic spray.

Everything smelled of antibiotic spray. The city was drenched in disinfectant. Rumor had it that grocery store shelves were picked clean of Lysol...and toilet paper. For some reason.

I found Evelyn waiting outside the hospital in a brand-new rental car—another Toyota hybrid, no less. She stepped out onto pavement dusted with snow and turned a winter-kissed face on me, light hair pulled back in a ponytail, lips red. She wore just a trace of makeup—just enough to cover the bruising she had sustained when her face crashed into my ribcage, and my ribcage crashed into the roof of a...what was it? A Lexus?

We stood six feet apart, just staring for a long moment, my body aching, her body a little slumped. Then Evelyn circled the nose of the Toyota and wrapped both arms around me. She rose onto her toes. She kissed me. I kissed her back, pulling her body into mine until I could smell the vanilla-lilacs.

Nothing on earth had ever smelled so good.

We kissed until it became awkward, which took a while. Evelyn pulled away, flashing a semi-awkward smile that took me right back to high school. It was a good feeling. She returned to the driver's seat and I piled into the passenger. The heat was cranked up and felt good on my face. She shifted into drive and we departed Madison, rolling past vacant streets and empty strip mall parking lots.

Everyone was "self-quarantining", an expression that was new to me. Essentially, they had barricaded themselves into their homes, drenched in a cloud of disinfectant.

I couldn't blame them.

"The CDC confirmed that the modified virus spreads via body fluids," Evelyn said. "It won't go airborne."

"That's a relief."

"You have no idea. It's still more infectious than regular Ebola, though. One of the modifications Coleus performed involves early onset coughing and sneezing—before fever or chills set in. So it feels just like a head cold...and spreads."

I shot her a look from the passenger seat. I didn't have to say what I was thinking. The disgust in my face sent the message for me.

"Not all smart people are wise people," Evelyn said softly.

Isn't that the truth.

We drove for another few miles before Evelyn cleared her throat, apparently ready to change the subject. "They're lifting the quarantine in Prairie Junction tomorrow afternoon. There will be a memorial for Jeter on Sunday. They already cremated his body...precautions."

Jeter. I pictured my friend kicked back at Millie's Place with a Tank 7 sweating in his hand, and a wave of sadness washed through my chest.

"What day is it now?" I asked.

"Friday."

I nodded. We didn't speak. I watched gray skies and empty white foothills roll by on all sides, a peaceful wasteland that lay refreshingly free of FMTVs and military roadblocks. I glanced to the compass on the dash and noted that we were pointed not southwest, toward Iowa, but southeast.

Toward Illinois.

"Müller is still stonewalling," Evelyn continued. "Nobody is willing to cut him a deal with so little information. The DOJ is a disaster zone. The attorney general himself is rumored to be micromanaging the proceedings... The NIH and the CDC are in a tailspin. I've been placed on administrative leave until further notice."

I squinted. "They're blaming *you* for this?"

Evelyn waved a hand. "Not blaming, no. I'm 'too close to the situation'." She made air quotes. "I think my boss just wants to take credit. It's bureaucracy at its finest."

I grunted in understanding. The military was no stranger to such politics. Neither was the Phoenix PD.

Evelyn grew quiet. Her fingers tightened around the steering wheel. A green highway sign flashed by, advertising

Chicago—one hundred twenty miles distant. I cocked an eyebrow.

"I spoke with Alex," Evelyn said quietly. "He did some more checking. We all know there must be somebody else beyond Müller...somebody powerful enough to hire an army of private mercenaries, manipulate the governor of Iowa, shut down cell towers, and contain this thing from the eyes of the regulators. Somebody...big."

I nodded. It was an assumption I had made early in my investigation. After learning just how much money a successful Ebola vaccine could be worth, my instincts only sharpened. I knew there had to be somebody further up the chain—somebody willing to risk thousands of American lives in the hope of striking gold.

Whoever it was, they were ultimately responsible for the murder of Clay Taggert, along with all the wild tactics designed to conceal the true, illegal research being conducted at the Coleus Biotech facility, not to mention the disastrous terrorist break-in.

There was a bigger fish, all right. Probably a few of them. And if I knew anything about corruption, I knew that Dr. Müller would never testify to their identities. He would be dead long before he could...a freak accident in a jailhouse shower.

"What did Alex find?" I asked.

Evelyn chewed her lip. Then she pointed to the Toyota's glove box. I opened it to find an iPad Mini. I clicked it on—it wasn't password protected. The screen opened to an email pane. I scanned the message. My eye caught on something. I hesitated, wanting to glance sideways. I felt Evelyn stiffen next to me. I read on.

Then my chest really tightened. I looked up.

"Are you serious?"

"It adds up," Evelyn said, still quiet. "He has the power to blind regulators and open doors for this sort of covert research. And if a vaccine were discovered, he would also have the power to fast-track it into mass production without too many questions as to its origin. He could make...*hundreds* of millions."

I looked back to Alex's email. I considered. Then I switched the iPad off and replaced it in the glove box.

"Where are we headed?" I asked.

"I'm headed to O'Hare. I have a flight booked for Dulles. He lives in Silver Spring."

"And you expect him to just roll over and spill?"

Evelyn said nothing. She didn't blink, either. I almost smiled.

"Look at you getting all practical."

"We have to know, Mason. He *can't* get away with this."

I settled back into my seat and closed my eyes. My body still ached. I was still tired despite a week of rest.

Or maybe I was just supremely relaxed so close to amazing company.

"Is there a spare seat on that plane?" I asked.

"I'm not asking you to come with me."

I opened my eyes. I met her gaze with a gentle smile. "And you'll never have to."

62

T he private home of Dr. Jeffrey R. Simmons, decorated virologist, veteran of the WHO, and current director of the National Institute of Health, sat in an exclusive gated neighborhood of Silver Spring, Maryland. Just a short drive from Washington DC. An even shorter drive from the NIH headquarters in nearby Bethesda.

Responsible for a laundry list of activities that relate to issues of public health, the item on the NIH's website that most interested me was that of biomedical research—and the funding of such research. Specifically, the NIH was the government agency responsible for issuing federal grants— millions of dollars' worth—to institutions around the globe that were engaged in developing cures for all manner of nasty afflictions.

Cancer. HIV. Heart disease.

Ebola.

Dr. Simmons had been director of the agency for six years. He'd pushed Congress for additional funding, testifying four times throughout his career about the dire risk of a mass pandemic triggered by under-researched infectious diseases. Simmons was a strong advocate for gain-of-function research. He was a known ally of major pharmaceutical companies that manufactured vaccines. He lived in a four-thousand-square-foot mini-mansion that far exceeded the purchasing power of his government salary.

And—wonder of wonders—he was a frat brother and long-time personal friend of one Lawrence Lawson Burk, Governor of the State of Iowa.

We rented another car after landing at Dulles. We rode in silence to Evelyn's CDC field office in downtown DC, where she left the car running and popped in for only ten minutes. She returned with an unmarked black duffel bag.

Then we were headed north again, crossing into Maryland and winding through Silver Spring. It was a nice place —exactly the sort of bedroom community a powerful bureaucrat with pockets full of dirty money might pick to establish an excessively large home address.

Five minutes outside the entrance of Simmons's gated neighborhood, I put up a hand. Evelyn stopped the car at the curb and faced me. I took my time processing my thoughts.

I felt zero qualms about what lay ahead. If anything, I only regretted that I hadn't thought of the strategy myself. But the part of me that held back, the part of me that hesitated, wouldn't let Evelyn charge ahead without at least attempting to stop her.

"You should let me do this," I said.

"Why?"

"You have a career to think about. An entire future. If this goes sideways you could lose everything. If you're wrong about Simmons...you could land in jail."

Evelyn's eyes hardened. "And you wouldn't?"

I shrugged. "I'm just a guy. I don't have a career or any particular future. And I've done this kind of thing before."

Evelyn didn't blink. "We have to know, Mason. *I* have to know."

I measured the stare. Then I nodded. I pointed down the street.

"Avoid the gate. There will be cameras. Park near the golf course and we'll walk in that way—golf courses don't allow fences on their perimeters."

Evelyn shifted back into gear. She powered the car around the bend. We parked on the curb well beyond the neighborhood's entrance. I piled out and surveyed the streets while Evelyn collected her bag.

Then we were slipping through the hedges, crossing the edge of a golf course and circling toward the back of the neighborhood where Simmons's house lay. There were no news vans parked along the curb—compliments of the gated community—but the darkened front windows told a story of a man in hiding. On a Friday afternoon Simmons might not be home. He might still be in DC, flailing to conceal this mess.

That was okay. We were content to wait. We circled a pool deck and I tugged on a pair of rubber medical gloves from Evelyn's bag before picking the lock on a patio gate. A sliding glass door stood beyond, providing access to a sprawling open-concept living room connected to an expansive kitchen. I detected a security system inside—motion detectors and magnetic sensors on the doors and windows. A control panel on one wall that glowed blue.

More irritation.

Locating the home's exterior breaker panel, I lifted the metal door and swept the breakers. There were several of them, but I only needed the primary. I flipped it with a heavy snap and returned to the sliding glass door. The clock on the stove was now black. The hum of the electric heat pump had died.

But the glow of the security system control panel persisted.

"Backup battery?" Evelyn asked.

I grunted, considering. Then I flipped my Victorinox open, returned to exterior breaker panel, and surveyed the conduit pipes emerging from the ground. Those carrying electric cables and phone lines.

A kick of my boot broke a conduit pipe free of its fixture. I located the thick black phone cable housed inside. I looped it around my knife blade and snatched.

On the third slice the cable separated. I returned to the glass door.

"It's still live," Evelyn said.

"Yep. But now it can't dial for help."

I knelt on the patio and went to work with my lock picks. Evelyn stood back and watched without comment. I wasn't sure if she was impressed or disturbed by my burglar expertise. Within seconds I had the door open and was stepping across polished hardwood, scanning walls packed with pictures and memorabilia—mostly related to big game hunting. The furniture was puffy and clean, the rug thick and dark. The TV oversized, the kitchen somehow...bare looking.

The whole place bore the undertone of a bachelor pad, albeit a very expensive bachelor pad. I raised an eyebrow at Evelyn as she followed me inside.

"Divorced," she said.

I slid the door shut. Evelyn wore matching rubber gloves, holding the bag over her shoulder as she absently swept her hair behind one ear. Her body was perfectly rigid, her tongue darting out at odd intervals to dampen her lips. I tried to put myself in her shoes and recall what it felt like to break into somebody's house for the first time—to color outside the lines.

It had been so long, I couldn't recall.

"Relax," I said. "Have a seat. We might be here a while."

I walked to the kitchen. I tugged the fridge open and surveyed an assortment of condiments along with six different kinds of beer—mostly craft pilsners. I selected one and cracked it open.

It was ice-cold. A little hoppy for my taste, but not half bad.

"What are you doing?" Evelyn asked.

"Having a drink," I said. "Want a beer?"

63

Director Jeffrey Simmons pulled into his driveway exactly ninety minutes later. Evelyn and I spent that time in the dark, relaxed on the couches, sipping beer and surveying the junk on the walls as sunlight slowly faded.

We didn't talk. We didn't touch. A strange sort of tension had developed between us. A growing discomfort that I couldn't quite put my finger on, but felt in my gut. When I glanced sideways at Evelyn, the gleam in her eye told me that she felt the same, and that redoubled my own discomfort.

There were words unspoken, I knew. Uncertainties in the air. An elephant in the room that we would need to address in the very near future...but not until we addressed the monster.

Simmons drove a Mercedes AMG. He pulled the sedan up to the garage and I stood by the window, watching him by the dim glow of street lamps as he repeatedly mashed his garage door opener.

Nothing happened. The power was dead in the garage also. After moments of frustration, Simmons cut his car off and climbed out. He glared at the garage and muttered something.

Then he circled for the front door, looking dark and very stressed. Crows' feet decorated his eyes, and his tie swung loose from his neck. He jammed his keys into the deadbolt and fought with the lock, cursing loud enough for me to hear through the thick oak.

I donned an N-95 mask, motioning for Evelyn to do the same. It wasn't a perfect disguise, but I thought it would suffice. Stepping behind the sheltered side of the front door, I flipped an empty beer can into the nearby kitchen trash. It was only my second, but craft beer hits hard. I felt good—relaxed and focused.

The door opened. Simmons bustled in. He hit the light switches and cursed again. He slammed the door and dropped his briefcase. He turned.

He caught my open palm right across the side of his head—hard enough to stun, not hard enough to leave a mark. He stumbled, eyes rolling. I spun on my heels and slipped an arm around his neck, pulling him tight into my chest and cutting off his airflow as his legs flailed and his arms pounded my already bruised ribcage.

It hurt—I gritted my teeth as each blow reignited the throbbing pain of my injuries from the totaled Lexus. But Simmons was overweight and out of shape. His panicked thrashing served no purpose other than to exhaust his oxygen supply that much quicker.

He went limp. I held him by the collar of his jacket and dragged him toward the kitchen table, where wooden chairs featured high backs and stiff arms.

"Tape," I said, pointing with my free hand.

Evelyn stood in the kitchen, a little wide-eyed but remaining calm. She retrieved a roll of duct tape I had located in a kitchen drawer and met me at a table chair. I set Simmons into it and secured his wrists to the chair arms. I wrapped tape around his chest, locking him to the chair back. I taped his ankles to the chair legs. Then I dropped the tape on the table and pointed again to the counter.

"Water."

Evelyn handed me a glass. I dashed it across Simmons's face, and he came to with a heave and a thrash. He pulled at his arms, made eye contact with me, then screamed.

I flat-palmed him again across the temple. His head snapped back, his eyes rolled. He choked on his own saliva.

I pulled a chair back and settled down, both hands resting on the tabletop. Simmons collected himself, sputtering and jerking in the chair. His gaze flicked from me to Evelyn, then back to me. His eyes bulged.

"What is this?" he snarled.

"This is the end, Jeffrey," I said. "The end of the line. The end of the party. The end of the music. The sooner you accept that, the easier this goes."

Confusion clouded his face. He squinted. He glared. He looked to my hands, maybe checking for a weapon. There wasn't one, but if he had half the IQ a doctor of virology should, he would know that I didn't need one.

"Who are you?" Simmons said.

"People who know the truth," I said. "And we're here to confirm it. I'm getting hungry and there's no food in the fridge, so I'll cut right to the chase. We know about Coleus Biotech. We know about the illegal, accelerated Ebola research. We know that Coleus was working on a vaccine—

breaking the rules and bypassing regulations to bring it to the market sooner. In medicine, it's all about being the first, isn't it? Something like that could be worth gobs of money."

Simmons squinted. He feigned confusion. But deep in his calculating eyes I saw the truth. He was panicking. He was scrambling for a response.

I'd hit him where it hurt...and I swung again.

"We also know that you hold majority shares in Coleus. A major no-no, of course, given your position as head of the NIH. A massive conflict of interest, which is why you hid that ownership inside an LLC owned by another LLC owned by your cousin...a stock broker twice investigated for fraud but never convicted. I have to admit, it's a pretty nifty arrangement. It took our contact at the FBI nearly a week to track down all the connections. If a network of Islamic extremists hadn't learned of your little project and breached the facility, it might just have worked out. But they did, and you tried to cover it up. You leaned on your buddy the governor and weaponized the Iowa National Guard to buy you time. You pulled strings to have cell towers and internet service suspended. You deployed a little army of ex-military killers to hunt those terrorists down...or bury witnesses, depending on the circumstances. I guess you actually thought you could recover—but of course you didn't, which leaves us here. In your house. Having this conversation. Because we all know what you did and why you did it... The only rub is, I'm not sure we can prove it."

Simmons's jaw closed tight. Smug anger flashed in his eyes, but he didn't speak. I noticed that he hadn't spoken since I began my monologue, which was telling in its own way. An innocent man would have pleaded. Interrupted. Asked questions. Appeared confused.

Jeffrey Simmons only seemed preoccupied—as though his mind were spinning at a thousand miles per hour, searching for a solution.

"You're out of your mind," Simmons said, at last. "I'm a *regulator*. I'm the director of a federal agency. Do you have any idea how deep I can bury you? You have nothing!"

"Actually," I said, "you're right. We have nothing we can take to court. That's where the confession comes in. You're going to supply one."

A snort. A derisive laugh. Simmons's gaze switched between us, eyebrows crinkling in incredulity. His façade of innocence was breaking down. He was pissed. He was losing control.

Simmons leaned forward, lowering his voice to a nasty hiss. "You want a confession?"

"We expect one," I said.

"Okay. What if I confess that I'm going to *burn you*? Both of you. I'm going to burn your lives, your careers, your families. Before I'm finished you won't have a pot to piss in. I am a *federal official*! You can't just come in here and throw me around like some kind of roving vigilante thugs—"

He kept ranting, voice rising in volume as spit sprayed from his lips. I stopped listening. I stood and circled behind him, snapping my Victorinox open. Evelyn unzipped her medical bag. Simmons began to panic, his head snapping back and forth as his face flushed. He cursed and jerked. I flat-palmed him in the temple, then used my knife to slice open his suit jacket and shirt sleeve, exposing his right shoulder.

Evelyn withdrew a syringe from the bag, thumping and depressing it to drive out the air. A tiny bubble of clear liquid emerged from the tip of the needle. Simmons grew suddenly still. He fixated on the needle. The breath caught in his throat.

"Wait. What are you doing?"

I pocketed the knife and wrapped my left arm around his throat, pulling him against the chair back. I used my right hand to pin his right arm in place. He jerked against the tape. Evelyn stood from her chair and approached with the needle. Simmons swore and thrashed, but I was much too strong for him. He couldn't move.

"Wait!" he screamed. "Don't do that!"

He was too late. Evelyn stuck him. She depressed the plunger, pumping his body full of that nondescript solution. Simmons choked. Then the needle was gone, the cap back on. Evelyn was packing her equipment as I released Simmons. He panted and craned his neck to view his needle-stuck shoulder.

"What was that?" Simmons gasped, real terror saturating his voice. I calmly deployed the Victorinox again, slicing the tape that bound him to the chair. I peeled it away and wadded it up, joining Evelyn at the end of the table.

"What *was that?*" Simmons shouted.

"Ebola virus," I said calmly. "Modified, of course. I hear there's a vaccine in the works...but all the files from Coleus's off-site data centers are now under the control of the FBI. I guess you'll have to place a phone call if you want the formula." I tossed the wadded-up tape into the trash. I turned for the door, then paused. I looked back over my shoulder. "Oh, and Jeffrey? You're gonna have to explain how you knew Coleus was developing a vaccine."

Simmons's face washed white. He looked to his arm, clawing the torn suit jacket back. His eyes turned wide. He fell out of the chair, calling after us.

We ignored him. We stepped out of the sliding glass door and circled through the golf course, peeling gloves and masks off, Evelyn walking with her medical bag slung over one shoulder. As we approached our latest rental car Evelyn thumbed the key fob, starting the engine. We climbed in and I dumped my gloves and mask into the floorboard.

"What did you give him, anyway?" I said.

Evelyn looked through the windshield, eyeballing Simmons's distant house. She looked as cold as I'd ever seen her.

"Nasty flu virus," she said. "It'll scare the piss out of him when the symptoms set in."

I grunted. "Nice going. I thought it was water."

Evelyn shifted into gear. She chewed her bottom lip. She glanced sideways at me.

"You really think this will work?"

I scratched a cheek, eyeballing Simmons's house too. He was just exploding out the front door, falling over himself as he descended the front steps and headed for the Mercedes. I didn't have to wonder where he was going. I knew the flu virus, whatever its variant, would be impossible to test this soon after injection.

If Jeffrey Simmons was going to save himself, he was going to have to fess up.

I leaned back in the seat, relaxing my battered body and closing my eyes. I felt good...not just to be alive, but good to be sitting next to Evelyn.

"Fifty-fifty, Landry," I said, answering her question. "Now let's find some lunch. I'm famished."

64

We held Jeter's memorial at Prairie Junction's First Baptist Church, just three blocks from the house he had called home since returning from Vietnam. The entire town was there—every member of the Prairie Junction police force wore dress blues and served as honorary pallbearers despite the lack of a casket. Even Schmuck the cat drifted in, curling up on the pew next to me and purring softly while the minister delivered a message about resurrection and eternal life.

I found myself drawn to his vision of a New Creation—a life beyond the carnage and tumult of a broken Earth. The person of Jesus was, of course, the central character. More strings drawing me back to that mysterious faith my late fiancée held so dear.

After the service everyone was invited back to Millie's Place for a memorial dinner. In truth, it was more of a life celebration. Millie catered the entire thing. Photographs of Jeter were posted to every wall. Flowers crowded the corners. Beer bottles stacked in trash cans while teary-eyed locals shared every favorite story of "the best chief this town ever had."

The time he pulled Mr. so-and-so out of a ditch with his banged-up patrol car. The time Jeter parked that car and climbed behind the wheel of a John Deere tractor to help a neighbor get his soybeans harvested before a storm blew in.

Or the time Jeter used his master keys to allow high school seniors into the locked school gym to pull off a dramatic senior prank. Rumor had it, he even provided the crime scene tape the kids used to outline a fake murder scene. He certainly responded with his siren screaming the next morning, participating in the harassment of the school principal until he could no longer keep a straight face.

That was Ransom Jeter. The locals called him a best friend. A mentor. A pain in the ass. A relentless civil servant. To them he was one in a million, but in a strange way, to me he was one *of* a million. Another face in the mental hall of fame I had constructed since leaving Phoenix two long years prior.

The old electrician who offered me a ride and a word of encouragement back in North Carolina. The ex-gangster in Atlanta who taught me that God doesn't demand perfection, just loyalty. The battered cop in Alabama who believed in community, scars and all. The campers and hotel residents at five dozen grimy spots from the Gulf Coast to the Midwest.

The good cops. The humble restauranteurs and street musicians. The *everyman*. The ordinary people who lived extraordinary lives, regardless of the price. The kind of people that a million Dr. Müllers and Director Simmonses could never erase.

I was half drunk, with a belly full of pot roast, when

Evelyn found me in a back corner of Millie's Place. She didn't say anything. She just held two fresh bottles of beer, the vaguest hint of a smile on her face. A slight tilt to her head.

I blinked, and I wasn't in Iowa anymore. I was in Phoenix, not in a diner but a bar. And that face, that invitation...

I blinked again, blocking out burning eyes. I accepted the beer and stood with a grimace as muscular pain ripped up and down my spine. I followed Evelyn through the crowd and out the front door, limping a little onto the snowy and silent Main Street. It was nearly ten p.m. and there were still half a dozen Iowa National Guard Humvees parked along the curb, even though the quarantine had lifted the day prior. A fresh snowfall left the blacktop dusted in white, but the sky had returned to clear. It was cold, but without a breath of wind to slice through our coats, it almost felt comfortable.

Evelyn extended her bottle and I used my Victorinox to remove our caps. Then we started off down the sidewalk, walking next to each other but not touching, only the crunch of our boots in the thin snow to break the silence. We sipped beer and reached the city square where Jeter had hosted a police department Christmas fair for the entire town. Lights, hot chocolate, and the mayor bumbling around in a Santa Claus costume. The memory brought on a smile as Evelyn and I stopped at the edge of the sidewalk and overlooked picnic tables and a gazebo. A frozen playground and an icy duck pond.

It was perfect. It was quiet. The only thing missing was Evelyn's hand in mine, and as I realized it my stomach twisted with sudden, desperate longing. A feeling I hadn't felt in...

Two years.

"Alex called," Evelyn whispered, breath clouding.

"Yeah?"

"Jeffrey Simmons turned himself in to the FBI this morning. He was puking his guts out, insisting that he had Ebola. He tested negative, of course...but he'd already said too much."

She looked up, a smile stretching her lips. "It worked. He even ratted out his buddy the governor. It's going to be a legal slaughter."

Our bottles touched with a soft clink. I sipped high-gravity beer and felt that wash of floatiness course through my brain, a warning that I was approaching the precipice of intoxication. I held Evelyn's gaze and noticed the inebriation in her own eyes.

Evelyn looked away first. We started walking again, reaching the gazebo and stepping beneath its metal roof. The benches were wooden and cold. I dusted the snow off with the sleeve of my coat before we sat. Evelyn leaned over her knees and stared at her bottle.

I knew she had something to say. I could feel it, but I didn't press. I thought I could wait this way, seated beside her, all night long.

"Alex..." she started. Stopped. A lump settled into my stomach, something hot and vaguely...jealous?

Evelyn lifted her head, gazing at the duck pond. "Alex and I talked. Or...he talked, anyway. He wants to meet when I get back to DC. Have dinner or something. I think...he wants to try to fix things."

I said nothing. Evelyn licked her lips. Her cheeks were

kissed with red from the cold, the tip of her nose matching. With a soft blue knit cap pulled over that bright blonde Scandinavian princess hair, I thought she'd never looked so beautiful.

"Do you want that?" The words left my lips before I could stop them. I flinched at the intrusion of my own question, wanting to kick myself.

But also glad that I'd asked it.

Evelyn's lip quivered. She swallowed. "Do...you?"

The question hit me like a pickup truck to the gut. My chest constricted. Evelyn didn't look away. Neither did I. The breath clouded between us but all else was perfectly still.

"I want you happy," I whispered at last. They weren't the words I wanted to say...but I knew they were the right words.

She smiled, just a little. She sipped beer. Closed her eyes.

Then, slowly, she slipped across the bench. She settled against my side. I slipped my arm around her shoulders. Her head rested on my chest, and that lump in my gut simply evaporated. My body relaxed. I bent and kissed her on the top of her head. Evelyn snuggled closer.

And despite the cold, I knew. It had been years since I felt this warm.

"Would that old truck of yours make it to DC?" Evelyn whispered.

I smiled. "You know...I think it might."

ABOUT THE AUTHOR

Logan Ryles was born in small town USA and knew from an early age he wanted to be a writer. After working as a pizza delivery driver, sawmill operator, and banker, he finally embraced the dream and has been writing ever since. With a passion for action-packed and mystery-laced stories, Logan's work has ranged from global-scale political thrillers to small town vigilante hero fiction.

Beyond writing, Logan enjoys saltwater fishing, road trips, sports, and fast cars. He lives with his wife and three fun-loving dogs in Alabama.

Did you enjoy *Lethal Action*? Please consider leaving a review on Amazon to help other readers discover the book.

www.loganryles.com

ALSO BY LOGAN RYLES

Made in the USA
Middletown, DE
19 December 2024

67699389R00239